**W9-CCE-845**

# Praise for the Novels of Gail Oust

## *'Til Dice Do Us Part*

"A well-written, entertaining mystery with a delightful heroine who has a very wry sense of humor, but a fierce sense of friendship and loyalty."  —The Mystery Reader

"An entertaining amateur sleuth as the Bunco Babes reject the notion of tossing dice during visiting hours to the state pen. Fans will enjoy the camaraderie of the BFFs as they Whack 'n' Roll their way through their investigation with humor, concern, and catching optimism. Gail Oust rolls an eleven with this enjoyable winner." —The Best Reviews

"Author Gail Oust gives readers a look into a group of feisty, lively retirees with a passion for bunco and for mystery-solving as well."  —Fresh Fiction

"Time will fly as you quickly devour Gail Oust's *'Til Dice Do Us Part*, laughing out loud as Kate and the other Babes socialize."  —TwoLips Reviews

## *Whack 'n' Roll*

"Feisty and intelligent, Kate is an admirable protagonist with genuinely clever detective skills. Far superior to the typical cozy, this uniquely capricious mystery will engage readers from the very first page to the surprising conclusion."
  —*Publishers Weekly* (starred review)

*continued . . .*

"A delightful amateur sleuth ... the Bunco Babes are a close-knit group who have each other's back like the Muske-teers, so Kate has a powerful geriatric support group. The spunky Kate and her BFFs are filled with so much energy that people half their age will admire them. Gail Oust pro-vides a complex whodunit starring a cast of eccentric sex-agenarians."
—The Best Reviews

"An engaging heroine ... well plotted ... a fine start to a series featuring some very enjoyable Southern sixtysome-things."
—The Mystery Reader

OTHER BUNCO BABES MYSTERIES BY GAIL OUST

*Whack 'n' Roll*
*'Til Dice Do Us Part*

# Shake, Murder, and Roll

## A Bunco Babes Mystery

# Gail Oust

AN OBSIDIAN MYSTERY

OBSIDIAN
Published by New American Library, a division of
Penguin Group (USA) Inc., 375 Hudson Street,
New York, New York 10014, USA

Penguin Group (Canada), 90 Eglinton Avenue East, Suite 700, Toronto,
Ontario M4P 2Y3, Canada (a division of Pearson Penguin Canada Inc.)
Penguin Books Ltd., 80 Strand, London WC2R 0RL, England
Penguin Ireland, 25 St. Stephen's Green, Dublin 2,
Ireland (a division of Penguin Books Ltd.)
Penguin Group (Australia), 250 Camberwell Road, Camberwell, Victoria 3124,
Australia (a division of Pearson Australia Group Pty. Ltd.)
Penguin Books India Pvt. Ltd., 11 Community Centre, Panchsheel Park,
New Delhi - 110 017, India
Penguin Group (NZ), 67 Apollo Drive, Rosedale, Auckland 0632,
New Zealand (a division of Pearson New Zealand Ltd.)
Penguin Books (South Africa) (Pty.) Ltd., 24 Sturdee Avenue,
Rosebank, Johannesburg 2196, South Africa

Penguin Books Ltd., Registered Offices:
80 Strand, London WC2R 0RL, England

First published by Obsidian, an imprint of New American Library,
a division of Penguin Group (USA) Inc.

First Printing, May 2011
10 9 8 7 6 5 4 3 2 1

Copyright © Gail Oust, 2011
All rights reserved

OBSIDIAN and logo are trademarks of Penguin Group (USA) Inc.

Printed in the United States of America

Without limiting the rights under copyright reserved above, no part of this
publication may be reproduced, stored in or introduced into a retrieval system,
or transmitted, in any form, or by any means (electronic, mechanical, photo-
copying, recording, or otherwise), without the prior written permission of both
the copyright owner and the above publisher of this book.

PUBLISHER'S NOTE
This is a work of fiction. Names, characters, places, and incidents either are the
product of the author's imagination or are used fictitiously, and any resemblance to actual persons, living or dead, business establishments, events, or
locales is entirely coincidental.
    The publisher does not have any control over and does not assume any re-
sponsibility for author or third-party Web sites or their content.

If you purchased this book without a cover you should be aware that this book
is stolen property. It was reported as "unsold and destroyed" to the publisher
and neither the author nor the publisher has received any payment for this
"stripped book."

The scanning, uploading, and distribution of this book via the Internet or via
any other means without the permission of the publisher is illegal and punish-
able by law. Please purchase only authorized electronic editions, and do not
participate in or encourage electronic piracy of copyrighted materials. Your
support of the author's rights is appreciated.

*To Greg, my warrior son.*
*The universe rewards courage.*

# Acknowledgments

Thanks to the elite of the McCormick Garden Club for your help making my plot blossom and grow. Special mention goes to Carol Mavity, a dear friend, who faithfully rides to my rescue whether with answers to dumb questions, a coffee cake, or an unscheduled trip to the dump. Joyce Isaacson, it's been a pleasure to discover a devious mind lurking beneath your kind heart. Mary Ann Beyer, you're a true gem. Your attention to detail makes me envious. I'm grateful you're a pack rat. Jean Randall and her assistants (Bet, Barb, Janet, and Pat) at the Friends of the McCormick County Library, have I told you how much I appreciate your efforts on my behalf? You host the best book signings ever! Sandy Mahoney, RN and First Responder, your experience added verisimilitude. As always, to Bob, husband and friend, for being my sidekick through thick 'n' thin. I can't write a book about yards and gardens without thanking our personal Shrub Patrol. Stouffer's, Montgomery's, Beyer's, and Byron, you made our house look like a home again.

And last but by no means least, my heartfelt thanks to my superlative agent, Jessica Faust of BookEnds, LLC, and my wonderful editor at New American Library, Sandy Harding, for your unstinting patience, support, and caring. Sometimes words just aren't enough.

# Chapter 1

"Honestly, Kate, I don't know why I let you talk me into this."

*A little cheese to go along with the whine? Cheddar or Gouda?* I wanted to ask, but I bit my tongue instead.

Monica, bless her heart, could be such a whiner. If anyone was entitled to whine, it should be me, Kate McCall. Along with the rest of the Bunco Babes, I'd voted to forgo our bimonthly bunco game in favor of a lecture on, of all things, gardening. Gardening! Imagine me and gardening. The two go together like John Dillinger and the FBI. Friends from Serenity Cove Estates to Toledo know my thumb isn't green. It's brown, brown, brown!

"Y'all, isn't this excitin'?" Connie Sue Brody fairly bubbled with enthusiasm. Connie Sue is our resident beauty queen and a former cheerleader. And once a cheerleader, always a cheerleader. "Just think, a real celebrity right here in Serenity Cove Estates!"

"I even went to the mall and bought a new outfit—in case there were photographers present," Polly, our group's septuagenarian piped. "I hear bright colors show up best."

Bright? More like neon, I thought eyeing Polly's pink and lime-green ensemble. But who said one needs to act one's age? Sometimes it's a heckuva lot more fun to kick up your heels and be a youngster again. In a retirement community for "active" adults such as Serenity Cove Estates, age is relative. Here a *youngster* is anyone ineligible for Medicare. Sixty is the new forty.

Gloria Meyers, Polly's long-suffering daughter, glanced at her watch. "It's almost time. Shouldn't they be opening the doors soon? It'll take a while for this many people to settle."

Tonight's crowd congregated to witness a mind-boggling PowerPoint presentation on drought-resistant perennials—I'm being facetious about the mind-boggling—were scrunched together like sardines in the hallway outside the auditorium of the rec center. Those who showed no desire to be sardines milled aimlessly about the lobby, waiting for Marietta Perkins, the assistant manager, to fling open the auditorium doors and admit the masses.

"I hope this isn't going to be a waste of time," Monica fussed. "You know how I hate to miss bunco."

"Hush, sugar. It won't hurt just this once. Isn't that right, Kate?" Connie Sue turned to me for validation.

I crossed my fingers behind my back. "Absolutely," I lied.

Wild horses couldn't drag it out of me, but secretly I agreed with Monica. I'd much rather be rolling the bones than listening to a botanist—even a glitzy, semi-celebrity cable TV botanist—expound on plants that didn't have the sense to wither when the thermometer read ninety-five in the shade. Yawn, yawn, and triple yawn.

Any of the Babes would gladly cut off their right arms, cheerfully surrender a kidney, or happily donate a gallon of blood, but if you ask us to give up bunco expect to hear some grumbling. Bunco, for the uninitiated, is a silly, mindless dice game. No skill, no strategy required. Just shake, rattle, and toss. Strictly social. We munch; we imbibe; but most important, we laugh. Bunco is our therapy.

Pam Warner, my BFF, hopped aboard my train of thought. "Bunco wouldn't have been as much fun tonight anyway. For one reason or another, half the group couldn't make it. For Rita's sake let's make the best of the situation."

"Pam's right," I concurred. "Isn't that what girlfriends are for, to support one another?"

"Y'all, this is quite a coup for Rita." Connie Sue fluffed her always perfect honey-blond locks. "What better way to end her term as president of Flowers and Bowers, Serenity Cove's very own garden club? Imagine her college roommate, none other than Dr. Sheila Rappaport."

"I never miss *How Does Your Garden Grow?*" Gloria confessed.

"I'd watch, too," Polly said, "but it comes on at the same time as *The Young and the Restless*. Y and R's got some hot new dudes."

Knowing it would only irritate Gloria, I tried not to smile. Out of the corner of my eye, I caught Pam hiding a grin behind her program.

"Did y'all know you should cut back lantanas in February and cover 'em with mulch?" Connie Sue asked, taking out her compact and inspecting her makeup. "You can learn a lot from watchin' Dr. Sheila."

Maybe I'd develop a better knack for growing things if I stopped watching *Law & Order* reruns and switched to HGTV. Merely thinking of such a sacrifice made me want to weep. *Law & Order* and *CSI* helped mold me into the woman I am today. A woman versed in the crime-solving trinity of motive, means, and opportunity. A woman who can rattle off acronyms like a reformed alcoholic does the twelve steps. Acronyms like DOA, COD, and GSR. I know TOD isn't a man's name but time of death. And I'm well aware CODIS and AFIS aren't the names of a movie star's twins.

"Oh, look, there she is—Dr. Sheila." Gloria Myers

pointed toward a striking couple standing somewhat apart from the rest of those assembled. The movement caused her many bracelets to jangle. What Gloria lacks in a trendsetter wardrobe, she makes up for with jewelry. She sparkles and shines. She glows. Bling is her thing.

"She's even better-lookin' in person than on TV," Connie Sue remarked after scrutinizing the woman. What better judge of beauty than our very own former Miss Peach Princess?

I half-turned to study the subject under discussion. Sheila Rappaport was perhaps five foot seven, slender as a reed, her body tight and toned beneath a silk wrap dress. Her blond hair, sporting both highlights and lowlights, was cut in an asymmetrical style, leaving the right side to swing free and follow the curve of her jaw. I had to agree she looked . . . *smokin'*. At least I think that's the current term for hot enough to steam bifocals.

"And isn't that . . . ?" Monica whispered.

"Dr. Vaughn Bascomb," Pam supplied. "I recognize him from his guest appearances on Dr. Sheila's show."

Vaughn Bascomb, I'd learned from Rita, was Sheila Rappaport's significant other. They'd been an item for nearly five years but never married. They say opposites attract and, in this instance, it appeared true. While Sheila exuded glitz and glamour, her partner was pleasantly plain and rumpled. Bascomb was slight of build with slouching shoulders and when it came to hairlines, well, let's just say the tide had definitely left the shore. Yet there was something oddly appealing about the man. I couldn't quite put my finger on whether it was his slightly perplexed expression or his scholarly persona. I wondered why botany was his chosen field. At first glance, the man seemed more suited for a classroom than digging in the dirt.

"Here you are," Rita Larsen's voice boomed from behind us. Intent on putting the team of Rappaport and

Bascomb under the microscope, we hadn't noticed her approach. No mean accomplishment considering Rita's nearly six feet tall and built like a running back for the Carolina Panthers. "Thanks for coming tonight. It means a lot to me."

"We wouldn't have missed it for the world," Monica gushed.

I narrowed my eyes and studied Monica. I may suffer "senior" moments now and again, those annoying little lapses of memory that plague the golden years, but I swore only minutes ago Monica was bellyaching about having to miss bunco. Yet here she was, oozing "nice" like an Oklahoma oil well. I wanted to ask, Who are you and what have you done with the real Monica Pulaski?

Polly didn't waste time satisfying her curiosity. "Were you and Sheila really college roommates?"

I caught Gloria giving her mother a cautionary elbow in the ribs. Knowing Polly, however, she might well have saved herself the effort.

Polly continued unfazed. "Seeing the two of you together, no one would guess you're the same age."

An awkward silence fell over our little band of bunco players. No one likes to hear they're growing old—especially not from a friend.

"What Mother meant was . . ." Gloria began.

Rita waved aside the apology. "I know what you meant, Polly, and I happen to agree. Sheila looks . . . fabulous."

Did I detect a note of envy in Rita's voice? If so, I could hardly blame her. Sheila Rappaport could easily have passed for forty.

Connie Sue leaned closer and lowered her voice. "Sneak into her bedroom, sugar. Find out what kind of beauty products she's usin'."

Rita feigned outrage, pressing a hand against her impressive set of 40 DDs. "Connie Sue Brody, are you asking me to spy on a friend?"

"You're darn tootin', sugar." Connie Sue grinned, unabashed. "If that fails, find out the name of the surgeon who did her work. And while you're at it, see if she's got his card."

"Let me introduce all of you before the doors open." Raising her hand, Rita beckoned to the guest of honor, who was now circulating through the crowd.

Sheila spotted Rita instantly—not that spotting Rita took special skill. Arm in arm with her significant other, Vaughn Bascomb, the esteemed botanist made her way toward us, doling out charm and glamour along the way like Halloween candy.

"Sheila, Vaughn, I'd like you to meet my best friends," Rita said, and then proceeded with the introductions.

If Sheila Rappaport was attractive from a distance, she was even more so up close and personal. I found myself marveling at her flawless complexion. Even at sixty-something, it appeared smooth and nearly wrinkle-free, giving her an ageless look. Now I ask you, why do some faces get wrinkly and saggy and others don't? Why do some waistlines stay trim while others get thick and lumpy? Two of life's greatest mysteries. Some things just aren't fair.

Introductions over, Sheila laid a hand on Rita's forearm. "Rita would you be a dear, and find me some ginger ale? My stomach's a bit queasy."

"Sure thing," Rita told her. "Wait here. I'll be right back."

"Rita, if you don't mind, would you bring one for me as well?" Vaughn asked tentatively, then turned to us, his tone apologetic. "Ever since lunch, I've been feeling a little under the weather. Must've been something I ate."

# Chapter 2

"It's all that fried food," Sheila stated unequivocally. "No wonder this region of the country is considered the Stroke Belt."

We shuffled out feet and looked elsewhere. None of us, it seemed, knew quite how to respond to this allegation, including Polly, who for once kept her comments to herself.

Finally Monica cleared her throat. "Actually, many possible causes for the high stroke rate have been investigated, but the reasons still haven't been determined."

For once, and perhaps the only time, I greeted Monica's love of quoting recent studies with enthusiasm. *You go, girl*, I silently applauded.

But Monica didn't need my applause, she was just warming up. "There are many hypotheses. However . . ."

"Nonsense," Sheila cut her off. "Take tonight for instance. The menu was a perfect example of Southern fried indigestion. The meal consisted of fried chicken, fried catfish, fried okra, macaroni and cheese, and fried green tomatoes."

"You're forgetting the hush puppies," Vaughn ventured.

"I may have forgotten, but you didn't. I noticed you helped yourself to seconds."

For those unfamiliar with Southern cuisine, hush puppies are small balls of cornmeal dough that have been—yep, you guessed it—deep fried.

Sheila was obviously unfamiliar with Monica's fondness for trivia. Once started on a tangent there was no stopping her. "There are a variety of legends on how the name 'hush puppies' originated," she expounded. "One such legend dates back to the Civil War."

Connie Sue wagged a French-manicured fingernail at her. "True Southerners, such as myself, will tell you that there was nothin' whatsoever *civil* about that war."

"They prefer to call it the War Between the States," Rita explained for Sheila and Vaughn's benefit.

"When we were in Charleston, I heard a tour guide refer to it as the 'late unpleasantness,'" Pam added.

"Meemaw," Connie Sue said, "called it the War of Northern Aggression."

My, my, I thought, we were off and running, trying to impress not one, but two, celebrities with our wit and wisdom. Connie Sue had even quoted her meemaw, Southern-speak for grandmother, to add to her authenticity.

"Hey, you guys," Polly interrupted, "let's get back to the subject at hand—hush puppies."

With a nod, Gloria picked up the conversational thread. "Folklore has it that Southern soldiers, who were gathered around a cook fire, sensed the presence of Northern troops and tossed their barking dogs fried cakes with the command to "hush, puppies.""

"I learned a different version in Charleston," Pam went on to explain. "The tour guide mentioned that slaves carrying their master's food from the outdoor kitchens to the house would throw the batter balls to the barking dogs, telling the 'puppies' to 'hush.'"

Gracious! I recalled Pam and her husband, Jack, had

spent a recent weekend there, but until now I didn't realize she'd memorized the entire tourist spiel.

Not wanting to be outdone in the pursuit of interesting but useless trivia, Polly jumped into the fray. "I heard on the radio that the new snack food in the South is batter-dipped, deep-fried butter."

"Ugh!" Sheila shuddered at the thought.

Vaughn dug his hands deep into his pants pocket and tactfully changed the subject. "The dragon lady who holds the keys to the kingdom ought to be opening the floodgates soon. In the meantime, if you ladies don't mind, I think I'll find a spot to sit down."

Sheila's brows knit in a frown as she studied her partner's pinched face. "You don't look well, darling. Are you sure you're all right?"

He smiled wanly. "Too many hush puppies is all. Now, ladies, if you'll excuse me . . ."

We watched him wend his way through the crowd. I had to agree with Sheila. Vaughn definitely looked a little green around the gills. Where the devil was Rita with the ginger ale? Did she have to drive clear into Brookdale—five miles or so as the crow flies—for it? And what was taking Marietta Perkins so long to open up? I guess we were still in the part of the program the brochure labeled as a "meet and greet." Heaven forbid Marietta veer from a set schedule.

An awkward silence followed Vaughn's departure.

Feeling it my sacred duty to keep the conversational ball afloat, I gave it a poke. "We're Rita's closest friends. We call ourselves the Bunco Babes."

Sheila gave me an odd glance. "No offense, but aren't you all a bit old to be considered 'babes'?"

*Old? No offense?* Those were put-up-your-dukes fighting words. "Babes," I informed our esteemed guest, "are the sum of attitude, style, and grace. Age doesn't enter into the equation."

Pam, always a diplomat, recognized the dangerous glint

in my eye and stepped in to prevent a brouhaha. "What Kate was about to explain is that a group of us women get together twice a month to play bunco."

"Bunco?" The term spilled from Sheila's tongue like a word in a foreign language. "Is that a card game?"

"Dice," Polly chirped. "We roll dice."

"Oh." Sheila nodded. "Like craps?"

Connie Sue shook her head. "Craps is different."

Gloria discreetly rechecked her watch. "Craps is only two dice. Bunco is three."

"And there's no money involved," I added for good measure, trying to fan a spark of interest.

"Mmm," Sheila murmured absently.

Sheila's eyes roamed the crowd, hoping, no doubt, someone would rescue her from women who toss dice for a hobby. Women with obviously too much time on their hands. I, too, wished a stranger would intercede with a pithy question about grubs or aphids. But no such luck. Folks seemed hesitant to approach her. Gee, I wonder why. Her personality, perhaps?

Monica, who's always up for a challenge, pasted on a bright smile. "The winner at bunco takes home a tiara."

Disinterested, Sheila continued to survey the throng that spilled out of the hallway and into the lobby.

"There's no strategy involved," Connie Sue, usually adept in the small-talk department, plugged away.

"No skill whatsoever," Pam concurred.

"What?" Sheila's head snapped around at hearing this. "No wagers, no skill, no strategy? If you ask me, bunco sounds boring."

I wanted to remind her that no one had—asked her, that is. "It's strictly social," I explained. "Bunco is all about fun, food, and friends. Most important, we laugh a lot."

"Hmm." Sheila shrugged a slender shoulder. "I don't have the time or inclination for frivolous pursuits. Work is all that matters to me."

The Babes and I exchanged glances. I didn't need to be a psychic to read their minds. It isn't often all of us agree, but I'd wager on this occasion we were of one accord. Dr. Sheila Rappaport would *never, ever,* be invited to sub at one of our bunco sessions—regardless of how desperate we were.

I went through a mental checklist for possible topics of conversation. Civil War versus War Between the States— check. Origin of hush puppies—check. Bunco—check. Yep, our supply of chitchat was depleted. Where in the world was Rita? I wondered. Maybe she took the easy route and ducked out the back door, leaving Sheila to fend for herself. Then inspiration struck. When all else fails, fall back on the old standby—blatant flattery.

"My friends all rave about your TV show," I said, mustering as much enthusiasm as possible without making myself nauseous.

"I watch *How Does Your Garden Grow?* every afternoon." Pam, bless her heart, rose to the occasion. I made a mental note to thank her later.

"I wouldn't miss it for the world," Monica simpered.

I couldn't believe it, Monica actually *simpered*. Thank goodness George Clooney didn't make a surprise appearance. We'd need EMTs standing by with paddles warmed and ready.

Connie Sue jumped on the flattery band wagon. *"How Does Your Garden Grow?* happens to be my very favorite show on HGTV. Don't y'all just love it?" Grinning broadly, she turned to us for support.

"That's very kind of you." Sheila gave a practiced smile, lips curving upward, but no flicker of warmth in her eyes. The lady was one cool cucumber, as we used to say as kids.

Gloria hitched the strap of her purse higher on her shoulder. "I have you to thank for saving my gardenias when their leaves started yellowing. Who would have thought that a mix of vinegar and water would green them up instead of some priccy concoction sold at a nursery?"

Sheila inclined her head, accepting the compliment like royalty. "I like viewers to know there's often simple solutions to pesky problems."

"And your advice on mealy bugs," Monica gushed. "I've never had a problem with them since I listened to your show."

"Bugs!" Polly exclaimed loudly. "You had bugs?"

"Shh!" Monica hissed, glancing over her shoulder to see if anyone had overheard.

Mercifully, just then Marietta Perkins deemed our wait over, and the doors to the auditorium swung open. The crowd surged forward, jostling and shoving in their haste.

Seemingly out of nowhere a petite brunette in a cherry-red dress barreled through the masses. Rudely nudging me aside, she looped her arm through Sheila's. "Sorry I'm late, darling," she said, sounding out of breath. "My plane was delayed getting in from New York. Then I had to rent a car and drive God only knows how many miles to get here."

"Relax, Betsy." Sheila patted the woman's hand. "You're here now, and that's all that matters."

"*Tsk, tsk*." Betsy clucked her tongue in disapproval. "Darling, you're looking a bit washed out. Luckily for you, I brought along my little bag of tricks, courtesy of Belle Beaute. I'll have those cheeks blooming like roses with a couple swipes of my magic brush."

"I see a side door. Let's get away from this madness."

"Did you hear that?" Connie Sue whispered, almost beside herself with excitement, as the two women slipped away.

"Hear what?" I asked, scanning the rapidly filling auditorium for a row that held six vacant seats.

"This Betsy person must work for Belle Beaute. Her company is the sole sponsor of *How Does Your Garden*

*Grow?* Take it from a former Miss Peach Princess, sugar, their cosmetics are the best! The *very* best. Rumor has it they're comin' out with a new product . . ."

I listened with half an ear while Connie Sue rattled on, spouting a lot of R words. Words such as retexturize, revitalize, and rejuvenate. If those products took years off my age as they seemed to for Dr. Sheila, I intended to try some on my next trip to the mall.

"Rita must be pleased with tonight's turnout," Pam commented as we scooted into our seats.

Leaning across her mother, Gloria said, "Rita told me that the editor of Sheila's book, as well as the producer of her TV show, are expected to be here."

"Hush, y'all," Connie Sue cautioned. "The program's about to start."

The lights dimmed, and Rita stepped up to the podium and addressed the audience. "Before I tell you about tonight's speaker, I'd like to introduce some special guests in the audience."

I craned my neck for a better view of those in the front row. Along with the board members of Flowers and Bowers, I noticed Betsy of the cherry-red dress, Vaughn Bascomb, and two gentlemen I assumed were Sheila's editor and her producer.

Rita, in fine fettle as mistress of ceremonies, introduced the illustrious guests. Betsy turned out to be Betsy Dalton, vice president of Belle Beaute, Sheila's cosmetic sponsor. The gentleman on Betsy's right was Roger McFarland, senior editor of a prestigious university press that specialized in horticulture. McFarland, a pudgy, carrot-haired individual wearing horn-rimmed glasses, looked like an aficionado of down-home Southern fried. The man on Betsy's left was Sheila's producer, Todd Timmons. Timmons, a small, intense young man with a high forehead and close-cropped brown curls, favored the unshaven look currently popular with male TV stars. Unfortunately for Timmons, he looked like a Chia Pet.

"Last but by no means least," Rita continued, "it's my privilege to introduce Dr. Vaughn Bascomb. Many of you may recognize Dr. Bascomb from his frequent guest appearances on *How Does Your Garden Grow?*"

Enthusiastic applause followed. Vaughn Bascomb, dabbing at his mouth with a folded handkerchief, rose to his feet and turned to the audience. He looked paler than Jacob Marley's ghost, I noted, but that could be a trick of the lighting. The man certainly needed to exert more self-control around hush puppies.

Rita forged ahead in her role as mistress of ceremonies. "Serenity Cove Estates garden club, Flowers and Bowers, is honored to host . . ."

Blah, blah, blah. . . . I stifled a yawn, wishing I was home channel surfing for *Law & Order* reruns.

". . . I could go on and on about tonight's guest," Rita paused, "but I won't." She smiled, waiting for the polite laughter to fade. "I know you're not here to listen to me, but to Dr. Sheila as she's known to her legion of fans. Ladies and gentlemen, it gives me great pleasure to introduce my esteemed friend, Dr. Sheila Rappaport."

After what seemed a lengthy pause, Sheila teetered out from the wings. Was she drunk? The thought flashed through my mind; then I noticed the rictus of a smile pasted across her ashen face and a slender hand pressed to her abdomen.

# Chapter 3

Sheila's entrance from the wings was met with wild applause. The audience, so it seemed, was willing to forgive minor imperfections in their idols.

I watched in morbid fascination as the renowned botanist tottered toward center stage. I tried not to be judgmental. I'd probably wobble too if I attempted to wear stiletto heels. Or worse yet, I'd probably fall and break my fool neck. Though it pains me to admit, all my pretty high heels are relegated to plastic shoe boxes at the back of my closet. Someday I'll part with them, but the time hasn't come when I'm ready to trade peep-toe pumps for orthotics.

Hanging on to her facsimile of a smile, Sheila grasped the podium with both hands and looked out over an auditorium packed with her admirers. Each person was ready to hang on to her every word, swallow her every syllable. Each eager to explore the mysteries of drought-resistant perennials.

"Sheila's complexion still looks a bit washed out," Connie Sue said, keeping her voice low. "Those roses Betsy promised to put into her cheeks failed to bloom."

I nodded sagely. "Hope she kept her receipt. Maybe she can get a refund."

Connie Sue looked at me strangely, obviously failing to appreciate my veiled attempt at humor. "Her receipt for the roses that failed to bloom. Get it . . . ?"

Giving me an eye roll, she turned her attention back to the stage.

"Ladies and gentlemen . . ." Sheila began, her voice resonating through the microphone. She stopped speaking and stared off into space, then, blinking several times, she cleared her throat.

"She drunk, or what?" Polly asked, forgetting to keep her voice down.

Gloria shot her a look. "Mother, please."

Sheila collected herself and began anew. "Ladies and gentlemen . . ."

Then the elegant, the sophisticated Dr. Sheila Rappaport, the darling of HGTV, author of a soon-to-be-published coffee table book, clutched her abdomen and spewed the contents of her stomach all over the stage.

As one, the audience gasped in horror. Vaughn Bascomb sprang to his feet and surged toward the stage, but before he could offer any assistance, he halted abruptly. Half-turning, he emitted a strangled cry. His eyes rolled back in his head. Then seconds later, he collapsed and began flopping around like a lake trout minus the lake.

Pandemonium broke out. The crowd rose to its feet, everyone talking at once.

As I watched in indecision, Sheila slumped to the floor like a marionette with its strings cut.

"Is there a doctor in the house?" Rita screamed into the mike. "Someone call nine-one-one."

Automatically I reached for my purse and started digging for my cell phone. I had to yell at the EMT dispatcher in order to make my voice heard above the din. "Hurry," I shouted.

I was sorely tempted to yell, "We need a bus," à la Mariska Hargitay, who plays tough cop Olivia Benson on *Law & Order: SVU*. Mariska/Olivia always manages to look sleek and exotic in black leather. Too bad as a Medicare card–carrying maven I can't pull off that look with the same aplomb.

I felt Connie Sue's nails dig into my arm. "They're goin' to be all right, aren't they, sugar?" she asked.

"Sure, they'll be fine," I assured her, lying through my teeth. I'd repent later.

A few brave souls hovered around Sheila and Vaughn, unsure what protocol to follow. Vaughn had ceased convulsing, but his body remained inert. Sheila was beginning to stir, but appeared disoriented. I found myself wishing for Janine, another of our band of buncoettes. Janine was a licensed RN and our go-to person for anything medical. If she were here, she'd know what to do. But she wasn't. No, Janine was in Barbados probably sipping margaritas and dancing in the sand, happily celebrating her wedding anniversary. Some people have no sense of timing.

Polly tugged my sleeve. "Do you think greasy food made them sick? Fried chicken's a favorite of mine. Suppose I should give it up?"

"I don't know, maybe . . ." I muttered, peering over my shoulder, hoping the EMTs would magically appear.

Behind her trifocals, Polly's faded blue eyes held a worried gleam. "Sheila's friend kept talking about all the hush puppies he ate. Suppose I should give up hush puppies, too?"

"Polly might be onto something," Pam said quietly. "This could be a case of food poisoning."

A commotion in the back of the room kept me from answering. I let out a humongous sigh of relief as a team of first responders, fluorescent orange bags in hand, rushed forward. Two of them knelt alongside Vaughn and turned him onto his side as he began to seize again. Another pair, led by a woman I knew only as Sandy, raced up the steps to the stage and wrapped a blood pressure cuff around Sheila's arm. I felt gratified to ob-

serve that Sandy had donned latex gloves. With all the
germs around these days, one can't be too careful.

Once—for about sixty seconds—I'd entertained the
notion of being trained as a first responder, then promptly
dismissed the idea. As a mother of two, I'd cleaned up
my share of blood and barf and wasn't eager to do it
again. Thank goodness not everyone shared my squeam-
ishness. These efficient and dedicated individuals are
first on the scene and arrive prepared for any emergency. Suddenly I no longer minded that Janine was in
Barbados. Vaughn and Sheila were in capable hands.

Within minutes EMTs hurried in, and the first responders stepped aside to allow them access. Rita hovered in the background, looking more shaken than I'd
ever seen her. Usually she's a rock. Gibraltar personified. But not tonight. It was one thing to see paramedics working on a stranger, another thing entirely when
the victim was a friend.

Odd as it was, no one made a move to leave the auditorium. Not a single soul. All around me, people gawked
unabashedly or talked on cell phones in hushed, excited tones. All eager to impart the scoop on what happened at the garden club lecture. Let it be said, when it
comes to gossip, Serenity Cove prides itself on its great
communication network. Its motto ought to be, *Faster
than a speeding bullet*. It would come as no surprise if
Dr. Sheila's prone form showed up on YouTube tomorrow. Or even sooner.

One of the EMTs, a man in his fifties with skin tanned
and tough as leather, barked orders. Two stretchers were
rolled in. Vaughn Bascomb was lifted onto the first one,
an oxygen mask strapped to his face, an IV dripping
into his arm, and quickly wheeled out. Sheila, complete
with oxygen and an IV of her own, was placed on the
second stretcher, then rushed out behind Vaughn.

The evening's entertainment over, people began to
file out. I kept hearing the words "food poisoning" ban-

died back and forth. What had started as a whisper gathered momentum, racing through the crowd more rapidly than a tsunami.

"Do you suppose . . . ?"

"I feel a little nauseous myself."

"I thought the catfish had a funny taste."

"I wonder if the cheesecake went unrefrigerated."

"I've heard of cooking oil turning rancid."

Was the emergency room at the local hospital about to be flooded with complaints of food poisoning? I wondered. Was the power of suggestion at work? Whichever, I was happy the banquet preceding the presentation had been limited to garden club members only. I'd sure hate to eliminate fried chicken or hush puppies from my diet.

"Oh, I think I'm going to be sick," Monica groaned.

Uh-oh, I thought. Monica's complexion was the moldy olive green I'd come to associate with her sensitive stomach. Fortunately, there were restrooms close by.

"Kate, find Rita and see if you can help," Pam, always the practical one, urged. "The rest of us will look after Monica."

A glance at Monica, who had one hand clamped over her mouth, assured me I hadn't drawn the short end of the stick. "Thanks, Pam."

The Babes flanked Monica, two on each side, and herded her toward the ladies' room.

Rita was about to push past me as she elbowed her way through those exiting when I grabbed her arm. "Rita, slow down. Where're you going?"

"I'm going to follow the ambulance," she explained, not breaking stride. "Sheila doesn't have any family nearby, so it's the least I can do for her."

"I'm going with you," I said, hustling to keep pace.

"Thanks, but you don't have to . . ."

"I'm going with you," I repeated, steering her toward my trusty Buick.

In spite of her protests, I could tell Rita wanted company. I knew Dave, her husband, was in Myrtle Beach golfing with his buddies. Her daughter-in-law, Tara, had begged off tonight since she expected a call from her husband, Mark, who was deployed to Iraq.

Before Rita even buckled up, I shoved the gearshift into reverse, nearly plowing into a Chevy that was edging past me. I ignored the angry blare of its horn and, shifting into drive, stomped on the accelerator. As we roared out of the parking lot, I found myself wishing for one of those flashing red lights to set atop the roof. A little gadget to make me look official. If I ever caught Sheriff Sumter Wiggins in a good mood—fat chance— I'd ask him where a concerned citizen such as myself could get one. I made a mental note to surf the Internet. It would be easier than confronting a man who thought I was an idiot. I put the pedal to the metal, and we headed down the highway

"Watch for deer," Rita said, the reminder mechanical.

This area of South Carolina was heavily populated with the critters. A deer population that treated newly planted shrubs and flower beds like their own personal salad bar. Deer that darted into roadways, changed their minds halfway across, then dashed back the way they'd come. And to complicate matters, they traveled in pairs. Several of my friends literally had had run-ins, resulting in costly repairs and minor injuries. I learned from their experiences. Mixing Bambi with a Buick doesn't result in a hybrid.

The night was dark as pitch with only a sliver of moon to guide the way. It felt like it took an eternity to navigate the twenty-odd miles of winding road to the hospital, but in reality it hadn't taken long at all. I dropped Rita at the emergency room entrance and parked the car in the adjacent lot.

When I entered through the sliding-glass doors, Rita

glanced up from a seat on one of the vinyl sofas. Except for worried parents of a fretful toddler and a man in coveralls, a bloody towel draped around one fist, we had the waiting room to ourselves.

"Hey," I said to Rita by way of a greeting. "Any news yet?"

She shook her head. "The doctor's working on them. The nurse told me it might be a while."

Just then a man who I assumed to be an ER doc in lab coat and scrubs shoved through the door that separated the waiting area from the treatment rooms beyond. His gaze skimmed over the toddler's parents and the worker with the bloody hand, then rested on the two of us. "You relatives of the food poisoning victims?"

Rita and I stepped forward. "Friends," Rita said. "We're just friends."

The doctor frowned. "By any chance, do either of you know how to contact their next of kin?"

My knees turned to Jell-O. "Are they . . . ?"

# Chapter 4

"Dead?" the doctor asked, supplying the dreaded D word.

We nodded.

"No, but they're both in critical condition. To be honest, ladies, it doesn't look good. If either of you know how to contact their relatives, now would be a good time."

With this he disappeared into the restricted area.

"Did you . . ." I cleared my throat. "Do you know her family?"

Rita shook her head. "Sheila has a sister, Debbie. Last I heard she was living in LA and had just remarried for the third time. I have no idea how to get in touch with her."

"What about Sheila's parents?"

"They both died years ago." Rita slumped down in a chair, cradling her purse in her lap. "I feel so helpless."

I did too. And didn't like the sensation any better than she did. "Why don't I try to find us some coffee? This is shaping up to be a long night."

Rita nodded dully. As I started across the waiting room on my quest for a coffee machine, the doors of the emergency room slid open and in walked a trio I recognized from the rec center. For some strange reason they reminded me of Peter, Paul, and Mary, folk singers from the sixties. Sixties? Yikes, the thought brought me up short. That makes me sound as old as Methuselah. How can I protest being "elderly" when I keep having these flashbacks? Isn't there some kind of pill I can take?

Betsy Dalton, the cosmetics VP, clung to TV producer Todd Timmons while Roger McFarland, Sheila's erstwhile editor, trudged two steps behind. "I know you don't care for Bascomb any more than I do," Betsy was saying, "but Sheila's another story."

Absently Todd patted her hand. "I've talked myself hoarse trying to persuade Sheila that she'd be better off without that dude. But did she listen? No," he said, not waiting for an answer. "I tried to convince her that Bascomb's responsible for the drop in ratings, but there's no reasoning with her. She insists he appear on her show time and time again. He's bland enough in person, but on camera, Bascomb projects the personality of a squid."

Squid? Did this mean Timmons didn't care for calamari? A pity, but then calamari might rank up there along with the other "fried" foods Sheila disdains. It struck me that neither Betsy nor Todd were members of the Dr. Vaughn Bascomb fan club. I filed this information away for later.

Waking from my eavesdropping coma, I decided to make myself known as a member of the Sheila and Vaughn cheering section. "Hello," I said, approaching the threesome with a smile meant to convey sympathy and friendliness. "I'm Kate McCall, a friend of a friend of Sheila's."

They stared at me. I felt like an alien from Mars.

But persistence could be my middle name, so I tried again. "Guess you could say that makes me a friend of Sheila, twice removed.

"Get it?" I asked, hoping to inject a little levity. "You know, it's the way Southerners describe relatives—aunts, cousins, what have you—once, twice, three times removed."

I waited for a glimmer of amusement, a glimmer of anything actually, but from their expressions I could tell I was wasting my wit.

Roger McFarland's chubby face puckered into a frown. "Have we met?"

I took this as encouragement. "No, but I saw you in the audience tonight. My friend Rita Larsen was Dr. Sheila's college roommate. She was instrumental in bringing Sheila here to Serenity Cove Estates."

Todd Timmons looked down his nose at me, not an easy feat considering he was vertically challenged. "Then you better hope nothing happens to Sheila, or that precious retirement community of yours will be hit hard enough with a lawsuit to knock it off the map."

Without another glance, the trio left me in the dust while they beelined for the registration desk. My attempt at Southern hospitality had been a total flop. My good intentions rebuffed, I decided to let them find their own coffee.

I returned fifteen minutes later carrying two Styrofoam cups filled with a liquid that had the consistency of mud and smelled like kerosene. Even so I counted myself lucky. The cafeteria had closed hours ago. It was nothing short of miraculous that I'd stumbled across a janitor—are they still called janitors these days, or are they custodial engineers?—who directed me to a bank of vending machines. Without the man's kind assistance, I'd still be wandering through a maze of dimly lit corridors, past shuttered offices, in the grim hope of finding sustenance. Sustenance in the form of caffeine *and* sugar. While waiting for the coffee to trickle into the cups, I'd plugged my last quarters into the candy machine. With each step across the waiting room, Peanut M&M's jangled merrily in my pocket. In times of stress, the sound was music to my ears.

I handed Rita the coffee and sat down beside her. "Still no word?"

She shook her head, took a sip of the brew, and grimaced. "I tried to persuade the nurse to at least let me keep Sheila company, but she said the doctors were with her. She told me that unless I was a blood relative I had to wait out here."

"I have an idea. What if I convince her I'm Sheila's sister from Spartanburg? I do have some acting credentials if you recall," I added for good measure.

Rita winced at the reference to my recent acting debacle in a production in which she'd served as stage manager. Under less dire circumstances, I would've been offended. Instead I tore open the M&M's.

The parents with the fussy toddler were finally called to be seen. The man with the injured hand kept his gaze fixed on a TV mounted high on a wall tuned to one of those twenty-four-hour news stations. I selected a green M&M and popped it into my mouth. When my children were young, I convinced them the green ones were for mothers only. This way I was assured my fair share. After all, a mother's duty is to protect their young. And all mothers know too much sugar isn't good for kids. So I made the supreme sacrifice and ate most of the M&M's myself. Thus saving my offspring from hyperactivity and bad teeth.

Peter, Paul, & Mary, as I was coming to think of the threesome of Todd, Rog, and Betsy had established squatter's rights in a configuration of vinyl chairs adjacent to where Rita and I kept vigil. Ignoring a sign prohibiting cell phones, Betsy pressed hers to one ear and jabbered away. The two men slouched in their seats. Roger scowled at the screen of a sleek laptop while Timmons played with a BlackBerry. I recognized the gadget, not because I owned one, but because I've seen the commercials. I even know about iPads and apps. As for commercials, I watch because I can. Jim, my late husband, was a medalist in the sport of channel surfing. Since the remote control was invented, I rarely saw a commercial and felt totally out of mainstream America. Now that he's passed, I'm commander of the remote.

Timmons struck me as the artsy type. He was dressed casually in designer jeans strategically faded at the knees, an unstructured blazer, and a shirt that had never met an iron, opened at the throat to reveal a dark T-shirt. Roger, on the other hand, favored rumpled chic. With his tie askew, well-worn cords, and tweed jacket sporting leather patches on the elbows, he was making a valiant attempt to impersonate a college professor. I gave the boy a B+ for effort.

Time crept by. One hour bled into two, then three. It was getting later and later. The toddler had been sent home with his much-relieved but weary parents. The worker had been stitched up good as new and advised in the future not to mix six-packs with power tools. Except for the five of us awaiting news of Sheila's and Vaughn's condition, the emergency room was deserted. I glanced up from my dog-eared copy of *Prevention*. I thought it an odd choice for reading material in a hospital. I ask you, is that sound business practice? If more people practiced prevention, they'd have little need for a hospital's services. With no patients, hospitals would have to close their doors. Just a thought . . .

I saw Timmons peek at a watch nearly the size of a dinner plate that probably offered more apps than an iPad. "I've had enough sitting around. I want to know what's going on, and I want to know now."

He sprang up and trotted toward the reception desk. His cronies followed suit, relentless in their determination to harass a poor, unsuspecting clerk.

"I have a good friend on the staff at Emory," Timmons announced loudly. "If I don't hear something soon, I'm calling him."

Emory, I knew from my brief time south of the Mason-

Dixon Line, was a highly respected university hospital in Atlanta. But our smaller, regional hospital wasn't exactly chopped liver. All anyone had to do was look at the many awards of excellence plastered over the walls to know this.

"Sir, if you'll just be patient—"

"We've *been* patient," Roger cut in. "Maybe this Podunk hospital isn't equipped to handle an emergency of this nature."

"Roger's right," Betsy concurred. "Perhaps we should insist Dr. Rappaport be airlifted out of here."

"I demand to speak to the doctor in charge," Timmons continued his rant. "If he isn't out here in the next five minutes . . ." He let the warning hang.

I felt sorry for the receptionist who had the misfortune to be working the night shift. "How rude," I whispered to Rita.

"Ignore them, Kate," she whispered back. "They're fools."

I returned to an article on green, leafy vegetables, but kept one eye on the large clock over the door. I found it strange that the PPM Trio hadn't expressed any concern whatsoever over Vaughn Bascomb. The poor man had been stricken as well, but they seemed mindless of the fact.

Timmons flicked his wrist and stared down at his watch, evidently prepared to make good his threat. But before he could cause the hapless clerk more grief, the sliding doors *whooshed* open, and the doctor who had asked about next of kin appeared.

"Are any of you related to Dr. Vaughn Bascomb?" he asked, addressing the waiting room at large.

When no one acknowledged kinship, he heaved a tired sigh. "I don't suppose any of you know how we might reach a relative?"

Rita and I exchanged anxious glances. Something in the doctor's tone put me on red alert.

"We're not here for that idiot," Timmons snapped. "As friends and associates of Dr. Rappaport, I insist on an update on her condition."

I had to hand it to the doctor. He showed remarkable restraint in dealing with a guy with an ego the size of Jupiter. If it had been me, I'd've—to borrow a former coworker's expression—laid him out in lavender right there on the emergency room floor.

I rose and stepped forward, propelled by sympathy for a man I didn't even know. "How is Dr. Bascomb? Is he going to be all right?"

The doctor's gaze shifted in my direction. I sensed Rita right behind me, breathing down my neck as we waited for his response.

"I'm afraid Dr. Vaughn Bascomb didn't make it."

"Didn't make it?" I repeated. The words echoed hollowly inside my brain, but I couldn't quite seem to wrap my mind around the concept.

"We did all we could . . . I'm sorry."

# Chapter 5

*Didn't make it . . . ?*

I struggled to process the doctor's words. *Vaughn didn't make it? Why . . . ? What happened . . . ?* This was an award-winning medical facility. The staff was trained to save lives. My throat felt like I swallowed a giant cotton ball, so dry I could hardly squeeze the words out. "Surely you don't mean . . ."

"The patient developed a severe arrhythmia, an irregular heartbeat. That happens sometimes in cases like this. In spite of everything we did to correct it, he went into cardiac arrest. I'm sorry, but Vaughn Bascomb is dead."

*Dead?* Denial kicked in, numbing me for what would follow later. How could a man I'd met only hours before go from feeling a little "under the weather" to D-E-A-D, dead? Denial, for those who might or might not know me well, is my all-time favorite defense mechanism when life gets too sticky to handle. With denial, the hard truth can be plain as day, yet you can't see the writing on the wall. I might be mixing metaphors again, but you get my drift.

"I wasn't aware Vaughn had heart disease. Do you know what might have caused the arrhythmia?" Rita, being the practical, sensible woman that she was, wanted answers. Rita, bless her heart, didn't let herself get bogged down by such trivial things as denial.

The doctor spread his hands and shrugged. "There are any number of causes. We'll know more after the autopsy."

"Could it have been food poisoning?"

The doctor shrugged again. "That's the likely scenario. We'll have a better idea once toxicology reports get back from the lab."

I saw Betsy clutch Timmons's sleeve, her red lacquered nails like splotches of blood against the dark fabric of his jacket. "You still haven't mentioned Dr. Rappaport's condition."

Roger the pudge shoved forward, his stance just short of belligerent. "Betsy's right. You still haven't said a word about Dr. Rappaport."

"Ms. Rappaport's condition has stabilized." In the far recesses of my mind, I registered the fact that the doctor hadn't used *doctor* when speaking of Sheila. Apparently he reserved that form of address for a degree in medicine, not one in plant reproduction.

Timmons pried Betsy's fingers from his arm. "Do you think your hospital can care for her adequately, or should we make arrangements to have her transferred elsewhere?"

Todd Timmons's tone could best be described as . . . snippy. Dr. Evan Michaels, according to the embroidery above the left breast pocket of his lab coat, dug balled fists deep into his pockets. I surmised it was to prevent himself from slugging the smug, little twerp.

"We're perfectly qualified to handle a case of this nature," Dr. Michaels replied, his voice equally snippy. "The gastroenterologist on call has already examined Ms. Rappaport. She's been given a sedative and is resting quietly. As soon as a bed is available, she'll be transferred to ICU."

"ICU?" Betsy's dark eyes rounded in her pretty doll-like face. "You said her condition was stable."

Dr. Michaels seemed to summon the last of his dwindling supply of patience. "This is only being done as a precaution. The ICU will allow us to monitor her more closely."

Betsy drew herself as tall as her petite frame would allow. "Well, I want to see her. In case you're unaware, my company, Belle Beaute, is the sole sponsor of her TV show, *How Does Your Garden Grow?*"

The physician seemed singularly unimpressed by Betsy's name-dropping. "Sorry, rules are rules. Once Ms. Rappaport is on one of the medical floors you can visit her all you like, but until then . . ." With a brisk nod, he turned and retreated into the ER's inner sanctum.

"Since there's nothing more we can do here," I said, turning to Rita, "we might as well get some sleep and check on Sheila in the morning."

Rita nodded wearily. "Just let me grab my purse."

"Give me a sec to power down my laptop," Roger said to Timmons. "I'm not one to speak ill of the dead, but at least Bascomb won't be able to meddle in the book business anymore. The man liked to think he knew more about editing than me, the editor. His constant interference threatened my entire vision for the finished product. Now at last I'll be able to make some progress."

Timmons, busy pecking away on his BlackBerrry, nodded absently.

"Well, I don't know about the two of you, but I'm exhausted." Betsy checked her cell phone for the umpteenth time, and then closed it with a *snap*.

"Thank goodness I had my assistant reserve a room at the B and B in town," Todd said, dropping his Black-Berry into a pocket as he strolled toward the exit. "What about you, Betsy? Staying here in Timbuktu, or heading back to Atlanta?"

"Me?" Betsy tucked her clutch purse more securely

under her arm. "Sheila and Vaughn rented a house in that old folks' place where that friend of hers lives. She invited me to stay with them. She gave me a key earlier tonight."

Roger hefted a bulging computer bag onto his shoulder. "Looks like you and me, buddy," he said to Todd, "are headed in the same direction. Not too much to pick from in a burg with only two stoplights."

"Guess beggars can't be choosers, eh?"

"Guess not."

"Wait up, boys," Betsy called as she hurried to catch up. "I need a lift to Sheila's place."

I looped my arm through Rita's. "It's been quite a day, hasn't it?"

"You can say that again."

I actually thought about saying that again just to see if I could make her smile. That, however, required more effort than I was capable of at the moment. It had been a long day, a very long day. Instead I reverted to the euphemistic, "Things always look brighter in the morning."

"I keep thinking about poor Vaughn. Regardless of everything those awful people said about him, he didn't seem like such a bad guy. Sheila, on the other hand, isn't always the easiest person to be around. Oftentimes, she's selfish, inconsiderate, and demanding. She can be quite the diva when things don't go her way. I've seen her throw a tantrum a time or two that would curl your hair."

I studied Rita more carefully, but she didn't return my look. "You don't sound as though you like her very much."

"Like?" Rita snorted. "Honey, I could write a book on the foibles of having Sheila as a friend and former roommate."

There it was again. That undercurrent of dislike—or envy—I'd noticed earlier. The Rita I'd come to know over the years was affable and easy to be around—usually unperturbed by the idiosyncrasies of others. But I'd wager Sheila Rappaport knew which of her buttons to push—and did so with regularity.

We made it almost to the exit when the voice of the admission clerk froze us in our tracks. "Wait up, y'all. Is one of you Rita?"

Had something gone wrong? Had Sheila taken a sudden turn for the worse? Next to me, I sensed Rita stiffen. No doubt, the same fear skittered through her mind.

"I'm Rita," she replied slowly. "Rita Larsen."

"Ms. Rappaport's been askin' for you. Dr. Michaels gave his okay, but said to keep it short—five minutes max."

"Has anyone told her . . . ?" I asked, but faltered.

"'. . . about Dr. Bascomb," Rita finished my sentence.

"Dr. Michaels broke the news. Go straight back. She's in the second exam room on the left." The clerk picked up a stack of forms and began to sort through them.

Rita headed for the door the clerk had indicated with me sticking to her like glue.

"Hey!" the receptionist called after us. "Dr. Michaels didn't say anything about letting both of you go back."

"I'm Ms. Rappaport's sister—from Spartanburg," I fibbed, not breaking stride. No way was I going to cool my heels in the waiting room while Rita got the scoop of the decade. Way I looked at it, I was doing her a favor. As a friend of Sheila's, Rita couldn't be objective about what she was about to see or hear. I, on the other hand, could be objectivity personified.

Cautiously, we cracked open the door of Room Two and peered inside to find a gray-haired nurse with a bad perm busily adjusting the dials on machines that went beep. "Ms. Rappaport needs her rest," she said, not bothering to look up. "Keep your visit short."

"Yes, ma'am," I said, fighting the urge to salute. The

woman had that kind of effect on me. If a casting call
came out for a remake of *One Flew Over the Cuckoo's
Nest*, I'd nominate her for the part of Nurse Ratched.

We sidled into the room.

Nurse Ratched gave Rita and me the once-over as
she checked a lead attached to Sheila's chest that led to
a machine with squiggly green blips. "Which one is the
friend?"

"That would be me," Rita volunteered.

The nurse eyed me with suspicion. "And what does
that make you?"

"I . . . um. I'm the sister—from Spartanburg."

"Funny, I don't see a family resemblance."

"Ah . . . um . . . we had different fathers. Mine was
shorter," I ad-libbed. "And a little chubby." My smile
felt taut as a rubber band about to snap. If I was being
cross-examined on the witness stand, I'd fold like a two-
dollar bill.

"Hmm . . ."

I could tell from her expression that I wasn't pulling
the wool over her eyes. I steeled myself to be kicked to
the curb.

Nurse Ratched stared meaningfully at her watch.
"Ticktock, ladies. Five minutes, then clear out."

The woman had clearly missed her calling. She'd have
made a dandy Marine drill sergeant. Things in nursing
had changed over the years, I mused. Crepe-soled shoes
had been exchanged for Reeboks. Starched whites had
been replaced by rumpled scrubs. But one thing was
constant—the knack nurses had for running roughshod
over unwanted visitors. That remained part of the standard curriculum.

The nurse left us amidst a lot of beeping, whirring,
and hissing machinery. Rita tentatively approached the
stretcher where Sheila lay. I edged close behind. At first
I thought Sheila asleep, or unconscious, but then I saw
her eyelids flutter open.

"Hey there," Rita said, gingerly grasping Sheila's hand. "You gave us quite a scare. How're you feeling?"

"Like I've been sucked through a straw," she said, her voice raspy. "I must look like hell."

She wasn't far off the mark, but I didn't want to tell her that. When someone's come that close to meeting their Maker, it's my policy to cut them some slack. Unless you're on a soap opera, it's hard to appear glamorous with oxygen tubes in your nose, IVs in your arm, and dressed in a gown that your grandmother wouldn't wear to scrub floors.

I cleared my throat. "We're sorry about Vaughn," I told her.

My presence in the cubicle seemed to register with Sheila at last. Sheila blinked back tears, and swallowed audibly. "The doctor said his heart gave out."

"It's such a tragic . . . accident," I murmured for wont of a better word. "Food poisoning is a terrible thing."

Sheila's gaze fastened on mine and held. "It wasn't an accident," she whispered hoarsely.

"What do you mean it wasn't an accident?" Rita asked sharply.

"I was poisoned."

"Poisoned?" I repeated, not sure I'd heard correctly.

Had the ordeal addled Sheila's brain? Left her paranoid and delusional? And what about the food poisoning theory? Even the doctor had said that was the most likely cause for their sudden illness. But poisoning . . . ? No one in Serenity Cove Estates ever gets poisoned. Bludgeoned perhaps. On rare occasions shot deader 'n a doornail. But poisoned? The whole idea sounded too Machiavellian for us straightforward, simple-minded folk.

"We've made our share of enemies." Sheila licked her dry lips. "Someone—I don't know who—but someone wanted Vaughn and me dead."

Rita and I exchanged nervous glances.

"I know it sounds crazy, insane even," Sheila persisted, her eyes riveted on mine. "But I've felt threatened for months now. Felt something menacing just waiting for the right moment to strike—and now it has."

I cleared my throat, not sure how to respond.

As if sensing my confusion, Sheila reached out and clutched my hand. "Please," she begged, "say you believe me."

# Chapter 6

"Psst," Marian, our tai chi instructor hissed. "Left foot, Kate. *Left* foot."

I heard a few snickers from the class as I hastily substituted my left foot for the right. *Focus, Kate, focus,* I scolded myself silently.

Instead of being chastised—however subtly—my presence here should be lauded. No one in this room could ever guess how hard it was for me to resist slapping the snooze button when the alarm sounded this morning. After the long night I'd spent with Rita in the ER, it was a wonder I'd slept a wink. But here I was dressed in my workout clothes and chipper as could be—given the circumstances.

"Imagine picking fruit from a tree," Marian crooned in the singsong voice she adopted when she wasn't busy hissing at recalcitrant students.

I reached for a pretend apple.

Next to me Pam calmly continued to pluck imaginary fruit from an imaginary tree. "So what happened at the hospital?"

I paused in my apple picking half-expecting to hear Marian admonish Pam to hush. When it didn't come, I whispered back, "Vaughn died."

"Died . . . ? How . . . ?"

"His heart stopped beating." I added another "apple" to my collection. It served only to remind me I was starving. After tai chi, Pam and I planned to meet Connie Sue and Monica for breakfast.

Pam froze, arms extended overhead, all thought of fruit—peaches, pears, plums, and cherries—temporarily forgotten. "Please, tell me you're joking."

"Keep in mind, class, gathering is one of the oldest activities known to mankind. A survival movement," Marian intoned, oblivious to the conversation in the back row. "Your search for food has been successful. Let's move on, shall we?"

My stomach lurched at the thought of food. Suddenly, visions of hash browns and crispy bacon vanished. Food was what had started this whole tragic chain of events. That and its kissin' kin—food poisoning. Would Vaughn Bascomb's death certificate read murder by hush puppies?

"The next exercise is the leg swing." Marian brought both legs together while keeping her left foot at a forty-five-degree angle. "Remember, class, this is a swing, not a kick," she cautioned, lest we become overzealous and tear a groin muscle.

I tried to appear graceful, but wobbled from side to side. Fortunately, I caught myself before going *splat!* Let me tell you, it's no easy task keeping your balance while standing on one foot. Human beings aren't designed like storks.

"This movement helps relieve indigestion," Marian singsonged.

Did she say indigestion? That quite literally stopped me in my tracks. Too bad Vaughn didn't know about the leg swing. Maybe he'd still be alive.

"Kate, Kate . . . ?"

With a shake of my head, I brought myself back to the present and realized Marian was speaking to me. I have to give her credit, this time instead of irritation she seemed genuinely concerned about my well-being.

"Are you all right? You look a little pale. Do you need to sit down? Some water perhaps?"

"No, I'm fine," I said, managing to find my voice. I slowly became aware that the entire class had stopped swinging their legs and was watching with curiosity. I drew in a deep, cleansing breath. In through the nostrils, out through the mouth, and then let it rip. "Dr. Vaughn Bascomb died last night."

"Oh, my God!" Marian exclaimed, looking shocked.

Bootsy Robert's hand flew to her mouth. "That's terrible!"

"I was there last night when he collapsed," Shirley Buckner announced to the class at large.

Trixie Hamilton quickly jumped into the conversation. "Me, too."

Further attempts at exercise were futile. Our chi abandoned us for Serenity Cove's all-time favorite sport— gossip. Normally I don't like to carry tales, but in this case I made an exception. I felt it my civic duty to impart the truth, the whole truth, and nothing but the truth. I would single-handedly save Serenity Cove Estates from a glut of false rumors. It was the least I could do.

Pam folded her arms across her chest, her head cocked to one side. "Spill it, girlfriend."

So I did. How could I refuse a request from my BFF?

The entire class, Marian included, surrounded me, eager to hear every single detail. "Well," I began humbly, relishing my role if not the message. I proceeded to tell them everything that had transpired from the time Vaughn Bascomb was wheeled out of the auditorium on a stretcher to Dr. Michaels informing Rita and me that he didn't make it.

My audience lapped up every morsel that fell from my lips. Bascomb's death was the most exciting event to hit town since various and sundry body parts started showing up on the golf course some months back. No one, it seemed, wanted to read news like this on the front page of the *Serenity Sentinel*. Not when they could hear the morbid details firsthand from someone who'd actually been on the scene. That someone being none other than little ol' me.

I'm not sure why, but I left out the part about Sheila claiming they'd been poisoned. Maybe I didn't want to panic the good citizens of Serenity Cove. They'd been through enough recently with not one, but two murders in our midst. No, there would be time enough for that later—if her allegations proved true.

When I finished my recitation, everyone started talking at once. And everyone, it seemed, had the same theory.

"Everyone I talked to said it must be food poisoning."

"I bet someone let the potato salad stand out too long."

"And what about the deviled eggs? They're chock full of mayo."

"I know of at least a half dozen people who complained of nausea and stomach pain afterward."

"I heard Monica Pulaski ruined practically new suede pumps she found on sale at Stein Mart because she didn't make it to the restroom in time."

This last tidbit didn't surprise me in the least. Monica had a reputation for turning moldy olive green at the slightest provocation. This wouldn't be the first time her supersensitive stomach caused the ruination of a pair of shoes.

"I'm going to let this be a lesson," Bootsy concluded. "From now on, I'm going to be extra careful what I put in my mouth."

Connie Sue and Monica had finished land aerobics and were waiting at the Cove Café when Pam and I arrived for breakfast.

"Aerobics finished early 'cause of all the gossip and speculation circulatin' about Vaughn Bascomb," Connie Sue said by way of a greeting.

I nodded noncommittally. Seemed to a lot of that going around this morning—a regular epidemic.

"Coffee, Miz McCall?" Vera McGillicuddy, the Babes' hands-down favorite waitress, appeared with a coffeepot.

I beamed her a smile. "Does a cat have whiskers?"

Vera, I noted, was looking particularly perky these days. Rumor had it there was a new man in her life. No wonder she was all smiles. A little nip and tuck, along with a divorce from her sleazeball husband, had done wonders for the woman.

I accepted the menu Vera handed me, knowing full well it was only a formality. I had the darn thing memorized. Bootsy Roberts may have decided to be extra careful about what she put in her mouth, but that didn't mean I had to follow suit. I wasn't going to let rumors of food poisoning interfere with a hearty breakfast, not when I was ravenous. Besides, if Sheila's claim did prove to be the case, the true culprit was more likely along the lines of arsenic or cyanide—not potato salad or deviled eggs. I made a mental note to haul *The Complete Idiot's Guide to Forensics* from the shelf and dust it off. I needed to check if the book had a chapter on poisons.

I felt exhilarated at the notion of taking my detective skills out of mothballs. Just thinking of this made me feel almost giddy. And hungrier by the minute. I could identify with the cast of *CSI*, one of my favorite TV shows, who always seemed to enjoy a hearty breakfast when working a case. Nothing like a little murder and mayhem to stimulate the appetite.

Pam frowned at the menu. "What're you having?" she asked, turning to me.

"My usual," I told Vera, returning the menu unopened. "Eggs, scrambled, bacon crisp, hash browns, and wheat toast."

Connie Sue shuddered when she heard my order. "Sugar, are you sure all that food's a good idea knowin' everyone's scared witless worrin' over food poisonin'?"

"But I'm starving." My pronouncement sounded dangerously close to a whine.

"Me, too." Once again, Pam proved to be a true blue friend, and much to Connie Sue's consternation, ordered the same.

"I'll have unbuttered toast, wheat, but I'll skip the fruit cup this mornin'," Connie Sue said primly. "And water with lemon, no ice."

Monica tucked a wisp of dark hair behind one ear. "My stomach's still a little queasy this morning. I'll just have a cup of Earl Grey tea."

"No one seems to have much of an appetite this mornin'," Vera grumbled.

Glancing around, I noticed the café was virtually deserted. "Where is everyone?" I asked. "Are the four of us the only ones hungry?"

Vera shrugged. "Guess so. If business doesn't pick up soon, the cook's threatening to leave early."

The instant Vera left to place our orders, Connie Sue leaned forward. "All right, sugar, tell us everythin' that happened last night after you left us to go chase the ambulance. And don't you dare leave out a teensy detail."

What could I do? I took the only recourse open to me and recounted the events of the evening. And this time I left nothing out—I repeat, nothing—including the part where Sheila claimed someone deliberately tried to kill both her and Vaughn.

Monica shook her head in disbelief. "You must have misunderstood."

"Nope," I told her. "That's what she said, all right." I took a sip of coffee—my first of the day, heaven in the guise of Columbian caffeine—and sighed with bliss. Downright orgasmic.

"Kate, darlin', I worry about you. You're watchin' far too many of those TV crime shows. They're startin' to soften your brain."

A scowl marred Connie Sue's brow. I didn't want to mention it, but if she kept that up she'd need Botox to smooth out frown lines. "If you don't believe me, ask Rita. She heard Sheila too."

"Who'd want to poison Sheila?" Pam asked.

"This is Serenity Cove Estates, a retirement community." Monica's mouth tightened into a line. "How is any of this possible?"

I took another sip of coffee and let the questions swirl around me.

"Every single person at land aerobics swore it was food poisonin'," Connie Sue remarked.

Looking across the table at my friend, I marveled at how the woman could look fresh as a daisy after a morning workout. Connie Sue represented a shining example of feminine engineering with nary a honey-blond strand out of place, her makeup always flawless, and with a stubborn refusal to admit the world is sometimes a bad place. It's not easy to have a friend so perfect. I thought of Rita and her former college roommate, Sheila Rappaport. It couldn't be pleasant hearing a friend the same age looked a decade younger. That was enough to make a saint envious. And Rita was no saint. Could envy have wormed its way into that friendship, making it rotten at the core?

"I know the whole thing sounds crazy," I admitted, albeit reluctantly.

We were uncharacteristically quiet as Vera returned with our orders. When we failed to respond to her cheery banter, she sauntered off muttering something about a fresh pot of coffee.

Pam speared a bit of scrambled egg and avoided eye contact. "With everything she'd just been through, do you think Sheila might have been confused?"

I sighed. I had to confess Pam made a good point. "That's what Rita seems to think." We'd discussed the matter at some length on the drive home. Sheila, Rita had insisted, had always been somewhat of a drama queen and loved the limelight.

Monica dunked her tea bag up and down in her cup. "Sheila's claim could possibly have been the result of the drugs she'd been given. Or it could be her electrolytes were off. Too much sodium or not enough potassium can do strange things to a person's mind."

How typical of Monica. I bit my tongue to keep from asking her where she'd earned her medical degree.

Pam cut to the chase. "But who would want to kill her?"

I set my cup down more forcibly than I intended. It was déjà vu all over again. Like last night, concern centered around Sheila Rappaport and not her companion. Poor Dr. Bascomb. No one seemed to be overly concerned that he had died. "Don't you mean who would want to kill *them*?"

Connie Sue looked crestfallen at the oversight. Reaching over, she patted my hand. "I'm sorry, sugar. Surely none of us meant to take his passin' lightly."

Pam and Monica nodded their agreement. "Dr. Bascomb's death is a terrible tragedy. I only met the man once, but he'd seemed a decent sort," Pam said.

"A little on the dull side—at least that's how he came across on TV—but decent," Monica hastened to add.

I felt ashamed of my little outburst. Blame it on lack of a good night's sleep. Although our acquaintance was brief, I'd developed a certain fondness for Vaughn Bascomb. It's hard to dislike a man with a weakness for hush puppies.

Pam toyed with her hash browns. If there'd been a dog around, she'd have slipped him some under the table. "What did the doctor say was the reason for Dr. Bascomb's death?"

I munched a slice of bacon while I gave the matter serious thought. Last night seemed light-years away. "Um, if I recall correctly, he said it had something to do with his heart."

"There you go, sugar." Connie Sue smiled for the first time. "No reason to think the worst when the man died from natural causes."

Natural causes hastened by a dose of cyanide? I wanted to ask.

Pam wagged her fork in my direction. "Kate, I hate to be the one to say this, but maybe you're looking for crimes where they don't exist. Think about it. Could you be getting some sort of vicarious thrill from playing detective?"

This . . . from my BFF? I could scarcely believe my ears. Just because I happened to be instrumental in solving several recent crimes committed here in Serenity Cove Estates didn't mean I fancied myself Nancy Drew. Wait a minute . . . Nancy Drew? Wasn't Nancy a teenager? At my more mature age, maybe I should liken myself to Jessica Fletcher of the *Murder, She Wrote* series. Jessica's fine, but I distinctly refuse to be compared with the "elderly" Miss Marple, of Agatha Christie fame. "Elderly" isn't a word in my vocabulary, as I try, with limited success, to make clear to my children.

"Pam's right, you know, Kate." Monica kindly pointed out. "And even if food poisoning isn't involved, Sheila mentioned she and Vaughn weren't used to deep-fried food. It's no wonder their digestive systems rebelled. Vaughn probably already had a weak heart, and the whole thing was simply too much for him."

I dove into my breakfast even though I was no longer hungry. In spite of arguments to the contrary, I simply wasn't convinced Sheila's shocking announcement had been the result of delusion, drugs, or too much sodium and not enough potassium. She had been lucid—and convincing.

Suddenly, I knew the course I had to take.

Ten minutes later, I was a certifiable member of the clean plate club. I needed to fortify myself for the ordeal ahead. I hoped Sheriff Sumter Wiggins had fortified himself as well.

# Chapter 7

My resolve wavered after leaving the Babes. The more I thought of confronting the lion in his den—the lion in this case being Sheriff Sumter Wiggins—the colder my feet got. Not that Sheriff Wiggins didn't need to be informed he had a murder case on his hands, mind you, but the sheriff isn't always—receptive, for lack of a better word—to help from concerned citizens such as myself. A lesser person could be downright discouraged by such a negative attitude.

Sumter Wiggins seems to have a selective memory when it comes to remembering all the assistance I've given him in the past. Honestly, by now he should offer to make me an honorary deputy. But I won't hold that against him. Still, I needed a battle plan of sorts before barging into his lair—a lesson I'd learned the hard way. I may be slow, but I'm not stupid.

While mulling over the best approach to a tricky situation, I decided to stop by the Piggly Wiggly. Nothing like browsing through aisles of canned goods and boxed dinners for inspiration. My thoughts kept circling back to Sheila lying in her hospital bed. The dear, she must be heartbroken at the loss of her significant other. Rita had mentioned Sheila and Vaughn had been an item for years, first as coworkers on a field assignment, then as friends who shared a common love of plants, and finally as lovers. Try as I might, however, my mind balked at thought of the pair in bed—naked.

Had I turned into a prude somewhere along the way? Couples didn't stop having sex when Social Security checks started rolling in. Jim, my wonderful, loving husband of forty-plus years, and I had had a healthy sex life up until his untimely demise in a bowl of guacamole on Super Bowl Sunday some years back. I've since lost my taste for anything with avocados.

I was pushing my cart, er, buggy—I sometimes forget that the grocery cart was rechristened here in the South—through the produce department when an idea struck. Before leaving the ER last night, Dr. Michaels had assured Rita and me that, barring complications, Sheila would be discharged within a day or two. Why not make a big pot of chicken noodle soup to bring her after she was released? Nothing better than chicken soup for the soul. I think I even own a book by the same name. With this in mind, I added celery to my cart/buggy.

"Terrible about that guy dying, isn't it?"

I turned and found Judy Sanders, a woman I'd sat next to during my one and only experiment with ceramics. The birdhouse I'd slaved over had made me the poster child for uneven brushstrokes.

"Hey, Judy."

Judy seemed to be in a quandary over choosing a bag of lettuce. I have to admit sometimes I long for the old days when a head of iceberg was the only option. Now one has choices. Too many choices if you want my opinion. Mediterranean, American, Italian, or European. Romaine lettuce comes classic, chopped, or leafy. And if that isn't confusion enough, there's spring mix, spinach, and arugula. Whew! No wonder Judy looked discombobulated.

Sighing, Judy surrendered and went for unoriginal iceberg. "Everyone I've talked to this morning says it was food poisoning."

"Is that right?" I murmured noncommittally, bestowing my undivided attention on the carrots. Not even carrots were an easy pick anymore. Baby, sliced, or julienne? They used to come in a bunch fastened together with a rubber band. I dropped a bag of babies into the cart and moved on to the fresh herbs with Judy right on my heels.

"I don't even feel safe serving salad since that lettuce recall tested positive for E. coli," she said.

"That was years ago, Judy. I think lettuce is pretty safe these days." I tried to reassure her, but what did I know?

Grabbing a bunch of parsley, I continued down the aisle, leaving Judy to ponder what to serve for dinner that night. It seemed every couple feet along the way, I heard whispers of food poisoning and once the B word: botulism. Talk like that was designed to strike fear in the hearts of the fearless.

Intent on crossing noodles off my list of ingredients, I entered pasta land. It was here my head started to pound. Old-fashioned versus whole grain? Yolk-free versus the hearty egg variety? Fine, wide, or extra wide? Decisions, decisions, decisions. I closed my eyes, picked a bag from the shelf, and tossed it in my cart. If I didn't get out of the Pig soon, I'd turn into a raving lunatic. My upcoming confrontation with the sheriff now seemed like a piece of cake.

In my mad dash to a checkout lane, I almost mowed down a tiny, snowy-haired lady wearing a royal blue smock emblazoned in yellow with BAM! A nametag pinned to her scrawny chest read WILMA.

"I'm terribly sorry, Wilma," I said, apologizing profusely as I helped her straighten the items on a card table that had been set up with a display of some sort.

"No problem, dearie," she replied cheerily. "You're the most excitement I've had all morning." She held out a pleated baking cup containing a chocolate-coated something. "Care to try a bite? They're quite tasty."

"What is it?" I asked suspiciously. It looked . . . interesting . . . but where I was concerned anything and everything covered in chocolate looked interesting.

"It's BAM! The new energy bar," she said, smiling. "BAM! is a wonderful source of protein and contains vitamins, minerals, and other dietary supplements. Sports nutritionists recommend BAM! to athletes."

Athletes? Hmm . . . My interest piqued, I asked, "Does practicing tai chi several times a week qualify me as an athlete?"

"I'm not exactly sure what tai chi is, dearie, but these bars are a great addition to a healthy diet. They're a convenient and easy way to limit portion control."

I had to hand it to Wilma. She'd obviously done her homework and had her lines down pat. I took a small bite, then another. "Umm, good," I mumbled around a mouthful of chocolate, peanut butter, and nuts.

"Business has been slow today. Help yourself." She held out the tray of treats. "Take two or three."

So I did. Too bad someone didn't patent a way of making broccoli taste this good. "Business is slow, you said?" I asked, making conversation as I sampled.

Wilma shook her head sadly. "I'm afraid so, dearie. No one even wants to make eye contact. Why, one woman actually backed away when I offered a BAM! You'd think I was trying to poison her."

"Imagine that!" I commiserated.

"I'm afraid my sales manager is going to be sorely disappointed when he returns and discovers I haven't sold a single box of product. I'm usually his best food demonstrator. My reputation will be ruined."

I'd certainly hate for this nice woman's reputation to

be ruined. Besides if these energy bars worked wonders for athletes, just think what they could do for a housewife on a fixed income. They could cut vacuuming time in half. "I'll take a box. Matter of fact, I'll take two," I said and was rewarded for my impulsive deed with a broad smile.

I left Wilma looking much happier at having made her first sale of the day. I peeled the wrapper from a BAM! as I settled into the Buick and headed off for my meeting with the sheriff. I'd need all the energy I could rustle up.

The Brookdale County Sheriff's office was located on a side street just off the town square. The sight of it never failed to elicit a flicker of disappointment. The single-story brick building was a clone of brick bungalows all over the country. If I had my druthers, I'd have chosen architecture that better reflected life in the South. Nothing as grand as Tara in *Gone With the Wind*, mind you, but at least one of those sweeping porches with a couple rocking chairs. A pillar or two would've been a nice antebellum touch, but one has to be practical.

As luck would have it—and not necessarily good luck—I found a parking spot right out front. Purple and yellow pansies in clay pots flanked either side of the entrance. Now that danger of a hard freeze was over, these would soon be replaced by more summery petunias or million bells. There you have it, folks, the sum total of my gardening expertise.

I approached the sheriff's office with some trepidation and when I got to the front door, I stood outside for a moment and gave myself a pep talk. *Put on your big girl panties, Kate, and deal with it.* Drawing in a deep breath, I shoved open the door.

Tammy Lynn Snow, the sheriff's gal Friday, sat behind a huge metal desk. She stopped pecking at a computer keyboard and looked up as I entered. Her tentative smile faded before it ever bloomed. I tried not to take it personally.

"Morning, Tammy Lynn," I said by way of greeting. "You're looking . . . fit."

Fit as can be considering the girl would give wallflowers a bad rep. Her lank, mousy-brown hair framed an oval face with delicate features. Her countenance was scrubbed clean and without a trace of makeup. Dressed in clothes that all but screamed thrift store, she could have blended into the woodwork and never been missed. Our little Brookdale County Cinderella was in dire need of a fairy godmother.

"Ah, er, if you're here to see the sheriff, ma'am, he's real busy," she said, shoving oversized glasses higher on the bridge of her small nose.

Gee, where had I heard that refrain before? Oh yeah, I remember. It was the last time I'd entered this office. Each and every time to be precise. "No problem, dear, I'm prepared to wait. I need to catch up on back issues of *Guns & Ammo*."

I'd tried repeatedly to improve the level of reading material at the sheriff's office, but to no avail. Copies of *Southern Living* and *Good Housekeeping* continually disappeared, giving way to more manly periodicals. Apparently felons and felons-in-training weren't interested in getting in touch with their softer, more feminine sides. It was disheartening, to say the least.

"I'll let Sheriff Wiggins know you're here."

Tammy Lynn spoke into the intercom in a hushed voice. I tried to resist, but the urge to eavesdrop was too strong. I caught whispered phrases such as "it's too late," "she'll wait," and "I did try." The words "sorry, sorry, sorry" punctuated their conversation. I wondered if Tammy Lynn turned to booze when her shift ended. Couldn't blame the girl if she hit the bottle.

Turning to me with a pained expression, she said,

"Sheriff Wiggins said he's finishin' up a report. He'll buzz when he's done."

I plunked myself down, prepared to cool my heels in this little waiting game we played. I leafed through a dog-eared issue of *Guns & Ammo* but, since I didn't own a gun and didn't intend to, it failed to capture my interest. And with no gun, there was no need for ammo. I put the magazine aside and picked up another.

"So, Tammy Lynn," I said when *Truck Trends* didn't fare any better as an attention grabber, "are you still seeing that nice young policeman, Eric Olson?"

The girl's eyes looked suspiciously bright behind her too-large lenses. "Ah, no, ma'am, not since he came off his crutches. He's workin' patrol again and doesn't have much free time."

"I'm sure his job keeps him quite busy."

"Yes, ma'am, it surely does. Eric's very conscientious when it comes to law enforcement. He's fixin' to make sergeant someday."

Tammy Lynn went back to her computer while I pretended interest in an article on monster truck rallies. It was a darn shame about Tammy Lynn and Eric. The two of them seemed to be hitting it off following Eric's unfortunate accident in which he'd broken a leg. Tammy Lynn had hovered over Eric, a regular Florence Nightingale, while his leg mended. Now that the fracture was healed, it seemed Tammy Lynn had once again been relegated to the role of his best friend's baby sister. A pity. The girl was clearly smitten, but from all appearances the attraction was a bit lopsided.

The intercom buzzed just then, startling me.

"The sheriff will see you now," Tammy Lynn announced primly. "He's in his office. I believe you know the way."

I'm afraid I knew the way only too well. Slinging my purse over my shoulder, I trudged down the hall.

"Miz McCall," drawled the sheriff in a voice better

suited to an *American Idol* contestant. "Long time no see."

I narrowed my eyes and looked at him skeptically. Did I detect thinly veiled sarcasm behind the greeting? "It hasn't been all that long," I reminded him, mentally doing the math since our last encounter. According to my calculations, a little over a month had elapsed between visits. He hadn't changed a whit. Skin still dark as Granny Ann's mahogany chifforobe. His smile, which was a rare occurrence, would reveal a flash of teeth white enough to rival those of Tiger Woods.

Not expecting an invitation, I perched myself on the chair opposite his desk. A chair that might bear a RE-SERVED plaque with my name engraved on it.

Sumter Wiggins lounged back and eyed me coolly. "To what do I owe the pleasure of your fine company?"

I shifted my weight—subtly, I hoped. I didn't want to give the man the upper hand early on in our meeting. The sheriff possessed a God-given talent for intimidation. Some might attribute this to his imposing physique. Six foot two, if I were to judge, with shoulders that would make a linebacker weep with envy. Others might say attitude gave him an edge. The term "bad cop" could have originated with him.

I cleared my throat and began. "After our last case together, Sheriff, I've learned my lesson."

"*Our* last case?" He gave me the one eyebrow lift thing he'd perfected. A gesture guaranteed to make a Methodist minister sweat buckets. A trick I often tried to imitate, but had yet to master.

"Ours," I repeated firmly, determined not to let him browbeat me. "Ours as in law enforcement and concerned citizens working together." I folded my hands in my lap, pleased with my little speech. Just goes to show it really does pay to have a battle plan.

"Hmm." He leaned back farther. The springs of his chair squeaked in protest at being abused by two hundred plus pounds. "Kindly explain what lesson it is that you think you've learned."

"The one about obstruction of justice," I replied promptly. "Not to mention the one about withholding information. Or the part about sins of omission."

"And all this time I didn't think you were payin' any mind." Folding jumbo-sized hands across a trim and toned waist, he asked with exaggerated patience, "I'm certain Tammy Lynn mentioned my busy schedule, so if you don't mind, let's move this meetin' along."

"Right," I said, clasping my hands a little tighter. "I'm sure you've heard what happened at the garden club lecture last night?"

"I'm assumin' you mean the food poisonin' incident?"

"Yes, that's the one."

"It's my understandin' two people were transported to the hospital. One survived. The other, unfortunately, succumbed."

Succumbed? A polite substitute for kicked the bucket? The remainder of my cockamamie battle plan sprouted wings and flew out the window. "What if it wasn't food poisoning?" I asked, getting down to the nitty-gritty instead of beating about the bush. "What if it was the real deal?"

"The real deal bein' . . . ?'

I huffed out a breath. The man was being deliberately obtuse. Did I have to spell it out for him? "Have you spoken with the survivor, Dr. Sheila Rappaport?"

He shrugged dismissively, his dark face impassive. "No reason to."

"What if it wasn't the potato salad? Or the deviled eggs?"

"Are you implyin' what I think you're implyin'?"

"Indeed, I am." I had the satisfaction of seeing my missile hit the bull's-eye.

# Chapter 8

"Dr. Sheila Rappaport happens to be a friend of Rita Larsen, a close friend of mine and a fellow Bunco Babe. In fact, Sheila and Rita were once college roommates. Rita, however, had to be content with a bachelor's degree in botany while Sheila went on for her PhD. Fortunately Rita had a business minor and was able to establish a career in banking. She ended her career as a branch manager," I added proudly.

"I suspect this is all leadin' to a point you're hopin' to make between now and suppertime?"

*Focus, Kate, focus.* Those words became my mantra. The sheriff had gone and done it again. Made me ramble on and on until I could have been kissin' kin with the village idiot. The man seemed to have that kind of effect on me. "The *point* I'm trying to make is that Rita and I were both at the emergency room last night."

"And . . . ?"

"And just as we were about to leave, Sheila asked to speak to Rita. Naturally, I tagged along."

"Naturally."

I ignored the blatant sarcasm. "It was no easy task convincing Nurse Ratched I was Sheila's sister from

Spartanburg, especially when she failed to see a family resemblance. I improvised and told her we had different fathers, so she let me stay. I thought under the circumstances, it was wise to have an extra set of ears present. Rita, being a good friend and all, might have a difficult time being objective."

"While you, on the other hand, would have no trouble at all."

"Exactly," I replied, grateful he recognized the logic behind my actions. He didn't always. "I thought with two of us, there'd be less room for a misunderstanding. Anyway"—I lowered my voice and scooted to the edge of the seat—"Sheila told us she and Vaughn Bascomb had been *poisoned*."

"Poisoned, eh?"

I nodded vigorously. "She said someone wanted both of them dead."

The corners of his mouth twitched. "So you're tellin' me the poisonin' was deliberate and not the result of 'em ingestin' too much of our fine Southern cuisine?"

"Can't put anything over on you, can I?" Guess it was my turn to inject a little sarcasm.

"Interestin' how Ms. Rappaport sent you instead of callin' me herself."

"I don't know why she didn't call you. Maybe she didn't think you'd believe her. Or take her seriously." Just like he wasn't taking me seriously. Whatever the reason, it was a shrewd move on Sheila's part to delay the hot seat in the sheriff's office as long as possible. "I know the story sounds off the wall, but what's the old saying, 'Truth is stranger than fiction'?"

"Don't suppose she mentioned the name of the person or persons responsible for this dastardly deed, now, did she?"

"She claimed she doesn't know."

Leaning forward abruptly, he picked up a pen from

the desk and tapped it against his blotter. *Tap, tap, tap* translated into *drip, drip, drip*, the old standby Chinese water torture. "What do you expect me to do with this bit of information?" he asked at last.

"Why, investigate, of course. It's your sworn duty. I'd expect nothing less from an officer of the law. I'm afraid if you don't . . ." My voice trailed off.

"Come now, Miz McCall, finish what you started to say. This isn't the time to be bashful."

He was right, of course. There were things that needed to be said. "I'm afraid if you do nothing people are going to overact. Do you want to have mass hysteria on your hands?" I was on a roll and couldn't seem to stop. "Why, just this morning, I happened to be in Piggly Wiggly. A sweet, little old lady named Wilma couldn't even give away free samples of these." I reached into my purse, pulled out a BAM!, and placed it on the desk in front of him.

He eyed it with blatant suspicion. "What's this?"

"It's a new energy bar. Full of protein, vitamins, and other supplements. Folks at the Pig were afraid to take a bite less they suffer the same fate as Vaughn and Sheila. Until a report comes back on the cause of Vaughn Bascomb's death, no one in Brookdale or Serenity Cove Estates will have peace of mind—or accept treats from sweet old ladies."

He growled something under his breath that I didn't care to hear him repeat.

Rising, I hefted my purse onto my shoulder. I made a mental note to find a smaller purse or lighten this one up. If I didn't, I'd either wind up with rotator cuff surgery or become permanently lopsided. Neither option appealed to me.

"All I ask, Sheriff, is that you check into it. Find out if it was indeed a simple case of food poisoning—or something more sinister. Don't be surprised to learn that you have a homicide and an attempted murder on your hands."

I glanced over my shoulder as I beat a dignified retreat. I saw the sheriff tear the wrapper from a BAM! and take a huge bite. From the grim expression on his dark face, he might as well have been chewing nails.

While chicken soup simmered on a back burner, I called the hospital to check on Sheila's condition. I was informed she was no longer in ICU but had been transferred to a room on the medical floor. Next I phoned Rita. We agreed to pay Sheila a visit that evening.

Rita was ready and waiting with a lovely bouquet of pink and white flowers when I pulled into her drive. "Pretty," I said.

"Just something from the yard," she replied offhandedly.

"Something" from my yard would have been a couple spindly branches off a shrub of which I no longer remembered the name. If I was feeling especially creative, I might've added a twig of holly. But Rita was a master gardener, and I was . . . Well, I just wasn't.

I carefully maneuvered my way out of Rita's winding drive. Reverse has never been my favorite gear. I've gained the reputation of someone who's been known to run over some of those fancy lights folks use to line the edge of their driveways. As far as I'm concerned they might as well have targets drawn on them. That's how good my aim has become. "Have you spoken to Sheila since last night?" I asked to divert Rita's attention away from my deplorable lack of reverse gear expertise.

"No, I've been busy."

I nodded. We were headed out of town before I broke the silence. "Do you think Sheila was telling the truth last night about someone trying to kill her?"

Rita shrugged. "I doubt it. Sheila tends to overdramatize. She thrives on being the center of attention. She was probably just confused after everything she'd been through."

"Mmm, I'm not so sure," I murmured. "She sounded pretty convincing."

"Sheila's state of mind could have been the result of medication, dehydration, or stress. Maybe all three. I wouldn't obsess over it if I were you, Kate."

I wished I could be as certain as Rita. I slowed while passing through a town smaller than many shopping malls. Once I'd forgotten that the speed limit dropped like a rock from fifty-five to thirty-five and received a hefty fine. I swear the policeman would have given his own mother a ticket—and smiled while doing it. Ever since then, I've been careful to heed the posted speed, real careful.

"Well, drama queen or not, it's nice the two of you have remained friends all these years," I remarked as I began to accelerate now that I was out of the danger zone.

"Not really," Rita admitted. "Years passed without any contact between the two of us whatsoever."

"Not even at Christmas?" I asked, appalled by the notion.

"Nope, not even a card." Rita stared out the window as farmland flashed by. "I once asked why the radio silence. Sheila blamed the lack of communication on traveling. Her work takes her all over the world. Besides, what does a globe-trotting botanist have in common with a lowly bank manager?"

I elected to ignore the bitterness in her voice. "How did the two of you happen to reconnect?"

"She called out of the clear blue one day. Said she was working on a book about perennials in the Southeast and asked if I could recommend a quiet place for her and Vaughn to stay while they completed it. She'd researched the area in and around Serenity Cove Estates and thought it would be ideal. I contacted a Realtor friend, and *voilà*!"

Rita's story didn't sound all that farfetched. I'd occasionally had calls out of the blue myself since moving south. Mostly old friends looking for a cheap place to stay during Masters Week. Augusta, Georgia, home to the famed golf classic, books up quickly. What better time for me to renew an acquaintance with a grade school buddy who happens to have a coveted ticket but not a hotel room? Something, however, sounded fishy about Rita and Sheila's relationship. They sounded more like rivals than friends.

At the hospital, I parked the Buick in the visitors' lot. By the time Rita and I reached the fourth floor, nurse's aides were efficiently collecting dinner trays from patient rooms.

As we approached Room 424, I stepped aside and let Rita enter ahead of me. Sheila's room contained more flowers than a state funeral for a former president. I also spotted a stack of glossy magazines, a wicker basket filled with fresh fruit, and a terrarium large enough to accommodate a rainbow trout. Rita's bouquet looked paltry compared with the larger, more elaborate arrangements. Sheila lay propped in bed oozing glamour and looking fabulous in a silk peignoir the shade of ripe apricots. Her near-death experience obviously agreed with her. The only concession to her status as a hospital patient was an IV dripping into one arm.

"Rita! Kate!" Sheila exclaimed upon seeing us. "So good of you to come."

Now that I wasn't distracted by all the frills, I noticed we weren't the only visitors. Betsy Dalton, chic in a sapphire-blue cashmere twinset and tailored slacks, had staked a claim on the room's only comfortable chair.

"Oh look, Betsy," Sheila exclaimed. "I bet Rita picked these lovely flowers in her very own backyard."

"They're the last of my camellias." Rita glanced over

the crowded hospital room, then frowned. "Let me check at the nurses' station for something to put these in."

"Here," I said, handing Sheila a BAM!

Sheila eyed the bar with obvious distaste. "I never eat candy. It's fattening."

"It isn't candy. BAM! is the energy bar of athletes. I figured with everything you've been through lately you could use all the energy you could get."

"How thoughtful. Isn't it, Betsy?"

"Thoughtful," Betsy parroted. I could tell she wasn't impressed—or maybe she didn't like being upstaged by an energy bar.

I gave Betsy a friendly smile, determined to outnice her. A little well-placed guilt can work wonders on the disposition. I stuck out my hand. "I don't believe we've been introduced. I'm Kate McCall. A friend of a friend of Sheila's."

Betsy shook hands, but I caught her surreptitious glance at a container of hand sanitizer.

"And I'm the friend," Rita announced as she returned carrying the camellias in a turquoise plastic water pitcher. "Rita Larsen. Nice to meet you."

"Oh yes, Rita, the old college chum." Betsy favored Rita with a polite smile. "I'm Betsy Dalton, vice president in charge of new products at Belle Beaute."

*Well, la-di-da!* Ignoring Miss I'm-more-important-than-you, I turned my attention back to Sheila. "You look vastly improved since the last time we saw you."

Sheila waved a dismissive hand, but I could tell she was pleased at the compliment. "If I do, I have Betsy and Belle Beaute to thank for putting the color back in my cheeks. Betsy's a veritable wizard with her magic wands and potions."

"It's all part of the job, sweetie," Betsy declared airily.

Betsy Dalton was indeed a wizard when it came to makeup artistry. Instead of trying to disguise the pallor that still lingered after Sheila's ordeal, she had accentuated it. The result was that Sheila looked as frail and ethereal as Greta Garbo when she played the tragic Camille in a vintage movie of the same name.

"How long do you plan to stay in Serenity Cove Estates, Ms. Dalton?" I asked.

"Call me Betsy," she said, "and to answer your question, Kate, I plan to stay however long it takes until Sheila is once again the glowing picture of health."

"I offered Betsy my guest room," Sheila said. "Having someone stay with me will help now that Vaughn . . ." Tears rolled down her cheeks at the mention of his name.

I had to give the woman credit. Not only did she *look* pretty, she cried pretty. No loud blubbering, no runny nose, no puffy eyes. Just delicately quaking shoulders while tears streamed silently.

"Forgive me," she sniffed, accepting the tissue Betsy proffered. "I still can't believe Vaughn's gone."

Rita patted her hand awkwardly. "There, there, it's going to be all right."

How many times had mothers around the world used that same phrase to comfort a child? A million? A billion? A trillion zillion? As banal as they sounded, the platitude seemed to bring about the desired effect because Sheila's tears subsided.

"I must look a fright." Sheila dabbed at her eyes. "If you'll excuse me for just a moment, I'm going to duck into the bathroom and freshen up before any of my fans see me like this."

Holding on to her IV pole for support, she swung off the bed and slid her feet into a pair of mules trimmed in pale peach marabou that matched her peignoir. She hadn't taken more than two steps when she glanced up and realized she had another visitor.

"Kel . . . ?" she gasped.

Upon uttering this, Sheila sank to the floor in a dead faint. Greta Garbo couldn't have been more graceful.

# Chapter 9

Quicker than you can say "Jack Robinson," Betsy flew to the door screaming at the top of her lungs. Her cries brought a pair of nurses on the run.

Sheila's eyelids fluttered, then opened.

The nurses quickly and efficiently took charge. The taller of the two wrapped a blood pressure cuff around Sheila's arm while the other felt for a pulse.

"BP's ninety over sixty."

"Pulse thready."

"Wh-what happened?" Sheila asked dazedly.

"You're going to be fine, hon," the shorter, dark-haired one assured her. "Milly and I are going to help get you back into bed." She speared us with a no-nonsense glare. "All of you—out! Now! Visiting hours are officially over."

Well, I've been kicked out of better places—including one of Toledo's finer dining spots, but that's a story for another day—I thought as Rita, Betsy, and I shuffled out into the hall. I noticed Kel, the man responsible for Sheila's swoon, standing a couple doors down, looking uncertain.

"Better page the doctor on call," I heard one of the nurses say as we left.

"... and put her back on the monitor," the other one added.

What the devil had just happened? I wondered. Sheila had seemed fine one moment, then bam! Just like the power bar.

"I don't give a damn what those nurses said. They can call security if they want, but I'm not budging until I know Sheila's all right," Betsy declared as she took up a stand just outside Sheila's room.

"I'm sure she'll be okay," Rita told her, her tone matter-of-fact.

Betsy, though, didn't appear convinced. "I don't know how Belle Beaute would manage if anything happened to her. Bascomb was expendable, but not Sheila. She's the heart and soul of *How Does Your Garden Grow?* The show simply couldn't exist without her."

There it was again, I thought. Bascomb was disposable—and not well liked. Sheila, on the other hand, was a candidate for sainthood.

"Who *is* that man?" Betsy pointed a finger at Kel, who lingered by the elevator.

"That's Kel Watson," Rita explained. "The county extension agent from Clemson."

Kel Watson? A name collided with the face. I should have recognized him by the ponytail alone. I'd seen him a time or two at various lectures I'd attended with Rita over the years. Clemson, like most universities specializing in horticulture, employ agents who share their expertise on matters relating to horticulture and agriculture. Need advice on topics ranging from beekeeping to ornamental shrubs, Kel was your guy. I studied the man in question. He seemed harmless enough. Tall, lanky, shiny bald pate and with what remained of his salt-and-pepper hair skinned back into a ponytail that trailed to his shoulder blades. His complexion had the leathery look of someone who spent most of his time outdoors.

"Well," Betsy huffed, "this whole thing is entirely his fault. Sheila was fine until *he* showed up."

"Hold on a minute, Betsy," Rita snapped. "Don't start the blame game. Sheila fainted before Kel even had a chance to say hello."

Something in Rita's voice warned Betsy to back off. Instead of further argument, she fished her cell phone out of her purse and flipped it open. "I'd better call the president of Belle Beaute. He'll want to know what's going on."

Rita motioned to me. "C'mon, let's blow this pop stand."

I craned my neck for a better look into Sheila's room, but the older of the two nurses spotted me and slammed the door. I can take a hint. I know when I'm not wanted "But what about Sheila?" I protested, hating to miss out on the action.

Rita started down the hall without me. "Does a cat have nine lives? Don't worry about Sheila, she'll be fine."

I hurried to catch up. I'd half-expected to find Kel Watson waiting alongside the bank of elevators, but he'd disappeared. This left me feeling vaguely disappointed— and more than a little curious.

"Kate, can you do me a huge favor and switch bunco dates with me?" Rita asked when she called the following afternoon. "I'm busy helping Tara get ready to move. Mark just found out that when he returns to the States he's being assigned to Camp Pendleton."

"That's wonderful news! Tara must be ecstatic that his tour is over, and they'll return to California." Tara's been living with Rita while her husband—Rita's son— served in Iraq. She put on a brave front, but we all knew Mark was never far from her thoughts. I was happy for the couple even though it meant losing one of our regular bunco players.

"She's over the moon. Now they can finally start the family they both want."

"And what about you? You must feel so relieved— and grateful—Mark's deployment is over and he's safe." I couldn't pretend to imagine a mother's fear knowing her son is in a war zone. My respect for these women knows no bounds. Through it all, Rita had remained calm and stoic, but I sensed it was only an act. Mark was never far from Rita's thoughts for long either. "Is there anything I can do to help?"

"Thanks, Kate, but I think I've got things under control. You agreeing to host bunco is one item I can cross off my to-do list."

"Sure, no problem," I said. "I'll see if I can round up a sub."

"Great! In all the commotion over Sheila, I haven't given Tara much help. She's flying out the day after tomorrow to look for a place to live."

"Speaking of Sheila, how's she doing?"

"The hospital discharged her this morning. I spoke with her on the phone, but haven't been over to see her yet. I suppose that makes me a terrible friend."

"I think I'll stop by, pay her a visit. I made some chicken noodle soup and, if I say so myself, it's pretty darn good. As a matter of fact, it's so good that if I don't deliver it soon, there won't be any left. By the way, is Betsy Dalton still here?"

"Sticking like glue."

I chuckled at her wry tone. "I take it you're not overly fond of the woman."

"What's to like? The woman's a barracuda in designer clothes."

"Well, even barracudas might have a soft spot for homemade soup."

After getting the address of Sheila's rental, we hung up. Since this was as good a time as any for a sick call, I hopped in the Buick and drove straight over. Minutes later, I was ringing the doorbell of an attractive, beige stucco ranch-style home. It took so long for someone to answer the door that I was beginning to think I'd scribbled down the wrong address when Betsy finally appeared.

"Can I help you?" she asked, giving me the evil eye formerly reserved for door-to-door salesmen peddling encyclopedias. The kind of purchase my father once made much to my mother's chagrin. In my youth I'd spent many an hour poring through random volumes, soaking up trivia. At the time, I'd been determined to be the darling of Sister Agnes. And the smartest kid in class. Do people even buy encyclopedias since the advent of the Internet? Britannica? World Book? Americana? Do they still exist? I'd have to check this out with Diane, our resident librarian and fellow bunco-tere.

"I said, can I help you?" she repeated, sounding annoyed.

I'd check into the fate of encyclopedias later; right now I was on a mission. "Remember me? I'm Kate McCall. We met at the hospital the other night. I thought I'd stop by and see how Sheila's feeling."

"She's resting. I'll tell her you were here." Betsy started to close the door.

If she thought I could be turned away this easily, she was mistaken. I placed my foot on a strategic spot on the sill. As I did so, I heard Sheila call out, "Betsy, who's at the door?"

"Guess naptime's over." I smiled as I pushed past her into the foyer.

Sheila emerged through the French doors of an adjacent room. Seeing her, no one would suspect she'd had a near brush with death. On closer inspection, however, she was still a trifle pale, but on her pallor was becoming. Again she reminded me of a heroine—tragic yet beautiful—in one of those lavish films of the thirties.

Greta Garbo in *Camille*. Or Bette Davis in *Dark Victory*. Vintage movies, I confess, are my newest addiction. They came in second only to my fondness for crime and punishment shows. *CSI*, *Law & Order*, *Bones*, *Criminal Minds*. Bring 'em on. The more the merrier.

"Kate!" Sheila welcomed me with a smile. "It's so kind of you to visit."

"I thought you might like some chicken soup." I held out the take-and-go container I carried.

"How thoughtful."

Betsy snatched the soup from me. "I'll put it in the fridge."

"And, Betsy," Sheila called after her, "while you're at it, be a dear and bring us some tea."

I didn't put a lot of stock in the food poisoning theory, but after glimpsing the expression on Betsy's face just then I wouldn't mind having an official food taster myself. When Betsy returned with the tea, I'd let her take the first sip.

"Let's talk, shall we, while Betsy fixes tea."

I followed Sheila into what was obviously the library. Not the hodgepodge room that served as den/study/library at my house, but a real honest-to-goodness library complete with floor-to-ceiling cherry bookshelves filled with books and tasteful art objects. A sleek flat-panel computer monitor sat atop a credenza, also of cherry, that snugged one corner. A sofa and matching chair-and-a-half with ottoman in butter-soft leather completed the room's furnishings. I felt envy rise up and take a bite. I wanted a room like this.

Sheila curled up in a corner of the sofa like a giant tabby cat and patted the spot next to her. "I took an instant liking to you, Kate. Something that doesn't happen often at first meetings. I hoped we'd get a chance to become better acquainted."

I cautiously sank into the cushions alongside her. For the life of me, I couldn't imagine why a nationally known botanist would want to get to "better acquainted" with a woman whose houseplants made suicide pacts on a regular basis

"Rita mentioned you were instrumental in solving two murders," she began.

I shrugged, not sure where this conversation was leading. "Rita may have exaggerated a wee bit."

"Rita *never* exaggerates. And neither do I." Sheila lowered her voice to a whisper. "Vaughn's death wasn't an accident, Kate. He was murdered. And whoever did it tried to kill me as well."

I tried not to look surprised, but don't think I managed to quite pull it off. I've never been known to have what gamblers call a "poker face." "I ... er ..." I cleared my throat and tried to assemble my scrambled thoughts. "Poison ... you mentioned poison. Why do you think you were poisoned?"

"Really, Kate." She huffed out a sigh. "I thought you more astute."

Somehow I felt I'd disappointed her. Should I explain I tended more toward "dense" than "astute"? Or should I let her find out for herself? I voted for the latter.

"Don't you see, it's the only logical explanation for what happened? Out of the all the people at the banquet, all consuming the same greasy food, Vaughn and I were the only two affected. And if that isn't enough," she continued, "if you do your homework, you'll discover our symptoms were a textbook case of poison victims."

"Why are you telling me this? You should be talking to Sheriff Wiggins, not me."

She snorted, a very unladylike sound, not at all like one belonging to Greta Garbo or Bette Davis. "You think he'd believe me? He'd think I was crazy, delusional, paranoid. Once toxicology reports come back from the lab, it'll be another matter, but for the time being ..."

Part of me wanted to object. Insist the sheriff would

easily be convinced. But that part of me shut up, re-membering I'd already gone that route. Sheriff Wiggins had all but laughed me out of his office. No, the man wasn't about to buy into the poisoning theory without something substantial to back it up. Substantial being lab reports bearing words such as arsenic or cyanide.

"What do you want *me* to do?"

"Keep your eyes and ears open. Let me know if you observe anything suspicious. Do what you do best, Kate. You're a puzzle solver. If my suspicions are correct, who-ever it was will make another attempt. Next time I might not be as lucky."

"But . . ."

She darted a glance toward the open French doors leading onto the foyer. "Please, Kate. I need a friend, a real friend, someone I can trust. I don't have many women friends. I don't know why," she said, shaking her head sadly, "but I've never been good at developing re-lationships with other women."

What to do, what to do? Outwardly Sheila Rappa-port had it all—beauty, brains, and success. But no women friends? No one to laugh or cry with, no one to com-plain or whine with? How lonely. How utterly tragic. A wave of sympathy threatened to swamp me. Reaching over, I gently squeezed her hand. "No promises, but I'll do what I can."

Her eyes looked moist as she squeezed back. "Thanks, Kate. I can't tell you how much this means to me."

At the click of high heels on tile, Sheila held a finger to her lips and shot me a warning glance. "Not a word of this to Betsy," she whispered.

*Umm,* I thought. *The plot thickens.*

Oblivious of the tension in the room, Betsy entered the library and, using the ottoman as a coffee table, set down the tray she carried holding a teapot along with cups and saucers. "I assume Sheila mentioned Vaughn's memorial service is planned for Friday?"

"N-no." The question caught me off guard.

Betsy nodded briskly. "I tried to convince her there's no need to rush, but Sheila insisted."

"I didn't see any reason to delay." Sheila accepted the teacup Betsy offered. "Vaughn's body's already been cremated."

It wasn't until after returning home that it dawned on me that I hadn't asked Sheila who would want both her and Vaughn dead. I also realized belatedly that Sheila hadn't volunteered the information. A fine detective I was . . . not.

# Chapter 10

I hummed to myself as I readied the house for bunco. After popping the blue cheese and bacon appetizer I intended to serve into the oven, I did a final inventory. Score cards: check. Pencils: check. Three dice on each table: check. Peanut M&Ms: check. I was good to go.

Tonight, we were one player short what with Tara flying off to California. As luck would have it, dear, sweet Megan volunteered to bring a friend to fill in. I'd failed to ask the friend's name, but I'm not going to quibble. A warm body is a warm body. All that was required was some wrist action. Shake, rattle, and roll them bones. Bunco couldn't be simpler.

I peeked at the appetizer. It was starting to bubble and smelled heavenly. No sooner had I taken it out of the oven and set it on a trivet than my guests began to arrive. Between all the chatter and hugs, one would think we hadn't seen one another in ages.

"Hmm, honey lamb." Connie Sue sniffed the air appreciatively. "Somethin' smells good."

Monica sniffed, too. "Bacon, do I smell bacon?"

I raised my hand to forestall a lecture on fat grams. "Yes, it's bacon, and I don't want to hear another word. It's a recipe from *Southern Living*."

"How was your cruise, Janine?" Pam tactfully changed the subject.

I could have hugged her for running interference. I was not in a mood to listen to monounsaturated fat versus polyunsaturated. I'd heard it all before.

"Wonderful!" Janine Russell, the Babes' very own Jamie Lee Curtis look-alike, enthused. She and her husband had just returned from a Caribbean cruise to celebrate their fortieth anniversary. "We've already booked another one for next year."

"Did you go to one of them nude beaches?" Polly asked. Tonight she wore a black T-shirt with BUNCO DIVA spelled out in rhinestones. "I heard that's where you can see all the hot dudes. You know, the ones with six-packs."

Gloria, Polly's long-suffering daughter, helped herself to crackers and spread and pretended not to hear.

"Where's Claudia?" Diane Delvecchia asked. Diane, a striking brunette in her midforties, is a librarian in nearby Brookdale and the computer guru of our group.

Right on cue, Claudia Connors burst into the room. "Yoo-hoo, everyone. I'm baaack."

Claudia was back, all right. Claudia's the Babes' answer to Auntie Mame—bold, brassy, and with a heart of gold. Thanks to a no-good scumbag, her life had recently taken a downward spiral, but that was all in the past. Claudia had learned the hard way that what happens in Vegas should stay in Vegas.

"Hey, Claudia," I said. I gave her a big hug, then stood back to admire her new sassy strawberry-blond do. "You look like a new woman after a week at the spa."

"It was fantastic!" she gushed. "I'm telling you, Kate, we need to go there as a group sometime. We'd have a blast. It would be such fun! After a hectic day of facials, massages, and aromatherapy, we could sit around the fireplace every night and play bunco. And the food"— she rolled her eyes—"to die for. I gained three pounds."

"Gained?" Connie Sue repeated, appalled. "I thought the object was to lose weight, not gain it."

"Sign me up," Polly said. "Do they have good-looking dudes to give massages?"

Claudia laughed, but shook her head. "Polly, you're asking the wrong person. I've sworn off men—for life."

Rita looked pointedly at her watch. "All right, ladies, we can chitchat while we play. Who are we missing?"

I selected a foil-wrapped piece of chocolate from a candy dish—dark chocolate, of course, the kind loaded with antioxidants. I subscribe to the three squares a day rule of thumb when it comes to chocolate—dark chocolate, that is. "Megan offered to bring a friend to sub in Tara's place."

No sooner were the words out of my mouth than in walked blond, perky Megan Warner, Pam's twenty-year-old daughter and the apple of her eye. "Hey, everyone, sorry we're late."

My jaw dropped at the sight of Megan followed by none other than Tammy Lynn Snow. I don't think I'd ever seen the girl outside the sheriff's office. But outside or inside, Tammy Lynn was the same beige Tammy Lynn. Her face was makeup free, her dishwater-colored hair pulled back and fastened with a scrunchie.

"I didn't realize you two girls knew each other."

"Hey, Miz McCall." Tammy Lynn ducked her head. "Nice place you have."

Megan gave me a friendly hug and waved at her mother. "Tammy Lynn and I got to be friends after Eric broke his leg," she said, referring to the handsome, young Brookdale police officer who had suffered a nasty fall.

"We're happy to have you, Tammy Lynn," I said, in an effort to make the girl feel welcome. "There are snacks on the island in the kitchen. Help yourself to wine or soda, and we'll get started."

"I don't drink spirits, ma'am, and I'm more nervous than hungry." She cast a worried glance at a table with its dice and scorecards. "I've never played bunco before. Megan said there was nothin' to it. That anyone with half a brain could play."

"Well, dear, half-brained describes our group pretty well."

Tammy Lynn flushed to the roots of her hair. "I—I didn't mean . . ."

"No offense taken, dear. Half a brain is better than no brain," I said with a laugh, then clapped my hands to get the Babes' attention. "All right, everyone, find a table and let's get started."

"Wait up, y'all." Connie Sue sprinted for her handbag, which she'd left in the great room. She returned with a glittery rhinestone tiara, which she proudly donned. "Now we're ready."

The tiara had been Connie Sue's idea, a holdover from her reign as Miss Peach Princess. The night's winner at bunco takes home the tiara. It's a silly ritual, I admit, some might even call it juvenile. But who decreed women had to act like grown-ups when it's more fun to be a kid again?

I tucked my arm through Tammy Lynn's. "Why don't you and Megan be partners for the first round? That way she can show you the ropes. And don't worry about keeping score. Tonight let your partners do it since you're new to the game."

Everyone managed to find a place and settle in. I'd set up a card table in the great room. The kitchen and dining room tables were also pressed into service. Three tables in all with four players each. I ended up at the head table, which happened to be the one in the kitchen, along with Megan, Tammy Lynn, and Connie Sue. I picked up the bell Pam had once paid twenty-five cents for at a garage sale and let it clang. "Ladies, let the game begin."

"What are we supposed to do now?" Tammy Lynn whispered anxiously.

"Just watch and learn, sugar." Connie Sue scooped up the dice, rattled them good, and let them fly. Magically a one appeared.

"There are six rounds in each set of bunco," I explained as Connie Sue continued to rack up points. "In each round, the player tries to roll the same target number as the set. The player scores one point for each target point. The round ends when partners at the head table—which controls play—accumulate a total of twenty-one points."

"Then is the game over?"

Megan giggled. "That means we're just getting warmed up. We roll ones in the first round," she explained, continuing the tutorial, "twos in the next, threes in the third, and so on and so forth."

"We usually play six sets, or games, before totalin' our scores. Winner takes home the tiara," Connie Sue was quick to add.

Uncertain, Tammy Lynn looked at each of us in turn. "You mean that's all there is?"

"That's it, sugar." Connie Sue grinned. "A game can't get any simpler, but that's why we like it. Bunco's strictly social. We'd hate to have thinkin' interferin' with our talkin.'"

"Or our drinking," Polly called from the great room.

When her turn came around again, Tammy Lynn cupped the dice, gave them a shake, and let them fly. Three ones appeared as if by magic.

"Bunco!" Megan hollered as she reached for the bell.

"What?" Tammy Lynn stared at her perplexed.

I took pity on the girl. Maybe bunco was a trifle more complicated than we had led her to believe. "Sorry, Tammy Lynn, I forgot to mention that three of the target number equals twenty-one points—a bunco."

As the Babes got up from their tables and started to circulate, I gave her a reassuring pat on the shoulder.

"Since you and Megan are the winners, stay where you are but switch partners. The losers, in this case Connie Sue and myself, go to table three. The winners from table three move up to table two."

"And the winners from table two advance to table one," Megan said, shifting seats.

Tammy Lynn rolled her eyes. "This game is downright confusin'."

"Sugar," Connie Sue drawled, "switchin' tables is often the hardest part of playin' bunco—especially if the hostess is servin' booze."

"Y'all are never gonna ask me to play again," Tammy Lynn moaned.

Megan's lips twitched in amusement. "None of us can keep it straight, Tammy Lynn. That's why directions are printed across the bottom of the score sheet. We call it our 'cheat sheet.'"

On my way to lowly table three, I paused to top off my wine and grab a handful of M&M's. They might not be loaded with antioxidants, but as far as I was concerned, they were comfort food. Fortified, I slid into the seat across from Monica.

The instant the bell sounded, Monica snatched the dice and threw them. When they failed to produce a two, she glared at them as though she'd like to pulverize them. "Don't know why I bother with this stupid game," she grumbled.

Who was she kidding? All of us Babes knew Monica was a fierce competitor—even in a nonsensical dice game. We also knew Monica coveted the sparkly band of rhinestones. Once I had stopped by to return a book she had loaned me and caught her wearing the tiara while mopping the floor.

"Are you going to Vaughn Bascomb's memorial service tomorrow?" Gloria asked, passing the dice.

I nodded. "I feel sorry for Sheila. She doesn't know many people here, but she's trying hard to do the right

thing for Vaughn. The man deserves a proper send-off."
My brief run of luck over, I shoved the dice toward
Connie Sue.

"I wonder why the rush," Gloria mused. "Surely his
memorial service could wait until she's fully recovered
from the ordeal. After all, she nearly died herself."

"No reason to put it off, I guess. The body's already
been cremated."

Connie Sue nodded sagely. "Sheila probably needs
closure."

"Closure" seemed to be the catchphrase these days
for "an end to." At least it is on *Dr. Phil*.

Monica absently tucked a dark brown strand of hair
behind one ear. "Why is Sheila responsible for funeral
arrangements? Doesn't Dr. Bascomb have family?"

"According to Rita, he has a sister in California, but
they've been estranged for years. Apparently he left a
will stating he wanted to be cremated, and his ashes
scattered in a botanical garden."

"Pay attention, Kate," Monica scolded. "You just rolled
a baby bunco."

"Well, how about that?" I murmured. I stared at a
trio of fours in mild surprise. Baby buncos, in case I forgot to mention, occur when a player rolls three of any
number other than the target number and count for a
whopping five points.

"Bunco!" Tammy Lynn's voice sang out from the
head table. The girl was certainly catching on fast.

In spite of my baby bunco, Monica and I lost out to
Connie Sue and Gloria by one measly point. I ignored
Monica's scowl and scooted to an adjacent chair relieved
someone else would be her partner this round. Rita
and Megan joined us at what I deemed the losers' table.

Play resumed, and Rita picked up the dice. "So, Kate,"
she began, simultaneously talking and tossing. I envy
folks who can multitask. I used to be able to multitask
myself, but seem to have lost the knack somewhere

between Social Security and Medicare. "The garden club is planning to visit a nursery in Georgia next week. Guests and prospective members are invited. You interested?"

I narrowed my eyes to study her more closely. I wondered how many glasses of wine she'd consumed, but she appeared stone sober. Rita, better than anyone, knew my God-given knack for killing all things living and green. I was growing weary of being the target of her thinly disguised condescension—spelled p-i-t-y. "Surely you're not serious?"

"Are you looking for anything particular on your trip?" Monica asked as the dice made the rounds. "We had a tree removed recently. I'm thinking oleander might work to fill in the spot."

"Oleander?" Megan wrinkled her nose. "Isn't that poisonous?"

"Yes, it is, but that's probably why deer leave it alone."

*Poison?* My ears perked up.

Monica, the expert on everything, gave Megan a smug smile. "Honey, half the plants in your mother's yard are poisonous. That includes not only oleander, but Carolina jessamine and even her pretty pink hydrangea."

Hmm. My interest was definitely humming. It all but sang a rendition of the hallelujah chorus. Poison. Plants. Botany. Gardening. Was there a correlation? Or did the words merely belong to categories on *Jeopardy!*?

I feigned a casualness I didn't feel. "You know what, Rita? Not only will I go to the nursery with you, but I've been meaning to join the garden club. It's high time I learn a thing or two about plants and flowers."

# Chapter 11

The clasp on my favorite bracelet was getting harder and harder to fasten. Who designs these things anyway? These darn clasps were intended for those with twenty-twenty vision. What about the millions of people who wear trifocals? Maybe it was time the AARP stepped in, took a stand.

Just when I almost—and I repeat, almost—had the clasp conquered, the phone rang. One small distraction and—bingo!—once again I failed to connect the two ends. Tossing the bracelet aside in frustration, I rushed to answer the blasted telephone. Was I in a tizzy or what?

"Hello," I barked.

"Kate?"

"Bill . . ." My irritability melted like a Popsicle at a Fourth of July picnic.

"Is this a bad time?"

It was never a bad time for Bill Lewis, my honey of a handyman, to call. But I'd never tell him that. Bill, you see, tends to be a bit on the shy side, and I don't want to scare him. Bill is Serenity Cove's version of Tim "The Tool Man" Taylor of TV fame as played by comedian Tim Allen—minus the numerous trips to the emergency room. Bill not only owns every tool stocked at Lowe's, but knows how to use them. Ever since he showed up on my doorstep to replace a faulty ceiling fan, he'd become my personal blue-eyed devil in sawdust-covered jeans.

"Sorry, if I snapped at you," I apologized. A glance at the kitchen clock told me I still had a half hour before Vaughn's memorial service was scheduled to begin.

"I've done some rough calculations on those bookshelves you want me to build. I'm thinking it might be a good idea if we drove down to Augusta together to look at materials. You might change your mind about wanting cherry once you see the price."

I'd had my heart set on cherry bookshelves ever since seeing the library in Sheila's rental, but being on a fixed income, one has to be practical. "Well, I suppose that makes sense," I acquiesced.

Bill cleared his throat. "Are you busy this afternoon?"

"I'd love to, Bill, but Vaughn Bascomb's memorial service is at two o'clock. Can we make it another day?"

"I wasn't sure you'd be attending the service, since you didn't really know the man."

"Granted, we met only the one time, but he seemed quite charming. Besides," I continued, "I feel sorry for the guy. His only sister refuses to come, says she can't afford to take time off from her job. Since Rita's an old friend of Sheila's, the Babes and I have decided on a show of support."

Actually, I had an ulterior motive for wanting to attend the service. I was worried, however, that if I told Bill my plan, he'd try to change my mind. Some things are better kept to oneself.

"Tomorrow's Saturday," he said. "Maybe after checking out a lumberyard or two, we could take in a matinee? I'll let you pick the movie. I don't mind if it's one of those girlie ones you seem to like. Now that I'm getting used to them, they're not half-bad."

Bill was my kind of guy, all right. He refused to let a

chick flick threaten his masculinity. "Throw in some buttered popcorn, and you've got yourself a deal."

"And, Kate, after the movie I thought we could grab a bite to eat at Bubba's Buffet Barn? I know how much you love their fried shrimp."

Dinner *and* a movie? This sounded like a bona fide date. I wanted to quote the line from *Jerry Maguire*, "You had me at hello," but didn't. Once again I didn't want to frighten the guy.

"Sounds great, Bill. See you tomorrow."

After agreeing on a time, we disconnected. Another glance at the clock told me I'd better get a move on if I wanted to make it to the chapel on time. I wanted to do a little victory shimmy, but it would have to wait.

In spite of my good intentions, I was the last of the Babes to arrive at the memorial service. Except for Tara in California and Megan and Diane, who had to work, we were out in force. Nine out of twelve ain't bad, considering Vaughn was a virtual stranger.

Sheila had secured the use of a small, private chapel at the mortuary/crematorium where she'd had Vaughn's body sent. Sunlight streamed through a stained-glass window, spreading a kaleidoscope of color over a pedestal supporting an ornate urn that I assumed contained Vaughn's remains. A simple lectern stood off to one side. Oak pews could accommodate several dozen mourners, but other than the Babes, only a handful of people were present.

I squeezed into a pew near the rear next to Monica, Pam, and Connie Sue. Polly and Gloria occupied the row in front of us. To my left, I spotted Claudia and Janine. Sheila occupied the front pew. She was flanked by Betsy on one side, Rita on the other. Considering their disdain for Vaughn Bascomb, I was surprised to find Todd Timmons and Roger McFarland also in attendance. Had they undergone a change of heart? Could I have underestimated them? Nah . . .

"You're late," Monica scolded.

"Sorry," I said, keeping my voice low.

Polly turned in her seat and gave me a conspiratorial wink. "Don't mind her. You haven't missed the good part."

*The good part?* What in the world did Polly consider the "good" part of a memorial service? Before I could come up with a plausible explanation, canned organ music blared through a speaker set high on the wall, playing a hymn I didn't recognize.

Time to put my plan into action.

Now, it's a well-known fact amongst investigative aficionados such as myself that killers always return to the scene of the crime. It's equally well known that murderers often attend the funeral—or in this case, a memorial service—of their victims. I'd watched enough crime and punishment shows throughout the years to know this to be SOP—standard operating procedure. Sumter Wiggins, in his capacity as sheriff of Brookdale County, should be on the scene scoping out the situation. But in his absence, I'd step up to the plate.

I discreetly slid my cell phone from my purse. Flipping it open, I made a production out of checking for messages while unobtrusively pressing the camera icon. Instantly the back of Gloria's head popped into the viewfinder.

Satisfied I had command of the situation, I leaned forward to compliment Polly on her subdued ensemble. "Nice threads," I said.

*Click!* Just like that, I'd captured Todd Timmons's profile for posterity. If I had to say so myself, it'd make a great mug shot. Now all I needed to complete my photo array of Mr. Timmons was a frontal shot.

With cell phone clutched tightly in my hot little hand and intent on my subject, I angled my body and leaned

as far to the right as gravity would allow. Just as my thumb
hovered above the TAKE button, I lost my balance. Fortunately, Monica grabbed on to my suit jacket and saved
me an embarrassing tumble into the center aisle. Unfortunately, however, my cell phone clattered to the floor.
The back flew off, landing two feet away. Not even the
canned organ music could drown out the noise. Heads
swiveled in my direction.

Heat crept up my neck. I felt a bead of perspiration
trickle down my spine. *This wasn't good*, said a small
voice in the back of my brain. I haven't had a hot flash—
commonly referred to as a power surge—in years, but
this flush was a vivid reminder. Cheeks burning, I crept
out of the pew and retrieved my phone and its back.
"Sorry, sorry," I said, unable to suppress a nervous giggle, which earned me an angry glare from Monica.

Seated again, I fumbled, trying to reassemble the con-
founded bit of electronic wizardry.

Before I could master the technique, Monica snatched
it from my hands and united Part A with Part B. "Kate,
for pity's sake, sit still!" she hissed under her breath.
"You're going to give me a migraine with all that bounc-
ing around."

"Sorry," I murmured again. Chastened, I sat quietly. I
decided to wait until later to take the rest of my snap-
shots.

A slender man with a narrow face and slicked-back
hair entered the chapel through a side door. Judging
from his solemn demeanor and dark suit, I guessed him
to be the mortician, John Dobbs.

"Dear friends and loved ones of the deceased, we
are gathered here this afternoon not to mourn the life
of Vaughn Bascomb, but to celebrate it. Though I never
had the privilege of meeting Dr. Bascomb . . ."

*Friends, Romans, and countrymen . . . Blah, blah, blah.*
I tuned out the eulogy.

My mind wandered; my eyes roamed. I hoped both

body parts would someday be reunited. At present, however, I was more interested in pinpointing a possible murder suspect. Once toxicology reports came back from wherever—probably Columbia—with proof Sheila and Vaughn had indeed been poisoned, Sheriff Wiggins would applaud my efforts. Concerned citizens such as myself made his job much easier.

I zeroed in on the back of Roger McFarland's freckled neck. That night in the emergency room had been a revealing one. Roger'd made no secret of his dislike for Vaughn. According to him, Vaughn was interfering with his creative vision for a coffee table masterpiece. Timmons, too, had verbalized hostility, blaming Vaughn for a drop in ratings of *How Does Your Garden Grow?* My gaze shifted to Betsy Dalton. She hadn't seemed overly fond of Vaughn either, though I didn't have a clue why. Perhaps Todd wasn't the only one upset over plummeting ratings. After all, as VP of Belle Beaute, the show's sponsor, Betsy had a vested interest in the show's success. Had dislike crossed the barrier into hatred for Todd, Rog, or Bets?

The mortician droned on, perhaps in the vain hope a camera crew would arrive to videotape his eulogy for a segment of *How Does Your Garden Grow*? I couldn't help but notice Betsy's fixed stare at the urn holding the ashes. She wore a peculiar expression on her doll-like countenance. I tried, but failed, to pin a name on it. Careful to make certain Monica's attention was elsewhere, I eased open my cell phone and snapped her photo before slipping the phone into a jacket pocket.

"Would anyone here care to share a few memories of the deceased?" John Dobbs asked, his stock of platitudes apparently depleted. His request met with an awkward silence. The mortician stared hopefully at Roger and Todd. "Gentlemen? I understand you were acquainted with the deceased. Would either of you care to speak?"

With vigorous shakes of their heads, they made known their wishes to the contrary.

"Well, then," Dobbs said with an unctuous smile, "I'll ask his dear friend and colleague, Dr. Sheila Rappaport, to do a reading from the Bible."

Sheila, looking as delicate as a Dresden figurine, stepped to the podium and began to read the twenty-third Psalm, "The Lord is my Shepherd . . ."

I bowed my head, my thoughts going back to Jim's funeral. Jim had had lots of loved ones. The church had overflowed with friends, relatives, and well-wishers. Some of his former coworkers had made the long trip South and graciously shared remembrances of Jim's career first as a salesman then as a district manager. Others offered amusing anecdotes, many dealing with his love for sports, especially golf. So different from this service, bereft of both family and friends.

"He leadeth me beside the still . . ."

*Still . . . ?* Not anymore. My cell phone picked that precise moment to start blasting the "Battle Hymn of the Republic." Sheila stopped midway through her recitation of the twenty-third Psalm. Once again, heads turned in my direction. And once again I felt the hot surge of embarrassment. I pawed through my purse, then remembered I'd slipped my phone into the pocket of my suit. I prayed I'd find it before the rousing chorus of "glory, glory hallelujah." I'd meant to set the phone on vibrate, but all the picture taking had distracted me.

His "truth was marching on" before I finally regained the upper hand. Flustered at being the center of attention, I squeezed the darn thing to within an inch of its life to smother the microphone. I relaxed marginally when I heard a *beep* signaling the call had gone to voice mail and made a mental note to change the ringtone.

I mustered a feeble smile for the unsmiling faces who'd turned to stare at me. "Sorry," I mouthed.

"Really, Kate," Monica growled, "sometimes you're worse than a two-year old."

Polly, on the other hand, seemed to harbor a fondness for toddlers. In the row ahead of me, she half-turned and gave me a thumbs-up.

Sheila completed her reading without further ado and returned to her seat. John Dobbs took her place at the podium. "Ladies and gentlemen, Dr. Rappaport has requested that you join her at a reception in Dr. Bascomb's honor at the Cove Café immediately following the service. Now, if you'll rise and join me in 'Amazing Grace.'"

Connie Sue's alto, strong and true, melded with Polly's quavery soprano. The rest of the Babes joined in, doing justice to the much-loved hymn. Then, the brief service over, the mourners—and pseudo-mourners—began to file out.

I wasn't sure I'd get another opportunity. Roger McFarland's mug was still on my Most Wanted list of suspects. I decided to rectify the oversight when he paused to exchange a few words with Sheila. Digging into my pocket, I hauled out the troublesome cell phone.

Connie Sue leaned across Monica and nudged me gently. "Really, sugar, don't you think you should give that thing a rest? A memorial service is no place to conduct a conversation."

She was right, of course, but I needed one more photo to complete the lineup of possible poisoners. Any second now Roger would turn in my direction. This was my big chance. "I'm just checking voice mail," I muttered.

My daughter Jennifer's name lit up on the screen. Jen lives in California—Brentwood to be precise—with my two granddaughters and her husband and former nerd, Jason Jarrod. Jason happens to be a lawyer to the stars, famous for drafting clauses the Terminator can't terminate. But instead of listening to my daughter's message like I pretended, I aimed the phone toward Roger, who had started down the aisle, and pressed TAKE.

*Perfect!* I thought, snapping the phone shut. A portrait photographer couldn't have done a better job. "It was Jen," I explained for Connie Sue's benefit as we drifted toward the exit. "I'll call her later."

# Chapter 12

Cell phones are marvelous inventions—that is until they're accidently dismembered during a memorial service. Even so, mine had held up admirably under the assault. Vaughn's memorial service marked the first time I'd ever used the camera function and—not to brag—I did so without reading the inch-thick manual. I could hardly wait to flaunt my ingenuity under the nose of the smug Sheriff Wiggins. But I'd bide my time. I'd wait until he was scratching his head, befuddled, when the toxicology report read: Cause of death—poison. Then I'd whip out my photos of possible suspects.

"Nice service, wasn't it?" remarked Pam. We found ourselves side by side as we headed toward the parking lot.

I crooked my arm through hers. "Yes," I agreed, "I might add it was also quite satisfactory."

"Are you going to the reception at the Cove?"

"I wouldn't miss it for the world." I caught Pam eyeing me strangely. "What I meant to say," I quickly amended, "is that I wouldn't miss this opportunity to support Sheila during her time of need."

Pam seemed placated by my concern for a woman I'd just recently met. I could hardly confess I was planning to use the reception to glean information to support Sheila's murder by poison theory. My friends, even Pam, my BFF, were beginning to think I had gone over to the dark side when it came to crime solving. Sheesh! I couldn't imagine why they'd leap to that conclusion. Blame it on coincidence that I happened to be instrumental in solving not one, but two recent murders here in Serenity Cove. Could my friends be a tiny bit jealous of my newfound talent?

Pam glanced at her watch. "I'm afraid I won't be able to join you. Megan's car is in the shop, and I promised to pick her up after work."

"I'll call tomorrow to let you know what type of wood I picked out for the bookshelves Bill is going to build."

Pam gave me a cheeky grin. "You can skip the wood and go straight for the good part."

The good part? That was the second time I heard that phrase used in one afternoon. "If by that sly remark, girlfriend, you're referring to my friendship with Bill, they're all good parts."

Pam's grin widened. "Things starting to get serious between you and the tool man?"

How do I answer that . . . ? Bill was cute as can be with his Paul Newman blues and a full head of silver-gray hair. Now, some men look great in a tux; Bill, on the other hand, looks awesome in a tool belt. Trust me, ladies. But were we getting serious? Bill, for all his wonderful attributes, had a bashful streak a mile wide. He was sweet as can be, but not the type to rush into things—especially things of the "serious" variety.

"For goodness' sakes, Pam, don't read too much into it. We're just going to a lumber yard in Augusta, then afterward take in a matinee and . . ." I caught myself, but it was too late. I'd already said too much. One didn't have to be an astrophysicist to know my friendship/relationship with Bill was the subject of much interest among the Babes. I'd like to preserve a small modicum of privacy where that was concerned.

"And . . . ?" Pam prompted.

I should've known Pam wouldn't let me off the hook so easily. I drew in a deep breath and let it out. "And afterward, we'll stop for a bite to eat at Bubba's Buffet Barn before heading back."

"Sounds suspiciously like a date, if you want my opinion."

"Wipe that smirk off your face, girlfriend," I said as I climbed into my Buick and waved good-bye.

By the time I arrived at the parking lot that serves both the pro shop and Cove Café, I discovered it filled by golfers enjoying a round in the balmy spring temperatures. Spring is my all-time favorite season here in South Carolina. Every other day, the highways and byways explode with a fresh display of color. One day sunny yellow Carolina jessamine twine and twist through branches. Soon after, bright purple-pink blooms of the redbud burst open, followed by dainty white dogwood. The grand finale comes when rounding a bend in a country road and encountering purple wisteria literally dripping from a stand of lofty loblolly pines. The sight simply steals my breath away. Gardens and yards also put on a show. There are the Lady Banks roses. And the azaleas . . . The mounds of vibrant pink azaleas are something to behold, but I digress.

My patience in finding a parking space was rewarded when I saw a golfer load his clubs into an SUV. I waited for him to pull out and swung into the spot he'd vacated. I hesitated at the entrance of the café to get the lay of the land. Normally the café is deserted at this hour, but apparently Sheila had arranged for a private party. Vera McGillicuddy and Mary, the waitress who usually works the dinner shift, circulated among guests, taking drink orders. A buffet table with chafing dishes had been set up along the far wall.

Off to my right, Sheila presented a striking figure in a trim black suit and wide-brimmed hat. Her flawless complexion retained that Greta Garbo–like ethereal beauty I envied. Did she come by this ethereal quality naturally? Or was her sponsor, Belle Beaute, responsible? On my next trip to Dillard's or Macy's, I intended to take some of their products out for a test-drive. Maybe that would crank up Bill's "serious" meter.

I fell into the queue, waiting to give Sheila condolences. I watched Claudia give Sheila an exuberant embrace, which she returned with reserve. "So sorry for your loss," I heard Claudia say before moving off.

Gloria echoed Claudia's sentiment but wisely omitted the hug. Next Janine stepped forward and offered her hand. "Dr. Bascomb's death must have come as a dreadful blow. If there's any way I can be of help, please don't hesitate to ask."

Leave it to Janine to always hit just the right note — something heartfelt and comforting. Unlike Janine, I tended to be more a blurter than a diplomat. Now it was my turn to console the grieving significant other. I really wanted to say, "Sorry someone poisoned you and Vaughn—and he died."

As I moved closer, Sheila tipped her head, and our eyes met in a moment of silent communication. "I'm sorry for your loss," I said. Even to my own ears the words sounded trite and clichéd.

She smiled wanly and took my hand. "Let's talk soon over lunch, shall we?"

Before I could open my mouth to reply, Betsy approached holding a glass. "Sheila, dear, you must be exhausted. I brought you some ginger ale."

I extricated my hand from Sheila's. There would be time later to speak with her when Betsy no longer guarded her like a mother bear with a cub. Summarily dismissed, I wandered off in the direction of the Babes who gathered nearby.

"Sorry. I can't stay," I heard Janine say. "Ray and I are attending a simulcast in Augusta tonight."

Polly gave her a quizzical look. "You've been holding out on us, Janine. Never would've taken you for a boxing fan."

"I'm not." Janine laughed. "There's a benefit being held for the new children's oncology wing. The hospital auxiliary is sponsoring a simulcast of the opera *Carmen*, direct from the New York Met."

"Opera?" Polly sniffed. "No offense, Janine, but those dudes at the auxiliary are making a big mistake. There's nothing like an old-fashioned boxing match to rake in the bucks."

Gloria shook her head, sending her hoop earrings swaying. "I swear, Mother, I don't know how you arrive at these conclusions."

"Dated a boxing promoter when I was younger. Told me all about these things. Really, Gloria," Polly said and this time she was the one who shook her head, "parents don't tell their children everything. They like to have some secrets."

"Just as I'm certain children don't tell their parents everything," Rita, the ever-sensible, pointed out. "There are some exploits best kept secret."

"Amen," Connie Sue added fervently.

"Can I get y'all something to drink?" Vera asked as she approached our little group, order pad in hand. "Maybe a nice glass of wine?"

If you don't count Monica, who is a teetotaler—except in times of stress during which she drinks bourbon, straight up—the vote on wine split fifty-fifty between red and white. While Vera went off to fetch our pinot grigios and merlots, Janine glanced at her wristwatch. "Sorry, but I've got to run. Ray and I have reservations for an early dinner at our favorite seafood restaurant."

I had a sneaky suspicion that the favorite seafood

haunt she referred to wasn't Bubba's Buffet Barn with
its hand-breaded fried shrimp. But to each his own.
Glancing around, I noted the reception in Vaughn's
honor had attracted more attendees than his memorial
service.

As if reading my mind, Rita nodded toward the half-
dozen women who had just entered the café. "I see the
board of Flowers and Bowers finally arrived."

"Why weren't they at the service?" Monica asked, her
voice sharp.

Rita hitched the strap of her purse higher on her
shoulder. "I spoke with some of the gals earlier. They
claimed they didn't feel comfortable partaking in a memorial service for a man they didn't know."

"But they feel comfortable enough to partake of the
free drinks and munchies," Claudia observed dryly.

Rita shrugged off the criticism. "I'm just grateful for
the Babes' support this afternoon. I'm sure it meant a
lot to Sheila to have you all there. It would have been
personally embarrassing to have an empty chapel."

Vera returned with diet soda for Monica and wine
for rest of us, then headed toward the Flowers and Bowers crowd. Drinks in hand, we resumed our conversation. Conversation is one of the things the Babes do
best. It's right up there with rolling dice.

"When I kick the bucket, I want a royal send-off,"
Polly stated matter-of-factly.

"Mother!" Gloria gasped. "I wish you wouldn't talk
like that. You know it upsets me."

"We all gotta go sometime, dearie. No one lives forever." Nonplussed, Polly sipped her wine. "None of that
depressing black for me. I want to be surrounded with
lots of cheerful colors. And music. Lots of music. Maybe
one of those funerals like they have in New Orleans. I
saw a movie once where this guy died, and they had a
parade down the middle of Bourbon Street. Had a band

and everything. People were singing, dancing, and having a gay old time. I think I'd like something like that."

I tried not to smile. I could just picture the Babes all decked out in their Sunday finery boogying down Oleander Avenue. That ought to make front-page news in the *Serenity Sentinel*. Unless, of course, Polly's funeral got upstaged by a hole-in-one or a thirty-pound bass.

Glancing about, I couldn't help notice that we weren't a very congenial crowd. Those present formed three distinct cliques. There was Sheila and her cronies, the inseparable trio of Todd, Rog, and Betsy. The garden club elite seemed to prefer their own company to ours. That left the Babes. Rita, a member of both groups, huddled with ours.

My wandering attention landed on the buffet table. "I'm hungry. Anyone care to sample the hors d'oeuvres?"

"Kate!" Monica's eyes widened in alarm. "Surely you're not going near *that* food?"

"Why not?" I asked. "I skipped lunch. Besides, if I eat here, it'll save me having to make dinner."

"But is it *safe*?"

The question hung in the air like yellow pine pollen on a windless day.

Connie Sue shifted her weight from one shiny high heel to the other. "Maybe Monica's right, sugar. It doesn't hurt to be careful."

"Surely you don't think we're in danger of contracting food poisoning?" I asked. Another triumph of my mind-reading skills.

"One can't be too sure," Claudia cautioned.

I couldn't believe my ears. I looked to Rita for support, but she avoided eye contact.

Gloria fiddled with the flotilla of gold chains around her neck.

Monica folded her arms across her chest, her expression mulish. "I don't know about the rest of you, but until we know for sure why Vaughn died, I'm avoiding anything not prepared by my own two hands."

"For crying out loud, Monica"—Rita huffed out a breath—"I'm tired of all this talk about poisoning—food poisoning and otherwise. Kate and I both heard the doctor say it was Vaughn's heart. Can't we just let it rest with that?"

Connie Sue looked doubtful. "If I'm going to splurge on calories, it'll be another glass of wine. A girl's gotta watch her figure, you know."

"Suit yourselves." I felt their disapproval and concern as I walked away.

"Wait up, Kate," Polly called after me. "I'm not one to pass up a nice spread."

It was, as Polly called it, a "nice spread." Trays were mounded with an assortment of finger foods that included egg rolls, chicken wings, and shrimp rangoons. But the buffet table looked virtually untouched. Was everyone watching their figures? Or had paranoia stolen the "serenity" from Serenity Cove? Whatever the case, I took a plate and dug in.

Alongside me, Polly helped herself to the shrimp rangoons. "Umm, yum," she said, sighing with pleasure. "I can never get enough of these shrimp things."

"Aren't you worried?"

"Nah. Like I told Gloria, no one lives forever."

I might've guessed Polly wouldn't let a little thing like food poisoning deter her from her favorite foods.

"You . . . !"

At Sheila's loud shriek, I almost dropped a chicken wing. Fortunately, I retrieved it in the nick of time. Curious, I turned toward the commotion and saw Kel Watson, the county extension agent, with Sheila. His rumpled demeanor seemed harmless and nonthreatening enough. But Sheila didn't look happy. This wasn't the first time her reaction at seeing him had been over the top. In the hospital, she had fainted at the mere sight of him in her room. My fledging detective antenna went *ping*! Something was up—but what?

"How dare you show your face?" Sheila demanded angrily.

A dull flush seeped across Kel's cheekbones. Embarrassment? Or guilt? "I just wanted to pay my respects. It was the least I could do."

"Well, you're not wanted here." Sheila's voice had taken on a strident tone. "Get out!"

"No need to get upset. I know you've been through a lot."

I had to give the man credit; he stood his ground. Almost of its own volition, my hand crept into my jacket pocket and withdrew my cell phone. "Time to check messages," I announced to no one in particular and punched the camera icon. In the blink of an eye, I'd captured Kel Watson's image for posterity. Ain't cell phones grand?

Without warning, Sheila tossed her drink in his face. "Out!" she shrieked.

The room went still. Everyone collectively held their breath waiting to see what would happen next. Instead of being angry, Kel kept his cool. Taking a handkerchief from his breast pocket, he wiped ginger ale from his face. "Sorry for your loss," he muttered, then turning, left the Cove Café.

"Now that's what I meant by the 'good part,'" Polly cackled.

Good part or bad part, I aimed to find out.

# Chapter 13

I waited until the following day to return my daughter Jennifer's call. If that makes me a bad mother, then so be it. Jen simply doesn't understand me. She thinks I should behave in an "elderly" manner. I tried "elderly" on for size once, and it didn't fit. Jen, bless her heart, heard the term "active retirement community" and assumed it would be a nice quiet place for her father and me in our ripe old age. Maybe she envisioned us in twin recliners, whiling away the hours tuned to the weather channel. I'd knit; her father would snore.

My daughter failed to note the adjective "active." Maybe "hyperactive" would more aptly describe life in Serenity Cove Estates. Most residents keep busy morning to night pursuing things they had never had time for in their nine-to-five lives. Sports such as tennis, golf, boating, and fishing keep our joints limber. Activities such as aerobics, both water and land, tai chi, yoga, line dancing, and Zumba, the latest fitness craze, are inked into our schedules. For those who enjoy games, mahjongg, sequence, bridge, hand and foot, euchre, and pinochle keep us mentally agile. Others find fulfillment in volunteer work in the schools, community, or church. All this busy leaves little time for cookie baking and rocking chairs. I've said it before, I'll say it again: Retirement isn't for sissies.

I felt a niggling of guilt as I punched in her number. I'd carefully taken the time difference between South Carolina and California into consideration, deliberately calling when I knew she'd be getting the girls off to various weekend activities. I'd also picked a time when I knew I couldn't talk long. Bill would be picking me up soon for our outing to Augusta. I refused to refer to our outing as a date for fear of jinxing our simple excursion to the big city. Bill tended to be skittish in the relationship department.

"Mother," Jen scolded upon hearing my voice. "Why did it take you so long to return my call? It might've been important."

"If it had been important, dear, you would have tried again to reach me." When had my daughter's voice taken on the same edge as Monica's? I wondered. "I was at a memorial service so your call went to voice mail. Besides, you know how slow I am at checking my voice mail."

"A memorial service . . . ? I suppose that's something you have to expect amongst all those elderly people."

I felt my blood pressure ratchet up several notches at hearing the hated E word. Drawing a calming breath, I called upon my inner chi—the internal energy—and started the conversation anew. "Actually, Dr. Bascomb wasn't a resident of Serenity Cove Estates, but merely a visitor when he passed." When had I started using "passed," the euphemism commonly heard in the South? Why couldn't I come right out and say he died, kicked the bucket, or vacated the planet? No, here it tended to sound more genteel. Something along the lines of "entered into eternal rest" or "departed this life."

"Dr. Vaughn Bascomb?"

Jen's question jerked me back to the present. "Yes. Have you heard of him?"

"Of course! I'm a fan of *How Does Your Garden*

*Grow?* Dr. Bascomb's a frequent guest on the show. I hadn't heard that he died—and in Tranquillity Cave of all places."

Up, up, and away on the blood pressure scale. "*Serenity Cove*, dear," I corrected. "I don't know why you have such a difficult time remembering the name of the place."

"Sorry. What happened to Dr. Bascomb?"

I peeked out the kitchen window, but no sign of Bill. "Rumor has it that it was food poisoning, but . . ."

"Food poisoning!" Jen's voice ping-ponged from cell tower to cell tower. "Mother, please, promise you'll be careful. All that fried food . . ."

"Folks are convinced it was the deviled eggs or the potato salad rather than the catfish or chicken," I said, cutting her off to forestall a diatribe on the evils of Southern cuisine. I swear the girl sounds more like Monica's flesh and blood than mine.

"I wish you'd put your house on the market and move to California. Your granddaughters would love to see more of you. That place where you live, *Serenity Cove*, isn't safe."

"It's perfectly safe," I said on a sigh. "The only other person to get sick was Dr. Rappaport, and she fully recovered."

"*You* know Dr. Rappaport? Isn't she awesome?" Jen gushed. "I've learned so much from her show. For instance, did you know English ivy . . ."

I stared out the window, half-listening to her ramble on about benzene and toluene fumes. My yard needed a makeover almost as badly as Tammy Lynn Snow. It could use a little pizzazz, some personality. It was . . . bland. Don't get me wrong, it was nice and neat with its holly bushes lined up like cadets on a parade ground along the front walk. The requisite azalea bushes planted next to the garage were almost ready to bloom, but my yard still needed something. Trouble is, I wasn't sure exactly what that something should be. More color? Greater variety? I'm glad I decided to take Rita up on her offer to tag along with Flowers and Bowers on their next excursion.

"Mother? Mother . . . ? Are you still there?"

"Yes, dear, I'm still here," I answered, glancing at the kitchen clock. Bill should be here any minute, and I wanted to check my makeup once more before our date that wasn't a date. "Jen dear, I'd love to talk longer, but Bill—"

*"Him? Again . . . ?"*

I mentally counted to ten. I really needed to count to a thousand, but I was short on time. Bill Lewis was a sore subject between my daughter and me. Jen was convinced he was out to usurp her father's place in my affections. She was also convinced he was about to usurp my pension and Social Security. In spite of my best efforts, nothing I said convinced her otherwise. "Bill has offered to build the bookshelves I've been wanting in the library. We're going to Augusta to order the lumber he'll need. He's a friend, Jen," I added, "and a very nice man."

"Fine," Jen said in the snippy tone she'd always used as a teenager. The one that made me grit my teeth—and was often punctuated by a slamming door.

Our conversation wound to a dissatisfactory conclusion. I promised myself I'd call soon and make amends.

Cherry, cherry, cherry.

We looked at oak; we examined maple; we studied pine, but in the end the final decision was easy. It all came down to cherry. After seeing the lovely library in Sheila's rental, nothing else compared. With visions of bookshelves dancing in my head, Bill and I took a little side trip through the garden center at Lowe's. Fueled by a desire to beautify the outside as well as the inside of my home, I wanted to view the plethora of plants and shrubs newly arrived for spring planting.

"There are so many to pick from that I get confused,"

I confessed as we strolled the aisles, careful not to trip over hoses used to water plants. "Azalea and rhododendron, are they one and the same?"

"Beats me," Bill said with a shrug. "You're asking the wrong person. You need to talk to someone from the garden club."

"I bet Rita could tell me. She's a master gardener, you know." I paused to admire a display of perky pink, white, and purple flowers with green centers. "Why do you suppose these are called Lenten roses?"

Perplexed, Bill scratched his head. "Another question for Rita."

"Just look at these hydrangeas," I cried, stopping before a display.

"Mmm, hmm," Bill murmured in that noncommittal way men frequently adopt when they're not sure of the right answer.

"My mother used to grow these in her garden." I reached out and touched the splashy lavender flowers the size of mop heads. "This is just the thing my yard needs to give it some oomph."

A half hour later we left the garden center pushing a cart loaded with perennials. Perennials? Or annuals? I tend to confuse the two. Perennials appear every year, don't they? Or is it the other way around? You'd think annuals would appear annually. Isn't that a logical assumption? Thankfully we had taken Bill's trusty Ford pickup so we had plenty of room for my purchases, which consisted of two hydrangeas, a couple lantana, and several Lenten roses. By now, we'd missed the movie we had planned to catch. It was too late for the matinee and too early for the evening show.

"Still hungry?" Bill asked as he slammed the gate of his pickup shut.

"I'm starving, but what about my hydrangeas? My lantana?" I cast a worried eye at the leafy greens sprouting from the truck bed. "What if someone with a hankering for flowers happens to come along and is tempted to help themselves?"

"Don't worry, I'll find a parking space up front where we can keep an eye on things. If anyone tries to run off with your hydrangeas, well, they'll have me to reckon with."

I couldn't contain the smile that blossomed bigger than the splashy lavender mop head I'd just bought to jazz up my yard. I loved it when mild-mannered Bill morphed into a superhero. From sweetie to swashbuckler in a flash. Be still my heart.

Ten minutes later we found ourselves seated in a red vinyl booth at Bubba's Buffet Barn with a clear view of the Ford pickup and its precious cargo. Bill glanced around the nearly empty restaurant. "Guess we didn't have to worry about a front-row seat. This place is virtually deserted."

The lone waitress stifled a yawn as she sauntered over with menus. "What can I get y'all to drink?"

"Iced tea—unsweet, with lemon," I said.

Bill smiled. "Make that two."

*Aren't we a pair?* I thought to myself as the waitress went off with our drink order. We even take our iced tea the same way.

"Where do you suppose all the people are? Even at this time of day, the place is usually jammed."

"Think it's the economy? People eating out less to save money?" I mused aloud.

"Nope. It ain't the economy." The waitress, returning with tall glasses of iced tea, had apparently overheard my remark. "It's that damn food poisonin' scare at some old folks' home up north a here. Business been off ever since. Don't pick up soon, Bubba's threatenin' to file bankruptcy."

Bill and I exchanged glances and wordlessly reached for the menus. Neither of us wanted to admit we were escapees from that "old folks home" on the lookout for a good meal.

# Chapter 14

When Sheila called and wanted to meet for lunch, I suggested either the Cove Café or the Watering Hole. Instead, she insisted we dine at the Chinese restaurant Su Me, located on Brookdale's town square.

"Has anyone actually done it, you know, sued them?" Sheila asked as she slid into a booth at the rear.

"Good question, but, no, not that I'm aware of," I responded.

Sheila glanced around. "It's a strange name for a restaurant."

"While I wholeheartedly agree," I said, "Su Me happens to be the name of the proprietor. The woman doesn't seem to have a good grasp of the American tradition of litigation."

Sheila looked much too elegant for this tiny restaurant with its leather booths, red flocked wallpaper, and effigies of gold dragons. She was dressed in coffee-brown slacks with a matching jacket and an ivory silk shell. Her dark glasses in designer frames might have been a bit over-the-top as was a floppy brimmed hat that partially concealed her face. Give her a trenchcoat, and she could audition for the role of Mata Hari. She had obviously gone to great lengths not to be recognized by her adoring public. But I ask you, doesn't her get-up just scream: I'm incognito, please don't recognize me? In an itty-bitty Southern town no bigger than a fly-speck, she needn't have bothered. And not to belabor my point, it was two o'clock in the afternoon, and we were the only customers in the joint. My guess was that Su Me's business had suffered from the same food poisoning blight that had befallen Bubba's Buffet Barn.

Su Me, a plumpish Asian woman of short stature and indeterminate age, approached our table with plastic water glasses in each hand and menus tucked under one arm. "You ready, order?"

"I'm not hungry," Sheila said. "Just tea."

"Only tea?" Su Me looked indignant. "Su Me make good egg foo yong. Make good chicken fried rice."

Sheila shook her head. "No, thank you, just tea."

Su Me's dark eyes held an angry gleam as she turned them on me. "You, lady, you no like Su Me's food?"

I quickly scanned the menu. Call me a glutton if you will, but I wanted something more substantial for lunch than a pot of tea. "I'll have General Tso's chicken."

The woman's round face crinkled into a smile of approval. "Very good, lady. What kind soup you want? Wonton? Egg drop?"

"Wonton," I replied promptly. "And I'd also like an egg roll."

Sheila glanced around nervously as Su Me shuffled off with my order, then reassured she wasn't about to be besieged by autograph hounds, took off her sunglasses. "This is nice, isn't it? Just the two of us. Gives us a chance become better acquainted."

Suddenly I was back in middle school, and the most popular girl in the class had singled me out to be her best friend. I was the chosen one. Special. The envy of all the other prepubescent schoolgirls. I felt flattered, yet uneasy. What if I failed to live up to Popular Girl's expectations? My quandary was postponed by Su Me returning with a pot of tea and two tiny porcelain cups.

Sheila poured tea and handed me a cup. If she noted my sudden attack of nerves, she ignored it. Or maybe she had grown accustomed to people being uncomfortable in her august presence. "You probably know after talking to Rita that we were college roommates. I tried, I really tried, to become friends, but Rita never returned the effort."

"Um ... I didn't know." I took a gulp of tea and burned my tongue.

Sighing, Sheila tucked a wing of frosted-blond hair behind one ear. "I'm afraid Rita and I were never close. What's the term used nowadays ... bonding? We never bonded."

I murmured sympathetically. At least I hoped the sound came out as sympathy not indigestion.

Sheila's eyes were downcast as she toyed with the edge of a paper place mat illustrated with Chinese New Year symbols. "I don't understand why, but I don't have many women friends."

This marked the second time I'd heard her sing this refrain. I get it, I wanted to say. No need to beat me over the head with it. Then I thought of the Babes and how much they meant to me, and instantly felt remorse for my lack of sensitivity. I was tempted to reach out and touch her, but remembered Sheila wasn't into touchy-feely.

"I'm sure Rita's very fond of you," I said instead. "Not many people maintain a relationship as long as the two of you."

"That's sweet of you, Kate, but the truth is Rita's always been ... jealous. In college, she envied my boyfriends, my grades, my scholarship. Later, she envied my success. First as a botanist, then as a host of my own TV show."

What's not to envy? I wanted to ask, but didn't. Sheila

had it all—beauty, brains, success. Half the women in America would give their eyeteeth to trade places with her, I felt like telling her. Wisely I kept silent.

"When I called to learn more about Serenity Cove Estates, Rita did everything she could to discourage me from coming." Sheila shook her head sadly. "It was almost as though she didn't want me here."

Thankfully the wonton soup arrived just then. I crumbled noodles into it, stalling for time while I digested all Sheila was telling me. "I'm sure Rita just needed time to adjust to the notion," I said on my friend's behalf.

"If Rita had had her way, I'd have found a quiet spot elsewhere for Vaughn and me to complete our book." Sheila's lips curled in a mirthless smile. "She changed her tune quickly enough once I offered to speak to her precious garden club."

"It turned out to be quite a coup for Rita personally," I said, sampling my soup and finding it delicious. "Not only did you attend Flowers and Bowers's annual banquet, but you graciously consented to be guest speaker afterward at a lecture open to the public."

"I also presented the Garden of the Year award," Sheila added modestly. "Contrary to what Rita might have told you, it was the board of directors, not her, who issued the invitation to appear."

"You don't sound as though you like her very much." Even as I said this I felt disloyal to a dear friend.

"It's more as if I don't . . . *trust* her."

I stared into Sheila's perfectly made-up, unlined face. "Surely you don't think she'd do anything to harm you," I asked, aghast.

Sheila daintily sipped tea. "I'm merely saying that Rita's been jealous of me since the day we met. Jealousy, Kate, tends to bring out the worst in some people. It can cause an insecure person to resort to extreme measures."

I resisted the urge to squirm. Girl-pal bonding or not,

I didn't like the direction of this conversation. "Even if Rita harbors a grudge against you," I said, clearing my throat, "why harm Vaughn, a man she barely knew?"

The question hung between us like dense fog on a winter morning.

Su Me returned, whisked away my half-finished soup, and replaced it with an egg roll and several cellophane packets of sweet and sour sauce. I shoved the egg roll aside, curious to hear what Sheila would say next. I didn't have to wait long.

"Don't get me wrong, Kate. I *never* meant to imply Rita would harm me in any way." She traced her fingertips along the condensate on her glass of ice water. "I only wanted to let you know how she feels about me."

She looked so dejected I couldn't help but feel a stab of pity. Beauty, brains, and success didn't necessarily spell H-A-P-P-Y.

"My poor, darling Vaughn," Sheila said with a catch in her voice. Grabbing a napkin, she dabbed at her eyes. "Every time I think of him, my heart breaks."

General Tso's chicken chose that moment of high drama to make its fragrant appearance, but I'd lost my appetite. I'm not saying I still wasn't hungry, just not as hungry. There's a fine line between the two. "I'm sorry for your loss," I mumbled, reverting to the tried and true. When it comes to clichés, I have a lifetime subscription.

Sheila sat up straighter, leaned forward, and lowered her voice. "I've given the matter a great deal of thought, Kate. At first I believed whoever did this evil deed wanted both Vaughn and me dead. But my mind's clearer now. I no longer believe Vaughn was the intended victim. It was me—and only me—all along. Dear, sweet, Vaughn unfortunately was collateral damage."

I speared a chunk of my General Tso's and chewed. Collateral damage? That seemed an odd way to describe the death of a loved one, a paramour. "What made you change your mind?"

"Vaughn was so easygoing, so low key." Sheila blinked rapidly to stem a flood of tears. "Everyone loved him; it was impossible not to. He didn't have an enemy in the world."

I don't know about his enemies, but I did know Sheila was delusional if she thought Vaughn was well liked. At least according to the bits of conversation I'd overheard. I decided then and there to work the case, so to speak, from two angles—Vaughn's and Sheila's. Both were victims, one more fortunate than the other—one being alive, the other cremated. It also occurred to me that if Sheila was right, and she was the intended victim, whoever was responsible might very well try again.

I poked at my lunch. My thoughts scattered, an occurrence I generally blame on menopause for lack of a better excuse. Maybe I should have ordered something that hadn't been baptized in a pot of hot grease. What was it about deep-fried that appealed to my taste buds? Belatedly I recalled Bubba's hand-breaded shrimp that I'd eaten Saturday night. With each mouthful I'd imagined ugly plaque clogging my arteries. When was the last time I had my LDL and HDL checked? How high were my lipids? And did I even want to know?

"Something wrong, Kate?" Sheila asked, interrupting my cholesterol triage.

"Who'd want you dead?" I asked as I scooped up a forkful of rice. "Surely you must have your suspicions."

Sheila leaned back in the booth, arms folded over her chest. "I've made my share of enemies over the years."

She sounded remarkably calm for a woman who feared for her life. I'd already begun my list of potential members of the Murder of the Month Club. But I couldn't help but wonder who topped hers. In for a penny, in for a pound. Only one way to find out and that was to ask. "If you had to venture a guess, who do you think would try to kill you?"

A mere hint of a frown marred Sheila's usually smooth brow. Whether a defect in Belle Beaute or Botox, I couldn't say. "I'd hate to point a finger without proof," she replied slowly, "but . . ."

"But . . . ?"

Her expression, from what I could see beneath the brim of her hat, appeared pensive. "Kel Watson," Sheila answered. "That man gives me the creeps. The way he persists in showing up where he isn't wanted scares me. He refuses to leave me alone. I feel as though he's stalking me."

"I couldn't help but notice your reaction at the hospital, and again at the reception following Vaughn's service." I pushed my plate aside and signaled for a to-go box. "How long has this been going on?"

"It all started when he came to the set of *How Does Your Garden Grow?*"

"What did he want?"

"Kel insisted on forming a partnership of sorts in some half-baked scheme he'd conjured up. He assumed that since we were both botanists I'd go along with his idea. Well, he was mistaken. I wanted no part of his wild scheme and told him so in no uncertain terms. But did he let the matter rest? No. He refused to take 'no' for an answer."

Kel Watson looked like an aging hippie, but a harmless one. During my brief stint as a detective-in-training, however, I'd learned appearances can be deceiving. I promised myself to check out the county extension agent first chance I got.

Sheila leaned over and clutched my hand. "Will you get to the bottom of this for me, Kate? I desperately need you on my side. You have an easy way with people that I admire. Everyone seems to like you. And best of all, you have an inquiring mind. From everything Rita's told me, Sheriff Wiggins values the help you've given him in the past."

I nearly choked on my egg roll at hearing this. "Well, I'm not so sure that's the case," I said, stifling a laugh, "but I'll do what I can. After all, what are friends for?"

She gave my hand a squeeze. "Thanks, Kate. I can't tell you how much this means to me."

Lounging against the booth, I reached for the fortune cookie Su Me had deposited along with the check. I broke it open and read the message printed on a narrow ribbon of paper: *Jealousy is the dragon in paradise.*

How apropos, I thought with a grimace. Would jealousy also be the dragon in Serenity Cove Estates?

# Chapter 15

No time like the present.

Instead of driving straight home after leaving Sheila, I decided that as long as I was in town anyway I might as well pay a visit to my extension agent—and prospective murder suspect. Though I'd never been there before I knew the Brookdale County Extension Office was housed on the second floor of the old bank building. The first floor of the weathered brick structure had been converted into an antiques store. I entered by a side door and climbed stairs creaky and concave from years of foot traffic. .

My tentative knock was answered by a gruff, "Door's not locked. C'mon in."

Kel Watson sat with his feet propped on a desk that to my unpracticed eye wavered in the nether region between just plain old and antique. He gave me a quick once-over as he swung his booted feet to the floor. He motioned me to have a seat on the one and only chair that wasn't piled a mile high with journals while he continued his phone conversation. From what I overheard, I gathered that the person on the other end of the line was having sod problems. The terms "fescue" and "zoysia" provided a solid clue. Kel Watson, much to his credit, was patient to a fault, diplomatic even, as he reviewed the merits of each.

I gingerly lowered myself into the cracked leather chair he'd indicated and took advantage of the opportunity to leisurely study him and his surroundings. No one could ever accuse the man of being handsome. His nose was too large for his narrow face, his mouth too wide. His skin was tanned the color of tobacco, furrowed by a lifelong exposure to the harsh Carolina sun without benefit of SPF. Hair, more salt than pepper, was skinned back into a ponytail. He would have blended seamlessly into the Haight-Ashbury scene back in the midsixties. Unfortunately for Kel, times had changed and Brookdale County was a far cry from Haight-Ashbury.

The office was much like the man himself—outdated. The hardwood floor showed wear and tear; the institutional beige walls cried for a fresh coat of paint. A computer, the once-white monitor yellowed with age, occupied a corner of the desk. Bookshelves along one wall sagged beneath the burden of reference books and journals. A rack on the wall next to the door was crammed with brochures with titles such as "Pesticide Safety," "Fire Ants in the Vegetable Garden," and "Food-borne Illnesses."

*Hmm. Interesting.* I was forever curious about others' taste in reading material. Whether at an airport or poolside, I could never resist sneaking a peek to see what people were reading. Whodunits versus romance versus bestsellers. I recalled how much fun a bunch of us regulars at a Florida time-share had floating around the pool with our foam noodles and casting the characters in a popular mystery series.

The debate between fescue and zoysia raged on. Bored, I started to dig through my purse for a nail file when I noticed a glossy brochure that must've slid off his desk and landed on the floor. Naturally I bent and picked it up. Much to my surprise, it had nothing to do with landscape gardening and everything to do with cosmetics—Belle Beaute in particular. The products listed promised to renew and regenerate, to revitalize aging complexions and smooth out wrinkles. Who could resist such claims? I darted a glance at Kel. Was he seriously thinking of purchasing creams and lotions promising to make him appear years younger? Was he trying to impress someone? Sheila Rappaport, perhaps?

I viewed my visit today as a reconnaissance mission of sorts. I intended to get the lay of the land, so to speak. Find out what made the man tick. Just because Kel Watson gave Sheila a case of the willies didn't give me a green light to come right out and ask him if he was a stalker.

Or worse yet, a crazed killer.

His call concluded, Kel hung up the phone and turned his attention to me. "Sorry to keep you waiting," he said.

His voice, though deep and pleasant, was no match for Sheriff Wiggins's smooth-as-molasses baritone. I held out the brochure still clutched in my hot little hand. "I've been told Belle Beaute has an excellent line of face creams and moisturizers. Expensive, but I'm thinking of trying them myself."

A dark flush spread across Kel's high cheekbones. Springing to his feet, he snatched the brochure from my hand, stuffed it into a desk drawer, and slammed it shut.

What was that all about? I wondered as I watched it disappear. Was he afraid folks would find out he was a closet face cream and moisturizer kind of guy?

Kel lowered his lanky body into his chair and asked, "How can I help you, ma'am?"

*You can start by telling me if you poisoned Vaughn Bascomb and Sheila Rappaport.* "Ah, I'm Kate McCall," I replied, reverting to the more conventional greeting. It's never wise to antagonize a potential killer if it can be avoided. It wouldn't do to come right out and accuse the man of being Sheila's nemesis and crazy stalker guy—at least not at our first "official" meeting.

Elbows planted on the armrests of his chair, he studied me over steepled fingers and quietly waited for me to speak. I noted he had the large, callused hands of a laborer, the fingers square-tipped, the nails clipped short. He wasn't wearing a wedding band and, from lack of a tan line, hadn't for some time. Note to self: Ask Rita what she knows of Kel's background.

I cleared my throat. "Please, call me Kate. It's less formal."

"All right, Kate," he said. Leaning forward, he folded those strong, capable hands on the desk in front of him, pious as a priest waiting for a confession. "Suppose you tell me your problem."

Instantly I felt guilty. *Should I cross myself or genuflect . . . ?* "Um, sorry. I bought too many plants at Lowe's and now I don't know what to do with them." Was my transgression horticulture gluttony or simple botanical lust?

"Well, that's not so terrible," he said, absolving me with a kind smile. "Now, tell me what you purchased, and I'll make some suggestions."

*Your sins are forgiven. Five "Our Fathers" and ten "Hail Mary's."*

"Lantanas . . . ?"

"Lantanas are a good choice." He nodded approvingly. "They're tough as nails. Thrive in our hot, dry summers. Butterflies are drawn to them like a magnet, but the deer leave them alone."

"What about Lenten roses?" I fumbled through my purse for pen and paper. This information was too good to trust to a memory susceptible to "senior" moments.

"Lenten roses, also known as hellebore, prefer full or partial shade. Deer also tend to avoid them."

I made a note of this on a Piggly Wiggly cash register receipt I'd found crumpled at the bottom of my purse. "And last but not least, hydrangeas."

"Pretty things, aren't they? Hydrangeas are a little trickier to grow than, for instance, lantana. Their color is affected by the pH in the soil—blue flowers require acidic soil, pink or red like alkaline."

I scribbled like mad to jot all this down. "Where do they grow best?"

"Plant them where they'll get morning sun, but light shade in the afternoon."

My head swirled with do's and don'ts as I rose to leave. Morning sun, light shade? I was going have to pack a picnic lunch and spend a day getting better acquainted with my yard. My respect for gardeners was growing by leaps and bounds. I had always ascribed to the dig-a-hole-in-the-ground-and-hope-for-the-best theory. No wonder I had so many failures. No wonder my late husband had hired a landscaper.

Kel rose too. "The whole time we've been talking, I've been thinking you look familiar. Have we met before?"

I tugged my lower lip while I debated my answer. Of course I could admit I was at the Cove Café after Vaughn's memorial service and witnessed Sheila's meltdown. I might even mention I was in Sheila's hospital room and watched her faint dead away at the sight of him. Nah, too much information. Instead, I took a chance he hadn't noticed me in the shadow of Rita's big knockers. "I, um, attended a couple of your lectures with a friend of mine."

My answer seemed to mollify him since he turned his attention away from me and toward his computer.

I was about to leave when I turned back with another question. "Why do deer leave certain plants and shrubs alone, but eat others like candy?"

Kel looked up from making an entry. "There are a

number of theories. Some folks insist deer sense which ones are poisonous, which ones aren't. Others believe poisonous plants aren't all that tasty. Guess you'll have to ask a deer to find out the real answer."

I stood, one hand on the doorknob, while I processed all this. "You just finished telling me deer leave lantana and Lenten roses alone. Are you saying they're poisonous?"

"Yep," he drawled. "Even your pretty hydrangeas contain low levels of cyanide." He resumed his hunt-and-peck typing. "Just don't eat them, and you'll be fine."

Poison in my very own yard—and in countless yards throughout the South, I marveled as I descended the stairs, careful not to touch the grimy banister. How convenient for someone with murder on their mind.

"I'm ready to officially join the garden club. Sign me up."

I sensed Rita's hesitation from three blocks away.

"Are you sure you've thought this through?" she asked.

"Positive. I'm turning over a new leaf." I giggled. I'd quite literally be turning over new leaves as well as old ones. "My ultimate goal is to have one of those cute Garden of the Month plaques in my front yard."

"Remember ceramics?"

Leave it to Rita to remind me of my failures. Ceramics, by the way, happens to be much more difficult than people realize. I tried it for a time with limited success. Then to add insult to injury, my masterpiece, a sweet, little birdhouse that had taken months to complete, had exploded in the kiln.

"Remember salsa dancing? Kayaking? Duplicate bridge?"

"This is different," I protested. "Gardening doesn't require coordination."

Rita heaved a sigh. "Kate, you ought to have a sign over your door that reads: DEATH TO HOUSEPLANTS.

Somehow you even managed to kill the ZZ plant I gave you. A plant practically guaranteed indestructible."

I felt bad, I really did, over the plant's untimely demise. In my opinion, ideal houseplants should be able to tolerate long periods of drought followed by flash floods. "Gardening can't be much different than cooking, right?" I asked, rallying my defense.

I heard Rita's groan on the other end of the line.

"All one has to do is read the recipe typed on those plastic plant-stick things and follow the directions. If I can make a soufflé, how hard can it be to grow a plant?"

"I didn't think you liked to get your hands dirty."

I could tell from Rita's tone I was wearing her down. "I'll wear gloves. They come in all sorts of pretty colors and patterns. And I've got the perfect straw hat to wear so I'll look cute in case Bill happens to drop by."

"Oh, all right, seeing as how I can't talk you out of joining. My term as president is up, but I agreed to serve as the new membership chairman."

"Great! Send me the papers, and I'll sign on the dotted line."

"Kate, this isn't like applying for a second mortgage. Consider yourself a provisional member of the club. Active membership is subject to a vote. And, Kate, you'll have to spend time working at our current beautification project."

"No *problemo*." I hung up feeling inordinately proud of myself. I'd not only beautify my yard, but I'd gain firsthand knowledge of which plants were safe and which weren't. Happy I was on the right track, I made myself a cup of herbal tea, then settled on the sofa in the great room with a good book — *The Complete Idiot's Guide to Forensics*. After scanning the table of contents, I flipped open to Chapter Eleven.

"Death by Poisoning" promised to be an entertaining read.

# Chapter 16

"Kate, this is Sheila. Are you doing anything special tomorrow?"

"Tomorrow?" I flipped through the pages of my imaginary day planner. What day was tomorrow anyway? Wednesday . . . ? Let me think. I mentally ran through my schedule: grocery shop, laundry, pay bills, clean the bathroom. "Nope," I replied. "Nothing special."

"Wonderful!" she enthused. "How would you and a guest like to attend the Masters?"

"Me . . . ?" I squeaked. "Attend the Masters?"

Sheila's pleased laughter tickled the phone lines. "It's only a practice round. Belle Beaute is hosting a hospitality suite, so I happen to have extra tickets. I understand Wednesday traditionally is the day for the Par 3 Contest. I'm not a golfer, but I've been told it's fun to watch."

*Only a practice round?* I sank into a kitchen chair and stared out the window. Tickets for even practice rounds were scarcer than hen's teeth. No tickets were sold at the gate. South Carolina has a lottery system in place for practice round tickets, but only a small percentage of those who applied are lucky enough to get them. Jim and I had been there once, and now compliments of Sheila, I'd be going again. The Masters Tournament wasn't just big, it was HUGE. People who can't tell a golf ball from a football know the Masters is golf's premier event. More than premier, it's legendary. Icons such as Ben Hogan, Sam Snead, and Byron Nelson were past champions. I was getting *verklempt* knowing I'd be walking the same fairways as past and present greats. Tiger, Phil, Vijay, ready or not, here I come!

"Kate . . . ? You still there?"

"Y-yes," I stammered. "I'm still here." What I really wanted to ask is, What should I wear? Shorts or capris? Golf chic would be the name of the game. And another bonus: I could shop while there. Their golf shops carried a fabulous selection of all things golf and all sport the Masters logo. I'd get a golf shirt for Bill, blue to match his eyes, and one for my son-in-law Jason. No one loved logos more than Jason. Jen once confided he even had them on his socks and underwear. And I'd find something cute for the girls, something pink. Before long, golf would be competing for their after-school hours along with violin, gymnastics, and soccer.

"I've never played the game myself—too busy," Sheila was saying. "Maybe I'll take it up when I retire."

"I'm so excited I hardly know what to say." I collected my scattered wits and hauled myself back to the present. I tried for cool, calm, and collected but failed on all three counts. "I'd love to go," I said, waving a hand to fan my flushed cheeks. Power surge to the max.

Sheila laughed again. "Great."

"Thanks so much for inviting me. I can't tell you how much I appreciate this." I was gushing more than BP's oil spill in the Gulf.

"Bring a friend. I'll have Betsy leave the badges at the gate. You'll also find directions to the hospitality suite Belle Beaute is hosting afterward at the Marriott. I hope you'll have time to join us for a drink."

Wow! The tournament and a hospitality suite. I felt

I'd hit the mother lode. I swallowed hard. "We'd be delighted."

"Oh, Kate, while I've got you on the phone I wanted to let you know Sheriff Wiggins paid me a visit this afternoon."

"Oh?" I felt my euphoria fade. Leave it to the mean ol' sheriff to rain on my parade. "What did he have to say?"

"Preliminary toxicology results came back from the crime lab in Columbia."

I picked a pencil off the table and began playing with it. "And . . ."

"He said they found no trace of either E. coli or botulism."

"Well, I guess folks around the buffet table will rest easy knowing it wasn't food poisoning."

Sheila lowered her voice. "That's not all."

I held my breath and waited for her to continue.

"He insinuated there were some elements that merited further investigation."

"Does he have any idea what they're looking for?" I absently tapped the eraser end of the pencil up and down on the table.

"No, but I think he's taking my allegation of poisoning seriously." An urgency had crept into Sheila's voice. "He agreed it's strange that Vaughn and I were the only ones at the banquet who were affected. Then he asked if we had any enemies. Anyone who would want to harm us."

"What did you tell him?" I could picture her elegant shrug.

"I told him with our success we were apt to make people jealous. The culprit could be any number of people. I also told him to look extra hard at Kel Watson and the reasons why."

When we disconnected a few minutes later, the day of fun and frolic I'd anticipated had been transformed into a day of work. Sheila had off-handedly mentioned

Roger McFarland planned to take publicity stills of her
with the Masters as a backdrop for his coffee table work
of art. Todd Timmons would be there as well, shooting
promo for upcoming episodes of *How Does Your Garden Grow?* Naturally, Betsy Dalton, smug in her role as
VP at Belle Beaute, would be flitting around. Tomorrow my search for the Big Three as I referred to them—
motive, means, and opportunity—would begin in earnest.
Business before pleasure is the motto of the Kate McCall
School of Private Detecting.

I resumed my impatient *tap-tap-tap* with the pencil.
Which friend should I bring? I pondered my choices.
Bill was the first person to spring to mind. Not only did
Bill make my heart go pit-a-pat, but he possessed the
ability to be objective and rational. Traits that sometimes eluded me. I was about to punch in his number
when I remembered he'd promised to drive a pal to the
airport in Atlanta. After considerable thought, I settled
on Polly as my number two choice. She liked solving
mysteries nearly as much as I did.

"Hey, count me in," Polly agreed readily after I explained the mission. "I've got the perfect outfit to wear."

"Polly, this isn't a play day, it's a work day."

"Don't mean I can't look spiffy for all those good-
looking golfers."

"No, but we don't want to blind them by one of your
neon-bright getups."

"Gotcha. We need to blend, be inconspicuous."

"Gates open at eight, so be ready by seven."

"Roger and out, girlfriend. I'll let you be Sherlock;
I'll be Watson."

I smiled to myself as I hung up. Sherlock and Watson, the Masters and the Big Three. Yessiree, tomorrow
promised to be quite a day.


Wednesday morning dawned bright and sunny with a
cloudless, blue sky. I'd been so excited I'd barely slept a

wink. I downed a cup of coffee and choked down half a bagel. And cautioned myself to stay focused, not to get distracted by all the hoopla. Not that I'd allow that to happen of course, but I warned myself all the same. Sheila's unexpected invite afforded me the perfect opportunity to mingle with my unfavorite trio of Todd, Rog, and Bets. I wanted to get a better handle on them, see if one of them stood out more sharply than another as a suspect. If Sheila's assumption was true, and she was the intended target not Vaughn, whoever was responsible might try again.

But what if Sheila was wrong? What if she, not Vaughn, was collateral damage? It was a sobering thought. My resolve hardened. I was more determined than ever to study the crime from both perspectives. Two sides to every story, right?

If the day was bright, it dimmed next to Polly. I felt positively dowdy in comparison. "If memory serves, I thought the dress code was going be on the conservative side."

"I don't remember saying anything about conservative," she said as she climbed into the passenger seat. "I said we needed to blend, be inconspicuous."

"You call that blending?" I asked, eying twiglike legs protruding from shocking-pink capris.

"Get a load of this." She opened her matching lightweight jacket to reveal a poison apple–green T-shirt with bright orange flames sprouting from the slogan ONE HOT MAMA. "Like it?"

*Like* is a little mild to express how I feel about Polly's wardrobe. "You've outdone yourself," I told her. And that was an understatement. "How do you figure that's blending in?"

"Simple." Polly snapped on her seat belt. "The green blends with the grass; the pink matches the azaleas."

"Of course. How silly of me not to see the connection."

"I read a while back that bright colors stand out best in a crowd." Polly settled back, ready for the hour-long drive. "The *Augusta Chronicle* says all the big dogs will be here filming: the Golf Channel, ESPN, CBS Sports and Jim Nance, along with crews from the local stations. We might even make the six o'clock news. I Tweeted everyone to be on the lookout for a cute blonde dressed in pink and green."

I sighed as I pointed the Buick south. If the cameras favored bright, Polly would be a star. "Just remember, our mission isn't to have fun. We're on the prowl for possible murder suspects. I need you to keep your eyes and ears open. Pay special attention to Sheila's sponsor, her editor, and her producer. I want to find out which one has the strongest motive and means."

"Gotcha." Polly gave me a wink. "Roger, Todd, and Betsy. Eyes and ears peeled."

We drifted into idle chatter as we drove along a winding highway lined with pine trees and interspersed with small communities bearing odd names such as Plum Branch and Modoc.

"Sure nice of Sheila to invite us," Polly said.

"Mm, hm," I agreed. "Sheila's gone out of her way trying to be friends. I feel kind of sorry for her. She doesn't seem to have many women friends."

"Too busy with her job, eh?"

"Something like that, I guess."

The number of cars on the road increased as we approached Augusta. I waited for the light to change and made a left. Traffic along Washington Road barely crawled. The atmosphere seemed charged. Restaurant chains flew colorful banners advertising Masters Week specials. Marquees in front of shops and strip malls welcomed visitors to Augusta, home of the Masters. NO VACANCY signs blinked at hotels and motels near the I-20 interchange. Ticket scalpers, some in vans, others in RVs, hawked tickets along both sides of the road, careful to maintain the mandated distance from the Augusta National. Tickets could be had apparently, but at a premium. It was Mardi Gras Augusta-style.

"Place reminds me of Vegas." Polly rubber-necked, not wanting to miss out on the action.

"You know Vegas?"

"Dated a blackjack dealer before moving in with Gloria and Stan."

I shot her a glance out of the corner of my eye. Somehow I could easily picture Polly shooting craps or feeding coins into slot machines. Once again the saying, what happens in Vegas stays in Vegas seemed to apply.

I turned onto Berckmans Road and spied a kid in a ball cap waving a yellow flag and motioning toward a grassy lot that fifty-one weeks a year served as a resident's side yard. I slowed to a stop and handed the kid a twenty, ransom money for parking in a spot close to the street. He pocketed the bill and pointed to a spot behind a Toyota. Hefting a well-stocked bag to my shoulder, Polly and I joined the throng of people migrating toward the gate.

We found our badges waiting just as Sheila promised. Slipping them into clear plastic holders fastened to a lanyard, we put them around our necks. I felt anticipation mount as we approached the security checkpoint. "Showtime," I announced cheerily.

"Halt!" a female voice called.

I stopped dead in my tracks. "You talking to me?"

A fresh-faced girl in her early twenties, a blond ponytail protruding beneath a cap with the Masters logo, held up one hand like a school crossing guard. With the other, she pointed at my bulging shoulder bag. "Ma'am, you can't bring *that* in with you."

"B-but . . ." I stammered. "It has all my . . . stuff." Once a Girl Scout, always a Girl Scout. I'd come prepared with stuff, stuff, and more stuff. Camera, cell phone, binoculars, autograph book and pen, wallet and credit cards, peanuts, orange sections, and for good measure, a couple bars of BAM! My purse must've weighed a good twenty pounds.

Behind me I heard a rumble of dissension. "What's the holdup?" one woman demanded querulously.

A man in the next line over jerked a thumb at a nearby sign informing one and all that purses could be no larger than ten inches wide by five inches high. "Can't you read, lady?"

My face burned with embarrassment at being singled out as an illiterate. Where was the infamous Southern hospitality? True Southerners were unfailingly courteous. I decided these rude people were aliens and ought to be deported for unsportsmanlike conduct.

"Sorry," the girl said. "Rules are rules."

When did these rules go into effect? Surely, since my one and only visit years ago. "But what about my camera, my cell phone, my autograph book?" I wailed.

"Cameras are allowed at the practice rounds, but no cell phones. For player safety, we adhere to a strict no autograph policy on the course. Now, ma'am, if you'll please step aside, you're holding up the line."

Polly tugged on my sleeve. "What're you gonna do?"

To make a long story short, I turned and started hiking back to the car. I left Polly behind to get a head start on souvenir shopping.

This was a less than auspicious start to a day of crime solving.

# Chapter 17

So much for getting an early start, I fussed as I trudged back along Berckmans Road. The day was heating up. I was both sweaty and cranky after my long hike. Although I might have to be scanned through security, I was grateful that at least I didn't have to step on a scale. Before tossing my purse in the trunk of the Buick, I'd jammed as much into the pockets of my navy capris as space would allow, including a camera and a couple BAM! bars for good measure.

Polly was waiting for me inside the course gate weighted down with two bulging shopping bags. "Wait till you see all my stuff."

"*Stuff* is exactly what got me sent all the way back to the car," I grumbled. "We won't make it until lunch if you have to lug those bags around with you."

"Ma'am?"

I turned to find a woman in madras capris and a visor standing next to me.

"Sorry, hon, didn't mean to eavesdrop," she apologized with a friendly smile. "But there are lockers right over there where y'all can store your packages."

I thanked the woman profusely for her suggestion. Now, there was an example of Southern hospitality at its finest. Polly and I might very well have walked right past the lockers, but there they stood, a bank of shiny metal just ready and waiting. After considerable huffing and puffing, we managed to squeeze Polly's souvenirs inside, slam the door, and twist the lock.

"Time's a wasting," I said. "Let's see if we can spot Peter, Paul, and Mary in this crowd."

Polly blinked up at me, confused. "Who?"

"Sorry," I replied absently. "I meant Todd, Roger, and Betsy." I opened the spectator guide to orient myself to the grounds.

"But what about golf?" Polly whined. "All these tanned and fit athletes, and me all dressed up."

"Don't forget, the motto of the day is business before pleasure."

"Right," Polly muttered. She looked more like a toddler about to have a tantrum than an AARP card–carrying senior citizen.

"There'll be time for that, too."

I studied a map of the course, then with Polly close on my heels, started off in the general direction of Amen Corner, a popular viewing spot for holes eleven, twelve, and thirteen, so named because of the critical action that often takes place there. We hadn't gone far before we were nearly mowed down by an army of spectators bent on following a threesome. One figure in particular stood out as he marched down the fairway like royalty.

Polly tugged on my sleeve. "Is that who I think it is?" she whispered.

"Tiger," I whispered back. "The one and only."

How many chances does a person get in one lifetime to watch one of sports greats in action? We wormed our way through the crowd until we were close enough to the roped-off green to watch him putt. I found myself behind a couple of brawny young men who looked to be in their early thirties. Each time I craned my neck

for a better look, one or the other inadvertently blocked
my view. Next to me, Polly seemed to be running into
the same trouble. She solved the problem by half-turning
and wedging her skinny body between the pair.

"Sorry, sonny." She returned their dirty looks with a
sweet smile. "Hope I didn't step on your feet. When you
get to be my age, dear, and know there isn't much time
left ..." she said, blinking rapidly as she sniffed back
crocodile tears.

"Sorry, ma'am," the darker-haired one replied. "Here,
let me make room for you."

I resisted the urge to roll my eyes, but I had to hand
it to Polly for winning herself a prime spot. When it
suited her, she played the age card with finesse. The
young men may have been taken in by her grandmoth-
erly wiles, but I wasn't. I was just miffed I hadn't thought
of it myself.

While the pros chipped and putted from various angles, I scanned the crowd searching for a familiar face. I
was about to give up when I spotted Todd Timmons
trotting alongside a CBS Sports crew like an obedient
puppy. Clearly in his element, he wore Ray-Bans, a classic polo shirt, and an ear-to-ear grin. Todd chattered
away in a futile attempt to engage an obviously disinterested cameraman in conversation.

I watched one of the marshals approach him. "Sorry,
sir," I heard him say, "but I'll have to ask you to step
outside the ropes. This area is restricted to media only."

Todd spread his hands and grinned even wider. "I'm
a TV producer."

The man didn't return the smile. "If you're media, why
doesn't it say so on your badge?"

"Todd Timmons." Todd extended his hand. "*How
Does Your Garden Grow*? You might have heard of my
show."

The marshal ignored Todd's outstretched hand. "If

you don't remove yourself immediately, sir, I'll have security escort you off the premises."

Todd shot a hopeful glance at his newfound cameraman buddy, but when no support was forthcoming, he ducked under the rope to stand with the rest of us peons. His expression mirrored anger and embarrassment as he stood, face flushed, arms folded, and watched the golfers. After the threesome moved on, he attached himself to a crew from ESPN and trailed along, careful to maintain established boundaries. Watching him, if only for a brief time, I realized Todd had an agenda— and wasn't one to give up easily.

In spite of intentions to the contrary, I fell under the Masters's spell. I forgot my plan to be organized and efficient and started to just enjoy the day. Under similar circumstances, I was certain Nancy Drew or Jessica Fletcher would've done the same. Polly and I roamed the course aimlessly. It was a magnificent setting. Banks of azaleas in full bloom and dogwood trees bursting with dainty white flowers made it seem more botanical garden than golf course. Acres of velvety grass rolled and stretched like the lawn of some grand country estate. The lawn . . . er, grounds . . . were interspersed with irregular patches of pristine white sand, a reminder that this wasn't a park, but Augusta National, home of the Masters.

We mingled; we watched. We oohed; we aahed.

Watching the pros practice their putting proved a revelation. I was amazed at their intensity. One after another, they'd squat on their haunches to study the slope of the green, conferring with their caddies whether it might break right or left. When I play, I tend to do more finger-crossing than actual strategy. Trying to figure out the exact angle reminds me too much of Sister Marie Frances's geometry class. No wonder I don't excel at putting. Geometry was the only class in which I'd ever received a D. And let me tell you, boys and girls, I'd been ecstatic that I didn't get an F. All those angles, planes, and point A's to point B's failed to register in my addled brain.

I was also impressed by Polly's rapt attention to the pros' techniques. To the best of my knowledge, she'd never been particularly interested in the game. Instead of her usual voluble self, she became uncharacteristically quiet. Then I observed her more carefully. She was watching the golfers, all right, but it was their bottoms and not their golf balls that commanded her attention. I shook my head, glad Gloria wasn't here to witness her mother's affinity for anatomy.

"Polly," I said, giving her a gentle prod, "it's lunchtime."

We wandered until we came across one of the concession stands that dot the course. Polly and I ordered sandwiches, pimento—a longstanding tradition at the Masters—for myself, and BBQ for Polly. We settled down at a picnic table under a stand of pine with our food. As much as I was enjoying the day, the time had come to get back to business. If I didn't make more of an effort to exclude names on my persons of interest list, I'd feel somehow I'd failed Sheila. "We're having way too much fun," I announced, wiping my fingers on a paper napkin. "We need to try harder if we're going to track down Todd, Rog, and Bets."

"But how?" Polly asked. "There are thousands of people here. It'll be like spotting Waldo in one of those *Where's Waldo* books."

"It's almost time for the Par 3 Contest. Maybe we'll have better luck there."

"Fine, but let's check out Magnolia Lane first. It's famous. I want my picture taken there so I can post it on Facebook."

While Polly chucked our sandwich wrappers and drink cups into a trash can, I consulted the map. "Looks like the clubhouse is that way," I said, pointing straight ahead. "Long as we're here, I'd like to see Magnolia Lane myself. Last time, all Jim wanted to do was watch approach shots."

We threaded our way through a milling throng of people toward the clubhouse. The clubhouse was a white three-story structure built in the low-country style with porches encircling the first and second floors. "According to the Web site, this is the original plantation house dating back to the 1850s. The course itself used to be an indigo plantation," I told Polly, showing off knowledge I'd gleaned the night before on the Internet. Only wished I'd paid more attention to the do's and don'ts. Knowing the size of handbags would have saved me a long hike. *Get over it, Kate,* I scolded, *the exercise probably did you good.*

"Look at them magnolias," Polly enthused, peering down the long sweep of drive that led from the clubhouse to an entrance gate. "Aren't they a sight for sore eyes?"

"Speaking of sore eyes, look who else is admiring the view."

Roger McFarland stood midway down the drive, staring through the viewfinder of a camera. Not just any old camera, but the long-lens type paparazzi might use. The type I'd expect from a man charged with editing a book about plants and shrubs. A man with an eye for detail.

"Enjoying the Masters?" I asked as Polly and I sauntered up.

He jerked at the sound of my voice, and I heard the shutter *whirr.* "Dammit," he cursed, turning on me. "I had the perfect mix of light and shadow until you ruined it."

"Here." Polly shoved her digital camera at him. "Take our picture, will you? I want everyone to see us on Facebook."

He let his Canon dangle from a strap around his neck. "Fine," he said in a voice heavy with resignation.

Polly pulled me closer, put her arm around my waist, and we smiled, smiled, smiled until our cheeks ached. "That oughta do it," Roger announced, returning the camera to Polly. "Say"—he squinted at us from behind horned-rimmed glasses—"haven't I seen you two before?"

"We're friends of Sheila's—good friends," I said. *And we're here to spy on you.* "Right, right," he muttered.

Judging from his baffled expression, he still didn't have a clue as to who we were. Apparently I hadn't made much of an impression. That happens to me a lot, but I try not to let it affect my self-esteem. "We met at the hospital the night Dr. Bascomb . . . expired."

"You might've seen us at his memorial service," Polly offered. "We were the two at the buffet table eating shrimp rangoons. Guess everyone else was afraid they'd get poisoned."

Roger's ruddy face turned even ruddier. "I, um . . ."

I could see the word "poison" was making him nervous. Good time to change the subject. "Are you taking photos for Sheila's book?" I asked.

"Ah, no." He rubbed a hand over his short carrot-colored hair, making it stand on end. "Horticulture is my true passion, not photography. I study plants and shrubs every chance I can."

Horticulture his passion? Hm, that would lend itself to my planticide theory. "That must help with your job as editor for a university press."

"Yeah, I guess," he muttered.

He turned to leave, so I fell into step alongside him. "How did you happen to go from a career with flowers and shrubs to book publishing?"

"Fate, timing." He shrugged. "Bad luck."

"How's that?"

"Someone else landed the job I wanted. Just because

a person happens to look more qualified on paper doesn't necessarily mean they're the right pick for the job, does it?"

"No, of course not."

Roger stopped and waved an arm back in the direction we'd just come. "Did you know, for instance, that those magnolias were planted from seed before the Civil War?"

"Um, no." Sad to say, but my homework last night hadn't included the history of trees. If this was a pop quiz, I failed miserably

"Say, Roger," Polly said, catching up with us, "could you snap a picture of me standing against that big tree over there?"

"We're surrounded by 'big' trees, lady," Roger said, sounding exasperated.

Polly was unfazed by the gruff tone. "The big one next to the clubhouse. The one with the purple flowers."

"Those purple flowers happen to be wisteria," he growled. "That particular vine happens to be the first wisteria established in the United States. It's believed to be the largest of its kind."

Polly handed over her camera. "You don't say."

While Polly posed for pictures, I mentally cataloged the information I'd gathered. Roger, the pudge, had not merely a liking, but a *passion*, for all growing things. That implied considerable knowledge of plants, both poisonous and nonpoisonous varieties. Aha, I said silently. Knowledge translated into M-E-A-N-S.

I recalled the conversation I'd overheard in the ER the night Vaughn . . . died, passed, or entered into eternal rest. Roger had complained Vaughn interfered with his vision of the coffee table masterpiece he was editing. With Vaughn out of the picture, literally and figuratively, he'd remove the obstacle that stood in the way of the book's successful completion. In addition, Roger harbored a grudge against the person who had beaten him out of a coveted position in a field he adored. Could that person have been Sheila? Or perhaps Vaughn? At some point had resentment spilled into rage? Rage and resentment spelled M-O-T-I-V-E. My fingers itched to jot this down in my little black book.

I returned to the course with a new bounce in my step. The day was starting to look up.

# Chapter 18

"Hey, Kate! Look at this!" Polly held up a wildly flowered notebook filled with scrawls. "I got me a whole bunch of autographs."

I blew out a breath. "Polly, the tournament adheres to a strict *no autograph policy*. You could've gotten us kicked out of here."

"But I didn't. The golfers were only too happy to oblige."

"You told them it was for your grandson," I said through clenched teeth. "You don't have a grandson."

"But if I did, the cute little bugger would be thrilled with all these autographs. Probably sell 'em on eBay and pay for his college tuition. Costs a pretty penny to become a brain surgeon these days, you know."

We were standing at the bank of elevators in the Marriott on our way to Belle Beaute's hospitality suite. Polly, bless her heart, hadn't been worth her salt as my assistant, Dr. Watson. Instead of searching for motive, means, and opportunity, she'd spent the day shopping for souvenirs, taking photos, having them taken, and collecting autographs for a hypothetical grandson. I, on the other hand, had stayed true to the course. I knew with certainty Roger McFarland possessed the unholy trinity of motive, means, and opportunity. Todd Timmons was next to come under my microscope.

When the elevator door *whooshed* open, we rode in silence to the top floor. We walked down a carpeted hallway and stepped into an episode of *Lifestyles of the Rich and Famous*. Only thing missing was Robin Leach. The large living room was filled with comfy overstuffed sofas and chairs in muted shades of green, gold, and burgundy. A giant flat-screen TV mounted on one wall replayed Masters coverage from previous tournaments. On the far wall, a floor-to-ceiling window provided a spectacular view of the Savannah River glittering in the late-afternoon sun. A long table in the dining area was nearly buried beneath trays of hot and cold hors d'oeuvres. A wet bar, complete with ice maker, held a vast selection of liquor, all top shelf, as well as wine, both red and white.

Polly stood transfixed on the threshold. "This sure is the cat's meow."

"Sure is," I echoed. I felt like the proverbial fish out of water, but I guess that's why the cat meowed.

People milled about, drink glasses in hand, laughing and chattering like they didn't have a care in the world. Some were in cocktail attire, but most wore casual chic. The cut of their clothes along with the flash and jangle of jewelry was the type only wealth could bring. In lieu of flash and jangle, I'd taken time to freshen my lipstick before mingling with the bold and the beautiful. I was glad I'd recently colored my hair and no gray roots showed in the ash blond.

"Been a long time since lunch," Polly muttered. "I'm a little thirsty, too. Think I'll get me something to drink. A nice cold margarita always hits the spot after a day on the links."

Sheila spotted me from across the room where she stood surrounded by a group of women. Fans? I wondered. She waved. I waved back.

Come to think of it, it *had* been a long time since lunch. And all the walking around had made me thirsty. I followed the same trail Polly had blazed. Sashaying over to the hors d'oeuvre table, I filled a plate with fruit and cheese, then helped myself to the shrimp and other goodies. Next I wandered over to the bar, where a nice bartender poured me a glass of pinot grigio. I sipped; I sampled; I eavesdropped.

Seeing Betsy Dalton talking to one of the up-and-coming young golfers, I sidled closer.

"I heard buzz that your company is coming out with a men's line," the guy was saying. He was tall, tanned, and gorgeous with sun-streaked blond hair and Nordic blue eyes. His name was Tyler or Trevor, or maybe Taylor, Something-or-other.

"Rumor's true. We plan to debut our new product line in time for the holidays." Betsy Dalton gazed up at him with a smile that all but whispered "Come into my web, said the spider to the fly."

He grinned engagingly. "My agent mentioned you're looking for endorsements."

"Also true," Betsy purred.

I tried not to choke on my meatball when I saw her reach out and smooth the guy's shirt collar—a collar which even to a woman with gradient lenses didn't need smoothing. "Naturally, we have a certain type in mind to best represent our products."

He flashed a blinding set of pearly whites. "Babe, you're looking at him."

Gag me with a spoon, will you? I can't believe a woman with Betsy Dalton's sophistication would fall for the corny "Babe" routine. But seeing, as they say, is believing. I watched her give him a coy smile and playfully run a finger down his cheek. "The company is searching for a man with certain . . . attributes."

I pretended more interest in a crab cake than it merited. Out of the corner of my eye, I saw him take her hand and brush a kiss across her knuckles. "Babe, I'm at your disposal," he said in a low voice.

"Really, Ty." Betsy gave his arm a playful swat. "I was referring to skin tone, but it goes without saying, good looks and a buff body are part of the total package."

"Feel free to check out my ... attributes ... anytime you like."

The Ty-guy dropped his voice so low that in order to eavesdrop I practically had to stand on one leg. I listed so far right I nearly lost my balance.

"There's a bed in the next room," I heard him say.

When Betsy didn't seem to object, he hooked a bronzed arm over her shoulders and led her toward the bedroom.

My, my, I thought taking a sip of wine to calm my nerves. If I wanted to watch this much action, I could tune into the afternoon soaps. I wasn't a prude but *sheesh*! The golfer was young enough to be her son. Right before my very eyes, I'd seen Betsy transform into Erica Kane, Susan Lucci's character on *All My Children*. Wait till Polly finds out what she missed.

Speaking of Polly, where was she? Left to her own devices, God only knew what mischief she might tumble into. People continued to arrive, making the suite even more crowded. I scanned the partygoers and found Polly in an animated discussion with one of the pros. Don't give my powers of deduction too much credit. I'll let you in on a little secret. Golfers are easy to spot. Just look at their hands. The right hand of a golfer always has a deeper tan than the left. Unless putting, they always wear a glove on the left. Clever of me, eh?

"Hey, Kate," Polly sang out. "Justin here was nice enough to give me his autograph."

"I'm happy to be able to cheer the poor little guy," Justin explained with a self-deprecatory smile. "He's a real trooper to go through all those operations. And lucky to have such a nice lady for a grandma. Now, if you ladies'll excuse me."

I wagged my head. "Polly Curtis, you're incorrigible."

Totally unrepentant, Polly tucked her autograph book away. "Where's the harm? It made him feel good to think he was helping a kid."

"And gave you an excuse to ogle a good-looking guy," I pointed our acerbically. "Keep it up, and I'm going to have to replace you as my assistant."

"All right, already, what do you want me to do?"

"Cozy up to Roger. See what else you can learn. I'll spy on Todd. And, Polly, go easy on the booze," I cautioned, eyeing the nearly empty margarita glass she held. "Remember how upset Gloria gets at seeing you tipsy."

"That girl is wound too tight. Takes after her father that way. Needs to loosen up."

We separated, working the room from opposite directions. I milled through the guests, smiling and nodding where appropriate, listening to snippets of conversation.

"Did you see Tiger's chip shot . . ."

"How about Phil's drive on number 5 . . .

"Trust me, that guy from the UK, what's his name, is the one to watch."

And so on and so forth.

I noshed my way through a plate of appetizers. The shrimp were a little chewy, but the baby bella mushrooms stuffed with crabmeat were to die for. Wish I had the recipe. They'd be a big hit at bunco. I was on the verge of going back for seconds when I spied Todd Timmons. He stood off to one side, studying the conglomeration of people. Then, his brow furrowed, his eyes narrowed, and he settled on his prey—a distinguished-looking gentleman with a well-endowed blond on his arm. I held my breath as I watched him stalk his potential victim. Again, I wished I could make note of this in my ubiquitous little book, but it might garner unwanted attention. I think my cell phone might have a record feature, but didn't have a clue how to use it. Shifting into stealth mode, I moved closer.

Todd waylaid the man, stuck out his hand. "Todd Timmons. Say, haven't we met?"

Hmph. That line failed to score in the originality category. I hope Todd has a better repertoire when he goes clubbing.

"Sorry, you don't look familiar." The man smiled politely. "Dick Phillips, Fox Sports."

"Are you in television, too, Rod?" the blond asked.

"That's Todd, not Rod," he corrected. "Yeah, I'm a TV producer. Maybe you've heard of my show, *How Does Your Garden Grow?*"

"Never heard of it," the blond said with a vacuous smile. "But then, I'm not into gardening. It ruins my manicure."

"I'm afraid I neglected to introduce my companion, Marlene Monroe." Dick placed a proprietary hand on the girl's curvy backside. "Marlene's been very helpful, showing me around Augusta."

Ignoring Marlene's generous cleavage, Todd zeroed in on Dick like a GPS locating an interstate. "Fox is a great station. Watch it all the time. Don't know another network that's better at taking the pulse of the people— or targets the right audience. It's innovative. Top-notch."

"You said you're a producer?"

"My show's on a cable channel. Small potatoes, I know, compared to Fox." In spite of air conditioning set on max, I noticed beads of perspiration dot Todd's hairline. "Here's the thing, Dick," Todd continued, "I'm ready to move on to greener pastures. I've done my time. Now I'm looking for more of a challenge. I'm hoping to land a job with a network such as yours, something with a larger market share."

"You're talking to the wrong guy, pal. With your background in the world of plants and shrubs, be happy you found your niche."

"No, no, you've got it all wrong," Todd said, making broad hand gestures. "That's just it. I don't know a damn thing about plants, shrubs, or flowers. I'm a techie, pure and simple. That's where my true genius lies. I can't tell a dandelion from a daffodil. Matter of fact, I flunked every science course I ever took."

"I promised the lady a drink." Dick urged Marlene-thanks-to-the-wonder-of-silicone forward. "Nice meeting you, Todd. Good luck in your search."

As the pair moved off, I heard Dick tell his companion, "It's all in the numbers, sweetheart. Unless his ratings are in the stratosphere, a network exec isn't going to give him the time of day."

I fiddled with a handsomely bound book lying on an end table, but my attention was still on Todd. A dark flush crept up from his collar. He clenched a fist and for a moment I thought he might punch something. Then, as I continued to watch, he reined in his temper. Taking a sip of his drink, he turned and scoured the crowd. He rolled his shoulders as though willing himself to relax, then sauntered toward a group I vaguely recognized as part of the CBS entourage.

I nibbled the lone cracker left on my plate. Todd blamed Vaughn for a drop in ratings. Was raw ambition motive to kill? And judging from the taut set of his mouth, Todd had a temper. Food for thought.

Suddenly I was ready to call it a day. As much as I'd like to fool myself into believing I can still dance all night, I can't. I'm not admitting to "elderly" mind you, but my dancing all night days are finished. Done. Over. *Finito*. Nowadays I'm lucky to stay awake late enough to catch the eleven o'clock news. Time had come to round up Polly and head back to the ranch—with one teensy detour along the way. First though, I needed to find our hostess and thank her for an extraordinary day.

I found Polly heading toward the bar. I plucked an

empty margarita glass from her hand and gave it to a passing waiter. "Let's say our thank yous like nice little girls and hit the road."

Polly made a token grumble, but I could see, though she'd never admit it, that she was fading too.

Sheila stood chatting with Betsy and Roger near the window. At close range, I could see the Riverwalk far below, a two-tiered park that runs along the Savannah. It was especially lovely this time of year with bold splashes of color along its pathways. Stay focused, Kate, I chided. This isn't the time to play tourist. I swung my gaze away from the Riverwalk and noticed the top button on Betsy's blouse unfastened—the only hint of her dalliance with a man young enough to be her son. Sheila acknowledged our inclusion into the tight-knit circle with a slight smile and nod.

"Sheila, my love," Roger was saying, "was the course all I bragged it would be?"

Sheila nodded her enthusiastic agreement. "It was truly amazing, Roger. Spectacular. The flowers alone made the trip worthwhile."

"There are thirty varieties of azaleas," Betsy supplied. "Most people aren't aware azaleas were first popularized in Augusta when Baron Berckmans and his son started a venture called Fruitland Nurseries, which later became the Augusta National Golf Course."

"Wow," I said. "I'm truly impressed that you know all this." And I was. Lipstick and night creams, yes. But the history of azaleas? No way, no how.

"Betsy's full of surprises." Sheila laughed. "You'd never guess it, but in college she double majored in chemistry and botany."

"Yeah," Roger agreed sourly. "Under all that fluff, she's a real brainiac."

Hmm. Another interesting tidbit to add to my growing list of interesting tidbits.

# Chapter 19

This was the big day. A red-letter day. The lumber for bookshelves in my soon-to-be library was due to arrive.

Bill arrived promptly as promised: nine o'clock sharp. He looked—to borrow Polly's favorite expression—hot. I'll kick that up a notch. He looked . . . smokin'. A tool belt slung low on his slender hips loaded with a handyman's ammo—hammer, screwdrivers, pliers—made him look like a modern-day Gary Cooper. Add to that a pair of killer Paul Newman baby blues, and it's the stuff hot flashes are made from. Mm, excuse me, I meant power surges.

"Morning, Kate." He gave me that sweet, unassuming smile guaranteed to make my pulse shift into overdrive. "Hope I'm not too early."

Who was he kidding? As if he could ever be *too* early. "No, you're right on time."

He sniffed the air appreciatively. "Mmm. Is that coffee I smell?"

"Starbucks Breakfast Blend." Starbucks wasn't the only thing steaming in my kitchen. I took a mug from the cupboard, filled it, then topped off my own. "Bought the coffee at the mall last night, along with a slew of Belle Beaute products, before Polly and I headed home."

"How was the Masters? Have a good time?"

"The best," I said, taking a seat opposite him at the kitchen table. "I still don't know what possessed Sheila to give me tickets, but as the old saying goes, don't look a gift horse in the mouth." For the life of me, I don't know where some of these clichés come from. They just seem to pop up out of nowhere. Why would anyone look a gift horse in the mouth? And what exactly is a "gift horse" any way? "Too bad you had to take your friend to the airport, or I would have asked you to come with me."

Bill chuckled. "When I heard you had tickets, I almost told him to start hitchhiking."

"Well, one thing I can say for Polly," I said, smiling, "things are never dull with her around."

"Hope she didn't try to tackle one of the pros to bring home with her."

"I'm sure the thought crossed her mind."

Bill glanced out the kitchen window, which had an unobstructed view of my drive. "Did the lumberyard call to say what time to expect delivery?"

"They called for directions about an hour ago, so they should be here soon."

Bill wanted to personally inspect each piece of wood to make sure they were blemish-free. At the price of cherry, he expected every board to be perfect. Afterward, he planned to recheck the room's dimensions. Bill happens to be a perfectionist when it comes to woodworking. I could hardly believe my library/study/den would soon be transformed into an honest-to-goodness library. If I closed my eyes, I could imagine shelves filled with works of favorites such as Nicholas Sparks, Nora Roberts, John Grisham, and Sandra Brown. I'd be the envy of every member of Novel Nuts, Serenity Cove's reigning book club.

Thinking *envy* made Rita pop to the forefront of my mind. There were no two ways about it—Rita envied Sheila. Her looks, her career, her success. Envy is a powerful motivator. It can make ordinary people do extraordinary things. The green-eyed monster had driven people to murder in the past. An awful thought wormed its way into my mind. Had Rita attempted to poison Sheila, not kill her of course, but perhaps give her enough of a substance to make her ill, to embarrass her in public? I immediately dismissed the thought as unworthy of my friend. Rita killed aphids and spiders—not people.

"Have you had breakfast yet?" I jumped up, grabbed the carafe, and topped off our coffee cups. "I can fix eggs."

"Er, no. I had cereal earlier." Bill looked at me strangely. If he thought my behavior erratic, he kept his comments to himself. "I loaded most of the tools I'll need for the job into my pickup. Hope you don't mind me setting up camp in your garage. I'll try not to get underfoot."

Mind? Quite the contrary. I'd been looking forward to his "getting underfoot." "Don't give it another thought," I said, striving for nonchalant. "I'll manage."

We sat in the breakfast nook, sipping our coffee and savoring the companionship. We watched a purple finch land on a branch of a sweet gum in my side yard. "It's nesting time," Bill commented.

Nesting. For some reason, the notion appealed to me. For forty years, Jim, my late husband, and I had shared a very comfortable nest, first in Toledo, then in South Carolina. But when only one bird's left, a nest can be a pretty lonely place. I wondered if Bill has ever felt that way since his wife died. I glanced across the table and caught a fleeting expression cross Bill's face. Had he experienced the same yearning I had? A yearning to cozy up. To nest, to become a couple once again.

Bill cleared his throat, and avoided eye contact. "Do you plan on sticking around this morning, or do you have items on your agenda?"

I groaned at the reminder. "I plan on paying Sheriff Wiggins a social call."

"Need backup?" Bill studied me over the rim of his coffee mug, his expression serious. "I can call a member of the Woodchucks to handle the delivery. Bernie Mason owes me a favor."

The Woodchucks happens to be Serenity's woodworking club where Bill had served several terms as president. I shuddered inwardly at the notion of Bernie Mason being given a task of any importance. The guy was a jerk, an accident waiting to happen. And in my experience, one never had to wait long. "Thanks, Bill, but I can handle the sheriff easier than anyone can 'handle' Bernie."

"You sure?"

"Positive," I said, finishing off my coffee and rising from the table.

"You're one brave lady, Kate." Bill's baby blues twinkled up at me. "Given a choice between visiting the sheriff or a root canal, most folks would choose the root canal."

"Well, you know my feelings about dentists, so I'll go the safer route." I checked my purse for car keys and other necessities. "If I'm not back when you're ready to go, just lock up."

"Most likely I'll still be here. You'll be seeing a lot of me over the next couple weeks."

Bill rose, too, rinsed out his coffee mug, and placed it in the dishwasher. There's something . . . so . . . so . . . irresistible about a man who cleans up after himself.

As I pulled out of the drive, I glanced toward the house a final time and saw Bill unloading a gazillion tools from the bed of his pickup. He was moving in, all right. Like he said, I'd be seeing a lot of him during the ensuing weeks. Those words were music to my ears.

"Sorry, Miz McCall, he's busy."

The first words out of Tammy Lynn's mouth rarely varied. But was I insulted? No, I was immune to words of unwelcome, vaccinated against a cool reception. Instead I plastered on a friendly face. "Now, Tammy Lynn, I thought after our fun evening of bunco, you'd call me Kate like I asked you."

She shot a nervous glance over her shoulder toward the sheriff's office. "Yes, ma'am, you surely did. And I will, swear to God, but just not here, okay?"

"That's quite all right, dear. I understand perfectly." Apparently there was some unwritten rule about not being on a first-name basis with a pesky senior citizens. "Don't mind me. I'll just kill some time reading the Most Wanted posters. I'd hate to ignore any new felon-in-training."

"No, ma'am. You might want to read the one I just posted about a bank robber in Raleigh."

Tammy Lynn turned to the intercom to announce my arrival. I moseyed over to inspect bearded faces pinned to a bulletin board. Certainly a motley crew. Surly, sullen, and shifty-eyed, they might as well have "criminal" tattooed on their foreheads. One glimpse, and I'd speed dial 911. Feigning interest in a man wanted in connection with an armed robbery of a gas station, I shamelessly eavesdropped. Phrases like "what should I tell her?" were punctuated with "you're in a meetin'?" and "plannin' session with mayor?" were bandied about.

Behind me, Tammy Lynn cleared her throat. "Mm, ma'am, sheriff told me to apologize for any inconvenience, but to tell you he's on a conference call. Said it could take hours."

I smiled and patted my handbag. "Tell him I brought my lunch."

"Yes, ma'am."

I returned to my study of fugitives from justice. Seems like aggravated assault was the crime du jour. Grand theft larceny was a close runner up with burglary a distant third. I was happy homicide hadn't made the top three. Wanted posters exhausted, I settled into one of the molded—and uncomfortable—plastic chairs. I deliberately chose a vantage point with a clear shot of the hallway. No way was the wily sheriff was going to duck out a back door. No sirree, not on my watch. I pulled out a novel, a nice, thick, six-hundred-page novel, prepared to play the waiting game.

One hour passed, then two. By now it was close to lunchtime, but I'd come prepared for every contingency. I pulled out a sandwich.

I heard the intercom buzz and Tammy Lynn whisper, "Yes, sir, still here." This was followed by a pause, then, "She's eating a sandwich—tuna, I think. And she brought a thermos."

After finishing my sandwich, I dug into my purse and pulled out a Ziploc bag filled with chocolate chip cookies. "Want one?" I asked, offering them to Tammy Lynn.

"Er, no, thank you . . . well, maybe just one."

"Take two, I have plenty."

Thirty minutes later the intercom buzzed again.

"Sorry, sir. I tried, sir, truly I did, but she's still here." Poor Tammy Lynn. She sounded a tad distraught. Another pause, followed by, "She's readin' a book, sir—a mighty thick one."

I pretended to be deaf and calmly flipped a page.

"Can't see the title exactly, sir." Tammy Lynn craned her head and squinted in my direction. "Nearest I can figure the cover has a skull and crossbones on it. Appears to be somethin' about dead men."

I heard a noise like a rush of wind. A monsoon? But South Carolina doesn't have monsoons. Occasional hurricanes along the coast, but no monsoons. Then I recognized the gust of air for what it was—Sheriff Sumter Wiggins's sigh of surrender.

I hid my smile behind the book. Sheriff should know better than to think I was easily discouraged.

# Chapter 20

Now that the hour had finally arrived, I walked down the hallway with the slow, measured tread of the soon-to-be-executed. The sandwich I'd just eaten threatened to turn into a cement block in the pit of my stomach. My nerves fluttered, but I blamed it on the Starbucks. I gave myself a little pep talk. After I explained the reason for my visit, the sheriff would be grateful. He'd applaud my efforts. He'd wish he knew more people with my dedication to law and order.

Sucking in a deep breath, I pushed open the door emblazoned in large gold letters: SUMTER WIGGINS, BROOKDALE COUNTY SHERIFF. "Good afternoon, Sheriff."

"I trust Tammy Lynn informed you . . ."

"That you're a busy man?" I cut him off in midsentence.

Sheriff Wiggins stared pointedly at his wristwatch. "I have a meetin' . . ."

". . . with the mayor?" I inquired sweetly. Not waiting for an invitation that might not be forthcoming, I plunked myself down in the seat opposite his desk, set my oversized purse on the floor, and folded my hands in my lap. "I trust your conference call came to a satisfactory conclusion."

"Conference call ... ?" His dark brows beetled in a frown, then realization dawned. "Ah, right, conference call. You know how those things are. They can take forever. Now, I'd appreciate it if you would kindly state your business. I have a meetin', I mean an appointment, and don't want to be late."

I swerved out of sarcasm and into businesslike. "I'm here to offer my assistance narrowing our list of suspects in the Vaughn Bascomb/Sheila Rappaport case."

A pained expression crossed his face, making me wonder if he suffered from acid reflux. I debated whether to tell him about some marvelous new drugs on the market. Some available without a prescription. But knowing how the sheriff resisted advice—mine especially—I remained mute on the subject.

I was about to demonstrate the reason for my visit when he suddenly leaned over and peered around the desk. Frowning, he studied me for a long moment, his dark eyes gleaming like onyx, until I squirmed uncomfortably. Was I wearing tuna on my sweater? Did I have a chocolate chip stuck between my central incisors? "Something wrong, Sheriff?" I asked.

"Aren't you forgettin' somethin'?" he drawled.

"Um, I don't think so." I ran through a mental checklist of supplies: tuna sandwich on rye, thermos of coffee, bag of cookies, bottled water, crossword puzzle book, mystery novel. Then it occurred to me with blinding certainty. Breath mints. I'd forgotten breath mints, and now I was polluting the air in his office with halitosis. I pawed frantically through my purse, hoping to find a stick of gum, or piece of hard candy, to remedy the oversight.

His lips twitched in a rare glimmer of amusement at my discomfiture. Rocking back in his chair, he laced his fingers together over a trim waist. "I tend to get suspicious when folks act out of character. Reckon it goes with bein' in the law-enforcement profession."

"Me, acting out of character?" I asked indignantly. "How?"

"Not a single present in sight. No nice green plant to leak all over important documents. No two-months-old 'Words of Wisdom' calendar. No chocolate chip cookies or lemon bars. If I've offended you in some way, ma'am, I'm beggin' your pardon right here and now."

I felt strangely flattered he remembered my gift-giving habit. "Aw, Sheriff," I crooned, "you had me fooled. All this time, I didn't think you cared for my small tokens of esteem."

"I didn't; I don't," he growled, reverting to type. The crabby, surly type, I'd come to associate with him.

"You're mistaken if you think I came empty-handed." Reaching into my giant purse once more, I withdrew my cell phone and, with a small flourish, set it on the desk directly in front of him. I didn't have long to wait for a reaction.

"A cell phone . . . what the blue blazes? You're givin' me a cell phone?" He recoiled back farther in his seat. "I should warn you, Miz McCall, a gift of this nature could be construed as bribin' a public official."

Well, golly gee. Slap me upside the head with a billy club. From the way he was carrying on, you'd think I'd just committed a capital offense. "Well," I replied, nonplussed, "bribing a public official seems a step up the ladder from the usual obstruction of justice charge you're forever threatening me with."

"No call to be flip, Miz McCall. Just figured a friendly warnin' was in order."

He jabbed a kielbasa-sized finger at the cell phone. "S'posin' we get down to business, and you tell me what this heah phone's all about."

"Heah" I've learned since moving south of the Mason-Dixon Line is Southern-speak for the Yankified "here." It takes one's ear a while to become attuned to the lazy vowels and slurred consonants. I'd dearly love to casually drop "y'all" into conversations with my children, but haven't quite mastered the technique without sounding like a bad actor in a third-rate film.

"Stop your woolgatherin', Miz McCall. My time's awastin'."

"Sorry." I scooted up straighter, took a deep breath, and readied myself for battle. "As I mentioned, I'm here to help you solve yet another murder case."

Did color actually leach from his dark skin? I wondered. Or was it a trick of the lighting?

Sumter Wiggins pinched the bridge of his nose. "Exactly what murder would you be referrin' to?"

"Don't play coy, Sheriff. I tried to convince you weeks ago that Dr. Bascomb and Dr. Rappaport were poisoned, but you remained a skeptic. At the time, it must've struck you odd that of all the people present at the banquet, all eating the exact same food, Vaughn and Sheila were the only ones to fall ill?"

He started to open his mouth, but I raised my hand and cut him off. "Now, I don't disagree that Dr. Bascomb's heart problems contributed to his death, but I'm convinced something triggered that irregular heartbeat. If it comes to light that an unsub deliberately put a poisonous substance into their food or drink then it's a crime—plain and simple. Call it what you will—murder, manslaughter, or criminal negligence—but it's a crime of some sort."

"Unsub?" He did his one-eyebrow lift thingy designed to intimidate even the most hardened of criminals. "You been watchin' more of that TV show you like so much— *Murder and Mayhem*?"

"No," I bristled. "I've branched out on my TV viewing. 'Unsub' is a term the FBI profilers use on *Criminal Minds*. It stands for . . ."

Stifling a groan—just barely—he waved aside my explanation. "I know, I know—unsub stands for unknown subject. You're forgettin' I'm the sheriff."

"Actually, the show you're thinking of isn't *Murder and Mayhem*. It's called *Law & Order*." He was being deliberately obtuse, and it irked me. I'd gone to all the trouble of ordering him a DVD of classic *Law & Order* episodes, hoping it would bring him up to speed on how big-city cops operate. He'd probably stuffed it into his sock drawer without ever watching.

"Why can't you be one of those grandmas who stays at home and bakes cookies?"

"I take it that's a rhetorical question?" Not waiting for a reply, I forged ahead. "Sheila—Dr. Rappaport—told me the lab's preliminary findings show no evidence of either E. coli or botulism. Is that right?"

"You tell me. You're lead detective on this investigation."

Lead detective? Wow! I'd been promoted from Nancy Drew wannabe to lead detective. I knew the man was being facetious, but I allowed myself a moment to savor the fantasy. Then back to reality. Rifling through my purse, I extracted my little black book, which coincidentally bore a close resemblance to the sheriff's little black book, and a pen. "What else did the lab rule out?"

He looked pained. "Can I take back the crack about you bein' lead detective? I don't want to be givin' you delusions of grandeur."

"Sorry, too late. Besides, whether you want to admit it or not, we work well together."

He mumbled something under his breath I didn't quite catch, then with obvious reluctance reached over and pulled a file from a stack on his desk and flipped it open. "Lab ruled out most common bacteria and salmonella. No trace of staphylococcus."

I scribbled furiously. I could correct misspelled words later. "What else did toxicology report?"

"Have you gone and taken some mail-order course on how to be a detective in six lessons?"

"Didn't have to," I replied, not looking up. "There's a

new invention. It's called the Internet." I couldn't believe I was actually sassing the sheriff. Then I remembered a phrase Colleen, a former coworker, used to say: Be old and bold. She had other sayings, too, but I have a certain image to uphold. "What else, Sheriff? Remember, time's a-wastin'."

He sighed; he scowled, but eventually he acquiesced. "The lab ran a tox screen for the usual suspects to rule out heroin, cocaine, PCP, meth, and alcohol. None of them turned out positive."

"So what's next?" I asked. "I assume toxicology will test the usual—blood, urine, and stomach contents. And what about slides from Vaughn's liver? According to the Internet, the liver's the organ most heavily involved in drug metabolism."

"I gotta be losin' my edge." He rubbed a hand over his close-cropped hair. "Why am I even havin' this discussion with a civilian?"

"Because, Sheriff"—I leaned forward and picked up my cell phone—"this *civilian* has a head start on compiling a list of murder suspects. In fact, I have their pictures right here."

"Unbelievable," he muttered.

I shoved the phone toward him. "I took these at Vaughn Bascomb's memorial service—and ought to be congratulated on my foresight. It's a known fact in the world of law enforcement that murderers often attend the funerals of their victims. That's why plainclothes detectives usually fill the back pew and are told to keep their eyes peeled. Now, during the age of cell phones, their job has become simplified."

"For the sake of conservin' your time and my energy, who are these *suspects*?"

"I have four so far." I wiggled to the edge of my seat, eager to expound on my theory. "First of all, there's Betsy Dalton. She's vice president of Belle Beaute, the sponsor of *How Does Your Garden Grow*? She intensely

disliked Vaughn, but I don't know why—yet. Next there's
Roger McFarland, editor of Sheila and Vaughn's coffee
table book. Roger claims Vaughn interfered with his
vision of the finished product. And I recently learned
someone—could be either Sheila or Vaughn—beat him
out of a position he thought he deserved."

The sheriff, I was pleased to note, hauled out *his* little black book and was making notes, albeit not happily.

"Then there's Todd Timmons. Todd's producer of *How
Does Your Garden Grow?* He's extremely ambitious. Wants
to move from cable to a major network. He blamed Vaughn
for the show's drop in ratings. I have their pictures right
here on my cell phone."

I was still a novice when it came to taking photos
on my cell so was slow retrieving them. I sensed Sheriff
Wiggins's growing impatience, which made it hard to
concentrate. I hit MENU, then CONTACTS.

Oops! False start. Better try again.

"You said there were four names. Who's the fourth?"

"Kel Watson, the county extension agent. Do you know
him?" I tried the MENU button again, scrolled down, then
selected MESSAGING. Drat! Still no luck. Apparently picture-
taking on the cell phone wasn't as easy as it seemed.

"Yeah, I know Kel. How'd his name get on this list
of yours?"

I felt a bead of sweat trickle down my spine. The
man was making me nervous. "Sheila thinks Kel has it
in for her—professional jealousy or some such. She fainted
dead away at the sight of him when he visited her in
the hospital. And if that's not enough, his appearance
at the reception following Vaughn's memorial service
sparked quite a scene."

"That doesn't make the man a killer," he commented,
his tone mild tone.

"You're the sheriff," I snapped. "Do I have to do *all* the
work?"

I know I took the darn pictures. Why couldn't I find

them? I gnawed my lower lip in frustration and started the process all over again. MENU, scrolled through the options, this time selecting PICTURES and pressing OK. Instant relief flooded through me. I felt vindicated, free to shed the label of imbecile.

But my relief was short-lived. The screen was blank.

I shook the phone angrily, hoping the photos would magically appear. No such luck. The screen remained blank. Disheartened, I slumped back in my seat, staring dejectedly at the electronic gizmo in my hand. "I know I took the pictures," I said in a small voice.

"Don't s'pose you pressed SAVE after you took 'em?"

My head jerked up, and I stared at him in dismay. "No. Was I supposed to?"

# Chapter 21

After yesterday's fiasco at the sheriff's office, my morale needed a boost. Hopefully today's special program with Flowers and Bowers would be just what the doctor ordered to snap me out of my funk. Rita had reminded me yet again that I'd be considered a provisional member until I'd served volunteer hours at the club's ongoing beautification project and attended a minimum of three regularly scheduled meetings. Piece of cake, she'd said, speaking in her official capacity as chairman of the membership committee.

I ran around in a dither, trying to get ready. I had dressed for the day in garden club chic—or how I imagined garden club chic should look. Jeans, denim shirt, starched and ironed to the max, over a snowy white T-shirt with a flower motif. One of those crushable straw hats completed my botanical ensemble. I loaded supplies into a canvas tote bag: sunglasses, sunscreen, water bottle, insect repellent, wallet, checkbook. I bumped into the coffee table as I rounded a corner and swore softly. Why hadn't I gotten everything together the night before like a sane person? As I rubbed my aching shin, it all came back to me. I hadn't done any of this because I'd fallen asleep watching *Law & Order* reruns and woken up to *The Tonight Show*. To add insult to injury, I'd forgotten to set the alarm clock.

I heard a car engine and, glancing out a window, saw Bill pull into my drive. Was he early, or was I running late? Bill, bless his heart, had offered me his truck for the day since the trunk of a Buick can't compete with the bed of a pickup when it comes to hauling plants and shrubs. If need be, Bill could always use my car. Rita and I were to meet the rest of the group in the parking lot of Brookdale United Methodist Church.

I raced to the door. "Hi," I said, sounding slightly out of breath.

"Hi, yourself." He gave me that gentle smile I found so endearing. "You're looking cute as a button in that getup."

I felt my cheeks get warm. *Aw shucks*, I wanted to stammer, *t'weren't nothin'*. "C'mon in," I managed to choke out.

"Ready for your big adventure?"

"Getting there. I have a nagging feeling I'm forgetting something." Darn those senior moments that plague the golden years. "Help yourself to the coffee. It's still fresh."

"Hope you're not worrying about driving my truck," he said as he headed for the kitchen and the coffeepot. "It's an automatic so shouldn't be any different than driving your car. Plus, you'll have room for plenty of plants."

I snapped my fingers. "Notebook!" The elusive object popped back into my mind. I was about to embark on a crash course in horticulture. I intended to ask tons of questions and take copious notes. But to do this, I needed pencil and paper. "Be right back," I called out as I hustled off to locate said items.

No sooner had I returned to the kitchen than the phone rang. I accepted a mug of coffee from Bill and picked up the receiver, expecting to hear Rita on the other end of the line. "I'm ready if you are."

"Ready? Ready for what?"

It took a split second to switch gears and realize the voice belonged not to Rita, but to my son, Steven. "Hi, sweetie. Everything okay?"

"Hi, Mom. Things couldn't be better on my end."

"Steven," I mouthed to Bill, lest he think I had another "sweetie" waiting in the wings.

"I got into the office early," Steven went on, "so thought I'd give you a call while the place was still quiet."

"It's always wonderful to hear your voice, but I've only got a few minutes." Usually, this line was reversed and Steven the one with only minutes to talk. Though based in New York City—Manhattan, where else?—Steven was constantly on the go to places with exotic names like Zimbabwe or Kuala Lumpur. Forever in the search for gadgets and do-gee-bobs for a fancy housewares chain. You'd recognize the name instantly, but it's not my nature to brag.

"Where are you off to this early?" Steven asked. "Your martial arts class?"

"Right, dear. I'm working on my black belt."

Bill just looked at me and shook his head.

"Black belt?" Steven repeated.

Hmph . . . as if there even was such a thing in tai chi. Serves Steven right for never paying attention when I'm talking to him. It would do the boy good to think his mother was learning to kick butt. Give him a reason to scratch his head and wonder.

"You're getting up there in age, Mom. Careful you don't hurt yourself, or you could wind up in one of those assisted living places yet."

I huffed out a breath. Recently Steven had put my name on the mailing list for every assisted living facility on the East Coast. When my recycle bin got too heavy to lift, I finally had to put my foot down. My children can't seem to get it through their heads that I'm not ready for a rocking chair and the weather channel.

"Friends refer to me as Kung Fu Kate." I was on a roll and couldn't seem to stop. "Bill prefers to call me Karate Kate."

Bill's brows shot up at hearing this, and he laughed out loud.

"Mom." Steven's tone sharpened. "Is someone with you? A man?"

"Just Bill, dear."

A lengthy silence ensued. A silence some novelists describe as a pregnant pause.

"You've heard me mention Bill before," I finally said, taking a sip of coffee in the hope the caffeine would jump-start my brain.

"Do you realize what time it is?"

I glanced at the kitchen clock. I was about to answer his question when I caught myself. Steven had just adopted the same aggrieved tone I used when he was a teenager who'd broken his curfew. I'd come full circle—and didn't like it. "No need for that tone of voice, young man," I scolded. "Remember who you're talking to."

"Mother, please tell me you're not sleeping with the man."

The switch from "Mom" to "Mother" was duly noted. Clearly not a promotion, judging from the coolness in his voice. For a moment, I was tempted to lead him on. Let him think I'm a Social Security Salome. But I caught myself in the nick of time. If I wasn't careful, he'd be down here in a flash. Serenity Cove Estates would top his list of exotic locales.

"What's that . . . Bill . . . person doing at your house this early in the morning?" he asked, his voice redolent with accusation.

As much as I wanted to let his imagination run rampant, I felt a motherly obligation to set the record straight. "I'm going on an excursion with the garden club this morning. Bill was kind enough to loan me his Ford pickup for the day."

"Oh . . ." I heard Steven exhale from an office high above Madison Avenue. "Since that's the case, let me get to the real reason for my call. I spoke with Jen last night. She's worried about you."

"Whatever for, dear? I'm perfectly fine." I cast a quick peek at the clock. I wouldn't be fine, if I didn't hurry. It won't do to keep the garden club members waiting on my very first event.

"Jen said there was a food poisoning epidemic where you live."

"No need to worry, sweetie. Sheriff Wiggins ruled out food poisoning." I absently skimmed the checklist I'd left on the kitchen counter. "We're treating this as a murder and attempted homicide. We're still waiting, however, for toxicology results from SLED to confirm COD."

"SLED? COD? What the hell does that mean?" Steven shouted. "Have you joined a cult? Are you speaking in tongues?"

I wanted to give myself a good swift kick. A sinking sensation in the pit of my stomach told me I'd blabbed too much. If I were any judge of character, Steven would be on the phone with Jen before the sun rose over the Santa Monica Mountains.

Time to beat a dignified retreat. "Wish I had more time to talk, dear, but gotta run."

I turned to Bill after disconnecting. "That went well, don't you think?"

Bill simply shrugged his shoulders and smiled. A Renaissance man if there ever was one.

"Ladies, I'm the bearer of both good news and bad news."

The announcement made by a man who introduced himself as Just-Call-Me-Thomas was met by eighteen groans. My groan would have made nineteen, but since

I was new to the group, I kept my comments—and my groans—to myself. We were clumped around the entrance to Dixie Gardens Nursery in North Augusta, South Carolina. Now this might sound weird when most know Augusta is in the state of Georgia. The city of North Augusta, however, resides along the opposite bank of the Savannah River in South Carolina. Got that? *North* Augusta is in *South* Carolina?

Dixie Gardens Nursery was housed in a story-and-a half building constructed of weathered gray siding that boasted a cute little cupola atop its red metal roof. Trim around doors and windows was painted a spanking bright white. Plants were everywhere, giving it a look of—what else?—a garden. Baskets of ferns hung from porch rafters. Planters spaced at frequent intervals overflowed with flowers, red, purple, pink, and white, and trailing vines. Someday, I vowed, I'd know all the names of these pretty blooms. But that was a little too much to expect on my first day as a *provisional* garden club member.

"Johnny Wade Barrow couldn't be with us today," Just-call-me-Thomas continued. "His wife's cousin twice removed passed unexpectedly. That's the bad news, ladies. Now for the good." Just-call-me-Thomas rubbed callused hands together in anticipation, clearly enjoying his time in the limelight. "I'm sure you'll be pleased to learn that Brookdale's very own county extension agent, Mr. Kelvin Watson, has agreed to give you a guided tour of our wonderful facility."

I noticed a lot of smiles, a lot of head bobbing, and murmurs of approval from the Flowers and Bowers bunch. With Kel as tour guide du jour, the day promised to become even more interesting.

"Kel and Johnny Wade's friendship dates back to when the Dixie Gardens was first established. I'm sure Kel will be able to answer any questions y'all might have," Just-call-me-Thomas said, completing the introduction.

As if on cue, Kel stepped out and was met with a

round of enthusiastic applause. He, too, had dressed for the occasion in gardening casual, which for him consisted of pressed denims and a plaid work shirt. His sharp, angular features were partially hidden by the brim of a woven hat. Each time he turned his head, I glimpsed the neat gray ponytail trailing between his shoulder blades.

Kel stuffed his hands into his jean pockets and rocked back on his heels. "Actually, ladies, Johnny Wade Barrow and I go back even further than Dixie Gardens. We knew each other as kids growing up in Ninety Six. The gang used to call him 'Wheel Barrow.'"

Ninety Six isn't a number, mind you, but a name of a town located east of Due West. Jim, my late husband, and I used to chuckle at some of the quirky names of small towns. Towns with names such as Ninety Six, Due West, Caesar's Head, and Travelers Rest. My friend Joyce recently mentioned there's actually a North, South Carolina. Sure enough. I looked it up on a map and found out it's not even in the northern part of South Carolina, but south toward Charleston. For trivia fans, I'll have you know North happens to be the birthplace of entertainer Eartha Kitt. But once again, I digress.

". . . about to have a behind-the-scenes tour of one of the finest wholesale nurseries in the entire state of South Carolina," Kel rambled. "And let me tell you, ladies, that's no mean feat. Afterward you'll have the opportunity to purchase plants not yet available in retail stores. Now, if you'll kindly follow me."

I kept close to Rita as we trailed Kel down a brick walkway. While the garden club members were friendly, they weren't overtly so. Could they sense my deplorable lack of a green thumb? "I'm thinking of relandscaping my yard," I announced to anyone within distance.

Rita rolled her eyes. "Kate, I swear, you could kill an artificial plant."

"Landscaping can be quite a project," said a prune-faced woman on my right.

"Maybe you should hire someone with experience," advised a Clairol blond by the name of JoAnn.

"How hard can it be? Dig a hole, pop in a plant, then sit back and watch it grow."

My statement set off a flurry of body parts. Eyes rolled; tongues clucked; heads wagged. I felt the sharp sting of censure. Apparently, I'd committed a faux pas. Was there more to gardening than I thought? To cover my embarrassment, I bent down and examined a plant that looked vaguely familiar.

"Ah, I see someone admiring our gardenias." Kel paused and shifted into lecture mode. "To my mind, no plant expresses the grace of the South better than the gardenia. Nothing can compare with their exotic fragrance. Gardenias were originally imported from China and are sometimes called Cape Jasmine. As you can see, the plant's snowy white blooms create a nice contrast against its glossy, dark green leaves. Remember, ladies, gardenias need good drainage and acid soil containing organic matter."

Acid soil and drainage, right. I pulled out my notebook and jotted this down.

"Since gardenias thrive in heat and high humidity, they're an excellent choice for this climate," Kel told the group.

"I have a question," I said, raising my hand. "Are they poisonous?"

"No, ma'am," Kel answered politely. I could see from his expression that he recognized me. "Let's move on, shall we?"

The group shuffled along, stopping here and there to check out a certain bush or shrub. Rita seemed to have forgotten my presence—or maybe her forgetting was accidentally on purpose.

Kel stopped in front of a display of lush purple-blue flowers. I was pleased as punch I recognized them by name—hydrangeas. The same plants I'd purchased from Lowe's. "Hydrangeas work well as single plants, massed, or in tubs on the patio," he explained. "Their color is affected by the pH of the soil. Bluest shades are produced in strongly acid soil. Pink or red in neutral to alkaline soil."

I actually knew this from my previous conversation with Kel. All right, on a written quiz I might've gotten my acid and alkaline reversed, but I knew color varied with soil. Most of the women nodded as if they'd been born with this knowledge embedded in their infantile brains. None of them looked like they'd be caught dead not knowing such a basic. Well, I wasn't too proud to ask questions so I raised my hand and felt Rita's elbow in my ribs. "Honestly, Kate," she hissed, "this isn't grade school."

"Fine," I muttered under my breath. Then instead of my hand, I raised my voice and called out, "Excuse me, Mr. Watson, er, Kel . . ."

He had been about to proceed farther into the nursery, but stopped and turned. "Yes . . . ?"

"Isn't it true that hydrangeas are poisonous?" I already knew the answer, but asked anyway. People should be aware of this. If the Freedom of Information Act didn't apply to plant life, maybe it should.

"They contain low levels of cyanide," he answered hesitantly.

"Mmm . . ." *Arsenic and Old Lace?* Or to paraphrase, Cyanide and Old Lace?

Rita glanced around as the group moved forward, then lowered her voice. "What is this obsession of yours with poison? You're starting to make everyone nervous."

"I have an inquiring mind." I shrugged off her concern; I was on a mission.

Kel paused, pointing at a collection of greenery. "Here, ladies, we have a fine selection of oleander."

*Oleander...?*

"I love oleander," gushed Judy, a long tall blond I'd seen at tai chi. "They make a great windbreak."

"I have one of every color in my yard—white, pink, red, and yellow," another added.

"I always caution folks not to burn oleander prunings," Kel lectured. "The smoke can cause severe irritation in the lungs. That aside, oleander makes a superb landscape plant. Few plants are as adaptable. They can tolerate salt spray, sandy soil, and drought."

"Is it—" I started to say.

"Yes, ma'am," Kel interrupted. "Oleander, as most folks know, is highly toxic, so I'd advise you not to take a bite."

The Flowers and Bowers ladies enjoyed a hearty laugh at my expense.

I scraped together some of my tattered dignity. "I was about to ask if they were deer resistant."

"Yes, ma'am, they are. Deer are sometimes smarter than we give 'em credit for. Now, if y'all continue the tour ..."

We wandered down row after row of colorful plants so pretty I wanted to buy them all. Maybe I didn't yearn for a garden as much as I yearned for a full-blown nursery alive with vibrant color—complete with a gardener to maintain it.

"Oh, isn't this lovely!" a woman exclaimed.

All of us stopped to pay homage to a plant with pendulous, trumpet-shaped flowers the color of a ripe peach.

"Angel's trumpet," Rita said for the benefit of the unanointed—namely me.

"Also known as brugmansia," the prune-faced woman chimed, a little too obvious for my taste, in her attempt to be teacher's pet.

"That's correct." Kel beamed his approval. "Only yesterday Johnny Wade brought this beauty out of his hothouse to impress y'all. A relative of the jimsonweed, angel's trumpet is native to subtropical regions of South America. Here in the lower South, you gals have to remember it needs to be heavily mulched in late fall."

Nonplussed, I gave Kel a sunny smile. "Is angel's trumpet . . . ?"

". . . deadly," he supplied. The woven brim of his hat kept Kel's expression shrouded. But his eyes glittered with something dark—and vaguely menacing. "'Everything is poison; there is poison in everything. Only the dose makes a thing not a poison.' That's not from me, mind you, but Paracelsus, a medieval Swiss alchemist and physician. Let's proceed to the shady side, ladies. Dixie Gardens offers a huge variety of hostas and hardy ferns awaiting your inspection."

I trailed behind, pondering his words. I may not have answers to a lot of my questions, but I did know that if someone wanted to poison another, they'd have to look no farther than their own backyard. How convenient. How frightening. And who better to know which plant to choose than one schooled in the science of horticulture or botany?

My goal today had been to learn more about plants of the poisonous variety. Mission accomplished.

# Chapter 22

Party, party, party.

Masters Week was always party central, but the impromptu varieties were invariably the most fun. Now that the tournament was winding down, Sheila had decided to throw a cocktail party. She insisted I invite a guest. Naturally I phoned Bill. She'd also requested the numbers of some of the Babes. I wished she'd invite all of them, but it was Sheila's party, not mine. She'd called the night before, right after I'd unloaded all the plants I'd bought at Dixie Gardens. And, boy, my Visa card had taken a beating. As tempted as I was, I didn't buy one of everything I'd seen, but I'd taken a good run at it. By the time I finished, my yard was destined to be Garden of the Month with a shiny brass plaque to prove it. I'll have my picture in the *Serenity Sentinel*.

Bill and I arrived promptly at eight. Already cars jammed the drive and lined both sides of the street. Our arrival coincided with that of Claudia and the Babes' all-time-favorite attorney, Badgely Jack Davenport, IV. Better known as "Bad Jack" to his adversaries and "BJ" to his friends. We numbered among the latter. BJ had rescued Claudia from a dicey situation a few months back. But with all the hoopla behind her, she was her old self again. I'm also happy to report that she had donated her flashy—rhymes with trashy—wardrobe to a local thrift store. She's back to wearing the classier style I associated with her. This time a sage-green number that looked terrific with her strawberry-blond hair. As they approached, I couldn't help but notice the couple were holding hands. When had that started? I wondered.

"Kate, darlin'." BJ, spiffy in his signature bow tie, enveloped me with a bear hug. "What's my favorite lady detective been up to these days? Stayin' out of trouble, I hope."

I hugged him back. "I'm trying, BJ, but it isn't nearly as much fun as getting into trouble."

Bill cleared his throat, then stuck out his hand. "Nice to see you again, Davenport."

BJ's hand enveloped Bill's in a hearty handshake. "What's with the Davenport? Much, much too formal for a party. Call me BJ as do these two lovelies. Ladies, we don't want to keep our hostess—or bartender—waiting." Placing an arm around both Claudia's and my shoulders, he guided us up the walk, leaving Bill to bring up the rear.

We entered the foyer and ran smack dab into a wall of sound. The house was filled with people, everyone chattering and laughing and having a gay old time. Spotting us, Sheila separated herself from a circle of guests and walked over to greet us. She looked smashing in a simple but elegant black cocktail dress, her hair and makeup flawless as usual. "I'm so happy you were able to come, considering it was last minute."

"Wouldn't have missed it for the world." We exchanged perfunctory air kisses like I'd seen celebrities do on TV, making me feel sophisticated and worldly.

Claudia and I introduced Bill and BJ; then Sheila pointed us in the direction of the library. "The bar is in there," she said. "I hired this marvelous caterer to supply the hors d'oeuvres. Feel free to circulate and enjoy yourselves."

Claudia and I inventoried the crowd while Bill and BJ left to get drinks. "Where do you suppose all these people are from?" Claudia asked. "Surely not Brookdale or Serenity Cove, seeing as how I don't recognize most of them."

No sooner were the words out of her mouth than reinforcements arrived in the form of Connie Sue and her husband, Thacker. Thacker Benton Brody to be precise. Sounds like a law firm, doesn't it? The Babes and I secretly refer to him as St. Thacker of Macon. "Hey, y'all," Connie Sue hailed us with a bright smile.

"Hey, Connie Sue. Hey, Thacker," we hailed back.

"My, my, don't you ladies look fine." Thacker gave Claudia and me each a peck on the cheek, then surveyed the crowd. "An affair like this must have cost Dr. Sheila a pretty penny."

Typical Thacker-like comment. He was a bottom line kind of guy. He'd left a cushy job in Atlanta to become chief financial officer of some hotshot company in Milwaukee. Don't get me wrong, I like Thacker well enough in spite of his smarmy charm. It's just that I hate the way Connie Sue caters to his every whim. She once confessed, after two glasses of wine at bunco, that if pot roast wasn't on the dinner table every Monday, Thacker'd pitch a fit. Her words, not mine.

Claudia did a who's who of Sheila's guest list. "I don't see Rita anywhere," she announced.

I glanced around. Rita's tall, buxom figure was usually easy to spot even in a crowd this size. "Surely she was invited."

"Maybe she and Dave had other plans." Connie Sue fluffed her blond locks. "After all, this was last minute."

"Maybe," I echoed, but wasn't convinced that was the reason for Rita's absence. I had the sinking feeling she hadn't been invited. And that the lack of an invi-

tation had been a slight, not an oversight. Rita made
no bones that she wasn't fond of Sheila. Sheila wasn't
president of the Rita Larsen fan club either. Then another thought hit me like a kick to the solar plexus. What
if Rita had been invited—and elected not to come.

Might she have a guilty conscience?

"Say," Thacker said, rocking back on his polished
loafers, "isn't that guy over there an announcer on one
of those cable sports shows?"

Connie Sue, Claudia, and I turned to give the guy in
question the once-over. Not that we'd recognize a sports
announcer if we tripped over one. Ask about the Food
Network or HGTV and it would be a whole different
story. I did recognize Todd Timmons though alongside
the man, his head bobbing like a hula doll on a dashboard.

"Oh, my God!" Connie Sue slapped a French-manicured
hand to her chest.

We stared at her in consternation. Time to dial 911?
Was my buddy, my friend, the grandmother of adorable
twins, having palpitations?

"Y'all, I'm not believin' what I'm seein'."

"Darlin' you're not makin' a lick of sense," Thacker
reprimanded gently. "Who—or what—are you talkin'
about?"

"It's Mary Jo Peterson. I met her years ago in Atlanta where we both worked as reps for different cosmetics firms. We occasionally ran into each other when
we called on mutual clients. Got to be friends of sorts.
We'd get together now and again to exchange industry
gossip over lunch." She gave Thacker's chest a wifely
pat. "Just girl talk, darlin', we weren't tattlin' company
secrets. The usual—who's sleepin' with whom, who's preg-
gers, who's gettin' divorced, those kinds of things."

"Well, then, you ought to go over and say hello," I
suggested. "Find out what she's been up to all this time."

"You're absolutely right, sugar. I'll do just that." With
a jaunty wave, Connie Sue disappeared into the throng.

"If you'll pardon me, ladies, I'm off to find the bar," Thacker said as he sauntered off in search of libation, which in his case usually took the form of scotch.

Bill and BJ returned moments later, drinks in hand.

"Chardonnay, my dear." BJ presented a stemmed glass to Claudia with a flirtatious wink that was duly noted by yours truly. "Bourbon and branch for me. Life is good."

"I hope this is all right," Bill said, holding out a wineglass.

"Perfect." Bill wasn't much of a drinker, I knew, and I suspected his highball glass held nothing stronger than ginger ale. I wasn't much of a drinker either, but I admit I sometimes enjoy a glass of wine. Or a margarita. Or a cosmo. Looping my arm through Bill's, I asked, "Shall we mingle?"

Leaving Claudia and BJ to their own devices, I steered our mingling toward Todd Timmons and his companion.

"Do you ever get the urge to break out of cable, hit the majors, CBS or NBC?" I heard Todd ask. Yep, the man was a sports announcer all right, and Todd was schmoozing.

"I don't have any complaints." The man shrugged, sipped his drink. "Cable's been good to me. Meet a lot of interesting people. Get to spend most of my time outdoors instead of cooped up in some stuffy studio."

Todd aped his mannerisms, sipping with studied casualness. "Not me. I'd walk away in a heartbeat if I got the right offer."

"To get the right offer, you gotta have the right ratings. It's all about the numbers, my friend. All about the numbers," he repeated. He looked at his empty glass and grinned. "Guess I need a refill. See you around."

Todd's eyes followed the man as he vanished into the crush of people. With Bill in tow, I quickly blocked Todd's path before he had a chance to move off. "Todd, isn't it?" I said, giving him a wide smile. "Nice to see

a familiar face in this mob. I was just telling my friend
Bill that you were an important TV producer. Bill's never
met anyone in television before, much less an actual producer." The ol' reel-'em-in-with-flattery technique works
like a charm most every time.

Todd summoned a weak smile and offered his hand.
"Nice to meet you."

"Bill's an engineer," I volunteered. "That is, he was
before he retired."

"That right?" Todd asked, his tone bored.

"A chemical engineer actually. Bill worked for one
of those big cereal companies in Battle Creek. That's
in Michigan, you know." Honestly, from the way I was
carrying on, you'd think I was Mattel's model for their
Chatty Cathy doll.

"Hmm." Todd's eyes swept the room for someone,
anyone, who might further his career. Someone more
powerful than a retired chemical engineer from Cereal
City. I'd seen that same cunning expression during Belle
Beaute's reception at the Marriott. A very ambitious
young man, Todd Timmons.

I proceeded to squeeze more grease on the flattery
wheel. "Bill, did you know Todd's program, *How Does
Your Garden Grow?* is the gardening equivalent of *Paula's
Home Cooking?*"

Bill, the dear, sweet man, rose to the occasion, trying
valiantly to keep the leaky conversation balloon afloat.
"That's quite an accomplishment. Your show must be
seen by millions of viewers."

"Don't I wish," he said glumly, then shrugged. "Now
that Bascomb's out of the picture maybe ratings will pick
up. The man had no presence on TV, none at all. Might
as well have been taping a statue." He held out his
empty glass and shook it, making the ice cubes rattle.
"Excuse me, folks, but I'm in need of further refresh-
ment."

"What's your impression of the guy?" I asked Bill

as Todd vanished into the crowd. Out of the corner of my eye, I spotted Claudia and BJ off in a corner ... canoodling, for want of a better word. My inner radar—sometimes referred to as women's intuition—went on red alert. There was definitely something going on between the pair.

Bill stared in the direction Todd had taken. "Timmons strikes me as a young man who'll go to any length to get ahead."

"Even murder ... ?"

The question still hung between us, unanswered, when Connie Sue hurried over with Claudia and BJ not far behind. "Wait till y'all hear what I just discovered." Connie Sue's words tumbled over themselves in haste.

We closed ranks around her, eager to learn what had put the sparkle in her eyes. I ruled out wine because we hadn't been here long enough. Even Bill stepped in closer, not wanting to miss a juicy morsel.

"All right, girlfriend, dish!" I ordered, not the most patient person on the planet.

"Well, y'all," Connie Sue drawled in that lazy Scarlett O'Hara way of hers, "Mary Jo and I got to rehashin' old times. When you haven't seen someone in an age, there's a heap of catchin' up to do. You know how it is."

"Connie Sue!" Claudia sounded exasperated. "Get to the point before my toes start cramping in these high heels."

Connie Sue smiled, a cat-with-a-canary type smile. "Mary Jo told me that Betsy Dalton was once engaged. Had her weddin' dress and everythin'—then got dumped."

Hmm ... Interesting, but hardly world-shattering. "I feel sorry for Betsy, of course, but she's not the first woman to get dumped. Why the big deal?"

"Because, sugar"—Connie Sue paused for effect, clearly reveling in her role as drama diva—"the 'dumper' in this case happens to be none other than Vaughn Bascomb."

"Betsy . . . engaged to Vaughn?"

Connie Sue nodded vigorously. "And that's not all."

Our little knot of people tightened.

Connie Sue dropped her voice. "The woman he dropped her for was none other than our hostess with the mostess—the esteemed Dr. Sheila Rappaport."

"That makes for an awkward situation," BJ said at last.

And that, my friends, as they'd say in the movie industry, is a wrap.

Or so I thought. But Connie Sue wasn't finished yet. "Here's somethin' else for y'all to chew on. Mary Jo said Betsy isn't the sort to forgive and forget. She's part Sicilian—and that part's out for revenge."

*Revenge?*

Bill and I exchanged glances. From the wink he gave me, I could tell we were reading the same page. Bill, I'll have you know, is the star pupil at the Kate McCall Motive-Means-Opportunity School of Detectivology.

I knew what I had to do. Digging my cell phone out of my purse, I started snapping pictures of "persons of interest."

And this time I pressed SAVE.

# Chapter 23

If I wanted to murder a person, how would I go about it?

I'd tried to sleep, but finally gave up and crawled out of bed. Every muscle in my body screamed in protest. Yesterday, I'd dug holes, planted the plants I purchased both at Lowe's and Dixie Gardens, and fertilized until I was ready to drop. Now I was paying the price. Bill had offered his help, but Sunday was his day to work as a ranger on the golf course. He told me to wait. But did I listen? No, I was too eager for those babies to sink their little tentacles—"roots" in garden jargon—deep into the red South Carolina clay. I hobbled into the great room and sank into a corner of the sofa. Moonlight spilled into the room, making it glow milky-white. Outdoors, tree frogs serenaded. I was content to sit in the semi-dark and think even darker thoughts.

How would I kill someone?

I tried to put myself in a murderer's shoes. Would I choose a gun? No, a gun was too noisy. A knife? Too messy. Strangulation? No, watching someone's eyes bulge out wasn't my cup of tea.

That left . . . poison.

Poison was an entirely different animal. A pill or two

sprinkled in the oatmeal. A drop of this or that in the tomato soup. *Voilà*, the victim keeled over. Nice and tidy. No noise, no mess, no bulging eyeballs. The perp could be miles away when his victim keeled over. Yes, poison would top my list.

If Sheila's hypothesis was correct, whoever tried to kill her and Vaughn would try again. In the meantime, the sheriff dilly-dallied, waiting for an incriminating report generated by a faceless, nameless technician in Columbia. The man needed my help; he just didn't know it yet. It was time to become proactive.

From my brief journey into horticulture, I'd learned weapons of destruction could be found in almost every home, yard, and garden. Veritable arsenals stockpiled in the form of toxic plants and shrubs. Oleander, hydrangeas, angel's trumpet, and even the ubiquitous azaleas were suspect. And who knew toxic plants better than persons schooled in botany or horticulture? I was inundated with a veritable garden of suspects. Roger, Todd, and Betsy were odds-on favorites. Kel Watson also ranked high on my list. Even Rita wasn't exempt from suspicion—even though in my humble estimation she wouldn't harm a fly. Though Rita might not have Sheila's credentials, she was my go-to person for all things green and growing. She stored a wealth of knowledge inside that head of hers and wasn't overly fond of her former roommate. Jealousy was a proven motive for murder and mayhem throughout the ages. Not that I suspected Rita. I've said it before, I'll say it again, my friends don't kill people.

Eventually I dozed, but woke at daybreak feeling energized. I knew exactly what I had to do to get this show on the road. By the time Bill arrived to continue work on my bookshelves I was showered and dressed for the day. I'd even baked blueberry muffins to go along with our morning coffee.

"I've got a couple errands to run in town," I said as I headed out the door fueled by caffeine and sugar. I'm not sure if Bill heard me leave over the buzz of the drill.

Twenty minutes later I slid the Buick into a parking space in front of the sheriff's office. Popping the trunk, I picked up Exhibit A and Exhibit B. Staggering under the weight of a three-gallon container in each arm, I nudged open the door with my hip.

Tammy Lynn jumped up and came around her desk. "Here, ma'am. Let me help."

"Thanks, Tammy Lynn," I said, handing her one that had started to slip.

"Miz McCall . . . Kate? Is that you behind all these leaves and stuff?"

"This place is much too drab. I thought it could use some brightening up." I knew this would get a rise out of her, and it did.

"Oh, ma'am, Sheriff Wiggins likes it nice and drab," she protested. "I heard him say many a time, 'No sense wastin' tax payers' dollars prettyin' up a place for a pack of no-accounts who can't manage to stay out of trouble."

I chuckled at hearing this. "Don't worry, dear, these beauties aren't decoration. I have a more utilitarian purpose in mind for them."

"Glad to hear that, ma'am. I remember the sheriff bein' none too pleased when you brought him that ivy some months back."

The ivy, I recalled, had been a disaster of the worst kind. It was meant as a simple friendly gesture. A small token of appreciation to a host or hostess, a custom ingrained in me since childhood. The ivy looked innocent enough. Until it sprang a leak that swiftly turned into a river, running all over a stack of summonses, subpoenas, and what-have-yous.

I deposited the pot I carried next to the one Tammy Lynn had placed on the floor near her desk and brushed dirt from my hands. "Would you kindly inform Sheriff Wiggins I'd like to speak with him?"

Tammy Lynn, her expression doubtful, looked from me to the tubs of plants. "Ah, ma'am, I, er . . ."

I exhaled a sigh. "Please, Tammy Lynn, just tell him I'm here. And," I added, "don't think for a minute I'm going to fall for one his lame excuses."

"Yes, ma'am."

I settled into my usual spot, prepared to wait it out, while Tammy Lynn relayed my message. Luckily, I'd had the foresight to drop by Books on Main, Friends of the Library's used book store, and picked up a couple paperbacks to help while away the time. One of the books was devoted to gardening tips in the South. I leafed through the yellowed pages hoping to identify even more plants with homicidal tendencies. I peeked up from my reading to find Tammy Lynn calmly sorting reports. I wondered how the girl could keep her calm working day in, day out, for a grouchy ol' sheriff. Maybe she was on antidepressants. Or a saint?

Tammy Lynn checked a wall clock, then turned to me. "Sheriff Wiggins said to have you wait ten minutes until he finished a call, then send you on back."

I tucked my book away, then hefted a plant in each arm. Crooking my head to the right, I managed to peek between the branches—barely.

"Sheriff Wiggins asked that . . ."

"I know, I know," I said as I marched down the hallway. "He's a busy man."

Tammy Lynn scuttled ahead of me and pushed open the office door. Taking one of the plants from me, she set it on the corner of his desk, then beat a hasty retreat.

"What the blazes . . . !"

"Morning, Sheriff." I placed the remaining plant on the opposite desk corner so I'd have only a partially obstructed view of my favorite lawman.

"Miz McCall, I don't know what you're up to, but I don't have time—or the patience—for a social call."

I took a seat, crossed my legs, and smiled grimly. "This isn't a social call. It's business—strictly business."

The way he glowered at the plants, I expected them to wither right before my very eyes. Amazingly, they continued to bloom. "It isn't Christmas, and it isn't my birthday. Can we call a moratorium on the gift-givin'?"

"Time's a-wasting, Sheriff," I said, borrowing a phrase from his dictionary. "I thought you might like a head start on solving a murder case." I sensed a scowl hiding behind a hydrangea.

"Kindly state your business, Miz McCall, so I can be about mine."

So this is the way he wanted to play it. No idle chatter about the weather, or the outcome of the Masters. No "how about those Braves?" Fine and dandy. Two could play this game. When it came to crime solving I could be a professional, too. "Have you heard anything further about Vaughn Bascomb's death?"

He gave me a look, part aggravation, part resignation. "The coroner and deputy coroner both agree that he died from an undisclosed cardiac event."

"What about Sheila? She nearly died, too."

"Ever think you're readin' way too much into all this? Could be coincidence, plain and simple."

But to my mind there was nothing plain or simple about it. Right or wrong, Sheila was convinced someone deliberately tried to kill her—and might try again. And Vaughn's ashes were resting in a fancy urn.

"Are further tests being conducted to rule out contributing causes? Causes that might have precipitated a cardiac condition?"

His swivel chair groaned in protest as he pressed his linebacker sized body against it. "No cause for worry on that home front. The lab's very thorough. All routine tests are bein' done."

I sat up straighter. "That's exactly what bothers me. 'Routine' might not be the right way to proceed."

He heaved a sigh that started in the soles of his feet and worked its way upward. "What are you gettin' at?"

"Has SLED been called in?" I asked. Once upon a time—when I'd been innocent in the way of homicide investigations—I'd naively assumed SLED was a conveyance on runners. I've come a long way, baby. I now knew that SLED is an acronym for South Carolina Law Enforcement Division. Some folks speak Spanish, some French, but not me. I'm fluent in acronyms.

"No need to call SLED at this time. The investigation is still in the preliminary stage." He pinched the bridge of his nose between thumb and forefinger and changed the subject. "S'pose you tell me why you dragged these plants in heah."

I made a sweeping gesture to encompass his desk. "I'd like you to send samples of these to toxicology. The one on the right is oleander, one of the most poisonous plants in the world. Did you know only a small amount can prove lethal?"

"Miz McCall, you might not be aware of this, you bein' new to these parts and all, but most every home in the South has an oleander or two growin' in their backyard. Don't see folks fallin' over dead because of it, either. Far as I can tell, everyone's hale and hearty."

"Precisely!" I beamed at him like a proud teacher at her prized pupil. "Oleander is everywhere. If a person wanted someone dead, they wouldn't have to look farther than their yard."

"So you want the lab to check for evidence of oleander?" he asked, deadpan.

My smile broadened. "While they're at it, they might want to look for traces of cyanide."

"Cyanide?"

"Yes, cyanide." I gave the hydrangea a gentle nudge in his direction. "Hydrangeas are also a staple in Southern gardens. I have it from a reliable source that hydrangeas contain low levels of cyanide."

He nudged the plant back my way. "Some reason you can't stick with the old standbys of arsenic or strychnine?"

"Think about it, Sheriff. Both victims, Sheila Rappaport and Vaughn Bascomb, were botanists. They became ill after attending a banquet hosted by the garden club where many of the guests were either master gardeners or, at the very least, experienced gardeners. So I ask you, who knows more about poisonous plants than experienced gardeners? *And* those schooled in botany or horticulture."

"You implyin' a garden club member tried to kill 'em?"

"No, of course not." The man could be thick as a brick. "Except for my friend Rita, who happened to room with Sheila in college, none of the garden club members had even met Vaughn or Sheila prior to the banquet. Why would they want them dead?"

He gave a mighty sneeze just then, the gust strong enough to flutter the papers on his desk. "So," he said, reaching for a box of tissues, "you insinuatin' this friend of yours . . . Rita . . . might be the guilty party?"

"No," I replied, aghast at his conclusion. "That's not what I meant. I base my investigations on the motive-means-opportunity principle. That's how I arrive at my list of suspects." Rita, unfortunately, happened to possess all three, but I left her name off the list based on personal recognizance.

I heard another groan; this time it didn't come from a chair. "Haven't you had your fill playin' lady detective? Hang up your shingle, Miz McCall. Pay the grandkids a nice long visit. Take up knittin'. Join a book club. Surely there must be other things that interest you."

"What if I'm right?" I fired back, irritated by his condescending tone. "Doing nothing could cost Sheila her life."

I started to rise, but he stopped me.

"Hold your horses. Bein' you're here, you might as well get everythin' off your chest once and for all."

"When toxicology verifies a weird substance was responsible for Vaughn's death, I'm willing to bet it'll be a botanical. Instead of lagging behind, you could get a leg up by listening to me."

He raised a brow. I always found it impressive how much the man could convey with the lift of a single eyebrow. Skepticism, intimidation, impatience. He was the grand master. "All righty then, Miz McCall, I'll listen," he finally relented. "But don't think gettin' lucky a couple times makes you a bona fide detective."

As concessions go, it wasn't much, but it was good enough. "I'm working under the theory that whoever killed Vaughn possessed an extensive knowledge of plant life. A number of people wanted Vaughn Bascomb out of the picture—permanently. In all probability, they may resent Dr. Rappaport as well."

"S'posin' for a minute that you're right. Who might these people be, and why would they wish either or both of 'em dead?"

"Thought you'd never ask." I brought out my cell phone, complete with photos.

I ran through my list of possible suspects—Todd, Rog, Betsy, and Kel—quickly, succinctly. After all, the sheriff *was* a busy man. When he actually began scribbling in his handy-dandy black book, I knew he was taking me seriously. The only one in my collection of suspects that I didn't have a picture of was Rita. But then, Rita's my friend and only kills mealy bugs.

"I'll do some background checks. Can't promise more'n that."

"Good enough," I said. "Now, was that so painful?"

Not waiting for an answer, I got to my feet and left. As I closed the door behind me, I thought I heard another sneeze.

# Chapter 24

Bunco rolls around like clockwork every two weeks.

Since tonight would be Tara's grand send-off before her move to California, Rita had volunteered as hostess. I'd arrived early to offer my help. Wonderful smells assailed me the instant I stepped foot into the foyer.

Tara came out of the kitchen and gave me a great big hug.

"Going to miss you, honey," I said, returning the embrace. "Sure you don't have an unmarried sister for my son, Steven? You're the type of young woman I'd like to see him with." Steven had a tendency to keep mum about his love life. He seemed to favor friends named Sam or Joe. I'd love to have him settle down and give me more grandbabies. Maybe then I'd follow the sheriff's advice and take up knitting.

"Sorry." Tara laughed.

A pity, I thought. Guess, Steven was on his own. Tara's a sweetheart. In the time she'd lived with Rita while her husband—Rita's son—was deployed to Iraq, I'd grown very fond of the girl. I knew the other Babes felt the same. Soon we'd have to put our heads together and find a suitable replacement for her. Though it's hard to imagine, not everyone loves bunco as much as we do. Some women prefer games where you have to be clever and employ strategy. We like bunco because neither is required.

"Kate, in here," Rita called from the kitchen.

Arm in arm, Tara and I followed the sound of her voice.

"Wow!" I said. Trays and platters filled the countertops. "You're pulling out all the stops."

"I told her not to fuss, but she wouldn't listen."

Rita donned a pair of oven mitts before pulling a tray of appetizers from the oven. "I want tonight to be special."

I eyed the tray of hot hors d'oeuvres, the platter of cheese and fruit, and another mounded with shrimp. "It'll be even more 'special' tomorrow morning when I get on the scale."

"Kate, I'm putting you in charge of the champagne. You'll find glasses in the china cabinet."

I had no sooner popped the cork on the first bottle of bubbly when the Babes started arriving. They came in pairs like Noah's Ark. Diane and Janine entered first, still debating the merits of a recent bestseller. Monica and Pam tooled over with Pam at the wheel of her cherry-red golf cart. Next came mother and daughter. Polly must have been going for a Jackson Pollock look in a wildly printed knit top. A look better suited for a large canvas in a museum rather than a diminutive septuagenarian. Gloria was decked out in enough bling to compete with the jewelry counter at Macy's. Connie Sue, regal in the rhinestone tiara she'd won last time, and Claudia were right behind. Judging from the exuberant greetings and laughter, you'd think we were a bunch of long-lost friends at a high school reunion. From the decibel level, no one would suspect we saw one another frequently even when we weren't rolling the bones.

The door bell chimed, the sound nearly smothered by the commotion. "I'll get it," I called out, not that anyone was paying attention.

I mentally did a head count. Who were we missing? The Babes never bothered with doorbells; they walked right in. Not long ago, I'd answered the door just as I was doing now only to find Sheriff Wiggins on the doorstep with an arrest warrant. When he and his deputies left, they'd been escorting Claudia to the hoosegow.

Would Rita be next? My heartbeat quickened as I swung the door open.

"Tammy Lynn!" I gasped.

The poor thing looked decidedly ill at ease standing alone under the porch light. She nervously shoved her oversized glasses higher on the bridge of her small nose. "I, ah, Megan couldn't make it. She asked me to sub."

"Welcome. C'mon in." I put my arm around her shoulders and drew her inside.

She balked on the threshold of the kitchen. "Maybe this wasn't such a good idea," she whispered.

"Nonsense." I clapped my hands for attention. "Everyone, Miss Tammy Lynn Snow will be joining us this evening in Megan's absence."

She was greeted with a flurry of hellos and welcomes and gradually some of the tension faded from her expression.

Connie Sue waved her hand. "Can I have y'all's attention?"

We quieted while Claudia ducked out and returned with a large box wrapped in fancy paper and sporting a big bow. "Tara, honey," she said, "this is a little something to help you remember us."

Tara's eyes grew suspiciously bright as she accepted the gift. "As if I could ever forget any of you."

"Open it," Polly urged. "Show us what you got."

Tara unwrapped the package and pulled out a glazed candy dish divided into three sections and adorned with—what else?—ceramic dice.

"The different sections make it perfect for entertaining," Pam pointed out.

Monica moved in for a closer look. "And the dice are changeable with the seasons."

"Look inside the box," Connie Sue instructed. "You'll find a Santa for Christmas."

"And a heart for Valentine's Day," Claudia added, causing me to look at her sharply. Did I detect a wistfulness in voice? I'd thought after her recent fiasco, she'd be content as a bachelorette.

"Or an anniversary," Janine piped up. She was still raving about the recent anniversary cruise. From her description, one would think they'd set sail aboard the Love Boat. If I sound a teensy bit envious, it's only because I am.

Polly peeked inside the box. "I see a turkey for Thanksgiving and bunny for Easter. Wonder if they come with little martini glasses."

"Thanks so much everyone." Tara dabbed at her eyes with a tissue. "If we don't start bunco soon, I'm going to turn into a slobbering mess."

Rita tapped a glass with a spoon to get our attention. I'm not a cowgirl, never even been at a dude ranch, but I swear getting the attention of eleven women must be trickier than roping a calf at a rodeo. No sooner get the attention of one, and another wanders off. "Ladies"— Rita raised her voice and tapped some more—"before we start, let's raise our glasses in a toast to Tara, an honorary Bunco Babe."

"Here, here," the Babes echoed, raising their glasses high.

I glanced at Tammy Lynn, who frowned into her glass of champagne.

"Anything wrong?" I asked in a low voice.

"No, ma'am. I never touch spirits, but . . ."

"But . . . ?"

"It's just that I've always had a hankerin' to taste champagne. Somehow it sounds so . . . so . . . sophisticated."

"Well, sweetie, now's your chance." I gently clinked my glass against hers. "Drink up."

We heaped our plates with snacks, refilled our glasses. I gravitated to a seat in the dining room across from Tammy Lynn, who appeared painfully timid and out of place. "Let's be partners, shall we, for the first round. I'll keep score," I added when I noticed she'd topped off her champagne.

Pam and Polly joined us as the rest of the Babes settled at tables in the living and family rooms. Diane rang the bell from her place at the head table, signaling the start of play. I picked up the dice and let them fly. Nada, nil, zippo, my usual luck—or lack thereof. I slid the dice clockwise toward Polly. When she failed to score, she passed them to Tammy Lynn.

"What's up with Megan?" I asked idly as Tammy Lynn nonchalantly rolled point after point. Do I know how to pick the right partner or what?

"Megan's at a Kenny Chesney concert at the BI-LO Center in Greenville," Pam said. "She won tickets on a radio show."

Polly crossed her scrawny arms over her even scrawnier bosom. "She didn't win those tickets fair and square. They should've been mine."

"Polly!" Pam paused in the middle of a dice toss. "Are you implying *my* daughter cheated?"

I sensed a rumble. The Sharks and the Jets kind of rumble straight out of *West Side Story*. Pam, my even-tempered friend had definitely had her feathers ruffled. She wasn't about to let any harm befall Megan, her still-in-the-nest chick. But Polly was one tough cookie. She might be our group's septuagenarian, but she never let age be a handicap. I wasn't sure on whom to place my bet. Quiet spread over bunco-land like a virus. A peek over my shoulder confirmed everyone had ceased play to watch and listen.

Polly's blond Clairol curls bounced as she cocked

her head to one side, her attitude just shy of belligerent. "Megan and I were on our way home from the mall— you know we shop at the same stores—when the DJ on Whistle 100, 100.5 on the dial, announced they were having this contest. The first caller to know Kenny's birthday would win concert tickets."

"So . . . ?" Pam challenged.

"Naturally we both grabbed our cell phones and called the station. I got through first. Problem was I mistook the twenty-six in the article I'd just read about Kenny for a twenty-eight." Polly's lower lip jutted in a pout. "Megan won the tickets and didn't invite me along."

"Ah, no wonder you're upset. Megan invited Eric Olsen instead." Pam resumed rolling the dice, promptly throwing a baby bunco for an extra five points.

Polly wasn't easily placated. "Folks at *People* magazine ought to use better ink," she fussed. "Switch to a kind that don't smear so much."

"Admit it, Mother," Gloria called from an adjacent table. "The ink wouldn't have smeared if you hadn't been eating greasy potato chips."

My turn again. Tammy Lynn and I made a good team. She racked up points; I kept score. "Since when have you been a country and western fan, Polly?"

Polly sniffed as she rolled a series of ones. "Ever since I accidentally tuned into the CMA awards and gotta eyeful of Kenny in a tight pair of jeans."

Oh, yeah. It so happened I caught the same CMAs— Country Music Awards—show myself and have to admit Kenny Chesney looked fine, mighty fine indeed, in those snug, faded blue jeans.

"'Fess up, Polly." Pam smiled, her good humor restored. "You finally realized what you've been missing all these months by postponing cataract surgery."

"Bunco!" Monica yelled from the family room.

When round five came along, I found myself sitting with Connie Sue, Claudia, and Rita at table two. That, by the way, is another one of bunco's perks. Every round we rotate players and tables. This gives us a chance to socialize with everyone instead of being stuck with a single partner for an entire evening. Now I'm not mentioning anyone by name, but some people are liked better in small doses.

"Did you enjoy Sheila's cocktail party, Saturday?" I asked Claudia as I shoved the dice toward her. I saw Rita's mouth tighten at this and realized she *hadn't* been on the guest list. Too late now. I'd gone and put my foot in my mouth.

"Sheila certainly knows how to throw a party. BJ and I had a great time."

There it was again, a certain note in Claudia's voice that had me scrutinizing my friend more closely. "I thought you weren't going to date until hell froze over—or words to that effect."

"I didn't . . . I wasn't," she amended, keeping her eyes on the dice. "But BJ's, well, BJ's . . . different. He's become a really good friend. Plus, he's loads of fun."

*Mmm.*

Connie Sue's hands were in constant motion, scooping, shaking, tossing. When her run of luck ended, she slid the dice to Monica. "Rita, you're a close friend of Sheila's. Did you know Vaughn was once engaged to Betsy Dalton?"

Rita helped herself to a foil-wrapped chocolate. "She bragged about it once, but I wasn't surprised. Sheila's been stealing other women's boyfriends ever since she hit puberty. Betsy probably hates her guts."

As we began our second set, Tammy Lynn and I found ourselves at a table with Diane and Monica. Tammy Lynn's eyes were bright, her face flushed, her manner more animated than usual. When I spied her nearly empty champagne glass, I knew the reason. The bell rang, and the rattling of dice commenced.

"By the way, Tammy Lynn," I said offhandedly, "did

the sheriff send those plants off to the lab?" Was I a bad person for taking unfair advantage of the girl's inebriation?

"He surely did, ma'am—I mean Kate—but he wasn't smilin'."

"Too bad." I marked down the points Diane had scored. "If the man smiled more often he could pose for a recruiting poster. Instead that frown of his scares everyone away."

"What kind of plants?" Diane asked, sorting through the mixed nuts. Not finding a cashew, she settled for a hazelnut.

"Oleander and hydrangea. I can't help but wonder if a plant or shrub made Vaughn and Sheila sick." I watched as Tammy Lynn rolled points like nobody's business. When it came to bunco, the girl was a natural.

"They're both toxic," said Monica the omniscient. "Did you know small children have died from mistaking Carolina jessamine, the state flower, for honeysuckle and sucking its nectar?"

"Many plants are toxic, but not all of them are deadly," Diane pointed out reasonably. She let the dice fly and earned two points. "If you like, Kate, I can do some research at the library."

"Thanks, Diane. I'm trying to narrow the list of possible culprits," I told her. Diane happens to be a whiz with computers and a superwhiz at research.

Tammy Lynn effortlessly rolled a series of ones that left us agog. "Meemaw," she continued once her extraordinary run ended, "has foxglove in her side yard. She said that's where heart medicine comes from."

Monica nodded. "Digitalis."

Foxglove? I made a mental note to check that out, especially in view of the fact Vaughn suffered heart problems.

"My meemaw"—Connie Sue's head swiveled in our direction—"had castor beans along her back fence. Used to threaten us kids with a dose of castor oil if we misbehaved. Kept us in line, let me tell you. These days the old dear would be charged with child endangerment."

Monica scanned her score sheet, pleased with the points she and Tammy Lynn were accumulating. "Did you know castor beans contain ricin, which is five hundred times deadlier than cyanide?"

I snapped to attention in midtoss. "How do you know that?"

She shrugged as if to say "no big deal when you're as smart as I am." "I watched a documentary not long ago about a political dissident—Russian, I think. It was called *The Case of the Lethal Umbrella*. The man was jabbed in the leg by a stranger with an umbrella while crossing a bridge. A couple days later, he was dead."

I leaned back, trying to process all this. "Diane, how soon can you get me the info?"

"Give me a couple days," she said absently, focusing on the game.

"Can you put a rush on it?"

"Drop by tomorrow. I'll ask one of the volunteers to shelve books."

The bell sounded the end of the round

When scores were tallied at the end of the evening, no one was surprised that Tammy Lynn was the big winner. Connie Sue smiled broadly as she placed the glittery rhinestone tiara atop the girl's mousy brown hair. "There you go, sugar."

Tammy Lynn tentatively touched her crown. "I feel like a princess."

Connie Sue tilted her head to one side, studied the girl, then stuck out her hand. "Honey lamb," she drawled, "meet your fairy godmother."

# Chapter 25

The following day, Diane handed me a thick manila envelope. "I found quite a bit of material."

"I owe you," I said.

"Not me, the library. That'll cost you fifteen cents a copy—library policy." Diane held out her hand. "Consider it a donation to the new children's playground."

I dug money from my wallet and gladly paid the fee—er, donation. "By the way, thanks for giving Tammy Lynn a lift home last night. Her brother brought her by this morning so she could get her car."

"Glad to do it. It wasn't much out of my way."

"The poor girl has absolutely zero tolerance for alcohol. Except for her first glass of champagne, Rita switched her over to sparkling cider, which is . . ."

". . . alcohol free." Diane grinned. "Polly, on the other extreme, can drink a stevedore under the table. The sparkling cider was Gloria's idea."

"I guess the margarita incident is still fresh in her memory." Recently, Polly had assisted me in crime solving. The episode we're referring to involved beer, cigarettes, and tequila.

Behind me, someone *harrumphed* loudly. Unbeknownst to me a line had formed. Glancing over my shoulder, I found patrons loaded with books, DVDs, and books on tape. It was time to get a move on.

I was eager to study the material Diane had unearthed. I could've gone home, but it was hard to concentrate over the buzz of a saw and the whine of a drill. Could've stayed at the library, too, but the library didn't serve coffee or lemon meringue pie. Besides, I deserved a treat. I'd rationalize this later, but right now my taste buds were set on autopilot.

Minutes later, I scooted into a booth at the Koffee Kup Kafé. "Kafé" was the newest addition to the sign above the door. The Kup's owner, May Randolph, thought it added a touch of class to her establishment. A handful of folks had protested the KKK aspect, but had given up after she'd catered the Ebenezer AME church supper free of charge. Many of them later become regular patrons at the Kup. AME, for those unfamiliar with the term—such as me before relocating south—stands for African-Methodist-Episcopal. AME churches are frequent sights along the highways in this part of the country.

May ambled over, menu in hand. "How y'all doin', Miz McCall? Keepin' out of trouble?"

Why is it everyone thinks of me as a troublemaker? Of course, the woman had seen me in action the night I corralled a killer a couple months back. "Glad to see business picking up again, May, after that food poisoning scare."

"Folks are startin' to trickle in for a piece of one of my pies. What can I get you this mornin'?"

"Coffee and a slice of your lemon meringue. Make that two," I added as an afterthought.

"Two . . . ?"

"Would you please put the second one in a to-go box? It's for a friend."

"Can do."

I knew Bill had a fondness for May's pies, so this would be a nice little surprise for my hard-working tool guy. Besides, lemon meringue was a healthy choice since it contained three of the basic food groups—fruit, dairy, and carbohydrates. Much better than ... say ... pecan or butterscotch.

Opening the manila envelope, I started to read.

Many of the plants Diane had researched were ones I'd never heard of before—not surprising considering my lack of gardening expertise. Then I came across the info about oleander. I sipped coffee and barely tasted my pie. My pulse quickened as I read through the symptoms for oleander poisoning. I was on to something, something big. I could feel it. I pawed through my purse for the highlighter I'd thrown in.

Nausea and vomiting. Excess salivation and drooling. Abdominal pain. Collapse. Seizures. Cardiac reaction.

Symptoms of oleander poisoning matched Vaughn's to a T. I couldn't wait to present my findings to Sheriff Wiggins. I gathered my things, tossed money on the table, and hurried out of the Kup. I was Nancy Drew, Miss Marple, and Jessica Fletcher rolled into one. I'd solved the case, but I'd forgotten the pie. May chased after me with the to-go box in hand.

I was breathless with excitement as I burst into the sheriff's office. "Tammy Lynn, I need to speak with the sheriff." She opened her mouth to protest, but I cut her off. "It's a matter of life and death."

The girl blinked owlishly from behind oversized lenses. "Yes, ma'am."

Energy zinged through me like a jolt of electricity. Not even the Most Wanted posters could distract me. Unable to sit still, I paced the worn linoleum floor waiting for the go-ahead.

"You all right, Kate?" Tammy Lynn asked anxiously.

"I'm fine. Just peachy." I looked at her closely for the first time. The girl looked a trifle peaked after a wild 'n' wooly night of bunco. That single glass of bubbly about did her in. But I didn't have time to worry about Tammy Lynn; I had more important fish to fry. "Kindly tell Sheriff Wiggins I need to see him *now*."

She gave me a worried frown, but obediently pressed the intercom and informed the sheriff of my visit. I overheard the words "of the utmost importance." Then I heard more whispering that I couldn't quite make out. Finally she turned to me and said, "Go right in, ma'am. Sheriff's waitin' on you."

I sailed into the office under a full head of steam. "Oleander," I said, plopping the incriminating pages in front of him. "Oleander's what killed Vaughn Bascomb."

"You been drinkin'?"

That certainly turned my steam valve down a notch or two. "What do you mean, 'drinkin'? For heaven's sake, it's eleven o'clock in the morning. Who drinks at eleven o'clock in the morning?"

He shrugged shoulders broader than a broom handle. "Tammy Lynn claims you ladies drink like fish once you get to gamblin'."

"She said no such thing." Surely Tammy Lynn wouldn't rat out her new best friends? "How many times do I have to explain we don't gamble, we play bunco. It's a dice game, no high stakes, no finesse. And we mostly talk."

"And drink?"

"On occasion, we have a drink or two, but we certainly don't drink like fish." I should have ignored the jibe, but the darn man put me on the defensive. Irritated, I tapped the pages on his desk. "I solved the puzzle. I know the poison used. All that's left for us to do is discover who administered it."

If he was excited about my epiphany, he hid it well. "Suppose you tell me what got you so all fired up, and make it quick. I've got a . . ."

". . . important meeting with the mayor?"

"I was about to say a dentist appointment."

"Right," I muttered. Leaning across his desk, I pointed at the items I'd highlighted in yellow. "See for yourself.

The symptoms of oleander poisoning are identical to the ones Vaughn and Sheila exhibited the night of the banquet."

This said, I plunked myself down in the visitor's chair, which I'd come to regard as mine.

Picking up the article, he read it carefully, nodding from time to time.

"Minutes before the lecture, Vaughn complained his stomach felt queasy and asked for ginger ale. I distinctly recall that he held a handkerchief to his mouth, which could be the result of excess saliva. When Sheila first came onto the stage, she clutched her stomach as if it ached. Then she collapsed. Vaughn had a seizure. Cardiac reaction occurred later at the hospital. Ergo, Vaughn's death first appeared to be a heart attack. It makes perfect sense, doesn't it?" I asked, unable to wait for his comments.

"Except for this." He reached into a file folder, extracted an official-looking report, and slid it over. "Tox screen trumps Internet."

Now, I wasn't a card player, but I knew enough to know my assumption was in deep doo-doo. I felt a sinking sensation in the pit of my stomach as I skimmed through it.

"Sorry to blow your theory to smithereens." Funny, he didn't sound the least bit sorry. "The state crime lab," he continued, "ran every standard tox screen outside the routine panel. All negative. This includes the old standbys of cyanide, foxglove—and oleander."

I sank deeper into my chair. I'd been absolutely certain that I'd been on the right track. My euphoria vanished in a puff of smoke.

Silence as oppressive as August humidity settled over the room.

"I apologize for wasting your time. I was so sure ..." My voice trailed into nothing.

He leaned back in his swivel chair, steepled his fingers, and pinned me like a butterfly to a mat with his unblinking stare. He looked inscrutable. Invincible. And I looked—and felt—like a fool. I started to squirm—the man had that kind of effect on me—but caught myself in the nick of time. Thank goodness, I wasn't the perpetrator of a serious crime, or I'd be pudding on the floor.

I attempt to leave, but his next words stopped me cold.

"There's more." Dropping his relaxed pose, he drew out yet another sheet from the folder. "This heah addendum states that the secondary tox panel detected a series of red flags. Further testin' is bein' done. Results pendin'. Unlike those TV shows you're so fond of, real-life answers take a whole lot longer."

I felt vindicated. My spirits once again started to rise. Even if it wasn't oleander, there were plenty more poisonous plants out there. I had only scratched the surface.

"Probably shouldn't have told you all this, but felt it's only fair since you persisted in bringing the matter to my attention." He rose and came around the desk to tower over me. Six feet two inches of hard muscle and bad attitude. "You've done your job as a concerned citizen, Miz McCall. Now, I'm tellin' you, step aside. Let law enforcement take over."

I debated with myself. Should I salute? Cower? I did neither, opting instead for a dignified retreat.

"I'm warnin' you, Miz McCall," he rumbled in that gruff baritone I was coming to admire less and less as time went on. "You could find yourself way over your head and in a heap o' trouble."

I stopped at the door, my hand on the knob, and gave him a cheeky grin. "Aw, Sheriff, you do care."

What exactly did "step aside" consist of? I wondered as I drove home. Twiddle my thumbs and do nothing? Forget two people had been poisoned? That Vaughn had died, and Sheila feared the perp would strike again? Contrary to the sheriff's opinion, I wasn't a foolish woman. And I wasn't stupid. I promised myself to be discreet, cautious, but I couldn't refuse someone who'd asked for my help.

My cell phone rang, interrupting my train of thought. Should I answer, or let it go to voice mail? I don't approve of people talking on their cell phones or texting while driving. A person has a greater chance of a cell phone–related injury than crossing paths with a dangerous psychopath. I decided to let the call go to voice mail only to have the darned thing ring again a minute later. Careful to keep one hand on the wheel and both eyes on the windy road, I excavated my phone from the depths of my purse. Jen's name lit up on caller ID. Even as a toddler, my daughter disliked being ignored, a trait she's passed on to her two daughters. Sighing, I pulled into the parking lot of one of those AME churches that dot the roadways. Might as well return the call and get it over with. Knowing Jen, she'd hit redial until I finally picked up.

"Hello, dear," I said cheerily.

"Glad you finally answered, Mother. I was wondering if I should call the paramedics to check on you. I must've seen the infomercial a dozen times about the . . . mature . . . woman who'd fallen and can't get up and always think of you."

"You almost said 'elderly' didn't you?" I stared out the windshield and counted to ten. Jen knew in no uncertain terms how I felt about the E word. Especially when applied to me.

"I don't know why you're so touchy. Face facts, Mother, you're not getting any younger."

"I shouldn't have to remind you, Jennifer Louise, but neither are you."

From the ensuing silence, I knew I'd struck a nerve. "It's only that I'm concerned about you," Jen said at last. "You need activities that increase the number of brain cells. I'm sending you an article on how mental stimulation decreases the risk of dementia."

I drummed my fingertips against the steering wheel. And prayed for patience. "No need to worry, hon. I'm constantly busy."

"How busy can you be?" she asked plaintively. "You're retired with all the time in the world and nothing to do. I don't see how you keep from being bored out of your mind."

I hoped I hadn't forgotten to take my blood pressure medication. "I manage," I said, my voice tight.

"Well, I hope the authorities got to the bottom of the food poisoning epidemic so at least I don't have that to worry over."

Idly, I watched a woodpecker peck away at a sweet gum. Apparently, Jen hadn't spoken with her brother and didn't know the case had turned into a homicide. "Oh, it wasn't food poisoning, dear. It was the real deal."

"What . . . !"

Oops! I slapped myself upside the head. Dumb, Kate, dumb! There, I'd gone and done it again. I suffer from a serious case of blurt-itis whenever I talk to Jen. The girl knew how to press all the right buttons. The thought of buttons triggered an idea. A brilliant idea. I'd turned down the volume on the radio to answer Jen's call. Now I jabbed the buttons and kept jabbing until I found what I was searching for—static. Nice, loud static. I cranked up the volume.

"Sorry, dear." I held the cell phone close to a speaker. "Poor reception . . . breaking . . . up."

Smiling to myself, I flipped the phone shut. I didn't feel a single blip of remorse. Nary a twinge. I was shifting into gear when I happened to notice the marquee in the churchyard: *Some minds are like concrete, thoroughly mixed up and permanently set.*

Yep. I nodded in agreement. That describes Jen.

# Chapter 26

I wasn't quite ready to head home. All that pounding, sawing, and drilling was giving me a headache. Instead, I'd take a detour and stop by Sheila's. She'd made it clear she wanted me as a girlfriend. And girlfriends visit. They have the unalienable right, guaranteed by the Coalition of Women Everywhere, to drop by unannounced. It's part of our credo. Only problem, I hated to come empty-handed. Especially since Sheila was a *brand-new* girlfriend. Then my gaze fell on the Styrofoam to-go box on the seat beside me with Bill's lemon meringue pie. Bill was a kind and generous man. Surely he'd say, *Go ahead, Kate, give Sheila the slice of my most favorite dessert in the whole wide world.* I was faced with a dilemma. It was either give Sheila the pie or go empty-handed.

In spite of Sheila's friendly overtures, I never felt completely comfortable around her. She was just too ... perfect. Even with the help of Belle Beaute products, my skin wasn't wrinkle-free and glowing. When I stood tall, shoulders back, I was still vertically challenged. Dressed in my found-it-on-sale finery, stains always managed to find me. That's the honest-to-goodness reason I make it a point to never order spaghetti unless I'm wearing polka-dots.

I needed to spend more time with Sheila, find out what makes her tick. Discover her likes and dislikes. Maybe even unearth a fault or two. I doubt if we'd ever become best buds like Pam, my BFF, and me. Pam and I have loads in common—tai chi, bunco, golf. We even have the same taste in books and TV shows. Best of all, Pam listens when I whine. Sheila and I, on the other hand, have practically nothing in common. The only whine I'd do with her would be either chardonnay or merlot.

Besides girl-bonding, I had an ulterior motive for wanting to visit Sheila. I needed to run through my "persons of interest" list with her. As I pulled into the drive of her rental, I spotted a sleek BMW with Georgia plates. Obviously Sheila had company. I sat for a minute, debating my next move. Then, after giving myself a pep talk, picked up the pie and headed up the front walk with a swagger worthy of a Welcome Wagon lady and rang the bell.

Second thoughts assailed me as I waited on the stoop. Not about the wisdom of my unexpected visit, but about giving away the slice of Bill's lemon meringue pie. I vowed I'd make up for the transgression by persuading him to stay for supper. There was still time to whip up tuna casserole, another of Bill's favorites. I didn't have to worry about not having the ingredients since I now bought tuna in bulk at Sam's Club. Even though I no longer had a cat to feed, I'd never run out if I lived to be a hundred.

I jabbed the bell again and waited some more. The folks inside had no idea how persistent I could be. Maybe persistent wasn't the right word. Maybe stubborn would be more correct. I'd learned to outwait, outpersist, out-stubborn the best. Need a testimonial? Just ask Tammy Lynn Snow or Sheriff Sumter Wiggins.

The door finally opened.

"Oh, it's you," Betsy Dalton said, her tone cool and

distant. "Sheila didn't mention you had an appointment."

"I didn't know I needed an appointment to visit a friend." I was determined not to let her irritate me.

"Since when are you and Sheila friends?" She swept me with a dismissive glance. "You don't seem her type."

"Didn't you hear that opposites attract?" I replied, trying for witty, but settling for cliché. Granted, Betsy—classy and sophisticated in tailored Armani and pricey stilettos—seemed more the type Sheila might choose to pal around with. I'm the complete opposite, tending to favor capris and sandals. And unlike Betsy, except for a swipe of mascara and a dab of lipstick, I rarely bother with makeup. But as much as I hated to admit it, this time I had to agree with her. Sheila and I did make an odd couple.

"Who is it, Betsy?" Sheila called out.

"It's me, Kate." Smiling sweetly, I sidestepped the fashionista and moved into the foyer.

"She's on the patio." Betsy's high heels click-clacked on the hardwood floors as she trailed after me. I gave Sheila's library an envious glance as I passed. It was hard to imagine, considering the present chaos, that I'd soon have a room like this. I found Sheila seated at a glass-topped wicker table on an enclosed patio overlooking a cove that sparkled in the sun. Have I failed to mention that Serenity Cove Estates is built around a tributary of Lake Thurmond, named after the esteemed South Carolina statesman Strom Thurmond? Oddly enough, Georgians don't share the same sentimentality for the former senator. On the Georgia side, the same waterway is known as Clarks Hill Lake. But I'm letting my mind wander again.

"We were working," Betsy said. She must've thought I was blind not to see the piles of files and folders spread across the table.

I felt a niggling of guilt for having interrupted, but quickly squashed it. Life here tends to be informal with friends popping in from time to time just to "sit a spell," as they say. And my visit today wasn't strictly social. I had business of my own to conduct.

"I brought you a slice of May Randolph's lemon meringue pie." I sank into a flowered cushion of a wicker chair without waiting to be asked. "It's so good, it'll make your tongue slap your brains out." Love that expression. First heard it from a waitress one New Year's Eve and have been waiting to use it ever since.

I darted a glance from Sheila to Kate and realized I was the only one smiling at my weak excuse for humor. "Sorry, Sheila," I said, trying to recover lost ground. "If I'd known you had company, I would've brought an extra piece. Perhaps you two can share."

"I don't eat sweets," Betsy snapped. "It's bad for the figure."

I forged ahead. "Pecan is another of May's specialties. But after our conversation the night of the banquet, I didn't think you were a fan of Southern cuisine."

"I'm not," Sheila admitted, "but I'm sure the lemon will be lovely, light and refreshing. How thoughtful of you, Kate, to think of me."

Betsy refused to sit, preferring instead to glower at me from the French doors at the patio's threshold. An awkward silence prevailed. The topic of pies depleted, I racked my brain for an equally compelling subject. I toyed with "Read any good books lately?" Then I thought about Netflix. Isn't it grand? Movies without having to leave home. Keep 'em as long as you want. No late fees. No dropping 'em off before the stroke of midnight dressed as the Unabomber. Sensing a lack of interest in Netflix, I happened to notice the photos spilling from an unmarked manila envelope. I pointed to one with silvery-green leaves and bright orange fruit. "That would look great in my backyard. What's the name of it?"

Sheila snatched the photo and stuffed it back into the envelope. "Hippophae rhamnoides."

"Hippopotamus ... ?" My tongue tangled trying to pronounce it.

"Common name sea buckthorn," Betsy supplied readily. "It doesn't grow around here, so you'll have to find something else for your yard."

*All righty, then.* I looked at the woman with burgeoning respect. "I didn't know you spoke botany."

"Betsy's more than a pretty face," Sheila said, smiling. "Her background in science was what first brought her to the attention of Belle Beaute."

Betsy shrugged off the praise, but I could see she was pleased. A tiny smile tugged at her mouth. "I'm sure Kate isn't interested in the story of my life." Her BlackBerry sounded just then. I recognized the ring tone. "I Feel Pretty," from *West Side Story*. How fitting for someone in the beauty trade. "If you'll excuse me, I've some calls to make. Can I get you anything in the meantime?"

"I shouldn't stay," I demurred. In reality, you couldn't pry me out of my seat with a can opener.

"Betsy, be a dear, and bring Kate and me a glass of iced tea when you come back. You know"—Sheila gestured vaguely toward the kitchen—"the special kind— Vaughn's favorite."

Emotion flashed briefly in Betsy's chocolate-brown eyes before it was masked. Anger? I wondered. Resentment? Grief? It had come and gone so quickly, I didn't have time to catalog it.

"Sure. Be right back."

Sheila turned her full attention on me. "Betsy does her own version of sweet tea by adding honey instead of simple syrup like most. Even if you aren't a fan of sweet tea, you'll love hers."

I shot a glance in the direction Betsy had disappeared, but there was no sign of her. I lowered my voice, and said, "The pie was only a ruse. I'm on my way home from the sheriff's office and wanted to tell you that he's finally taking our poisoning scenario seriously."

"Yes, I know," Sheila replied calmly.

"How do you know? Did he call?" Sheila was one cool cucumber, all right. Most women would be a ball of nerves knowing there was proof positive someone tried to off them. I envied that kind of composure.

"He dropped by earlier to inform me of the toxicology results."

I brought out my trusty little black book and flipped it open. "I wanted to go over my list of suspects with you to see if any name in particular stands out."

She arched a brow in a fair imitation of the sheriff's. "You actually made a list of people who might want Vaughn or me dead?"

"It's the way I operate." Did I sound official, or what? Hearing those words, one might think I actually knew what I was doing. I cleared my throat and got down to business. "Let's start with Todd Timmons."

"Todd . . . ?" she scoffed. "You can't be serious?"

"Serious as a heart attack." I said, not cracking a smile. Where in the world had *that* come from? Funny how the brain works. "Todd's extremely ambitious. I've watched him schmooze everyone he thinks might advance his career."

She dismissed my theory with a flick of the wrist. "If ambition was a crime, I'd be guilty myself. Why, most of the people I know would be behind bars."

"Todd blamed Vaughn for a fall in the ratings of *How Does Your Garden Grow?*" I persisted. "Without ratings, the networks aren't interested in hiring him."

"True," Sheila said, "the kid's ambitious, but he's dumb as a box of rocks. He narrowly missed flunking out of college. Todd can barely remember the way I prefer my coffee."

My mind balked at the thought of crossing Todd's name off the list. "If he's as dumb as you say, how did he wind up being a TV producer?"

"As fate would have it, Todd landed a summer internship at a cable TV station and worked his way up." A wry smile curved her mouth. "It didn't hurt that his daddy had a friend in the business."

I scribbled this down, striving to appear semi-intelligent and not as "dumb as a box of rocks," then consulted my notes. "Next on my list is Roger McFarland."

"Roger . . . ? Mild-mannered, borderline-OCD Roger?"

From her mocking tone, I gathered Todd's name wouldn't be the only one erased. "I heard Roger complain that Vaughn interfered with the 'vision' he had for his project, *Springtime Perennials of the Southeast*."

"Nonsense! Honestly, Kate, I don't know how you arrive at these conclusions. Roger's been given complete creative control over the project."

"There's more. I also found out Roger's true passion is horticulture, not publishing or photography. He deeply resents the person who once beat him out of a coveted position. I suspect that was either you or Vaughn."

"Ridiculous!" Sheila shook her head emphatically.

"The person in question happens to be none other than me," Betsy said from the doorway, and I found myself wondering how much of our conversation she'd overheard. "The rest, as they say, is history."

I stared at the woman openmouthed.

Betsy smirked, enjoying my reaction. "I was imminently better suited for the job. Since then I've been promoted to vice president in charge of new products."

Sheila helped Betsy make room on the table for a tray with tall glasses of sweet tea. "Trust me, Kate, Betsy was a much wiser choice."

"Mmm," I murmured, taking a sip of tea to buy myself time to mull this over. And found it delicious.

"The secret's in the honey," Betsy said. "I order it special from a farm in the upcountry."

The upcountry seemed like a long way to go for a jar of honey when you can buy it just as easily at the Piggly Wiggly. But to each his own, I guess. The upcountry Betsy referred to consisted of the scenic northwest pocket of the state. Maybe someday I'd check it out. Might even buy some honey of my own when I'm there.

Sheila raised her glass, but didn't drink from it. "I think you should tear up that list of yours and concentrate on the real suspect—Kel Watson."

"Why Kel?"

"That's precisely what I wish you'd find out before he tries again." She shuddered delicately. "I'm telling you, Kate, the way he skulks about gives me the creeps."

"Making you feel uneasy isn't a motive for murder," I reminded her.

Sheila scooted closer and dropped her voice. "I don't like to gossip, but it's rumored the man's on drugs. Possibly hallucinogenics. For all anyone knows, he might even grow his own. The man's not all there. For pity's sake, just take a good look at him. Kel Watson's caught in some kind of time warp. He's an aging hippie, a loner. I've seen a strange vehicle parked outside the house late at night. I believe he's stalking me. Aren't we always being told to trust our instincts? Well, mine are screaming the man's dangerous."

I couldn't fault her logic. I'd once heard an expert expound that "trust your instinct" should be the rule of thumb when it came to personal safety. "I'll do what I can," I promised. "I'll leave the two of you now to get back to work."

"Let me show you out," Betsy hastily offered.

I bid good-bye to Sheila and left my iced tea half-finished. Betsy escorted me to the front door, transparent in her haste to be rid of me. Did she worry I'd steal the silver or rifle through her underwear drawer?

At the door, she turned to me. "Woman to woman, may I offer a word of advice?" Not waiting for a reply, she continued. "Try Belle Beaute's skin replenishing cream. It'll work wonders on those fine lines of yours."

As I walked back to my car, I wondered if it would also work on the steam coming out of my ears.

# Chapter 27

"Saturday? Saturday—as in tomorrow?"

"I know it's last minute, sugar." Connie Sue sounded contrite from two blocks away on Magnolia Lane. "But chances like this don't drop in our laps every day. I couldn't believe my luck when Chateau Spa called with a last-minute cancellation. They'd had an entire bridal party booked for hair, makeup, manicures, pedis—the whole shebang—then the bride caught the groom cheatin' with her maid of honor after the rehearsal dinner. How tacky can you get?"

I peeked in the oven. The rolls were browning nicely, the casserole bubbling. From the half bath around the corner, I could hear Bill washing up before dinner. "That's tacky, all right," I agreed absently. "I take it the wedding's off?"

"Darn tootin'. The bride told the receptionist that the 'sumbitch'—that's her word not mine—and her no-account friend are usin' the honeymoon tickets. The pair plans to fly to Cancun and work on their tans. But enough about the two-timers. Say you'll come. Pretty please with sugar on it."

"Don't get your panties in a twist." It was hard to refuse Connie Sue when she switched into Scarlett mode. "Spa day? I wouldn't miss it for the world."

"Whew!" Connie Sue gave an exaggerated sigh. "You had me goin' for a minute. Not everyone can make it on such short notice, but with Tammy Lynn there'll be eight. We can all pile into Gloria's SUV."

We disconnected after agreeing on a time and place to rendezvous.

"Sounds like you've got big plans for tomorrow," Bill said, returning to the kitchen. He smelled faintly of soap mixed with a hint of sawdust. His silvery hair looked newly combed, and a familiar sparkle brightened his baby blues. "Sure nice of you to fix my favorite dinner."

I felt a twinge of guilt as I thought of the slice of lemon meringue pie that had nearly been his. Somehow I doubted Sheila'd even taste it, much less share it with Betsy. I removed the rolls from the oven and popped them into a bread basket. "That was Connie Sue. It seems the Babes are kidnapping Tammy Lynn Snow tomorrow for a makeover and a day at the spa. We'll probably drop by the mall afterward for a little shopping."

"Tammy Lynn Snow? The sheriff's girl Friday?"

"One and the same." I set the salad on the table. "Tammy Lynn has a mad crush on that nice young police officer, Eric Olsen. Eric, however, can't see beyond eyeglasses the size of Granny Ann's picture window or the dishwater-brown hair. Eric looks at her as his best friend's baby sister. Time's come to shake the boy up."

"What can I do to help?"

"To shake him up or to help with dinner?"

He grinned. "Whichever . . . you know I'll have your back."

I felt my insides turn soft and gooey at hearing him say that. "Sit down. Dinner's ready," I said to hide a rush of emotion.

I placed the casserole on a trivet. A plume of steam

escaped when I removed the lid. I poured coffee, then took the chair opposite Bill at the kitchen table.

"Exactly what is it you ladies do at a spa?" Bill asked, digging into the mound of tuna casserole I'd heaped on his plate.

"Good question, but I'm not exactly sure. The usual, I guess," I said, buttering a roll. In the recesses of my mind, I could hear Monica's voice. "Step away from the trans fats!"

"Mmm," he said, sampling the salad. "I like those little red things you put in it. And who'd ever think of adding nuts to a salad?"

He was referring the handful of dried cranberries and walnuts I'd added to make a plain salad look fancy. I wasn't even sure he'd notice. His praise made me feel like a cross between Rachael Ray and Julia Child. All those subscriptions to cooking magazines had just paid off in spades. "Glad you like it," I said, trying not to simper.

"Just what constitutes the 'usual' at a spa?"

"Hair, makeup, manicures, pedicures, waxing."

He looked up, fork poised midair. "Waxing?"

Did my intrepid tool man actually pale at the notion? "You know, hot wax to get rid of unwanted body hair. Many young women, I've heard, have bikini waxes these days."

"And that kind of stuff takes an entire day?" Bill chowed down salad, but I could see he'd lost his heart to the casserole. Wait till I brought out the pièce de résistance for dessert—lemon bars. Not pie, but not exactly a sharp stick in the eye, either.

"Claudia talked about a spa she'd been to in Asheville. She said they did all kinds of body treatments— green tea and sea salt, pomegranate and ground cranberry seed." My eyes half-closed, I envisioned myself in a den of iniquity. Candles flickering. Water tinkling. A Swedish masseuse. "As for massages, you can take your pick,"

I rhapsodized. "Hot stone, Swedish, deep tissue, or reflexology. Connie Sue said Claudia already booked a seaweed wrap. It's guaranteed to firm, tone, and detoxify."

"Maybe that's supposed to be fun, but it sounds more like torture. Give me poker and a six-pack any day."

I smiled to myself. Bill was such a guy's guy, but that's why I loved him. *Loved him?* Where had that come from? Out of left field, that's where. I liked Bill sure, but love? Love was a whole other dimension.

Suddenly I'd lost my appetite and shoved my plate aside.

"Aren't you hungry?" Bill frowned, noticing my dinner was half-finished. "Sure you feel okay? You're not coming down with something, are you?"

I rose to refill our coffee cups. "I'm fine," I said. *A little shaky about the love thing, but fine.*

We finished our meal, polished it off with more coffee and lemon bars. Afterward, Bill helped me clear the table and load the dishwasher even though I told him not to bother after a long day building bookshelves.

"Care to stay awhile, watch some TV?" I asked once the kitchen was tidied. "If we channel surf, we might catch some *Law & Order* reruns."

"Tempting as that sounds, I need to shower off the sawdust, and you've got a big day ahead."

"Soon then," I replied. "Let me at least walk you to the door."

We stood for a moment on the threshold. It was the time of day I liked best, when day gracefully surrendered to night. When light, rosy and soft, seeped into darkness. A single star burned bright overhead. I was acutely aware of the man beside me. The man who "had my back." A notion I found tremendously appealing. I was overcome by a combination of nerves and anticipation—reduced to being a sixtysomething-year-old teenager. It was then I noticed a smudge of sawdust on Bill's shoulder that had escaped his attention. I reached to brush it off, but he caught my hand. He smiled, and my bones felt they were made of Silly Putty.

Turning my hand over, Bill pressed a kiss into the palm and I felt a jolt all the way to my toes. Then he bent down and kissed me. My lips parted under his, whether in surprise or as a reaction I don't know, but my arms wound around his neck and I kissed him back.

Neither of us was smiling when the kiss ended. Had Serenity Cove experienced an earthquake? I wondered. Were we on a fault line? I'd distinctly felt the earth move. I could still feel the aftershocks.

My, oh my.

Our first stop of the day had been at an eyeglass center that advertised fast service on contact lenses. Hooray! Gone forever were Tammy Lynn's oversized glasses. Already the girl looked better. Chateau Spa was next on the agenda. Or "the Chat" as we dubbed it.

Our intrepid band of Babes—and lone Babette— congregated in a reception area tiled in imitation marble. To the best of my knowledge, except for Claudia and Connie Sue, none of us had ever been inside a pampering palace. "Who would have guessed?" Claudia marveled. "Here I traveled all the way to Asheville with this place just down the road."

Tammy Lynn gazed around doubtfully. "I don't know, y'all. This place looks way too expensive. I think we shoulda settled for the Cut 'n' Curl in Brookdale. Ethel Rae gives great perms."

Connie Sue put her arm around the girl's shoulders. "Don't worry about a thing, honey lamb. Not with your fairy godmother on the job."

Silently, however, I agreed with Tammy Lynn. Like her, I, too, found the opulent surroundings somewhat intimidating. Chateau Spa was a living, breathing testament to faux French. Lots of gilt. Oodles of red and gold. A mini-Versailles? Though I'd never been there, I'd seen pictures. I hoped the proprietor hadn't gotten faux chateau confused with faux brothel. Hadn't been in one of those either, but I'd heard tales. Would the Babes be mistaken for extras in *Moulin Rouge* at the end of the day? If so, I vote to rename Tammy Lynn . . . Fifi.

"Mornin', y'all." An attractive blonde greeted us with a friendly smile. "My name's Terri. So happy y'all could make it on short notice. Bridezilla demanded we schedule our full staff, then bam! 'Sorry folks, weddin's off.'"

"Poor thing," Pam commiserated. "It must have been devastating."

I rolled my eyes. Leave it to my BFF to sympathize with a woman referred to as Bridezilla.

Connie Sue urged Tammy Lynn forward. "Terri, this is Tammy Lynn Snow, the reason for today's little excursion. We want her to get the full treatment, includin'"— she ruffled Tammy Lynn's dingy locks—"highlights, cut, and makeup."

"We want her to look like a new woman when you're finished," Gloria added.

"Ladies, y'all came to the right place. Tammy Lynn's own mother won't recognize her by the time we're finished."

"Are you sure this is such a good idea?" Rita whispered in my ear. "Maybe we should've just called the Cut 'n' Curl."

"Have you seen some of Ethel Rae's customers?" I whispered back.

"Good point," Rita agreed after a moment's consideration. "My ninety-one-year-old mother-in-law gets better results at the nursing home."

Polly, who had been uncharacteristically quiet until now, piped up. "Say, Terri, you have any hot dudes that give massages?"

"All our clients love Randy. They rave about his magic fingers."

"Randy, eh? I was wishing for a guy named Raoul."

"I promise you won't be disappointed." Terri snapped her fingers and a young woman in a white smock appeared and led Polly down a hallway.

The rest of the staff materialized at an invisible command from Terri. Instructions were given, assignments made. The place might look like a whorehouse, but was run with military precision and efficiency. Claudia and I opted for facials. An antiaging one for her. I heard the esthetician—wait till Bill hears me bandy that around—use the term antiradicals. For myself, I selected a facial that promised a deep-pore cleansing with a citrus-based cocktail of alpha hydroxyl acid. My vocabulary was increasing by leaps and bounds.

"Think I'll have a hot stone massage," Rita said after scanning the list of services.

"Does the herbal linen wrap really relieve stiff muscles and joints?" Gloria asked the attendant.

"Yes, ma'am," Terri assured her. "Our clients love it."

"Guess I'll start with a manicure and pedicure," Pam, the ultraconservative, decided. "Maybe after lunch I'll try a massage."

Halfway through the facial, I reached a conclusion. I was going to treat myself to a spa day on a regular basis. After all, ladies, we owe it to ourselves to be the best we can be. I'd even forego Peanut M&M's to pay for the luxury. Perhaps next time, a spa day could include those who couldn't come this time. Diane, Janine, Monica, and Megan deserved to be pampered, too.

Lunch was served after the first round of beauty treatments. Fancy little finger sandwiches, herbal tea, and fresh fruit. Chateau Spa left no stone unturned when it came to making its clients feel special.

Then it was time for round two.

We exchanged grins and flashed newly lacquered nails as we circulated from room to room. Lots of smiles, laughter, and happy faces. Connie Sue was the only one who didn't indulge in the spa services. Instead she stuck with Tammy Lynn like lichen on a rock at Hickory Knob State Park. I caught a glimpse or two of Tammy Lynn, her head covered in strips of aluminum foil.

"Highlights and lowlights," Connie Sue said in response to my unspoken question.

Rejuvenated, destressed, detoxified, and antiaged, we reconvened in the anteroom.

"Any of you happen to have Raoul use his magic fingers?" Polly asked. She drew something from the pocket of her purse. "See, I got his card. Told him I was coming back. I haven't felt this good in years."

"Raoul?" Gloria snapped her compact shut. "I thought the guy's name was Randy."

Polly made a face. "He's way too cute for a Randy. I told him Raoul suited him better. He's thinking of changing it—for professional reasons."

Claudia ran her hand over her cheek. "My skin's as soft as a baby's behind."

Rita nodded knowingly. "Bonnie, the esthetician who did my facial, was talking about a new line of skin-care products that Belle Beaute is developing. It's supposed to be hush-hush."

"She mentioned it to me, too," I said. "Bonnie thinks it'll revolutionize the industry."

Careful not to chip her manicure, Rita fished her checkbook out of her handbag. "I'm considering buying Belle Beaute stock. I've been following it on NASDAQ. Could make a killing if rumors prove true."

"What's a NASDAQ?" Polly asked.

"It's a stock exchange, Mother."

"Don't trust it. I'll stick with the tried and true—my mattress."

Claudia turned to me. "Have either Sheila or Betsy mentioned a word of this? They should have the inside track."

"No," I replied slowly. "The subject never came up."

Which was odd, now that I thought about it. Something of that magnitude surely should have cropped up at some point. Then again, maybe not. Sheila and I had only been friends a short time. There was still a lot to learn about each other.

"All right, y'all, I want your attention," Connie Sue announced from the doorway of a treatment room. "May I present the guest of honor, Miss Tammy Lynn Snow."

We gasped in unison as Tammy Lynn stepped forward. The transformation was complete. Our little caterpillar had turned into a butterfly—and a lovely one at that. Gone was the mousy brown and in its place a warm blond with sun-kissed streaks. Her makeup was subtle, both youthful and natural. Delicate pink blush, artfully applied eye shadow and mascara, and rose-tinted lip gloss had turned the girl into a knockout. I wished I could be a fly on the wall when Eric Olsen saw her.

"You look . . ." I groped for the right word.

"Hot," Polly supplied. "And you'll look even hotter after we swing by the mall. I know just the place to get you some cool new duds. Megan and I shop there all the time."

I groaned inwardly at the thought of Polly picking out clothes for Tammy Lynn.

We said fond farewells to the staff at Chateau Spa and piled into Gloria's Expedition. Amid chatter about facials, wraps, and massages, I found my attention drifting. Were rumors true about Belle Beaute's marvelous new skin care line? How would this impact Sheila? Did it contain some kind of new mystery ingredient?

It was late when Gloria dropped me off, but I felt an overwhelming sense of accomplishment. Under all the drab, the spa had unearthed Tammy Lynn's natural beauty. In true Connie Sue fashion, she'd insisted on footing the bill for the girl's transformation. No amount of persuading could convince her otherwise. There can only be one fairy godmother, she'd insisted, and she was it.

End of discussion. Tammy Lynn kept saying over and over that she felt like a princess. Connie Sue beamed.

I wandered from room to room and switched on lights. The house was quiet, much too quiet. Times like this it would be nice to have someone to come home to. Share the day with. I strolled into the library/study/den to see how the bookshelves were progressing. Bill had left the room neat and tidy, or at least as tidy as possible, all things considered. Soon it would be time to seal and stain the wood and the project would wind to an end. I'd miss seeing Bill on a daily basis. Coffee in the mornings. Often for lunch. An occasional dinner.

Shutting off lights as I went, I drifted back to the kitchen, where I brewed myself a cup of chamomile tea. While waiting for the water to boil, I leafed through the stack of mail on the island. I slit open an envelope with an unfamiliar return address. I frowned as I read the enclosed letter. *In reply to a request from your son, Steven J. McCall, we're sending the enclosed information.* What the . . . ?

Living will . . . ? Power of attorney . . . ?

I shoved the papers into a drawer. Dear, misguided Steven. I probably should be angry, but I was amused. Knowing Steven as I did, I'm certain he assumed a madman was running rampant, poisoning residents of Serenity Cove, and thought I should be prepared for any eventuality. At least he'd given up sending me information on assisted living centers and nursing homes.

Tea in hand, I went into the great room and settled into my favorite spot on the sofa. Picking up the Belle Beaute brochures that had been gathering dust, I began to read through them. Maybe like Rita, I should consider buying shares in the company. A windfall in the stock market might be just the ticket to keep my children from thinking of me as old and feeble-minded.

# Chapter 28

A tisket, a tasket. A green and yellow basket.

I hummed to myself as I loaded an assortment of plants into a wicker basket. I'd come up with a quasi-clever plan that morning and was feeling quite smug. A few houseplants, straggly but alive, along with several small plants I'd purchased at Dixie Gardens, but hadn't yet planted, were added to the motley collection. I'd painstakingly removed any clues to their identity. Who better than the county extension agent to tell me their names and what I should do with them? Granted the excuse was borderline sneaky and downright flimsy, but I needed a reason to pay Kel Watson another visit. Sheila was certain he was responsible for the poisoning. Others, I knew, had motive, too, but Kel was becoming the front-runner in my little investigation.

Later in the day I'd arranged to meet Rita on the driving range. As for golf, it was time to get back in the saddle, so to speak. I'd lost interest in the game after finding a dismembered arm in a Walmart bag some months back. Funny how something that simple soured my desire to play. But I had a more pressing reason for wanting to speak with Rita. I planned to pump her for information. Rita and Kel seemed to have formed a relationship of sorts from her years in the garden club. And I intended to exploit that relationship by finding out everything I could about his personal life.

It was midmorning when I arrived in town. I parked the Buick in the side lot and, retrieving my basket, climbed the creaky stairs to Kel's second-floor office. I didn't think it possible to sneak up on him, but apparently I succeeded. I found Kel, his feet propped on his desk as usual, eyes closed, a trade journal open on his lap. Music blared loudly from a stereo set into a dusty bookcase. Seventies music. Rolling Stones? Bee Gees? ABBA? I hadn't a clue. Truth to tell, much of the seventies was lost in a haze of diaper changing. I was more likely tuned to an episode of *All My Children* than some station playing pop hits. In my world of Enfamil and Pampers, the happenings in Pine Valley overshadowed those of the music industry.

"Ahem . . ." I cleared my throat to get his attention.

At the sound, Kel's eyes popped open. He swung his legs to the floor and switched off the stereo. His journal slithered to the floor unnoticed.

"Sorry," Kel muttered. "How can I help you?"

I plunked the basket down on his desk and smiled—the epitome of innocence and light. "I find myself in need of your expert opinion."

His shaggy brows drew together in a frown. "You look familiar. Have we met before?"

They say the mind is the first to go. Either that or I was pathetically forgettable. I chose to think it was Kel's mind, and not my scintillating personality. With considerable effort, I kept my smile in place. "I'm Kate McCall, but call me Kate."

"Right, Kate."

Sheila had heard rumors the man used drugs. Did drugs affect one's memory? "Silly me, I bought all these cute plants then realized I had no idea what they were or where I should plant them. I thought, who better to ask than a county extension agent?"

He pulled the basket closer, gave it a cursory glance. "Most nurseries include information as to the type of plant and how to care for them. Next time make sure you know what you're buying before leaving the store. It saves time."

I knew what he meant. Saved his time not mine. "Already great advice. No wonder everyone sings your praises." I hoped he couldn't see where I'd scrubbed the labels off.

He picked a plant out of the basket at random, held it up, examined the leaves. "This one here is a common houseplant. Zamioculcas zamiifolia is the generic name, common name ZZ plant. It's a true survivor. Tolerates low light. Best to err on the side of dryness rather than overwatering."

My kind of plant the ZZ—a survivor—which explains why Rita gave me a cutting. "It's wonderful to have someone as knowledgeable as you around to help us amateurs," I said, lathering on flattery.

He grunted, but didn't look up. "This one here is Monarda didyma—bee balm."

"Odd name for a plant," I commented. "Does that mean bees like to bomb it?"

He looked at me with ill-concealed disgust. "Not 'bomb,' lady. Balm, b-a-l-m, balm."

*Well, excuuuse me.*

"Bee balm serves as a host for butterflies. Native Americans used it for its antiseptic and medicinal properties."

"Medicinal . . . as in poisonous?"

I watched recognition dawn across his craggy face. "Now I remember you," he said, aiming a callused finger at me. "You've pestered me before. You're the lady who keeps asking about poison."

Bingo! That's me, all right. "Getting back to the bee balm, poisonous or not?"

"Not," he growled.

Touchy, touchy. "I'm friends with Dr. Sheila Rappaport, but I hate to bother her with all these silly questions, knowing how busy she is."

He glared at me. "She's busy, and I'm not?"

*Not so busy you can't take a nap in the middle of the morning.* "Do you know Dr. Sheila?" I asked, deciding to play dumb. Or at least dumber than usual.

"Sorry, I'd like to talk, but I've got a meeting with the Brookdale Beekeepers Association." Kel rose, snatched a scuffed briefcase, and headed for the stairs. "Don't want to be late." Which, translated, meant, don't let the door hit you on the way out.

Grabbing my basket, I scurried after him. "What about Dr. Bascomb? Did you know him?"

Kel rattled off the name of a reference book. "I suggest you buy a copy."

Kel Watson was in full flight. Had I forgotten to use mouthwash? Had my deodorant failed? Or had my questions struck a nerve? I voted for the latter.

I reached the bottom of the stairs in time to see Kel climb into the cab of a faded gray pickup that had seen better days. I hurried to my Buick. I sat for a moment, drumming my fingers on the steering wheel and debating my next move. I wasn't exactly a novice when it came to the art of snooping. I'd read *The Complete Idiot's Guide to Private Investigating* cover to cover. At this point, any detective worth his or her salt would follow the suspect. So I started a tail. At least I assume that's the correct term. I had most of the jargon down, but there's always more to learn. As I pulled out of the lot, I wondered what it would take to get licensed as a PI. A course on the Internet? Class work? Mentoring? Would Sheriff Wiggins be willing to mentor his ace pupil? I laughed out loud. I might be dumb, but I'm not stupid.

Kel drove north away from town with me trailing.
Even though we were the only two cars on the road, I
maintained a discreet distance so he couldn't spot me
in his rearview mirror. Where was this so-called beekeepers meeting supposed to take place? I'd expected
it to be held in one of municipal buildings, but there
was no law against a member hosting it in their home.
Problem was, we weren't passing any homes—a few ram-
shackle trailers, a dilapidated gas station with a rusted
Sinclair Oil sign—but nothing that resembled a suitable
meeting place for a gaggle of beekeepers.

Ahead of me, the truck's brake lights flashed. I slowed
accordingly. Surprised, I saw Kel turn left onto an un-
paved county road. Naturally I turned, too. From the
corner of my eye, I noticed a historic marker half-hidden
behind a clump of pines. Huguenot Cemetery. The words
rang a bell. I vaguely recalled hearing Rita mention
Flowers and Bowers were adopting the cemetery as a
project. Volunteers were scheduled to meet there and
begin a massive cleanup and beautification project. As
chairman of the committee and me as the garden club's
newest recruit, Rita asked if I'd be interested. I told her
yes as long as someone with more experience showed
me the difference between a weed and a wildflower.

Together, the Buick and I bumped down the rutted
dirt road. A quarter mile farther, and no sign of Kel or
his truck. I braked to a stop when I came to a fork in
the road and weighed my options. Right or left? Turn
around and leave? Or continue on? Here I was, out
in the middle of nowhere, alone with a man who might
be a crazed stalker. And that was the best-case scenario.
He could also be a stone-cold killer. Part of me—the
sensible part—wanted to beat a hasty retreat. Yet another part—the adventurous, impulsive, curious part—
tempted me to stay. So I compromised. I'd venture
forth on foot. If I didn't come upon Kel Watson within
ten minutes, I'd leave.

Parking my car in an overgrown turnaround, I proceeded on foot down the left fork of the road, which soon became little more than a grassy trail. A trail with fresh tire tracks. Another hundred yards farther, I came upon a clearing and spotted Kel's truck. I quickly eased into a stand of scrub pines, which afforded me a decent view.

I spotted Kel Watson, garbed in a white jumpsuit, inspecting stacks of white rectangular boxes—beehives?— piled on top of each other ten or twelve high. He wore a safari-style pith helmet veiled in heavy netting and sturdy gloves to protect his hands. He walked slowly as he waved the wand of a smoke-producing apparatus. I had no intention of going any closer. Bees loved me, but the affection wasn't reciprocated.

If this was a meeting of the Beekeepers Association, Kel was the sole attendee. Unless, of course, one counted the dozens of bees circling drunkenly around their hives. Other than the fact they produce honey, I have to admit I don't know a lot about them.

Are the white boxes called hives? Houses? One thing I did know for certain, however, is that I didn't want to antagonize them. When bees were angry, they retaliated. And when they retaliated, I reacted.

It wasn't pretty.

I remained hidden until my legs started to cramp. Kel continued working diligently among the hives. Finally, when it appeared nothing sinister was about to happen, I took my leave. Far be it for me to come between a man and his bees.

# Chapter 29

I plucked a range ball from a yellow mesh bucket. "I'm telling you, Rita, it was strange. Very strange."

As agreed upon earlier that day, the two of us met at the driving range. It was time for me to get back on the horse that threw me and, once and for all, get over my reluctance to play golf. I'd never excelled at the game. Doubted I ever would. But golf provided a great excuse to get outdoors for a little exercise with my best friends. Chasing a dimpled ball over acres and acres of land all the while trying to avoid strategically placed pitfalls of sand and water, was simply a means to an end.

"Yeah, it's strange, but ..." Rita's nice easy swing sent the range ball soaring into the wild blue yonder.

"He practically *ran* out of the office." When Rita failed to respond, I got down to the business of golf. I balanced the range ball atop a tee in the center of a rubber mat. Mentally I ran though a checklist of things to do: feet shoulder width apart, arms straight, knees flexed. I took careful aim, drew back for a calculated swing—and watched as my ball dribbled down a grassy incline. I heaved a sigh. Some things never change.

"Next time keep your head down," Rita counseled.

"I wanted to see how far it went." My excuse sounded lame. Why couldn't I just concede I was a better bunco player than a golfer? Truth is, I'm not even all that great at bunco. My scores have been so lousy that I haven't taken home the tiara in nearly a year.

"Watch how I do it, okay?"

"Okay." I was content to watch Rita until the cows came home, but in my heart of hearts, I knew that wouldn't help one iota. Golf required rhythm along with a good amount of coordination. I lacked both. Over the years, I'd developed the theory that being a good golfer was directly proportional to being a good dancer. Therefore, if one could dance, one could golf. And vice versa. Take Pam for instance. Pam can watusi, cha-cha, and recently won a shag—the official dance of South Carolina—contest. Pam can also drive a golf ball one hundred fifty yards down the fairway straight as an arrow. Suddenly I missed Pam. My BFF wouldn't matter-of-factly tell me to keep my head down. She'd know I needed a "poor-baby" pat on the head. Thinking of Pam made me wish I'd asked her for pointers instead of Rita. Why hadn't I? Oh yeah, I remember. I planned to pump Rita for information about Kel Watson.

"So, Rita," I said, casually picking another range ball out of the bucket. "Tell me everything you know about Kel Watson."

Rita groaned. "Please tell me you're not playing detective again."

"Can't help it if I have an inquiring mind." I placed the ball on the mat. This time I wiggled my hips as I took my stance in the fond hope wiggling would simulate dancing. "I noticed Kel doesn't wear a wedding band. I take it he's not married?"

Rita rested her hands on top of her Big Bertha driver and cocked her head to one side. "Why do you ask? Thinking of trading Bill in for a newer model?"

"Chalk it up to the ponytail." I took a practice swing,

then stepped up to address the ball. This time it managed to leave the tee, but its departure wasn't exactly a Kodak moment.

Bending, Rita dug out a ball, placed it on the mat. "Kel's been divorced for years."

"What happened?"

"Same tired story." Rita adjusted the position of her hands on the club. "His wife left him for another man."

Since my driver didn't seem to be working properly, I exchanged it for a 3-wood. "Did Sheila and Kel know each other before Serenity Cove?"

"Hard to say." Rita hit several drives while I looked on under the guise of studying her swing.

"Why is it so hard to say whether they've met?" I persisted when Rita paused to take a break.

She shrugged. "I suppose it's possible they might have met at a seminar or conference over the years. After all, they are in the same field."

I wasn't making much progress—either with golf or my interrogation—but I wasn't ready to give up. "Sheila's convinced Kel was stalking her. You know the man better than I do. Do you think that's possible?"

Rita whiffed, completely missing her ball. Almost unheard of for a golfer of her caliber. "Jeez, Kate," she cursed. "Next you'll try to convince me Kel is responsible for Vaughn's death."

*Well, if the shoe fits . . .* I didn't need to be clairvoyant to sense Rita's growing frustration, so I quickly asked my next question before she stonewalled me. "Do you suppose Kel uses marijuana?"

"Who knows? Whether he does or not, it's none of my damn business." Rita took another practice swing, but I noticed she'd lost her rhythm.

"Think he might be growing pot?"

Rita whiffed again. "Those are only rumors. Unfounded, malicious rumors."

Hmm, I thought to myself as I took a swipe at a range ball. Much to my amazement, I seemed to be getting the hang of a semi-mediocre swing. The quality of Rita's drives, however, seemed to be deteriorating.

My small bucket of range balls nearly depleted, I mused out loud, "I can't help but find it odd that a man would lie about a beekeepers meeting."

"He probably wanted to get rid of you, but was too polite to say so. Look, Kate." Rita rammed her driver back into her bag, a surefire sign my lesson was finished. "Kel Watson is one of the good guys. He's always been ready to lend a hand with garden club projects either as a speaker or to help with the actual planting. I suspect Sheila's spreading gossip. It would be just like her to stir up trouble."

"Why would she want to do that?"

"You're Nancy Drew. You figure it out." Rita's mouth compressed into a hard line. "Maybe Sheila views the man as a professional rival. I stopped trying years ago to figure out what was going on inside that woman's head."

"Didn't mean to upset you." I returned my clubs to the bag. "How about lunch, my treat?"

"Sure," Rita relented. "Didn't mean to be so touchy."

"Sorry if my questions made you lose your rhythm," I said as we trudged toward the Watering Hole, often referred to by golfers as the "Nineteenth Hole."

"I didn't lose my rhythm as much as I forgot it," Rita confessed.

I hoisted the golf bag higher on my shoulder. "How so?"

Rita grinned down at me. "If you promise never to tell anyone, I'll give you my secret."

The day seemed full of secrets, but I'm always up for a few more. "If this darn golf bag weren't so heavy, I'd cross my heart and hope to die."

"Stick a needle in my eye." Rita completed the childhood phrase. "Suzie and the boobs," she said then, giving me a conspiratorial wink.

I looked at her, puzzled. "Who is Suzie, and what do her boobs have to do with your golf?"

"Simple." Rita's grin broadened. "Whenever I take my swing, I always chant the words 'Suzie and the boobs' to the tune of 'Bennie and the Jets.' 'Suzie' is the position of my hands before my stroke. 'Boobs' is the downstroke." She shrugged, looking a bit sheepish. "It helps me find the rhythm."

I shot my friend an envious glance. Rita's boobs were impressive 40DDs. As we deposited our clubs in a stand outside the Watering Hole, I caught myself wondering if invoking Suzie would help a modest 34B.

Inspiration, like lightning, doesn't usually strike twice. Today, however, was an exception. An idea occurred to me as I stepped onto my deck, morning coffee in hand, and surveyed my yard. The shrubs and flowers I'd recently planted were coming along nicely. The combination of warm, sunny days and occasional April showers had blessed them with a strong start. Plants, I'd discovered, often hid deadly secrets beneath their colorful faces. Hard as I tried, I couldn't rid myself of the certainty that Vaughn Bascomb had been poisoned.

And that the culprit was as plain as the nose on my face.

With this thought relentlessly looping through my brain, I went inside, picked up the phone, and began dialing. The Babes always came through in a pinch. I knew this would be no exception.

They didn't let me down. An hour later, fortified by caffeine and armed with optimism, I started my rounds.

Gloria appeared from the back of her house carrying a plastic trash bag. "Iris and narcissus as requested. Didn't know what else to put them in."

"The society garlic was my idea," Polly said as she joined us. "Don't smell too good, but it wards off evil spirits. I know this for fact 'cause I've been watching one of those vampire shows on TV."

"Perfect." I laughed. "Maybe society garlic will fend off evil spirits at the sheriff's."

Janine's was the next stop on my route. Seeing me, she stopped pulling weeds from a mulched bed near her front porch and waved. "Here's the loropetalum, which, by the way, I'm pretty sure is harmless," she said, handing me a woven basket. "Even though it broke my heart, I threw in some cuttings from my azaleas, roots and all. They're blooming like mad right now. I'd hate to think I did something to stop the show."

"Drastic times call for drastic measures."

"I think it's, desperate times call for desperate measures," Janine corrected.

"Whatever. Drastic or desperate, it's all a part of the elimination process." I placed her offerings on the floor of the Buick next to Gloria's.

A frown marred Janine's smooth brow. "I hope you're mistaken, Kate."

"The worst my little experiment can do is to prove that I'm on the wrong track. It won't be the first time. Thanks." I waved as I drove off.

As promised, Pam had left a box containing her contributions—lantana, camellias, and calla—on the porch. Since this was Megan's day off, the two of them had gone shopping. Sweet, I thought. I have to confess that I often envy their mother-daughter relationship. On my last visit to California, Jen had taken me to Rodeo Drive. A quick glance at price tags, and I'd developed a severe case of sticker shock. I'd broken down and admitted Kohl's and Stein Mart were more my speed. Jen swore she'd never heard of either.

Humming "Bennie and the Jets," I drove into Brookdale. I wasn't finished yet. Not by a country mile. A

Jeep pulled out of a parking space near the sheriff's as I drove up. I took this as an omen, a good one, and pulled in. I maneuvered close to the curb and turned off the ignition. Going around to the passenger side, I gathered my arsenal and, colors flying, marched off to battle.

# Chapter 30

Deepening my voice, I adopted a phony-baloney Southern drawl. "Delivery for Sheriff Wiggins."

"Go right on in," Tammy Lynn replied absently, not glancing up from her filing. "Down the hall, on your left."

Camouflage. Why hadn't I thought of it sooner? All I needed was to hide behind an armful of greenery, and *pow!* Immediate access to the inner sanctum. No cooling my heels reading dog-eared magazines. No memorizing the mugs of hooligans pinned to a bulletin board. No listening to lame excuses. Just grab a bunch of plants and trot right in.

I eased open the door with my hip. "Delivery," I sang out.

"What the Sam Hill?" a familiar voice thundered. Even in thundering mode, the deep baritone held a certain melodious undertone. I wonder if felons appreciated the fine quality of the sheriff's vocal range.

"I brought more samples for you to test," I said from behind a veritable forest of branches and leaves.

My announcement was greeted with a sneeze.

I dumped the entire conglomeration—bag, box, and basket—down in front of him. "The rest should be arriving shortly."

"'Tammy Lynn," he bellowed. "Get in here." The melodious quality I previously mentioned was beginning to sound somewhat nasal.

When Tammy Lynn failed to appear in response to his summons, he rose from his desk to glower at me. "What in blue blazes . . . ?"

Just then Connie Sue, followed closely by Claudia, breezed in. Both women, bless their hearts, carried plants of some sort. Like I always say, if you can't count on girlfriends, who can you count on?

"So, this is where y'all are hidin'." Connie Sue shoved aside a neat stack of folders to make room for her donation.

Claudia deposited the three-gallon plastic pot she carried on the floor next to the desk. "Nice to visit, Sheriff, when I'm not a guest of the county."

Sumter Wiggins sneezed again.

"*Gesundheit,*" we chorused in three-part harmony.

Sheriff Wiggins turned away and began pawing through a desk drawer. Paper clips, pens, and Post-it notes spilled onto the floor before he produced a box of tissues and loudly blew his nose. "Ladies," he began. He probably aimed for *stern* but had to be content with *congested.* "Kindly state your business, then take those . . . those . . . things out of heah."

"I'm afraid we can't do that, Sheriff," I said sweetly. "The Babes and I have discussed this. All of us agree that the crime lab needs additional samples of everyday plants."

"For instance, did you know that water hemlock is one of the most dangerous plants in the whole country?" Connie Sue asked, showing off her newly acquired knowledge.

"Yes, yes, I've been informed, but . . ." He reached for another tissue.

Connie Sue, never afraid to seize the moment, continued. "I didn't have any hemlock, so I brought along both hyacinth and daffodils. If there's any left when that lab of yours is done testin', they'll make a right pretty bouquet."

"I brought gardenias." Claudia pointed at her contribution. "Don't know if they're poisonous or not. They won't bloom for another month or so, but when they do their scent is absolutely divine." Turning, she directed her next words to Connie Sue and me. "I just splurged on an expensive perfume, White Gardenia, to wear next time I go out with BJ. He loves gardenias. The clerk said it's practically guaranteed to bring a man to his knees."

I smiled to myself when I saw the sheriff blink moisture from his eyes. The lawman seemed genuinely touched by our unsolicited offer to help solve the case. We were the poster children for caring individuals everywhere. Our actions set the bar high.

"I thought I heard voices," Diane said, poking her head in the door. "Where do you want all this?"

Diane, as promised, had raided the woods behind her big old farmhouse. She had filled a large carton with samples of Carolina jessamine, dogwood, and red bed.

"Over there," I said, pointing to a spot next to the wastepaper basket. The office seemed to shrink under the barrage of plant life, which filled every nook and cranny.

"What the . . . ?" The sheriff's tirade was cut short by a trio of sneezes.

Diane brushed off her hands, then shoved a brunette strand behind one ear. "According to my research, all parts of the Carolina jessamine, or yellow jessamine as it's sometimes called, are poisonous."

Claudia shook her head sadly. "Hard to imagine those bright yellow flowers with that wonderful aroma could be harmful."

"Did you know Lenten roses—hellebores—were responsible for the death of Alexander the Great?" Diane asked.

"No," I replied aghast. "I just bought some at Lowe's."

"Well, sugar, don't put them in your salad," Connie Sue cautioned dryly.

Sheriff Wiggins dabbed at his watery eyes with a crumpled tissue. "Ladies, please . . ."

But that didn't deter Diane when she was on a roll. "Many historians believe Napoleon didn't die from natural causes, but was poisoned."

Lordy, how that girl loved her trivia. Even Alex Trebek on *Jeopardy!* would give one of his rare nods of approval.

Claudia shook her head in disbelief. "You don't say."

"Arsenic." Diane nodded, her expression somber. "And speaking of arsenic, I came across a case where sixteen members of a Lutheran church became deathly ill after drinking coffee in the church hall. One man died a short time later. Come to find out, the coffee was heavily laced with arsenic."

"Coffee . . . ?" Claudia arched a brow and cast a meaningful glance at the large mug resting on the sheriff's desk.

The rest of us stared at it, too. After Claudia's previous encounter with Sheriff Sumter Wiggins, the thought of lacing his coffee must have been awfully tempting.

Scowling, the sheriff followed the direction of our stare. Reaching over, he shoved the mug aside. "Tammy Lynn," he bellowed,

"Hey, guys, sorry I'm late." It was Rita not Tammy Lynn who appeared as if by magic. "This is the angel's trumpet I told you about. Just be careful," she warned. "It's beautiful, but deadly."

"Tammy Lynn," the sheriff called again. He looked toward the doorway, his expression hopeful, clearly expecting his gal Friday to rescue him from an onslaught of crazy women. "Where in the blazes is that girl?"

"Tammy Lynn?" Rita asked. "She's out on the front walk flirting with that cute young policeman, Eric Olsen." Rita gave us Babes a broad wink. "And from what I could tell, Eric was flirting right back. The two didn't even notice me."

"Woo-hoo!" Connie Sue pumped her fist in the air. "The makeover was a resoundin' success. Let's hear it, girls."

Our cheers sent Sheriff Wiggins fleeing.

"Tammy Lynn," we heard him yell. "Where are my allergy pills?"

"This room needs repainting," I mused aloud.

"Hmm . . ." Bill murmured.

The two of us sat side by side in the library/den/study admiring Bill's handiwork. I occupied Jim's sturdy but shabby recliner, the footrest up. Bill sat next to me in the desk chair, his feet propped on an upturned box. The bookshelves were complete. And as I'd known he would, Bill had done an excellent job. His craftsmanship impeccable. A testament to the man's talent with hammer, saws, and drills. In spite of the lovely cherry shelves, however, the room still didn't resemble the elegant room I'd envisioned.

"Maybe a different color. Soft, but not too soft. What do you think about butternut?"

"If we're talking squash, I like mine baked."

I shot him a look. "No, silly, I'm talking paint colors."

Bill shrugged. "They make paint in squash colors?"

"Sage green might be a nice contrast with the cherry stain."

"Green's good," Bill agreed amiably. "Can't go wrong with green."

I continued in the same vein. "And then there's the

matter of furniture. This room could definitely use new furniture. I'm thinking leather, or perhaps one of those new microfiber fabrics that resemble suede. Which do you like best?"

Bill shifted—squirmed might be more like it—in his seat. "Either, er, both are fine with me."

I sighed. "Then there's the matter of window treatments. Sheila's rental has custom-made blinds and valances, but I've always been partial to plantation shutters. What do you think would work best?"

"Umm, uh . . . is it warm in here?" He jumped up and headed for the kitchen. "I'll go see if the coffee's ready."

I wanted to laugh out loud at Bill's obvious discomfort. The guy looked like he'd been about to break into a sweat. In some respects Bill and my late husband, Jim, were much alike. Confident and fearless, they made decisions on big-ticket items such as refinancing the mortgage or the amount of liability insurance, but ask them for an opinion on paint color or window treatments and they ran for cover. Or in Bill's case, the coffeepot.

Bill returned minutes later, a steaming mug of freshly brewed coffee in each hand. "Your pot roast tonight tasted great," he said, apparently finding food a safer topic than interior decor.

"I know pot roast, along with tuna noodle casserole, is high on your list of favorites." I accepted the mug, crossed my ankles. "I thought we needed something special to celebrate the completion of the bookshelves. I even considered champagne."

"Nah." Bill shook his head. "In my mind, pot roast tops champagne."

*Men!* I gave him a fond smile and decided to let him off the hook. "Think I'm going to ask Connie Sue for help. She's a whiz at decorating. She once spent an entire day going store to store comparing paint samples."

We lounged back in our respective seats, cradling our coffee mugs.

"I confess," Bill said, "I don't know a danged thing when it comes to furniture and window blinds. That was my wife's department. If paint color was left up to me, I'd wind up with azalea pink or daffodil yellow."

"Hearing you mention 'azalea' and 'daffodil' reminds me of my visit to the sheriff's office this morning."

He peered at me over the rim of his cup, his expression serious. "And how did that go?"

"Not well," I said, summarizing the meeting in two words.

"Care to talk about it?"

"The Babes and I delivered a variety of plants and shrubs common to this area. My intention was that he send these to the state toxicology lab for testing. Unfortunately, the sheriff has allergies, so our meeting was cut short."

Bill chuckled. "So you found the mighty Sumter Wiggins's Achilles' heel."

"Guess the man's human after all," I said with a laugh, remembering the watery eyes, the runny nose, and the mad scramble for allergy pills. Then I sobered. "I'm operating under the assumption that Vaughn and Sheila were poisoned with a substance easily accessible to anyone knowledgeable in horticulture."

"I suppose you have a list of suspects?"

"Thought you'd never ask." I quickly rose and left the newly christened library, and returned minutes later with my little black book. "I've wanted to brainstorm with you. Keep in mind the motive, means, and opportunity method of criminal investigation."

"I worry about you, Kate. Maybe you should let the sheriff handle things." I opened my mouth to object, but he wasn't finished yet. "If your theory's correct, the person you're dealing with is dangerous—and devious. Think how easy it would be for him or her to put a drop or two of poison in your drink or mix a little into your food. Promise you'll be extra cautious until whoever did this is caught."

*Aw, he cares. Or was it a nice way of telling me I am crazy?* "You're right, of course," I said meekly. "I promise, I'll be careful."

Maybe I was crazy, certifiably insane, to disregard the advice of family, friends, and even the sheriff. I'd become a dyed-in-the-wool crime and punishment addict. I wouldn't quit until the puzzle was solved, justice done. Crime solving had become my OCD du jour. I was doomed. Should I see a shrink? Or find the killer? I didn't have to ponder long; I already knew the answer.

"I've already ruled out Rita as a person of interest." I flipped open my notebook.

"Rita Larsen?" Bill nearly choked on his coffee. "Rita, your friend and fellow Bunco Babe?"

"The Babes don't murder people." I skimmed through my notes. "Besides, Rita was too obvious in her dislike of Sheila. What was the word you just used?" These darn senior moments happen at the most inopportune times. Then it came to me. "Devious! A killer, especially one who uses poison, would have been more devious, more subtle than Rita, so hear me out."

Bill listened attentively as I ran though my list of suspects—Todd, Roger, Betsy, and Kel—including possible motives, means, and opportunities. "Well," he said when I finished, "since you want my opinion, I'd say Todd Timmons, boy producer, has motive and opportunity, but lacks know-how."

"What about Roger McFarland?"

"You just said Roger has sole creative control over that fancy flower book he's editing. That, combined with the fact Betsy, not Sheila or Vaughn, beat him out of some high-paying job he coveted rules out motive."

"But he has means and opportunity," I whined.

"Sorry." Bill was ruthless. "Without motive you can't make your case. Let's move on."

Sighing, I turned a page. "That brings us to stuck-up Betsy Dalton. She has motive up the wazoo. I have it on good authority that Vaughn and Betsy were once engaged. Then Vaughn threw her over for Sheila. What's the saying, 'Hell hath no fury like a woman scorned?' Betsy wanted revenge, bided her time, then '*Gotcha!*'"

"Just because you don't like the woman doesn't make her guilty," Bill pointed out, sounding irritatingly like the voice of reason. "You're forgetting Betsy wasn't there. If you recall, her flight was delayed, and she arrived late."

I slumped in my chair. Bill was becoming one tough critique partner. "True, I don't like the woman," I admitted grudgingly. "Betsy's arrogant and likes to intimidate me, but I couldn't resist putting her on the list. There is one more . . ."

Over a second cup of coffee, I ran through the pros and cons of Kel Watson—the lone person left on my list—as the possible perp.

Frowning, Bill shook his head. "Granted, the man has means and opportunity, but what motive could Kel possibly have to harm Sheila or Vaughn?"

I shifted in the recliner, trying to find a more comfortable position. Motive was the weak link in the Kel Watson scenario. Circumstantial, but no hard evidence. "I believe Kel's a stalker. Why else would he keep showing up, first at the TV studio, and then wherever in Serenity Cove Sheila happens to be? At the banquet, the hospital, and even at the reception after Vaughn's memorial service? I think he's obsessed with Sheila and viewed Vaughn as a rival for her affection. If Kel couldn't have her, no one could."

"Mm, I don't know." Bill looked doubtful. "Sorry to

burst your bubble, Kate, but to be honest your theory seems a bit contrived. More like a plot one of those made-for-TV movies on the Lifetime channel."

I felt deflated. I was reaching, and I knew it, trying to catch a killer before they harmed anyone else. I wanted to stick out my lower lip and pout like a petulant two-year-old, not very attractive for a woman over sixty. Dejectedly, I gazed at my pretty new bookshelves, which at present held only two volumes: *The Complete Idiot's Guide to Forensics* and *The Complete Idiot's Guide to Private Investigating*. I wondered if perhaps I wasn't the living breathing version of the complete idiot.

# Chapter 31

"Sorry, Kate, I thought I'd made this clear." Rita's impatience transmitted itself across the phone lines. "Even provisional members of the garden club are expected to participate in our community service project."

"But a cemetery . . . ?" I'd been awake only long enough to down half a cup of coffee. I squinted out the window. Was the sun up yet? I wasn't a morning person by nature. Never was, never will be. My body clock just doesn't tick that way. Even when I was up and functioning, I didn't function. If that makes me a bad person, then so be it.

"Most of the members have already put in their time. All that's left for you to do is weed around the gateposts at the entrance."

"You want me to go out there—to a deserted cemetery—all by myself?" I heard a whiny note creep into my voice, but didn't care. A deserted cemetery plus weeding equals resistance. It doesn't take a math major to come up with the correct answer.

"Don't be such a baby, Kate. Deserted means there's no one else around; you'll have the place to yourself. Think how quiet and peaceful it'll be. You can commune with nature."

If I wanted to commune with nature, I'd sit on a beach in the Bahamas and watch the ocean while sipping a margarita. "Left to my own devices at the cemetery, I might be dangerous. I could pull out something that turns out to be a flower and not a weed."

"If it looks like a weed, chances are it is a weed. If it looks like a flower leave it alone. I'd go with you if I could, but I have a dental appointment."

Given Rita's choice of the dentist's office or a deserted cemetery, I knew which one I'd pick hands down. The cemetery. But not Rita. She was a glutton for punishment. "Fine," I acquiesced with obvious reluctance.

"And, Kate, one more thing. The club needs it done today if possible."

"Today?" The whine was back, the volume turned up. I had things to do, places to go. In other words, I had muffins to bake and library books to return.

"Let me know when you're finished. The club wants to send out a photographer from the *Serenity Sentinel* to take some pictures. Sorry, Kate. Gotta run, but don't worry. The job shouldn't take more than an hour at most," she added before hanging up.

The call had left me feeling cranky and out of sorts. I needed to work on crime solving, not weed picking. The toxicology lab in Columbia was slow as molasses in coming up with the possible cause of Vaughn Bascomb's death. They needed a boost. I couldn't help but wonder if Sheriff Wiggins even bothered to send along the samples the Babes and I had collected.

I popped a bagel into the toaster and poured myself more coffee. Eventually the bagel was demolished and the coffeepot drained. Time had come to put on my big girl panties and quit procrastinating. I donned an old pair of jeans and an even older T-shirt. No sense fussing with hair or makeup for old dead people and a bunch of weeds. It wasn't as if I was going on a date. I'd take a shower and freshen up when I got home in case Bill happened to drop by. I collected a pair of gardening gloves and a few basic tools. I tossed these into a canvas tote bag along with my wallet, then grabbed my car keys. I was good to go.

I turned down the same road I'd taken the day I followed Kel Watson. Today promised to be a beauty, the air already warm, the sky a bright Carolina blue. Birds chirped; insects hummed. It was hard to remain grumpy on such a lovely spring morning. I bumped along listening to Kenny Chesney, Polly and Megan's number one stud muffin, warble something about no shirt, no shoes, no problems. I, on the other hand, had shirt, shoes, and a boatload of problems. The first and foremost being who killed Vaughn Bascomb and nearly succeeded in killing Sheila.

I stopped when I came to the fork in the road. On my last visit I'd discovered Kel, costumed as if ready to explore outer space, inspecting stacks of rectangular white boxes, which I'd since learned on the Internet were called "supers." Was the man really the crazed stalker that Sheila had intimated? Was he mentally deranged? A psychopath? I'd seen plenty of movies where a man becomes fixated on an attractive woman. They usually involved a cat-and-mouse chase through a darkened house that culminated in the woman narrowly escaping with her life. The sort of movie that had me double-checking the locks, looking under the bed, and sleeping with a light on.

Since Kel's beehives were on the left, the cemetery had to be down the right fork. Brilliant deduction on my part, if I do say so myself. No reason to hurry. The weeding could wait.

I slowly idled down the rutted track I'd traveled two days ago. To my surprise, the road didn't end with the Queen Bee and her dominions, but continued on. Feeling adventurous, I decided to do a little exploring. Even though this wasn't far from my home, I'd never been out this way. I knew from local lore that the very ground I now traveled over was once home to the Huguenots, French Protestants who'd fled to the Carolinas to escape religious persecution in the eighteenth century. Many of their descendants still lived in the area. I once heard a local historian say this place had been a "hotbed of dissent" during the American Revolution. It was still a "hotbed" in my estimation. Due to several recent murders, Serenity Cove was no longer so serene.

I drove a goodly distance past the hives and was about to turn around when the trees thinned to form a meadow. In the middle stood a small garden plot. A strange place for a garden, but one nevertheless. I stopped the Buick and climbed out for a closer look. Why in the world would someone plant a garden in the middle of nowhere? But plant it they had. Whoever owned it had even gone to the trouble of constructing a sturdy chicken-wire fence to protect it from marauding Bambis and bunny rabbits. And to add to the mystery, the fence was locked with a shiny chrome padlock.

*Curious and curiouser, cried Alice.*

I picked my way through ankle-high grass to get a better look. The plants filling the enclosure were approximately a foot high with slender serrated leaves. This would be a sure-fire test of my new plant life identification skills. I squatted down for a better look. Leaves in groups of five or more fanned out from a central stem. They didn't resemble any common houseplant, or any of the plants I'd seen at Dixie Gardens. I made a made a mental note to seek Rita's expertise in giving them a name. Taking my cell phone out of my pocket, I snapped a photo, remembering to press SAVE. Some leaves were poking through the fence, practically calling my name so I snipped off a few with the clippers I'd brought along and tossed them in my tote bag. Later, I'd bring them to the sheriff for testing.

Intent on the mystery leaves, I started to rise.

I sucked in my breath at a sharp, burning pain in my forearm, which was simultaneously accompanied by a loud *pop!* I looked down just as a bee, its dastardly deed done, flew off. It had left its stinger behind as a calling card. *Uh-oh,* I thought. This spelled trouble with a capital E—E as in epinephrine. E also as in ER. Last time I'd been stung, the doctor had warned me not to take chances. Advice I planned to heed. Digging out my phone again, I dialed 1-800-BILL.

My arm felt like it was on fire. Odd how such a tiny pinprick can be the cause of so much pain. Forcing myself to remain calm, I slumped down beside the fence to wait for Bill's arrival.

"Sorry for all the bother," I said, my tongue staring to feel thick and clumsy.

Bill guided me toward his Ford pickup. "You're never a bother. Got here as fast as I could."

"I didn't trust myself to drive." I allowed myself to be helped into the truck and have the seat belt fastened.

"Want me to call nine-one-one?"

"Just put the pedal to the metal," I lisped.

"Consider it done." Bill executed a three-point turn, and we were off like a rocket.

Meanwhile, I could feel hives starting to pop like Orville Redenbacher's Kettle Korn along my arms and legs. I was about to scratch the most annoying one when I noticed a steady trickle of blood coming from a tear in the sleeve of my T-shirt. "I'm bleeding," I mumbled.

Bill took his eyes off the road long enough to glance at me worriedly. "What the . . . ?"

I shrugged off his concern. "I must have caught my shirt on the fence." By this time, I was beginning to feel a bit light-headed and tried not to panic. Closing my eyes, I leaned my head against the headrest. "I'm sure there's no cause for alarm, but could you drive a little faster?"

Bill complied, and the rest of the drive was a blur. I didn't open my eyes again until we reached the ER. Ignoring my feeble protest, Bill rushed to get a wheelchair. Good thing, too, since I didn't think my legs would support me. He wheeled me inside and spoke with the admissions clerk. I was immediately whisked into an exam room and lifted onto a stretcher.

"Hope I'm not making too big a deal out of a teensy beesting," I wheezed. My chest felt as though it had a sack of cement on top of it.

"Don't give it another thought, hon," the nurse assured me as she hooked me up to oxygen. "You did the right thing getting here as fast as you could."

The ER doc—the same one who'd treated Vaughn and Sheila—flew into the cubicle and rattled off orders in quick succession. I heard words like Benadryl and epinephrine and steroids. Music to the ears of anyone having a serious reaction. I gave Bill, who hovered nearby, a feeble thumbs-up.

"Make a fist, sweetie," the nurse instructed as she prepared to start an IV. Then her tone sharpened. "Dr. Michaels, I think you'd better take a look at this."

My eyes, which had been half-closed, snapped open.

The doctor pushed up the sleeve of my T-shirt. A frown furrowed his brow. "Mrs. McCall, did you realize your arm's been grazed by a bullet?"

"What . . . ?" If I had trouble breathing before, this bit of information knocked the rest of the wind out from my sails.

Unbelievable! Then I recalled the *pop* I'd heard the same instant as the beesting. Could that have been a gunshot? And what's more, who would want to shoot at me?

# Chapter 32

"Who do you s'pose would want to shoot a nice, but nosy, lady such as yourself?" Sheriff Wiggins drawled.

*Hmph!* Me, nosy? "Is that any way to speak to a person who's been wounded—perhaps by a sniper?"

"Sniper, eh?" He scratched his head. "Don't reckon many of 'em 'round these parts. 'Course, a big place like Serenity Cove Estates is another matter."

Even in my weakened state, I could recognize sarcasm when I heard it. The ER doc had insisted he was legally bound to notify the authorities of any and all gunshot wounds. He'd promptly phoned the sheriff, who'd arrived posthaste. The bullet had only grazed my upper arm, but required suturing. Would I have a tale to tell at bunco! I could hardly wait to see the expressions on the Babes' faces. If it wasn't for the five stitches, they might think I'd fabricated the entire story.

Bill and I were still in the emergency room, but I was hoping to get my walking papers soon. I'd had enough of hospitals now that I was beginning to feel like myself again. The shot the nurse had given me had dulled the pain in my arm to a persistent ache. The steroids and anti-histamines had also done their jobs. Better living through pharmaceuticals, just like the ads on TV say.

"What are you and your men doing to find the person who did this?" Bill demanded. Judging from his grim expression, he didn't seem happy with the sheriff's laid-back approach to my predicament.

The sheriff shifted his gaze from me to Bill. Most men would quail upon being skewered by those laser-bright eyes, but not my Bill. His blues didn't blink as he returned the look. I thought I saw the sheriff make a slight, almost imperceptible nod, before answering— but I could've been mistaken, considering all the drugs I'd been given.

"My men are combing the area. Now," he said, and this time it was my turn to be on the receiving end of the lawman's piercing stare, "let's go over this again. You say you didn't see or hear anything out of the ordinary?"

"We've already been through this." I sighed. "I was bending down to examine some strange-looking plants when I was stung by a bee. I vaguely remember a popping sound, but at the time I was too worried about having a reaction to the bee sting to pay much attention."

The sheriff jotted this in his omnipresent notebook. "Seems to me a person, a curious person such as yourself, would look to see where the poppin' noise was comin' from."

"Last time I was stung—years ago—the doctor told me not to waste time seeking medical attention or the results could be serious."

"Doc Michaels told me you should've been carryin' one of those gizmos allergic folk are s'posed to keep handy."

He was right, of course, which made me feel guilty as sin. Unable to meet the censure that seemed to radiate from him, I dropped my eyes and picked at the adhesive holding my IV in place. "I do have one of those 'gizmos,'" I admitted miserably. "An EpiPen. I'm supposed to keep it with me, but I forgot it when I switched purses."

It was Sumter Wiggins's turn to sigh. Why is it men can't understand a woman's compulsion to accessorize? If Jim had had his way, one purse, probably black, would have sufficed. No need to coordinate a handbag with shoes or the event or the outfit. Or the season. A woman *needs* variety, large purses, small purses, black purses, brown purses. *One fish, two fish, red fish, blue fish.* And so it goes. Dr. Seuss had the right idea.

The sheriff's cell phone rang just then, and he turned away to answer.

Bill stepped closer, took my hand, and squeezed it. "Kate, promise me you'll get one of those damn gizmos for every single purse you own."

"EpiPens," I corrected with a wan smile. "It's a promise."

His call completed, the sheriff returned. "That was Deputy Preston callin' to report they'd recovered a shell casin'."

"Good," Bill and I said in unison.

"By the way," I said, "did your men check out the secret garden I told you about? The plants I described could be the type used to poison Vaughn and Sheila. They must be important. If not, why bother to secure it with a padlock?"

"Oh, they're important, all right." Sheriff Wiggins chuckled, actually chuckled. "But I think we can rule them out as the killer poison."

"What makes you so sure?" Bill asked.

"The mystery plant isn't a mystery any longer. It has a name—cannabis."

I mentally reviewed my lexicon of things green and growing. "The name doesn't ring a bell."

"Most folks refer to it as marijuana. Some call it pot, others weed or grass."

"Ahh, marijuana. So that's what all the fuss was about."

"Uh-huh." The sheriff nodded. "My guess is the person growin' it saw you and didn't take kindly to someone pokin' their nose in his business. Doubt they intended to kill you. More likely wanted to scare you off is all."

I played with the sheet covering me, pleating it first, then smoothing it. "What if they'd killed me—accidentally?"

"Guess you'd be dead instead of sassy as ever."

I thought about this for a long moment. I know everyone dies someday, but I wasn't ready to go yet. Especially with a departure hastened by some kook defending a patch of illegal drugs.

"I warned you, Miz McCall, snoopin' around can be dangerous. Next time you might not be so lucky. You could find yourself seriously injured—or worse."

"For your information, I wasn't 'snoopin' around,'" I retorted, highly offended by his assertion. "I happened to be out there on behalf of the garden club."

"You sayin' the garden club is growing marijuana?"

"Don't be ridiculous," I snapped. "The club's service project happens to be the beautification of the Huguenot Cemetery."

He tugged his earlobe. "If memory serves, the cemetery's in the opposite direction of where you were shot."

Busted! Time to fess up. "I admit that the other day I followed Kel Watson as far as the beehives. Today I wanted to see where the road led, so I went a little farther and that's when I found the . . . marijuana."

The sheriff raised his brow—one dark intimidating brow. "Just curious, Miz McCall, ever get around to doin' any weedin' or flower plantin'?"

"No," I said, affronted by the smirk he was trying to hide. "But I had every intention of doing so. Why else would I go out in public without taking the time to do my hair or makeup?"

I groaned inwardly. With everything that had transpired, I'd completely forgotten my dishevelment. I must look like Babezilla. I wouldn't blame Bill if he ran for cover.

Sheriff Wiggins snapped his notebook shut and slid it into a pocket. "I'll keep you informed of our progress on findin' the shooter."

And that was that. The grillin' was over.

"Bill, would you hand me my tote bag?" I asked after Sumter Wiggins departed. "I didn't even bother with lipstick this morning. I'm a wreck." How like me to always keep an extra tube of lipstick handy, but no EpiPen. Dumb, dumber, and dumbest!

"Hey," Bill said, smiling as he passed it over. "As far as I'm concerned, you still look pretty as a picture. Now let's see about those discharge papers."

Turns out getting in was easier than getting out.

Dr. Michaels, it seemed, was a proponent of due diligence, a bona fide conservative. He insisted I hang around for observation. Said things like wanting to make sure I was stable before he'd sign off on my case.

By the time we finally pulled into my drive, it was growing dark. Instead of leaving, however, Bill informed me that he intended to spend the night. I made the requisite halfhearted protests, but relented without much of a fight.

The day had taken its toll. First the beesting, followed by the wild ride to the ER, and finally discovering I'd been shot. Besides, the Benadryl the doctor had prescribed was making me groggy. While I relaxed in a nice hot bath, Bill fixed grilled cheese sandwiches and tomato soup. When I finally joined him, wrapped in a pink fleece robe, the simple meal tasted like a gourmet dinner. It's been a long time since I'd had a man fuss over me. And it felt terrific.

Afterward, we cuddled on the sofa while watching *American Idol*. My eyelids drooped shut before Ryan

Seacrest announced which contestant would be sent home.

"Kate, honey," Bill said as he gently shook me awake. "I think it's time for you go to bed."

I sat up, yawning—and hoping I hadn't drooled. "Make yourself comfortable in the guest room," I told him drowsily. "I think you'll find everything you need."

He kissed my forehead. "You gave me quite a scare today. I've already lost one woman I loved, I don't want to lose another."

Love . . . ? Did I hear the L word? Or was I tripping out on drugs? I fell asleep the instant my head hit the pillow with a smile on my face.

I awoke the next morning to an incessant ringing. I rolled over, jammed the pillow over my head, and wished the caller would give it a rest and hang up. My upper arm ached from the gunshot wound; my forearm was swollen, sore, and itchy from the beesting. As for my disposition . . . well, just call me Miss Cranky Pants.

A light tap on the door was followed by Bill's voice. "Kate, honey, I think you'd better take this."

I stifled a moan as I swung my legs out of bed. Anyone who knows me knows better than to call before nine o'clock. How many times do I have to tell people, I'm not a morning person? Shoving the hair out of my eyes, I reached for my robe as Bill entered the bedroom, a cordless phone in one hand, coffee mug in the other. "It's your son," he whispered.

*Thanks*, I mouthed. My teeth felt furry; my hair was a disaster. This definitely didn't resemble a cute morning-after scene in one of those vintage romantic comedies I dearly loved. Katharine Hepburn or Claudette Colbert never subjected Spencer or Clark to halitosis or bed head. But this wasn't a movie classic, it was twenty-first-century reality. I accepted the phone along with my fate. "Hey, sweetie . . ."

"Mother," Steven said, his tone harsh, "don't try to tell me that man—Bill What's-his-name—didn't spend the night."

I shot a cautious glance at Bill. Wordlessly, he handed me the coffee mug.

"You might fool me once, but not twice," Steven continued his tirade. "This is the second time I've called early in the morning and found him there. I demand to know what's going on."

"Nothing is 'going on' as you so eloquently phrase it. I shouldn't need to remind you that I'm a grown woman and don't owe you an explanation—even if something was 'going on,' which it isn't." I took a gulp of coffee and scalded my tongue. Did I overdo the "going on" part? I wondered. Doth the lady "protest too much?" Or merely engage in wishful thinking?

Silence spun its sticky web. "Sorry, Mother," Steven muttered at long last. "It's just that Jen and I are concerned with you so far away and us never having met this guy. You must admit it seems suspicious when I call early and he answers the phone."

It was sweet of them to worry, I suppose, but unnecessary. "Bill did stay the night, dear, but not because of any prurient interest."

Hearing this, Bill raised a brow askance, but I merely shrugged. Prurient was a word I'd been waiting for the just the right moment to whip out. I only hoped I'd used it in the right context. Nothing like taking a new word out for a vocabulary spin and then using it incorrectly. Time to get back on track. "I was stung by a bee yesterday, and Bill drove me to the emergency room," I explained.

"I don't recall you being allergic to bees."

"I've become more allergic since you went away to college."

"Are you all right?"

"A shot of epinephrine and a couple stitches, and I'm right as rain."

"Stitches? Since when does a beesting require stitches?" Steven, bless his heart, sounded stricken. "What *aren't* you telling me, Mother?"

Note to self: Never have a discussion with your first-born without being fortified by lots of caffeine. I took another gulp of coffee and crossed my fingers that the caffeine would bypass my stomach and go straight to my brain. "No need to be upset, sweetie. The sheriff assured me whoever shot at me only wanted to frighten me away from his marijuana patch."

Another lengthy silence. During that time, I seriously considered having my jaw wired shut to prevent me from blabbing. "Steven . . . ? Dear, are you still there?"

"That does it, Mother! Sam and I are coming down for a visit."

"S-sam . . . ?" My mind stuttered at the notion of Steven's upcoming visit. And the fact he was bringing someone along named Sam.

"I want to meet this Bill person. And find out once and for all what kind of place you live in. We'll be there as soon as Sam can rearrange her schedule. See you soon," he said, disconnecting.

"Sam's a she." I handed Bill back the cordless. "Is it too early for a margarita?"

# Chapter 33

It never fails. Just when you think things can't get any worse, they do.

My garbage disposal growled like a heavy metal band. I think it ate a fork. Next I stubbed my toe hurrying to answer the phone only to hear the canned spiel of a telemarketer. And then when I went out to water my plants, I discovered mud daubers had built their tunnel-like nests all around my front door. I don't recall pesky mud daubers in Toledo. But down here they pose a nuisance. Now, for the uninitiated, mud daubers are wasps. Fortunately for someone like me who's allergic to insect stings, the daubers tend to have a nonaggressive nature. Unless you're a black widow spider, that is. Trouble is the daubers' nests aren't a aesthetically pleasing. Comprised of dirt—and dirt in these parts means red clay—their nests need to be knocked down, then the area scrubbed to remove the reddish brown stain they leave behind. After last week, I wasn't about to take any chances. I'd have to have my EpiPen in one hand and a scrub brush in the other when I cleaned up the mess. One trip to the ER was quite enough, thank you very much.

Hearing Tammy Lynn's voice on the phone was the

cherry on top of the sundae. Apparently her boss wanted
to see me pronto, ASAP, and get-your-butt-in-here-this-
minute fast. Sorry as I was to delay my attack on the
mud daubers—I'm being facetious—I hopped into the
Buick and pointed it toward Brookdale. I barely had to
steer. I'd made this trip so many times my car could
find its way all by itself.

"Hey, Kate," the new improved Tammy Lynn greeted
me warmly. "Sheriff Wiggins said to go right on in. He's
waitin' on you."

The Buick wasn't the only one to operate on autopilot. I could find his office blindfolded, I thought as I
walked down the hall and pushed open the door. To my
surprise, I found Sheila Rappaport seated in what I'd
come to think of as *my* chair. "Sheila!" I exclaimed. "What
brings you here?"

Sheila crossed her legs and smiled serenely. "Kel Watson made another attempt on my life."

"He what . . . ?" I could scarcely believe my ears.

"I just finished giving the sheriff my statement."

"What happened? Are you all right?"

"Yes, thank goodness, but Kel's been arrested. He
tried to poison me, but luckily this time I was onto his
tricks."

I was at a temporary loss for words—in my case usually a short-lived affliction. Spying a molded plastic chair
alongside a filing cabinet, I dragged it closer and plunked
myself down. I gave Sheila the once-over, but didn't see
any telltale signs of bodily harm. In spite of her ordeal,
she looked as elegant and poised as ever. An amazing
woman, Sheila Rappaport. Unlike me, I bet she'd never
rush off to pull weeds in a deserted cemetery unless her
hair and makeup were perfect. She looked chic in tailored navy blue linen slacks and a crisp white blouse
with turned-back cuffs and pearl buttons. I marveled at
the feat. I always look like an unmade bed whenever I
wear linen.

"You haven't mentioned why *you're* here," Sheila reminded me.

I shook my head. "Honestly, I have no idea. Tammy Lynn called and said the sheriff wanted to see me . . . so here I am. Where is he, by the way?"

"He said something about official business. Should be back any minute."

"In the meantime, tell we what happened with Kel. Or is it classified information?"

Sheila flicked an imaginary speck of lint from her slacks. "Kel turned up on my doorstep this morning unannounced. Insisted he wanted to make amends, to set the record straight. He kept repeating that he never meant for us to be enemies. He refused to leave until I heard him out so, against my better judgment, I invited him in."

I glanced nervously toward the partially open door, half-expecting the sheriff to appear and spoil my fun. Seeing as how he already considers me a busybody, I didn't want to give his belief any more ammunition. "Then what happened . . . ?"

"Well, I asked him to join me on the screened porch. Before he arrived, I'd been enjoying a glass of iced tea while reviewing galleys Roger had FedExed. Kel went on and on about how sorry he was for frightening me on the set of *How Does Your Garden Grow?* He told me how much he admired the show, said he viewed it regularly. Then he chatted about some mutual sites we'd explored, independently, of course. He said he needed a favor. He wanted to know if I had a photo of a certain ornamental we've come across in our travels. He claimed he needed it for a slide presentation for the garden club." Sheila brushed a wing of highlighted blond hair from her cheek. "Anything to get rid of the man, right?"

"Right," I agreed, hanging on to her every word.

"After I returned with the photo, Kel made a rather

abrupt departure and I returned to work on the galleys. I was about to take a sip of tea, but for some inexplicable reason I hesitated." A shudder raced through her. "I'm convinced at that precise moment, Vaughn's spirit reached out and saved my life. Suddenly I remembered his agony, the way his body had convulsed. Then I thought of Kel Watson's strange behavior."

I was at the edge of my seat. "And then what . . . ?"

She reached out and clutched my hand. "Thank God, Kate, I didn't drink the tea. It contained arsenic."

"Arsenic . . ."

Sheila nodded vigorously. "Of course I didn't know it at the time, but I was suspicious all the same. I immediately placed a call to the sheriff and demanded he send a sample to the lab for testing. He refused at first, but I was adamant. I even threatened to bring a lawsuit against him for failure to act on my behalf. Eventually, he conceded and agreed to have one of his off-duty men drive it to Columbia. The lab did a rush and faxed the results an hour ago."

"Wow," I said for lack of anything more eloquent. I leaned back trying to digest everything she'd just told me. Apparently the mystery was solved. Arsenic. Plain, old, ordinary arsenic. I'd recently watched the film *Arsenic and Old Lace* on a classic-movie cable network. Cary Grant and his sweet aunt Martha. One line in particular stayed in my head: *Well, dear, for a gallon of elderberry wine, I take one teaspoonful of arsenic, and add a half a teaspoonful of strychnine, and then just a pinch of cyanide.* Aunt Martha could have skipped the strychnine and cyanide and still won a blue ribbon at the county fair.

I felt deflated. Foolish. I'd been so positive I'd been on the right track. So certain that the poison came from a garden-variety botanical. I'd even enlisted the Babes' help to gather samples. I'd inundated poor allergy-suffering Sheriff Wiggins with plants until his eyes watered and his nose ran. Time to hang up my detective's shingle. Playing Nancy Drew had been fun while it lasted, but all good things must come to an end. It was time to resume my role as a senior citizen in a retirement community for "active" adults.

"Soon as I'm home, I'm going to start packing," Sheila said, seemingly oblivious to my dejection. "My lease is up at the end of the month. The book is essentially finished and *How Does Your Garden Grow?* hasn't been renewed for another season, so it's a good time to ... explore other avenues."

I nodded politely, my mind still on Kel's treachery. "Do you have any plans?"

"The past month has been stressful." She reached into her Louis Vuitton bag, brought out a gold compact, and studied her image. "I think I might travel. I've always wanted to spend time in the south of France. I've heard it's lovely this time of year."

When it comes to glamour, a burg like Serenity Cove Estates can't compete with the likes of the south of France. The south of France has the Cannes Film Festival and celebs like George Clooney and Brad Pitt. Serenity Cove, on the other hand, has the Babes and Bill. Think I'll stay put.

My ruminations were interrupted by the arrival of Sheriff Wiggins.

"Ladies," he said with a brisk nod. "Sorry to keep y'all coolin' your heels." He lowered his bulk into his chair and slid several sheets of paper across to Sheila. "This heah is your typed statement, Miz Rappaport. Kindly read it carefully before signin'."

"It's *Dr.* Rappaport, Sheriff." Ignoring the ballpoint he offered, she dropped her compact into her pricey handbag and extracted a slim Mark Cross pen.

While Sheila reviewed the document, the sheriff turned his focus on me. "Miz McCall, s'pose your wonderin' why I called you down heah?"

"'The thought did enter my mind," I replied. "Tammy Lynn said it was urgent."

"Based on the attempt on *Dr.* Rappaport's life, I asked Judge Blanchard to issue a search warrant for Kel Watson's home and property. We found arsenic in a storage shed behind his house. And"—he paused for effect, doing that eyebrow lift thing I'd come to anticipate—"we located a .22 rifle, recently fired. I trust ballistics will show a match with the shell casings at the site where you were shot. Plus, we unearthed a rather large stash of marijuana. We suspect Watson mighta been dealin.'"

*Wow*, I said, silently this time. While I'd been preoccupied looking for motive, means, and opportunity for Todd, Rog, and Bets, Kel Watson was blithely plotting murder and mayhem. "So," I said, trying to absorb all this, "has Kel confessed?"

"Not yet." Sheriff Wiggins leaned back and laced his sausagelike fingers over his trim abdomen. "It's only a matter of time before he talks."

In spite of everything, I felt sorry for the guy. Kel didn't stand a snowball's chance in hell in coming through an interrogation unscathed.

"Matter of fact, I just came from the jail. The man's insistin' he's innocent. Claims he's bein' railroaded."

"Humph!" Sheila snorted derisively. She shoved the signed papers toward the sheriff. "A likely story. The man's a nutcase. Probably spends all his free time watching *Law & Order* reruns on the boob tube."

Along with Kel, I'd just been relegated to being a "nutcase" and was none too happy about it. I also wasn't pleased with the smirk the sheriff shot in my direction as he collected Sheila's signed statement and slipped it into a folder. "Guess this wraps things up," he said.

"Not so fast," I protested. "What if Kel doesn't confess?"

"He will." The sheriff shrugged off my question.

"But if he doesn't?"

"Even if Watson doesn't man up to poisonin' Vaughn Bascomb, we have him cold for attemptin' to kill Dr. Rappaport. The prosecutor's certain he can get a conviction for attempted murder. If the shell casings on the .22 match like I 'spect they will, he'll face an additional charge of aggravated battery with a dangerous weapon."

Sheila gracefully rose and extended her hand. "Thank you, Sheriff. I'm gratified this matter is finally resolved. You're to be commended for your efficient handling of my complaint."

If this were an old-time Western, the sheriff would have blushed profusely and muttered something to the effect of "Aw shucks, ma'am, weren't nuthin'." But Sumter Wiggins was made of sterner stuff. He simply acknowledged Sheila's praise with a brisk nod and a tight smile.

Sheila turned to me next. "Thank you, Kate, for all your efforts—even though misguided—on my behalf."

And that, ladies and gentlemen, as they say, is that. Sheila sailed out of the office without a backward glance, leaving me in the dust. So much for girl bonding. What happened to our becoming BFFs? Where was my invitation to vacation in the south of France? I didn't need to be hit with a brick to know when I wasn't wanted. Not trusting myself to speak, I gave the sheriff a feeble wave as I left the rarefied atmosphere of his office for probably the last time. My term as junior-grade detective/ private investigator had expired, and I wasn't nominated for reelection. Tomorrow I'd return to life in the private sector—a world of golf, tai chi, and bunco.

# Chapter 34

Case closed. I should feel ecstatic. Instead, I moped around as if my dog had died. Tai chi usually mellowed my mood, but today it failed to work. The Babes, bless their hearts, rushed to my rescue, valiantly trying to cheer me up over breakfast at the Cove Café.

"Don't be so hard on yourself, sugar," Connie Sue counseled. "Remember, you did solve two murders. That alone makes you smarter 'n most."

"I should've zeroed in on the perp sooner."

"I was sure you were on the right track." Pam reached over and patted my hand. "With the abundance of botany and horticulture experts, it made perfect sense that the poison came from a simple source."

"Thanks," I muttered. That's why Pam's my BFF, my sidekick. I'd pick her to ride in my patrol car any old day.

Monica speared a bite of egg white omelet with her fork. "Historically arsenic was quite popular as a method of murder in the Middle Ages. I've read that the Borgias and de Medicis had their own private supply."

I spread strawberry jam over a toast triangle and reserved comment.

"Did the sheriff say whether arsenic was found during Vaughn Bascomb's autopsy?" Monica continued, nonplussed by my silence.

Was Monica secretly trying to usurp my role as former detective, junior grade? I frowned at her over the rim of my coffee cup. "No," I replied morosely. "He didn't say."

"I would've thought arsenic along with cyanide and strychnine would be the first poisons to be ruled out," Monica added a trifle smugly.

Should I give Monica my copy of *The Complete Idiot's Guide to Forensics*? My new bookshelves would seem empty without it. "It is, er, they were," I amended. "The sheriff said something about the lab running further tests. In any event, they know for certain that arsenic was in Sheila's iced tea. That's enough to charge Kel with attempted murder."

"Then there's his attack on you," Pam said. "That should get him sent up the river for a good long time."

Monica raised her cup of Earl Grey. "I'll drink to that."

"Kel's was the only name left on my persons of interest list. It was only a matter of time before I was onto him," I explained. Even to my own ears, I sounded defensive.

Silence thick as maple syrup spread across the breakfast table. Everyone suddenly concentrated on their food.

"Well," Connie Sue said at last, "on the bright side, y'all have to admit we're all lookin' fabulous since discoverin' Belle Beaute."

"Connie Sue's right, you know," Pam was quick to agree. "Just yesterday Jack told me I didn't look a day older than when he married me."

"Your Jack's a regular sweetie pie," Connie Sue cooed. "Thacker, on the other hand, tends to be stingy in the compliment department, but I love 'im anyway. I swear, y'all, we're lookin' mighty fine considerin' we're no spring chickens."

"Speak for yourself," I groused. "You're as old as you feel." And right now I was feeling every one of my sixty-something years.

Pam leaned forward, her blue-gray eyes dancing with merriment. "Claudia bragged BJ was flattering her left and right. He's been wining and dining her, sending flowers, bringing Godiva chocolates. She told me she's rethinking her decision to avoid serious relationships."

Connie Sue smiled knowingly. "In this part of the country, sugar, winin', dinin' and chocolate are what gentlemen do when they come courtin'. Sounds serious if y'all want my opinion."

"Rita had her financial planner buy shares of Belle Beaute stock," Monica said, obviously disinterested in Claudia's love life. "Rita said she had it on good authority that they were about to hold a press conference and announce a revolutionary antiaging formula."

"Y'all remember the mantra from the brochures?" Connie Sue asked, her enthusiasm contagious.

We bobbed our heads as obedient as altar boys at high mass.

Connie Sue reverted to cheerleader mode. "Give me an R!"

"Revitalize!" I sang.

"Restore!" Pam called out.

"Regenerate!" Monica supplied right on cue.

Pleased our memories hadn't been entirely corroded by senior moments, we reached for our wallets to pay the checks Vera had unobtrusively slipped us. We were on our way out the door when Pam turned to me. "Want me to pick you up for bunco Thursday night?"

"Bunco . . . ?" I'd completely forgotten about bunco. Goes to show my state of mind. "Sure, whose house is it at this time?"

"Janine's," Monica replied impatiently. "Honestly, Kate, you need to be more organized. You should write these things in that little book of yours so you'll remember."

I bit my tongue. I wanted to inform Monica that my soon-to-be-retired black book was strictly for professional use. For things like clues, and suspects, and motives. But I didn't think she'd understand.

When I returned home a short time later, quiet blanketed the house like a heavy quilt. The kind of quiet where the tick of a grandfather clock would seem overly loud. Or it would, provided I owned such a clock, which I don't. Jim swore he'd never sleep a wink with the infernal ticking and bonging. Now that he was gone maybe I'd buy myself one for times like this when the house grew too quiet for comfort. Or I could get a pet. I'd had a cat for a short period not long ago, an orange stray with a fondness for tuna. But it had betrayed my friendship and deserted me for a pregnant brunette. The experience had soured me on cats. If I ever got another pet, it would be a dog. Dogs are faithful and loyal—and wouldn't interfere with my supply of tuna.

Listless, I wandered into the bedroom and peered at my reflection in the mirror above the dresser. A round face, which I pretended was a perfect oval and a pair of green eyes that I liked to think were my best feature, peered back. Even with bright sunlight spilling into the room, I had to admit my skin did look better, firmer and smoother. Maybe like Rita, I should invest in Belle Beaute. Their products certainly worked miracles on Sheila. The woman looked years younger than her actual age. I bet Sheila had tons of Belle Beaute stock. No wonder the south of France figured in her travel plans.

I meandered back to the kitchen, took a pitcher of iced tea from the fridge, and poured myself a glass. I was about to add sweetener when I recalled Betsy's trick of using honey instead. Honey made me think of bees. And bees made me think of Kel Watson. Remembering Kel made my stitches itch. To take my mind off the itching, I took my tea out to the patio. It was peace-

ful there, a good place to think. I sank onto a lounger
and watched a tiny green gecko scamper across the flag-
stones. I noticed my azaleas were almost done blooming, their vibrant pink blooms nearly spent. Not even
azaleas had been exempt in my quest for a possible
poison. Jim and I had planted ours when we'd first moved
to Serenity Cove Estates. Their showy flowers graced
the gardens of grandiose Southern plantations and humble cottages alike. And they managed to thrive in spite
of my ineptitude. An ideal plant.

I sipped my tea, but relaxation eluded me. I missed
the whine of the saw and whirr of the drill. Most of all,
however, I missed Bill in and out every day. Then, for
no particular reason, my errant thoughts circled from
Bill to Kel. Try as I might, I couldn't understand why
Kel would choose common arsenic for his second attempt on Sheila's life. I'm no expert, but arsenic—a readily detected substance—seemed amateurish compared
with his previous effort. The poison in his initial attempt,
however, had been so sophisticated that it still remained
a mystery. And why did Kel want to kill Sheila? Was
he a thwarted admirer? An obsessed stalker? Or was there
another, a more sinister, reason that caused him to strike
out again and again?

A bluebird flitted through the trees and landed on a
branch of a dogwood. Sheila was a lot like that bird, I
mused, a colorful being everyone admired as she flitted
place to place. Sighing, I stared up at the puffy white
clouds scuttling across an azure sky. Rather than answers, I came up with more questions. Sheila's attitude
at the sheriff's office also puzzled me. For a woman who
had narrowly escaped death, not once but twice, she'd
seemed remarkably unperturbed. Almost nonchalant.
Her whole demeanor seemed out of proportion for
someone who'd narrowly escaped the clutches of a deranged stalker. But maybe that was normal after what
she'd been through. After all, she no longer had to keep

looking over her shoulder, wondering where or when the next attack would come. With Kel behind bars, she was free to get on with her life.

But I still had questions and only one person had the answers. I decided to go straight to the source.

"That's correct, Officer. I'm his third cousin twice removed." Removed from what exactly, I hadn't a clue. It didn't seem to matter though because the guard on duty buzzed me through. I happen to be a veteran when it comes to visits to the county jail. I didn't so much as bat an eye as I was patted down, wanded, and had my purse searched for contraband. I endured the indignities grateful I didn't have to step on a scale. Even I have limits as to how far I'd go to solve a case.

I was ushered into the waiting room by a tall, skinny guard wearing a bored expression. I guessed him to be thirty-something, but then again he might be one of those people who perpetually look thirty-something. I gingerly lowered myself into a grimy plastic chair, carefully avoiding the even grimier counter. Smudged Plexiglas separated the visitors from the inmates. Where were sanitary wipes when you needed them? Next visit, I vowed to slip a can of Lysol spray into my bra and pray I didn't set off the metal detectors.

Finally the prisoner shuffled in accompanied by a guard I recognized from my friend Claudia's recent incarceration. I gave the guard, whom I fondly nicknamed Jabba the Hutt, a friendly wave, which, by the way, he didn't return. At a glance, I could see prison life didn't agree with Kel. The orange jumpsuit he wore didn't flatter him any more than it had Claudia. The bright color lent a sallow cast to his complexion. The lines and wrinkles in his face appeared more pronounced. I could recommend a good skin care product, but under the circumstances doubt he'd appreciate the offer. His dark eyes looked more sunken than usual, his salt-and-pepper hair, though still pulled into a ponytail, looked stringy and unkempt.

Kel's eyes widened in surprise at spotting me on the other side of the Plexiglas. "Mrs. McCall . . . ?" His Adam's apple bobbed. "You're the last person I expected to see."

"Hey, Kel," I said, opting for the casual. I was becoming amazingly adept at jailhouse etiquette. Amy Vanderbilt, Emily Post, consider this fair warning: The book's my idea. "Hope you don't mind my coming, but I've some questions I'd like answered."

"Go ahead. Shoot," he said, then cringed at his poor choice of words. Dark red spread across the sharp ridges of his cheekbones. "Say, I'm sorry about that—the shooting that is. Was just trying to warn you away from my . . . plants . . . when you moved."

Sheesh! The nerve! He was making it sound as though getting shot was my fault. What's the world coming to? Doesn't anyone accept responsibility for their actions? "My mistake. I shouldn't have zigged when I was supposed to zag."

"Never meant you any harm."

"Don't give it another thought. The bleeding stopped even before we got to the hospital. Five stitches and a tetanus shot are no big deal." I didn't bother to hide the sarcasm.

I was gratified to see him wince. Serves him right for taking aim at a senior citizen. "I'll forgive you if you tell me why you were stalking Sheila Rappaport."

"Me?" His expression went blank. "Is that what she's telling people?"

"It is."

"That's a lie, a goddamn lie. And once more, I never tried to kill her or that fancy boyfriend of hers."

"If that's the case, why show up on the set of her TV show?" I waited a beat. "Then again at the hospital, and after the memorial service?"

Folding his hands, he leaned into the Plexiglas. "I dropped by the set 'cause I needed her advice."

"Advice . . . about what?"

"We're in the same profession." He made a face as if to say that should explain it all. "In the past, we've even worked some of the same sites. Added to that, the woman's got an 'in' in the cosmetics industry. I thought she might be willing to help a fellow botanist."

Hmm. I don't know what I'd expected to hear, but that certainly wasn't it. "Why is Sheila's connection to Belle Beaute so important?"

His expression became shuttered. "Doesn't make any difference now," he said, picking at a hangnail. "Sheriff Wiggins is going to hang me out to dry. No one's going to take my word over that of the respected Dr. Sheila. Especially after the sheriff's deputies found arsenic in my shed. Do you think I'm stupid enough to leave a murder weapon in plain sight? I haven't the foggiest notion how it got there. Someone's trying to frame me."

*Yeah right.* I wasn't buying into his argument. "I don't know, Kel. Maybe you thought with Sheila dead there'd be no one to point the finger at you."

At this, his resistance crumbled. Lowering his head, he covered his face with his hands. "I didn't kill Vaughn Bascomb. Didn't even know the guy, so why would I want him dead?" His head came up, and he pinned me with a look of sheer desperation. "I swear on my mother's grave, Mrs. McCall, I never tried to poison either of them. Sheila called this morning and invited me over. Said she was sorry about the way she's treated me and wanted to talk, smooth things over. She even offered me suggestions on my discovery. I thought we had ourselves a real nice visit over a glass of iced tea. She was fine when I left. You can imagine my surprise when the sheriff turned up and arrested me."

Kel made a good point. Who would take the word of

an aging pot-growing, pony-tailed hippie over that of the elegant and accomplished Dr. Sheila Rappaport? Sheila was the darling of the garden-and-weed set. Kel an ordinary county extension agent. It would amount to a case of he said, she said.

I rose, more than ready to get the heck out of Dodge with its stale smells and gritty floors. I was nearly at the door when I turned with one final question. "You failed to mention what advice you sought from Sheila."

He shrugged narrow shoulders and seemed to reach a decision. "I did some experimenting a while back and discovered a method of extracting oil from a certain plant—sea buckthorn—that contains properties that might apply to the cosmetics business. I figured Sheila, being a fellow botanist, might know how to get it to the attention of the right people. Point me in the right direction, so to speak. Guess it hardly matters anymore."

Or did it matter? I wondered as the jail door clanged shut.

# Chapter 35

She sells sea shells by the seashore.

As I drove toward home, the childhood tongue twister tormented me until it turned into Sheila sells seashells.

Sea shells . . . ? Sea buckthorn . . . ?

Wasn't sea buckthorn the same plant Sheila and Betsy had been studying the afternoon of my impromptu visit? I remember vividly because its generic name sounded something like hippopotamus. Betsy had snickered when I'd stumbled over the pronunciation. Then Sheila had quickly stuffed its photo back into a folder. Almost as if she didn't want me to see it. Almost as though she'd been trying to hide it. I tapped my fingers on the steering wheel, willing myself to recall the gist of the conversation. Betsy, Little Miss Snippety, had informed me sea buckthorn didn't grow in these parts, so my backyard would have to do without. Too bad, so sad.

He said, she said . . . by the seashore.

Variations of the stupid rhyme kept humming through my brain. What if Kel *was* telling the truth? What if he really was innocent? My stomach knotted at the possibility. Why should I take his word over Sheila's? Why should I believe a man who'd shot at me, might've killed me? Sheila, on the other hand, liked me, wanted me as a friend. She'd even given me tickets to the Masters. Why all the doubt? Why couldn't I just let it go?

But I couldn't.

And all because of a plant whose name was similar to that of a barrel-shaped mammal. Could sea buckthorn be the key to the mystery?

I concentrated as I drove along the two-lane highway trying to remember the photo. As I recalled, the plant had been large, nearly the size of a small tree, which is the reason I thought it a perfect choice for the empty space at the back of my yard. I'd also been attracted by the silvery-green leaves and clusters of bright orange fruit. I clutched the steering wheel tighter as a thought occurred to me. What if sea buckthorn had nothing whatsoever to do with cosmetics as Kel claimed, but everything to do with poison?

I couldn't resist a glance at the marquee as I passed the white clapboard AME church. *Forbidden fruits create many jams.* Were the sea buckthorn's pretty orange clusters forbidden fruit? Who better to ask than Sheila?

Only one way to solve this quandary once and for all. Rather than turning for home, I headed for Sheila's rental.

I parked in the drive next to her Lexus. The woman had expensive tastes, I noted, and not for the first time. There must be big bucks in having your own TV show. And she was an author. Sheila must be raking in the dough. Maybe someday I'd try my hand at writing a book. Easy peasy. How hard can it be?

Climbing out of the Buick, I marched up the walk and rang the bell. I waited, then rang it again, before the door finally swung open.

"Hi," I said.

"Kate, what a surprise," Sheila returned, her tone frosty.

She was dressed in the same clothes she'd worn at

the sheriff's office earlier that afternoon. Her navy linen pants remained unwrinkled, her white shirt still stain-free. It was hard to relate to a woman so perfect. "I was beginning to think no one was home. Hope this isn't a bad time."

"I didn't expect to see you again this soon."

Yep, there was a distinct chill in the air. What happened to our being best buds? If this was the way she treated other women, small wonder no one ever invited her to play bunco. "I've just come from seeing Kel at the jail," I told her. "We need to talk."

Sheila held her ground. "Sorry, this isn't a good time. I'm right in the middle of packing."

"This won't take long." Sheila apparently hadn't been informed of my middle name—Persistence.

"Very well." She stood aside, but didn't invite me farther into the house.

I didn't let that bother me. Faking an end run, I dashed past her into the great room and plunked myself down on the sofa. "Just a couple questions, then I'll leave you to your packing." Packing that was nonexistent. The house was in its usual pristine condition, not a knickknack out of place. And Sheila, being Sheila, didn't surround herself with ordinary knickknacks, or bric-a-brac, she had objets d'art. Crystal and statuettes, all of which appeared very breakable and super expensive. La-di-dah!

Sheila didn't sit, but stood, arms folded, watching me. "Really, Kate, most people call before dropping in. It's the civil thing to do."

No one had *ever* accused me of not being civil. Suddenly, however, I'd become the guest who overstayed her welcome. I swept my gaze over the room, and it landed on a single champagne flute on an end table along with an open laptop. Next to it rested a nearly full bottle of chilled champagne. From where I sat, I could read the label: Dom Pérignon. I knew the stuff was priccy, probably fifty dollars a bottle, maybe more. I was impressed, but I'm impressionable.

"Looks like you're celebrating," I said.

"It's not every day your attempted murderer gets what's coming to him. Care to join me for a glass?"

I mulled over the proposition—for half a second. When would I get another chance to drink fifty-dollar champagne? "Sure, I'd love to."

While Sheila went for another champagne flute, I couldn't resist taking a peek at her computer. To my way of thinking, since it was open for all to see, the laptop fell into the category of public domain. I jiggled the mouse and, lo and behold, up popped her e-mail. I quickly skimmed a congratulatory note from Betsy Dalton. Betsy extolled Sheila's discovery of a breakthrough method of extracting oil from the bark of sea buckthorn. She went on to say this brilliant find would revolutionize the cosmetics industry—and Belle Beaute would be the first to reap the benefits. *Promise you'll invite me to visit your villa on the Mediterranean*, the e-mail concluded. Clicking open an attachment, I viewed the final packaging of Belle Beaute's new antiaging formula, Forever Young.

Brilliant discovery? Breakthrough? Villa? But whoa, wait a minute . . . Didn't Kel mention an identical find? Wasn't that the reason he gave for seeking Sheila's advice? Evidently the discovery was worth millions.

"You just can't leave well enough alone, can you, Kate?"

I started at the sound of Sheila's voice. Was it a federal offense to read another person's mail? Or did that only apply to stealing or tampering? E-mail was another matter entirely, wasn't it? "Guilty as charged," I admitted with a feeble grin.

A grin that faded when I noticed the gun in Sheila's hand.

"If you didn't want to share the Dom Pérignon, all

you had to do was say so." I desperately hoped this was some sort of sick joke.

"If you think for one second I'm going to let a busybody such as yourself spoil all my planning and hard work, you're mistaken. I'm becoming quite proficient at eliminating people who stand in my way. I've no qualms about doing it again."

"Is that thing real?" I asked, motioning to the compact gun she held. With its candy pink grip and shiny chrome, it looked like it belonged to Shoot 'em Up Barbie. "Does it come in other colors?"

Sheila didn't crack a smile. "Did Rita ever mention I medaled in skeet shooting? Imagine the damage I'd do at close range."

I swallowed past the golf-ball-size lump in my throat. Puzzle pieces started to click into place. "You, not Kel, poisoned Vaughn."

"Congratulations, you finally figured it out." Her laughter sounded like breaking glass. "Sorry, but you're too late. Yes, I'm the one who poisoned Vaughn—and myself as well. Naive, unsuspecting Vaughn was becoming tiresome. It was simple actually—almost as simple as planting the arsenic in Kel's shed. I only needed to add a larger concentration of my special honey to his tea than I did to mine. I'd even experimented giving myself small doses of the toxin to lessen my sensitivity. Naturally, I was aware of Vaughn's heart disease. It wasn't difficult to cause an arrhythmia. The idiots at the crime lab in Columbia still haven't figured out his death was a case of Mad Honey Disease."

I inched along the sofa. If I could distract her, I'd bolt for the door and run like crazy. "Mad Honey Disease . . . ?"

Considering the gravity of the situation, Sheila seemed almost relaxed and in no great hurry to shoot me. Besides, everyone knows how hard bloodstains are to remove from carpeting. "Vaughn preferred tea sweetened with honey," Sheila continued. "The honey I used to sweeten our tea was distilled from the nectar of azaleas. It contains grayanotoxin, which in Vaughn's case proved deadly. While I exhibited similar symptoms, they weren't to the same degree as his."

I cautiously rose to my feet, my legs rubbery. "Why?"

"Chalk it up to the oldest motive known to mankind. Pure unadulterated greed." She shook her head at my stupidity. "I'm not talking penny-ante cash, Kate, but millions. In addition to copious amounts of Vitamin E, Beta Carotene, and antioxidants, sea buckthorn is high in essential fatty acids. Vaughn and I had nearly perfected a method of extracting its oil and were about to present our findings to Belle Beaute for further testing. Then along comes Kel Watson, a bumbling, local yokel of an extension agent, who not only made the same amazing discovery, but found the solution to our little problem. Well, that would never do. After I convinced Kel to explain his process to me in detail, I needed to eliminate him as a threat to my financial future."

"But what about Vaughn? I thought you two were lovers. Why kill him?"

She snorted a laugh. "I've never been the type who likes to share. This was no exception."

Wasn't it nice we were finally having a heart-to-heart girl talk? Too bad it was with a gun pointed at my chest. It detracted from the warm fuzzies I usually feel when sharing secrets with a pal. Angling my body, I took a small step sideways. "What do you plan to do with all that money?" Not that I gave a hoot, but it bought me precious time.

"I'm ready to move on." A humorless smile twisted her mouth. "I've worked hard all my life, now I'm ready to reap the rewards. I'll be able to live as I please. Clothes, cars, homes, travel, they're all within reach. Now"—she motioned with the gun—"let's go for a drive, shall we?"

# Chapter 36

"Are you going to shoot me?"

Though the line was cliché, it summed up my fear in a nutshell.

"No, I have something much more original in mind." Sheila's cunning smile made her a shoo-in for the role of Cruella de Vil in the Disney classic *101 Dalmatians*.

I reviewed my options as Serenity Cove Estates vanished in the rearview mirror. I could stomp on the gas, veer off the highway, and probably hit a tree. Just my luck, I'd wind up deader 'n a doornail, while Sheila would be rescued by a cute EMT, and the pair would live happily ever after in the south of France. Plan B: I could try to fast-talk my way out of this, but I needed snappier dialog than "Are you going to shoot me?" Problem was I didn't feel particularly snappy at the moment. Sheer terror has that effect on me. Plan C: Duh! I didn't have a Plan C.

"Just drive." Sheila casually flung my purse in the backseat, where it landed on the floor with a thud. "I'll tell you where to turn."

I shot her a sidelong glance. Sheila was much too calm for my liking. The woman had nerves as hard and cold as granite. Her gun hand was rock steady and remained leveled at my chest. Then lightning struck. Plan C came to me in a flash. I'd wait until we met a car coming in the opposite direction and swerve into oncoming traffic. The instant our cars collided, I'd jump out and yell for help. Problem with Plan C was it depended upon oncoming traffic. One of the perks of living in a rural area such as Serenity Cove was that there wasn't any traffic. It used to be a running joke between Jim and me that if we ever encountered two or more cars at an intersection, we'd have to move.

"You know, don't you, Kate, that you brought this whole situation on yourself?" Sheila said, her tone conversational.

*My fault . . . ?*

I stifled the urge to bop myself on the head and exclaim, "Gee I could've had a V8," but was afraid Sheila'd shoot me if I took my hands off the wheel. Was this another variation of Blame the Hapless Victim? Kel had tried the same tactic. Well, I refused to play the game. I needed all my energy to formulate Plan D.

"All you had to do was follow the bread crumbs," Sheila graciously explained for my slow-witted benefit. "The trail would have led straight to Kel Watson's front step. But did you do that? No," she answered before I could open my mouth. "You stubbornly refused to follow my lead. After listening to Rita brag how you solved a murder or two, I thought you'd achieved a certain level of credibility with the sheriff. I was certain that if I pointed you in Kel's direction, the sheriff would follow. But Wiggins regards you as pathetic. A nuisance. A rank amateur."

Her words stung. "Did Sheriff Wiggins really say those things about me?" I asked in a small voice.

Impervious to my wounded pride, Sheila continued. "I'd all but painted a bull's-eye on Kel's back—but what did you do? You suspected my coworkers. I nearly laughed myself silly at the thought. Imagine thinking

Todd Timmons smart enough to pull off a caper this complex. He's almost as simpleminded as you. As for Roger, the man can barely get his head out of a book long enough to go to the bathroom, much less plot a homicide. Betsy would have been the most logical candidate. She's the only one of the three with enough guts to off Vaughn. Too bad she was miles away when he ingested his fatal dose of honey."

I had no idea where we were heading, but knew it was nowhere I wanted to go. Houses along this stretch of the road were nonexistent. State forest occupied both sides of the road with an occasional dirt fire road thrown in here and there. Take your pick; any of them would be the perfect spot for a murder—namely mine.

"Turn here," she ordered abruptly.

I swallowed hard. This road led to the Huguenot Cemetery—and the beehives.

"Do it, or you'll be sorry. I'm an excellent marksman, and I'll start with your left foot."

With dread churning my stomach, I did as she commanded. Even though it was nearing the dinner hour, the days were noticeably longer as spring edged toward summer. At this time, most residents of Serenity Cove would be home with their loved ones. Soon they'd be eating pot roast or ordering gas station pizza. It was highly unlikely we'd encounter anyone idling down a dirt road in the middle of the woods. Panic showed its claws and dug in deep. My palms grew slick with sweat; my pulse hammered in my ears. I had things left undone and unsaid. I wished I'd been a better mother. More patient with my children's well-meaning attempts to micromanage my life. Did the Babes know how much their friendship meant to me? I wanted to say the L word out loud to Bill and risk the consequences.

I slowed to a stop when I reached the fork in the road. I looked longingly toward the one leading to the Huguenot Cemetery. I regretted not being a better garden club soldier and pulling my share of weeds. Rita had wanted the cemetery to look special for the photographer from the *Serenity Sentinel*, and I had let her down. I wish I could tell her I was sorry.

"Quit stalling," Sheila snapped. "Take the road on the left."

The Buick continued down the rutted road. My only chance was once I stopped the car, I could distract her long enough to make a getaway. I'd read somewhere it was harder to hit a moving target. Maybe I'd run a zigzag pattern. Or did that only apply when being chased by an alligator? One thing I did know, though, at close range Sheila was certain to hit a vital organ.

"I've heard all about your unfortunate reaction to bee venom." Sheila performed her Cruella impersonation again. "Pity you'll be stung again so soon. Death from anaphylactic shock can be quite dramatic. You won't suffer long. The onset should be within minutes."

The idea of being stung by bees nearly paralyzed me. My throat was too dry to swallow. Cardiac arrest seemed imminent.

Judging by her expression, Cruella, er, Sheila seemed to relish my fear. "Left untreated, shock and death can occur anywhere from a few minutes to an hour or more. First you'll experience swelling of the tongue and face, especially the lips and around the eyes. Next your body breaks out in nasty red, itchy welts."

I shivered convulsively at the picture her words painted.

"Then you'll wheeze and gasp for air. Finally your blood pressure will drop. You'll lose consciousness, lapse into a coma, and die." Her voice was clinical and detached as she described the gruesome symptoms.

I moistened my lips with the tip of my tongue. "Friends will never believe I was stupid enough to come out here knowing what happened last time."

Sheila shrugged nonplussed. "Who knows why peo-

ple do things? For a while, I imagine your poor judgment will be gossiped about over coffee or in line at
the drugstore. Eventually life moves on. People cease wondering and get on with it. Enough chitchat," she said,
her voice taking on a sharper edge. "Stop near the hives."

Even from a distance, I could see bees swarming
around the boxes, or supers or whatever the darn things
were called. Given my druthers, I'd rather take my chances
with a bullet than try to outrun a swarm of angry bees.
My brain scrambled for a means of escape. Did I have
my EpiPen handy? Good news: Yes, I did have it with
me. It was in my purse, probably in the nether region
fraternizing with tubes of lipstick and ballpoint pens.
Bad news: My purse was on the floor of the backseat
where Sheila had tossed it. I doubted whether she'd delay my execution while I retrieved it and rummaged
through the contents for a lifesaving medication.

"You'll never get away with this, Sheila." I resorted
to another slick cliché, but any cliché in a storm, right?
If I got out of this alive, I vowed to give up clichés forever. I'd stop watching the classic movie channel and
switch to the Food Network.

"We'll see about that. Now start walking!"

I opened the car and cautiously stepped out. My hand
was on the door handle when I heard a familiar voice.

"Kate . . . ? That you?"

Turning, I spied Rita's Honda Accord ten feet behind me. My knees sagged with relief. And then the adrenaline kicked in. The drama inside the Buick had been
so intense I hadn't realized we were being followed. From
the surprised look on Sheila's face, she hadn't been aware
of it either. This wasn't the time, however, to question
Providence. It was the time for action. I sprinted for the
safety of the Honda as if the hounds from hell nipped
at my heels.

"Hurry, Kate," I thought I heard Polly holler. "Get in
the frickin' car before you get stung."

The back door of the Honda swung open, and I tumbled inside. When I clumsily righted myself, I found myself surrounded by Babes. Rita was at the wheel, Connie Sue riding shotgun. Polly and Gloria, and now myself, occupied the rear. Was I hallucinating? Had I died and gone to heaven? Were the Babes angels in disguise? "What the . . . ?" I mumbled.

Rita squinted through the windshield. "Was that Sheila in the car with you?"

"We have to stop her," I panted. "She killed Vaughn—and almost killed me."

As all of us watched, Sheila climbed over the console of the Buick and into the driver's seat. Any second now, she'd hook a U-turn and make a run for the border.

"Cut her off," I screamed in Rita's ear. "Don't let her get away."

"Hang on!" Rita set her jaw. "High time she gets what's coming to her."

Connie Sue rolled her window down a crack and let out a rebel yell that could be heard clear to Augusta. Not to be outdone, Gloria cranked down her window partway and began pelting the Buick with any object she could lay her hands on. Water bottles, sneakers, garden trowels sailed through the air, hitting their target with uncanny accuracy.

The loud cry and all the pelting must have had an unsettling effect on Sheila because she jerked the wheel hard to the right. Rita gunned the motor and took after her in hot pursuit. Leaning over the seat, I grabbed hold of the steering wheel and charted a collision course. To avoid a direct hit, Sheila made another sharp turn and this time clipped the corner of a stack of supers. Hives flew upward, then landed with a crash on the hood of the Buick that had come to a precipitous halt. Rita, always quick-witted, shoved the Honda into reverse and backed down the road.

We sat for a moment in stunned silence and let the dust settle. Sheila sat slumped behind the wheel, a nasty gash on her forehead from hitting the windshield. No sympathy from me. That's what she deserved for not fastening her seat belt. Honey dripped over the Buick in thick, syrupy rivulets. Bees were everywhere. The queen and her cohorts were none too happy about losing the fruits of their labor. They swarmed over the car in a dark angry cloud. Sheila would have to have a death wish to leave the safety of the Buick.

"Well, that got the blood pumping," Polly chortled.

I let out a giggle comprised of tension mixed with relief. "Doesn't look like Sheila's going anywhere anytime soon,"

"Guess you could say we foiled a honey of a killer," Rita said, and we groaned at the pun.

"Thank you, guys. I owe you my life," I said, tearing up now that the adrenaline rush was fading.

"As it turns out, Kate," Rita said, "it's a good thing you never found time to do the weeding for the garden club."

Gloria searched for her sneaker; then her expression cleared, apparently remembering she'd used it for ammunition. "Rita called and asked if we'd do it for you."

Polly nodded eagerly. "We agreed that if we all pitched in, it wouldn't take us long. So here we are."

"Connie Sue's the one who spotted your car heading in the opposite direction. We decided to see what you were up to."

"Lucky for me you did. Sheila almost got away with Kate-icide." I sniffed back tears. "Does anyone have a cell phone I can use?"

Polly handed me one studded with rhinestones. "Here, use mine."

I tried to make the afternoon dispatcher at the sheriff's office understand that we had a killer—and we had bees. In spite of repeated explanations, she seemed fixated on the idea that we'd been attacked by killer bees. At any rate, she promised to send assistance.

I leaned back in the Honda, wedged securely between Polly and Gloria, and felt my body relax and my mind drift. Wouldn't my children be proud to learn their mother had brought yet another criminal to justice? Nah, I decided. They'd probably freak out. Just to be on the safe side, though, when Steven comes to visit I'll ask his help to fill out the living will and power of attorney he'd sent.

# Chapter 37

"Y'all should've been there," Connie Sue said as she poured herself a glass of pinot grigio. "It was a sight for sore eyes."

"You can say that again." Gloria's bangle bracelets jingled as she spread hummus on a wheat cracker. "EMTs, sheriff's department, firefighters. It caused quite a commotion."

"Bees must've covered every square inch of Kate's Buick." Polly's faded blue eyes twinkled behind her trifocals. "Then these cute guys, all gussied up in baggy white suits and hats with veils, came and waved smokers to quiet the bees."

Rita wore a look of smug satisfaction. "Firemen had to hose down the car before Sheriff Wiggins could haul Sheila out and read her her rights."

For the time being, I was content to sit back and listen to my friends' chatter. The Babes were gathered in Janine's kitchen waiting for a couple stragglers to arrive so bunco could begin. Somehow I had the feeling we'd spend more of the evening talking than rolling the bones. But that was okay. Recent events would be the chief topic of gossip and speculation around Serenity Cove for weeks to come.

"Did Dr. Sheila ever confess to poisoning Dr. Bascomb?" Megan asked, wide-eyed.

Feeling myself the center of attention, I paused in the act of dredging a taco chip through salsa. "Not yet, but Sheriff Wiggins said it's only a matter of time. He thinks Sheila's hoping for a plea bargain."

"Well, at least they have her cold for what she tried to do to you," Pam said. "Attempted murder isn't a charge to be taken lightly."

"Mmm." I munched on my chip. The salsa was spicy just the way I like it, but not enough I'd need an antacid. "With the new information the toxicology lab faxed over this morning, I think the sheriff's planning to amend the charge to first-degree murder. Sheila's plea bargain might amount to no more than taking the death penalty off the table."

"New information?" Monica looked at me sharply. "What new information?"

Smiling serenely, I helped myself to more chips and salsa. "The lab confirmed Vaughn's death was due to grayanotoxin just as Sheila claimed."

"Grayanotoxin?" Monica frowned, obviously unhappy there was a subject on which she wasn't well versed. "Never heard of it."

"Azaleas," I replied succinctly.

It took a few moments for this to sink in.

"Azaleas." Janine shook her head in wonderment. "Who would have guessed?"

"I did some research online after Kate called this morning," Diane said. "Azaleas produce bacteria that can mimic food poisoning."

"Stomach irritation, abnormal heart rhythm, seizures, coma, and even death," Janine enumerated the symptoms, her RN background rising to the fore.

"Exactly," I agreed.

"The honey Sheila added to Vaughn's tea was made

from the nectar of azaleas, or rhododendrons, and is known as 'mad honey,' " Diane explained.

Gloria hoisted herself onto one of the stools bordering the breakfast bar. "What I don't understand is why it took so long for the toxicology results."

"Real life isn't like TV," Pam, my crime-show buddy, lectured. "As much as I love *CSI* and *Law & Order,* in reality most crimes aren't solved in a day, much less an hour like on TV."

"More like forty-five minutes." Polly nodded sagely. "Gotta have commercials."

"I asked Sheriff Wiggins the same question, Pam," I said. "Once poisoning is suspected as COD—cause of death, for the less well informed among you—he told me the lab rules out common sources first. Arsenic, cyanide, strychnine, benzene, bromide—you know, the usual suspects." I rattled off the list, trying to impress the Babes with my wisdom and expertise. "You have to give the lab credit for finding the true culprit. There are many lesser-known toxins out there, and finding the right one must've been like looking for the proverbial needle in a haystack."

"Hey, y'all." Tammy Lynn burst into Janine's kitchen, looking flushed and happy. "Sorry I'm late, but Eric wanted to drop me off."

Well, well, well. Seems like our little Cinderella has found her Prince Charming. Tammy Lynn was decked out in a short, flirty skirt, scoop-necked red sweater, and heels. Heels, mind you, not sneakers or scuffed loafers. Who could have guessed the girl possessed a pair of Betty Grable legs beneath all the frumpy polyester?

"I heard y'all talkin' about the lab report," she went on. "Sheriff Wiggins said the technique for this specific test is labor intensive and requires an experienced forensics toxicologist. To complicate matters, the person most qualified to run this test had been away on family leave."

"But at the banquet Sheila became ill and had to be rushed to the hospital, too. Are you implying she poisoned herself?" Pam asked.

I started to take another corn chip, but changed my mind. All this talk of poison was affecting my appetite. "Sheila administered a small amount of the 'mad honey' to herself. Just enough to divert suspicion away from herself."

"And it worked like a charm. Should've known she'd do something like that." Rita clucked her tongue with disgust. "All the while everyone was thinking poor, poor pitiful Sheila."

"What would make a person do something like this?" asked sweet, naive Megan.

"Money, sugar," Connie Sue drawled. "Oodles and oodles of money."

Tammy Lynn bypassed the wine in favor of a diet soda. "Sheriff Wiggins confirmed Belle Beaute agreed to pay Sheila Rappaport a small fortune for somethin' to do with a plant."

"Sea buckthorn," I supplied. "Seems as though it shows great promise for skin care products. Unfortunately Kel Watson made the same discovery, but made the mistake of confiding in Sheila Rappaport. He unwittingly sought the advice of a fellow botanist—and we all know how that turned out."

"Sheila's not the sharing type," Rita said. "Not even in college. No way she'd share a humungous sum if she could keep it all to herself. Evidently Vaughn was expendable."

"Don't tell the sheriff I'm blabbin'"—Tammy Lynn lowered her voice—"but the pharmacist at the drugstore is willin' to testify Sheila picked up Dr. Bascomb's heart medicine. He said her knowin' how he had a pre-existin' condition and all will add weight to the case against her."

Pam looked at me fondly. "If it weren't for Kate, Sheila might've gotten away with murder."

And I'd nearly lost my life in the process. We were all silent for a moment, our thoughts probably traveling the same track.

"We're much too serious," I said, striving to lighten the mood. "Now, for some good news. Betsy Dalton called to thank me personally. Belle Beaute is so pleased we uncovered Sheila's duplicity, they want to send each of us a year's supply of their products."

Firmer, smoother skin. Fewer lines. Diminished wrinkles. Revitalize, rejuvenate, regenerate, recharge, restore, reenergize. Buzz words flew through the air thicker than lovebugs in mating season. And, ladies, anyone who's ever driven through Florida in October knows what I'm talking about.

"Where in the world is Claudia?" Connie Sue asked when the chatter died down. "She said she'd be late, but it's headin' toward ridiculous."

Janine craned her head and peered toward the foyer. "Speak of the devil . . ."

"Yoo-hoo, everyone." Claudia waved as she entered.

Polly gave her the once-over. "Don't you look spiffy."

"Spiffy" was indeed the adjective of choice to describe her stylish black cocktail suit with its slim skirt and fitted jacket. Claudia did a mean pirouette and, grinning ear to ear, waggled her left hand for all to see.

The sight of a huge, sparkly diamond solitaire—had to be at least two carats—was greeted with squeals of delight. Fine detective I was. Claudia's engagement shouldn't have come as a surprise. She had a certain twinkle in her eyes, a certain bounce to her step these days. And Claudia tended to be impulsive—no, "spontaneous" was perhaps a better word—when it came to her relationships with the opposite sex.

"I know that in view of my recent fiasco, I vowed to

swear off men for life," she confessed as the Babes clustered around for a closer look, "but BJ is such a charmer I couldn't resist. Neither of us is getting any younger, and we don't want to spend our golden years alone. And"—she paused for effect—"I'm asking all of you to be my bridesmaids."

Bunco was definitely on the back burner. We laughed. We cried. We toasted. A killer'd been caught, freebies granted, and a fellow Babe engaged. I sighed with contentment. It all added up to a wonderful evening.

"Ladies!" Janine clapped her hands to get our attention. "Let's play at least one round of bunco to commemorate the occasion."

As we made our way toward the tables, Claudia whispered in my ear, "BJ wasn't the only one shopping at the jewelry store. He recognized a certain blue-eyed tool guy hovering over the ring counter."

My heart skipped a beat. "Bill . . . ?"

Claudia winked.

I glanced down at my left hand, which was bereft of jewelry. I didn't need a sparkly diamond on the ring finger to know I loved Bill—a sweet, gentle man with the soul of a warrior. And with all my faults, I know in my heart he loved me right back. No need to rush things. What was it some philosopher once said? It came back to me as I took my seat at the table next to Connie Sue and rolled the dice.

Life is about the journey, not the destination.